Other works by Tony Irons

Hoover's Children

Praise for Tony Irons

"Tony Irons is equally gifted at creating characters and vividly rendering a troublesome history. He is a natural storyteller, with an original take on America..."

—Virginia Prescott
New Hampshire Public Radio

Published by RiverRun Select
an imprint of Piscataqua Press and the RiverRun Bookstore
142 Fleet Street | Portsmouth, New Hampshire 03801 | USA
603.431.2100 | www.riverrunbookstore.com

Printed in the United States of America

ISBN-13: 978-1-939739-01-8
LCCN: 2013909795

Visit Tony Irons on the World Wide Web:
www.tonyirons.com

DENGMAN GAP

A Novel

TONY IRONS

RiverRun Select
An imprint of RiverRun Bookstore

For Lee

To Mike & Rebecca

Tony Iko

Keep close to Nature's heart....
and break clear away, once in a while,
and climb a mountain
or spend a week in the woods.
Wash your sprit clean.

John Muir

1

Old Man

HIGHWAY 21, A NARROW TWO-LANE ROAD called the Cherokee Road by the folks who lived out there, ran flat and straight alongside Chestnut Creek for a stretch of ten miles or so. J.D. turned off the paved road where cordwood was stacked at the entrance to a straight dirt drive. He downshifted into first, spinning sheets of mud into the wheel wells of the pickup. Indian summer in late September had brought light rains to the Blue Ridge Mountains. Rivulets still trickled down the hillsides from high on the rhododendron ridges, and the ground was damp. Bunch grasses on the floor of the longleaf pine forests held on to a pale summer green. By morning, all the wet-warm clouds had blown north on cool winds out of Georgia.

A quarter mile down the dirt road, he could see the wooden plank bridge that spanned Chestnut Creek. The road rose up just before the bridge, and he knew the gravel would be mud-soft from the bridge runoff at the top of the rise. He upshifted into second, gaining speed. He didn't want to get stuck out there. Nobody lived within two or three miles, and Old Man was getting to be a really old man who wouldn't be able to help him get unstuck.

When J.D. saw him last, his backbone was permanently bent, no spring left in it at all. He walked with a hickory stick cane, face and chest nearly parallel to the ground. He'd given up lacing his boots and buttoning his black and red checked wool shirt. He just stuffed the shirt tails inside his suspenders. His hands, long and callous hard, had become claw-like. Knuckles like walnuts.

"Little Boy," he said—J.D. had to stoop when coming in the cabin door, and his shoulders were broad enough that he had to turn a bit sideways, but Old Man always called him Little Boy—"When I pass through that long vale of tears, you're going have to build me a casket shaped like a donut." J.D. had gotten the whiskey jug from the mantel, pulled the cork out, and handed it to him.

"Don't be talking like that, Old Man. You're still a spring chicken." The old man smiled, wiped the whiskey dribble off his chin stubble with his sleeve, and handed the jug back.

"Mighty long spring for this chicken," he said.

J.D. was a day late. He'd promised the old man he'd be there on the first of October, but coming down off Purgatory Overlook, his '58 Chevy Apache Stepside, black with a fire-engine red stripe down the side, had begun squealing and pulling hard. He'd spun a bearing in the front right wheel. He left the hood up, put a note on the seat: *Spun a bearing. Gone to fix it. Back before sunset.* He crossed the Parkway, tucked in his shirt, straightened the collar, stuck his thumb out, and hitchhiked twenty miles back into Roanoke. Everybody knew where an auto parts store was, but nobody knew how to get to any of them. He walked and asked, walked and asked, walked and asked until he found a garage that specialized in front-end work. They had a bearing for his truck in its original box, wrapped in oily brown paper. He bought it with a small tub of wheel-bearing grease and then hitchhiked back down the Blue Ridge to mile 95.

By the time he got set to pack the grease and put the new

bearing in, he had to use a flashlight propped on a rock. Old Man, fifty miles south in Dengman Gap, would have been turned in, and the cabin dark as a knothole. When the bearing was fixed, J.D. pulled off at the next exit, found a flat, grassy spot on the side of the road well off Parkway land, unrolled the patchwork quilt Old Man had given him, and slept in the bed of his truck, snuggled in against the night chill, his rifle beside him.

This was the third time in a year J.D. had driven two hundred miles south from his home in Rappahannock County, Virginia, to the cabin on the North Carolina border. He first met Old Man on the anniversary of the day the old man's son had died. Or at least the day the old man said he found out about it. Nobody knew when he actually died. He said a couple of coon hunters out with their coon dogs had found a shallow grave in a stand of oaks and a short hank of rope hanging from a stout branch not far away. That was twenty years ago, in 1948. His son was twenty-two, and Old Man still grieved. Not that he had ever specifically recounted the details of it to J.D., but when he sat back in his rocker by the wood stove and talked about the raucous days of Prohibition and the moonshine still he'd built in a barn up the hill behind the cabin the year his son was born, his blue eyes, a little cloudy and pale with cataracts, would get even paler, more cloudy, and damp, like the inside of a fresh opened robin's egg. Then the Revenuers came, he said, and burned the still to the ground. He told J.D. he was middle aged when his young wife gave birth to their son, their only child. He was nearly ninety now, eighty-five anyway if you figure he remembered the floods of 1888 taking half of his family house away—the kitchen, dining room, and parlor—just ripping it all off and spewing it right down the road with his mother in it, in her bathrobe. She'd been stuffing sheets and towels and blankets at the doors to keep the water out. He was getting far on in life. Almost down to the end of the plank. Most of his anatomical parts were either busted or gummed up. He said his pecker gave out when Eisenhower was president. Oh, he could still pee all right, but the whole process took up most of the morning. "How you like that, Little Boy," he said, "standing out in the yard leaning on a tree the whole damn day, just staring off into space waiting for the thing to do something. Like it's got a mind of its own. Its own little pecker brain."

J.D. was worried about being a day late, missing the anniversary. He'd promised to be there, and he had a feeling that the old man might conclude he wasn't coming and decide to just end it all. Ease on through that long vale of tears. J.D. had to talk to him. Had to find him alive. There were things Old Man knew that he wasn't telling about. Secrets. Stories that didn't add up. As far as J.D. knew, nobody else ever came to see him. He was pretty sure he had no family, no relatives at all. There were no photographs, paintings, or keepsakes and never a reference to any kinfolk. He'd never even mentioned a friend or acquaintance or anyone stopping by to visit. Maybe they did, but J.D. doubted it. A girl named Abigail, who ran two stores in town, was the one possible exception. J.D. was sure they were connected in some way, but neither of them would speak a word about it. Both of them flat-out denied even knowing the other existed.

Once a week, at noon on Saturday, rain or shine, the old man would drive his '47 Ford one-ton flatbed a half mile to the end of his driveway and pick up groceries driven out to him by the stock boy at Food Mart in Mount Airy, twenty minutes south. He always got the same thing, he said. Dozen eggs, stick of butter, two cans of B&M baked beans, two cans of chicken noodle soup, half pound of bacon sliced to fourteen strips, half pound of sliced Virginia ham, small head of lettuce, big cucumber, loaf of bread, chunk of cheddar cheese, quart of milk, and a pint of Maker's Mark whiskey. Once a month they would add a pound of Maxwell's "Good to the Last Drop" coffee. He got the same thing every week for as long as he could remember, which, he said, wasn't very long anymore. He paid the delivery boy in cash with a fifty-cent tip, handed him his small bag of trash and empty whiskey bottle from the week before, and drove back down the road to his cabin. The boy probably would have been happy to drive up to the cabin and carry the bags inside, but Old Man apparently didn't want him to. He said he would have preferred to buy his "provisions," as he called them, from Van Dunn's Meat and Produce in Galax where things were cheaper and fresher, but Galax was a dry town in a dry county. Haskell Van Dunn couldn't sell him his whiskey. It could only be bought in a bar. He'd thought about buying just the food from Haskell, but it would be unseemly to have someone drive nothing but a bottle of hooch all the way up from North Carolina.

Once a year, the last week in September, Bingham's Fuel would deliver two cords of dry, split hardwood for the fires and stack it neatly at the end of the drive. It was the best burning wood around, mostly hickory and ash cut short to 12-inches, so it would fit in both the cook stove and the little heating stove. Two boys drove the dump truck from over by Fancy Gap, dumped the whole load, and then ricked two ends by cross stacking four-foot squares eight feet apart. They filled in the center four feet wide and four feet tall, just as straight and clean as could be. The Bingham Gas truck would deliver two hundred-pound tanks of propane and a five-gallon can of kerosene and stack them at the front end of the wood pile.

When J.D. got there a year ago, he and the old man took the Ford flatbed, loaded up the wood in four trips, and J.D. stacked it in the shed off the kitchen. He never said it outright, but it seemed like the old man didn't want anybody to come to his cabin. Nobody, that is, but him. Nobody but J.D.

The planks rattled as J.D. sped up over the bridge. His rifle rattled in the gun rack behind the seat. He gripped the steering wheel hard. Something wasn't right. Something was wrong. Up ahead the cabin sat still, no smoke coming out of either stone chimney. It was too cold for no fire. Too far from summer for no smoke.

2

Winchester Model #94

J.D. GOT HIS RIFLE ON HIS SIXTEENTH BIRTHDAY. He didn't want it. He didn't tell his mother straight out that he didn't want it because she was all smiles and bubbly when she handed it to him in its leather zippered carrying case with a shoulder strap and a bright red plastic-covered hunting permit. The case smelled and felt of fresh rubbed saddle soap. The permit was clipped to the shoulder strap, and she handed it to him gently with both hands partway out like a person hands a baby to another person.

"You know, J.D., you're the man of this house." She laughed a giggly laugh.

"I know that, Mom," he said as he knelt down on one knee, unzipped the bag, and took the rifle out. "I don't really feel like shooting anything though." He didn't feel like shooting at all. He didn't even feel like holding it in his hands. It was heavy. It was a machine made for men to use for a singular purpose. The wide butt of the carved stock where it fit the shoulder, the hammer, the lever, the rigid, blue oiled barrel, menacingly straight and long, and the fat, curved trigger were not made for women and children, not made for small, soft, timid hands. He could feel himself being pushed from the thatched cup of the belly of the nest to the hard edge, the rim where there was nothing but the world beyond. "What kind of gun is it?"

"Mr. Cobb said it was a, ah … let's see if I get this right … a 'Winchester model 94 lever-action 30-30, the best and most popular hunting rifle ever made.' He said three of them are in the White House. He also told me that both Junior Benoit and his brother Dirk, go out hunting every year. I think they'd be happy to have you to go with them. They know the woods around here, and if you shot a deer, they'd show you how to drag it out. I guess they drag them out, or maybe they carry them. I don't know, but then we could have venison in the freezer. What do you think?"

"Carry a dead deer with deer blood running out of him where his guts used to be. Cripes, Mom, I really don't think I want to do that." He held the gun lightly, just pinched in his fingers, as if were he to go ahead and grasp it, it might shoot. He stared at the gun. His mother stared at him, still smiling.

"Maybe. Maybe I could," J.D. said. "If I did go out hunting with Junior and Dirk, I think it takes all day, then you could walk over with me and stay and visit with Mr. Benoit for a while. He's probably kind of lonely. I've seen you talking to him in Harley's Diner."

"Jeremiah Dixon, you stop that right now. John Benoit's wife died a painful death only a year ago, and I am not presently in the market for a beau. Aside from that, he's not my type. We just happen to run into each other sometimes at the diner. There are some bullets in that box on the mantel. Maybe you could take it out back to the woods and see how it works."

"Mom, did my father have a rifle?"

That was the end of the smiles and bubbly giggles. J.D. knew it the moment he said it. He didn't know where the question came from or why it got into his mind right then or why it should even have mattered to him. She turned foul whenever he asked anything about his father. As Amanda Dixon walked away into the kitchen, cinching her bathrobe tighter around her narrow waist, she said, with her back to her son, "No, he didn't have any guns. If he did, I probably would have shot him with one." He heard coffee pouring in a cup and the tin pot bang on the counter. Then she said really loudly, almost shouting, "The less you're like that man, the better off both of us are going to be."

J.D was flicking his ear with his finger when she came back into the living room and put her hand on his shoulder. "I'm sorry, J.D., but that's part of why I bought this gun. So you'd get outside, maybe learn to love the woods. Get stronger, more confident in yourself. I know you like to spend a lot of your time alone up in that room you've made in the attic, but I'm worried about you. I just think it would be better if you spent that time outside, where the sun shines. Do you know what I mean?"

Her husband, William Wentworth III, had been a geology professor at the University of Virginia. Six years ago, he had died in a car wreck, hit broadside by a speeding truck while pulling out of the parking lot of the Jack & Jill Motel on Route 29 between Washington and Baltimore. A witness said the truck sped away from the scene. It was never found. The passenger lived. He was his teaching assistant. One of two specially selected graduate students to have become familiar with the velveteen picture of Elvis, the Naugahyde chair, and the threadbare carpet at the Jack & Jill, where rooms were rented by the hour and an easy ride through a master's thesis was traded for sodomy. The boy still talked day in and day out about Professor Wentworth's head lying in his lap, looking right up at him, unattached to his body, as he rocked back and forth in the sunroom on the main floor of Pickett House at the Skinner Bluff Lunatic Asylum.

Any time she heard Paul Anka singing "Put Your Head On My Shoulder," she felt sick to her stomach. It had been playing on the radio in the county morgue while she was identifying the head and torso of her husband's body. Confirming they were a match. The coroner had tried to be sensitive about it. He had placed the head where it normally should have gone, but it was clear it wasn't attached. There was no neck. Some part of the front of the truck had come right through the side window and obliterated the neck and took it all away. She never told her son anything about the death except to say it was a car accident.

J.D. overheard Mr. Benoit and his buddies talking about it in their garage. They all worked for the grounds department at the university and got together every Sunday afternoon to drink Budweiser, watch the Baltimore Orioles or their beloved Washington Redskins, and talk shit about their bosses, the administrators, and the professors. J.D. didn't get much of it because the TV was loud and they were laughing so hard, but he did get that it had to do with sex in a motel and can you fucking believe the university didn't do anything about it, scared shitless about a scandal, and who the hell hires these weirdoes anyway … Throw me a can of Bud … Can you believe that shit? … Jesus H. Christ! … Freakin' professors … Bunch a friggin' doosies!

When he enrolled in fourth grade, his mother signed him in as Jeremiah Dixon, not Jerry Wentworth. She had put a note on the enrollment form: *Please call him J.D.* Amanda Wentworth had gone back to her maiden name within two months of her husband's death. Professor Wentworth had spent his married life teaching and huddled up in his office writing books. He had been a full tenured professor for fifteen years, written a dozen textbooks, with royalties still rolling in on eight of them, and invested his money in IBM. She inherited everything: an eight-room farmhouse built in 1836, a barn, carriage house, apple orchard, thirty acres of fields and hardwood forest, a new Buick, a Chevy pickup, $50,000 in stocks and savings, a $15,000-a-year spousal pension, and a $5,000 life insurance policy. She fired the muscular boy her husband had hired to tend to the yards and barns. She gave the $5,000 away to a charity that counseled troubled youths. She threw away most of her nylons, skirts, and blouses and bought boots, blue jeans, and sweatshirts, letting her coiffed auburn hair grow long, clasping it back in a ponytail. She sold every piece of jewelry she owned. Dr. Amanda Jane Dixon began her second life squared up with the world as good as she could get it. She kept her job as a research scientist. Three days a week, she would drive two hours south to the university medical school to work in the epigenetics laboratory, looking into the relationship between chemicals and intelligence.

J.D. walked into the woods behind their house with his new gun and one bullet. The gun felt smooth and smelled like oil. There was a small compass set right into the walnut stock, and the metal was solid and steel blue. He found the springed chamber slot on the side and slid the bullet in, then swung the lever down and back up like he'd seen Junior do when he was shooting at a deer target in his backyard. He backed himself tight up against a big maple tree, pushing his shoulder as hard as he could into the bark, raised the barrel, put the butt of the stock right up under his chin, aimed at another big maple, slid his finger onto the smooth, curved trigger, squeezed it, and broke his collar bone.

"What are you, a fuckin' numb nuts?" Junior Benoit said. "Everybody knows you stand with your feet apart, leaning into it a little bit, and let your body give a little. No wonder you broke your neck, backed into a tree like that. Jesus, that's 90 percent half mental." Half-mental numb-nuts or not, Junior agreed to bring him out hunting with them when deer season opened in late October. Junior figured with three of them, two

11

could herd a deer right up to the third guy, like stuffing it through a funnel.

The first year out, Dirk drilled a beauty straight through the brain at almost fifty yards. The beast took one step to a run and fell over dead. They didn't slit its throat or carve its guts out on the mountain. They dragged it down the hillside and humped it into the back of the truck. Back home, they hung it by its Achilles tendons, bled it, gutted it, skinned it. Little Dickey, Junior's boss, a master meat carver, came over with his bag of knives and sliced the buck from deer to venison.

The second year out, J.D. left his boyhood behind. Down at Little Dickey's garage he became known as "Fixin' Dixon, the Yes! Yes! Man." The Benoit boys were herding a buck up through the funnel, following his hoof prints through the last night's light snow. J.D. was halfway up the mountain, settled into an outcropping near an old logging road, his rifle loaded, crosswise on his knees, his haunches on a flat spot and his back against a scoop-out in the rock face. Down the hill through a thicket of scrub oak, he saw a hard-top Jeep. A guy and a girl were in the front seats, and he was ripping her shirt off, and she was flailing at him, pushing him away. He could hear her screaming, "Get off of me! Stop it!" J.D. froze, his back pushed hard into the cold rock until he knew he could no longer stay inanimate, could not pretend he wasn't there. He crept off down the hill, going fast from behind one tree to behind another, coming up crouched low to the ground behind the car. He crawled along the side, held his 30-30 pointed straight up to the sky outside the open window, no more than six inches from the guy's head, and pulled the trigger. The guy jumped so hard he smashed his head into the metal roof. Junior yanked the door open and pulled the guy out onto his back on the ground. His pants were down around his knees. The guy reached out and grabbed J.D.'s ankle, digging his

12

fingernails into the flesh, and J.D., intending just to quell him with some gentle pressure, jabbed down with the butt of his rifle and broke the guy's nose. The girl didn't say a thing, sat there staring at him. The guy had parked right next to a tree, so she couldn't get out. The girl crawled across the seat, her shirt and bra hanging off her, got out, stood beside the guy, and kicked him in the ribs. "You animal!" she screamed, not even trying to cover herself up. J.D offered his orange hunting jacket. She shook her head.

"Who's he?" he said, pointing at the guy.

"My Uncle Bennie, the pervert. He said we were just going to smoke some dope." She was not pretty. She looked about eighteen, scraggly brown hair, skinny with an overbite, and bad acne. The guy was lying there moaning, one hand over his face, one hand on his side.

J.D. stepped over him, started the Jeep, and said, "Let's go. I'll take you home."

She knelt down beside the guy, who seemed to have slipped into some kind of coma, fished in his pants and took out a dope pipe, a bag of weed, and small tin tube with a rubber stopper in the end. "Creep!" She kicked him again. "Okay," she said as she flung her bra into the back of the Jeep and put her shirt on, unbuttoned. She climbed across the driver's seat and uncorked the tin tube, pushed shut one nostril, and sucked in a snort through the other. She began fiddling with the dope and pipe. Partway down the mountain she got it lit, sucked in a full charge, held her breath with little squeaks, and handed the pipe to J.D.

While the buck ran through the thin snow up the hillside past the outcropping, J.D., parked under a pine tree, blew her dope and let her take his hand and put it onto her breasts, let her unzip his pants. She moved around the small front seat like a cat in a cage—belly up, belly down, head and arms out the window, screaming, "Yes! Yes! Yes!" That's what the Benoit boys heard. They heard it on and on and on until J.D. got a cramp in his hamstring, and then it all went quiet. The boys met them at the foot of the mountain where she put her bra on, buttoned up her shirt, and drove off in the Jeep. He never asked what her name was or where she lived.

Over the next three seasons, J.D. and the Benoit boys bagged three bucks, two six-pointers and an eight-pointer, all from the forests between Blue Top Mountain and Merrymeeting Lake. Amanda's freezer was full of venison. It didn't seem to run out. Venison steaks, venison ribs, venison rounds, rumps, briskets, burgers, and frozen venison stew. In the days after a kill, there were fresh dripping kidneys, hearts, and livers. She became tired of deer parts, realized she had never liked venison in the first place, and asked J.D. to henceforth give his entire take to the Benoits. "They can have my freezer if they want. I'm looking forward to seeing Mr. Poggio again. He has such good hamburger and chicken."

He spent all his time in the woods or the fields, on riverbanks or in hunting cabins in the mountains, watching, smelling, feeling, tasting the ferns, the berries, listening, just listening to the hoot of the owls, the yip of the coyotes, the child-like cry-scream of a fisher cat, writing, reading by the light of a gas lantern. First thing each morning when he got to school, he went to the principal's office where he took his knife and sheath off his belt, gave it to the coiffed, scarlet-lipped and drawn-tight Miss McManus, the school secretary who put it in her drawer, and he picked it up from her when school was done. Other than that, it was always on his belt. He thought there was some kind of secret side to Miss McManus. The way she took his knife and gently stroked the leather sheath before putting it in her drawer, and how she pulled her lips together, but the slight curl of a smile always crept out on one side or the other. She never once said he shouldn't bring a knife to school, that it was against school policy. J.D. thought that maybe when she wasn't at school, all painted-up and stiff-backed, when she was home alone (she didn't wear a ring) or out on the town, she might be a wild thing like the girl in the Jeep.

J.D graduated first in his class from Shenandoah High, one of the best high schools in the state. For a week, Amanda had been meeting the mailman at the end of the driveway, bringing the mail inside and putting the letters from universities in a small pile on her bureau. The afternoon she knew they were all there, she fixed herself a pot of tea, sat on the sofa, put the letters on the coffee table, and waited for her son to come home from town. J.D. opened each one, read each acceptance letter from the Ivy League schools, and handed them to his mother. The letter from Appalachian School of Forestry, three miles away, he put on the coffee table and tapped with his finger. "This is the best forestry school in the country. I'm going to study trees."

3

The She-Boar

IT WAS TUESDAY, SEPTEMBER 30, 1969. J.D. banged the steering wheel of his truck, shouting, "Goddamnit! Son of a bitch!" alone in the cab as he drove south, headed anywhere but where he was. It was his first trip away from home all by himself, and he didn't know how he could ever go back. He did know it was going to be awhile before he could see his mother again. On the last Tuesday of each month, his Economics of Timber Management class went on a three-day fieldtrip to the Shenandoah Mountains or the hardwood timberlands of West Virginia or Maryland to study different wooded environments and their impact on the local and regional economies. They met with loggers and landowners, the businessmen of paper mills and furniture companies, and, as often as could be arranged, state and local officials. Except this Tuesday. This trip had been canceled. Both the professor and his graduate assistant had come down with the same flu. J.D. walked home in the late afternoon, three miles through the cow pastures, over Huckleberry Hill, past the Benoits' garage, and to the back door of his home on Cherry Lane. He opened the door and heard crashing and wailing from the upstairs. He walked up the stairs, quiet on each step as Amanda wailed. There was an empty bottle of scotch in the hallway, and she was kneeling on the floor of her bedroom, punching the glass in a framed photograph, screaming, "How could you do this to us?" She didn't see him watching her. She didn't hear him breathing short breaths through dry lips. She didn't hear him across the hall stuff clothes into a pillowcase, get his sleeping bag, get his gun. He didn't know if she heard the truck start and drive away, and he didn't care.

When he wasn't banging on the steering wheel, he drove with his left elbow out the window, and with his right hand, he flicked his right ear, like a dog scratching fleas. He had always done that when he was sad or scared or confused, and he was sure that was why that ear, not the other one, was cauliflowered. His mother had told him it was hereditary. His Uncle Danny's ear had looked like that before it got chewed off. J.D. intermittently flicked his ear as he drove through the eastern foothills of the mountains in the Shenandoah National Park and George Washington National Forest to Lynchburg, then west, over to the Blue Ridge Parkway. He flicked his ear and tried to figure out why he only felt confused, not sad or mad or even betrayed. Just confused. Long after dark, he pulled off, slept in the bed of his truck, and awoke to the morning sun flooding down through the great valley, the same sun reflecting back in his eyes off the shiny silver badge of a National Park Ranger.

"It's illegal to camp overnight on the Blue Ridge Parkway. Can I see your license and registration, please?" J.D. was happy he'd slept in his clothes. The papers were in the glove compartment, and he had the ubiquitous crack-of-dawn boner. "You're from Rappahannock County. What are you doing down here?" His mother's bent back and...black it out...fists pounding...black it out...chocking and sobbing...black it out...

"I came down to do some deer hunting, sir."

"Do you have a rifle in your truck?"

J.D. flicked his ear. "Yes, sir. It's not loaded though. Don't

TONY IRONS

have any ammunition."

"Good answer, Mr. Dixon. It's morning now, so I'm just going to give you a verbal warning; don't carry loaded weapons in your vehicle and don't sleep on this parkway. No camping allowed. Good luck with your hunting."

"Thank you, Officer. By the way, where's a good place to hunt deer? And, oh yeah, where do I go to get a new permit? Mine's expired."

"You can get one at any police station, gun shop, or hardware store. Dengman Gap, an hour south down by Galax, is a great place to hunt. That's where I always go."

The wooden plank porch in front of Harrelson's Hardware was long and sloped toward the road. There was no railing, just two steps up. A young man, red-headed, stocky with a wide face and round blue eyes, wearing denim overalls and black rubber boots with red soles, sat on a hay bale on the porch, leaning back against the storefront, silent, just staring at J.D. as he got out of his truck, crossed the road, and stepped up onto the porch. J.D. said good morning to him, and he didn't blink or move a bit. Silent. Staring with an utterly blank expression. Not a flicker. Not a twitch. J.D. shivered in the warm air and walked into a store that hadn't changed in a lifetime. It smelled like fresh-cut hay and bag balm and molasses oats horse feed. Lined up along the wall were wooden casks filled with nails of various sizes, each cask with a small rake and a metal scoop. A tin bucket scale with sliding weights stood in the center. Along the other wall were stacked burlap sacks of oats and bales of alfalfa. All the tools of farmers, ranchers, plumbers, and carpenters stood stacked in a wide center aisle. Behind the sales counter, rifles and bows were lined up on a shelf. At the end were the two biggest guns J.D had ever seen. He went to them and read the marking: Westley Richards. A beautiful pair

19

of single-barrel shotguns. A two-foot-tall National brass and oak cash register with typewriter keys and a lever crank handle sat in the corner. Saddles, blankets, and tack were set out on saw horses. There was no one there. Hollering out didn't raise anybody. No one came. He walked around, smelled the alfalfa, felt the smooth tooled saddle leather. No one came. More hollering and still no one came. Back out on the porch, the young man stared at him with the same blank expression. Not a muscle twitched. As he stepped off the porch to leave, a girl, twenty or so, came running around the corner, braid bouncing wildly behind, saying, "I'm so sorry, Mister. I should have come sooner, but I was all gummed up with wrenches trying to fix that dadburned warshin machine in the laundermat. I am truly sorry." She held the screen door open for him and followed him in.

"How did you know I was here?"

"There's a button out on the porch beside that boy. It rings an electric bell in the laundermat. When I'm over there, he lets me know when someone's at the store." She walked around the counter and sat up on a high wooden stool.

J.D. looked around at the saddles and hay bales. "How do you know he always pushes the button?"

"That's a darn good question. Nobody's ever asked that before. But, yes, I do know that he always pushes the buzzer. I know that because that's why he's sitting out there. For one reason only, to push the buzzer. When your life has only one thing in it you have to do, you do it. He wouldn't miss a chance."

"Is he, ahh, how should I say this? Is he okay?"

"He's about as good as a person gets. He's like my brother. I've known him for a long, long time. He might seem duller than a sack of rocks, but he's not. He just got that way in the last year. He's also a very sweet person. Billy Talikonoge wouldn't hurt a fly."

"Talikonoge? What kind of name is that?"

"It means something like Two Wings in Cherokee. When he was little, he couldn't be left alone. He'd be scared and cry. So Chief John named him that, hoping it would straighten him out and he could fly by himself. He used to be better; talked and laughed and everything. I don't know now, though. He's just like that all the time. Sometimes I think he even might forget who I am, so I go out back and take my shirt off—I put another one on, of course—and I lay it in his lap, and he smells it and remembers everything, just like a dog, like people would if we hadn't forgot how to smell. I gave him the name Billy."

"Chief sounds like a really smart guy."

"Well, I truly don't know how smart he is. He just knows everything, that's all."

"I see. Yeah, I see how that could be."

"Now, all that being straightened out, what can I do for you?"

"Okay," he said, shaking all the questions out of his head. "I need a hunting license and a box of 30-30 shells, please." J.D. laid his wallet on the counter open to his driver's license, fished in his pocket for money, and waited while she filled out the permit.

"What about those two big shotguns up there?"

"Those there are Mr. Harrelson's. They're not for sale."

"What are they?"

"They're both almost a hundred years old. Single-barrel ten gauge. His granddaddy brought them over from England. That's where they were made. One slug will take down any big game: elk, boar, bear with one shot. Where are you going hunting?"

"Dengman Gap," he said.

"Dengman Gap? That's next to the Cherokee Reservation.

You can hunt there all right, but you be careful. It's the best hunting in this part of the state, but it can be dangerous. Things can happen up there. Don't go on the reservation; there's no public hunting there. It's not really a reservation. Nobody lives there. It's just thousands of acres of burial grounds the government gave the Indians about fifty years ago. It's sacred. You can tell if you're at it 'cause there's a strand of wire runs around the whole thing, miles of it. Miles and miles of one thick strand of wire. Some places there are bird feathers and teeth and branches tied to it and big signs about every hundred feet so you can't miss 'em. Nobody goes there, ever. That's how it's supposed to be." She leaned on her elbows on the counter, lowered her head a little bit, put her eyebrows up. "You be real careful now, y'hear?"

J.D. took his box of shells and his permit, stuffed his change in his pocket, contemplated her dark, dark blue, up-tilted, almost Oriental eyes with bright gold-green specks in them, her high cheekbones, the field of freckles on her face and neck, and the rhythmic pumping of her blood just below the open collar of her gingham shirt. She smelled like oranges.

"I'm very careful. Things can happen anywhere. I'll be fine. You're a really sweet person."

"Thank you Mr. ..." she looked down at his driver's license. "Mr. Jeremiah Dixon, so are you. You coming back to town?"

"Not likely. I'm not much in the killing mood. Mostly I just want sit with my rifle across my knees and think about things. Even if a deer came up to lick the salt off my neck, I'd probably just let it go on its way. I'll probably be headed north in the morning."

"Then what are you getting a hunting permit for?"

"Mood might change."

Acorns from the oaks carpeted the hillside floor, dropped off branches when the leaves turned brown so the squirrels could most easily gather the fresh, plump ones, stuff them in their squirrel mouth pouches, and scurry back to their autumn nests. Broad-winged hawks circled up and up, sweeping smoothly on a thermal cone while crows, helter-skelter, dove at them, nipping at their wings. There was no sound at all. Still. Warm. Blue sky and blue forest.

J.D. had ten rounds of ammunition, a hunk of cheese, a hunk of salami, and a bottle of ginger ale slung across his back in a Guatemalan pouch he'd bought at the Dollar Store in Galax, an eight-inch gutting knife on his belt, and his rifle, loaded with five shots, slung the other way across his back. Before he locked his truck, he realized his wallet was not in his back pocket. Not in the glove compartment or in the seat or on the floor. He checked all the pockets in his pants, shirt, jacket. He'd left it with his driver's license on the counter in the hardware store. *Might have to go back into town,* he thought. *That's all right; give me a chance to see her again.*

As J.D. set out, each step was careful, considerate, making sure no twig snapped, no squirrel startled. He had been walking uphill for an hour, and the oaks were getting shorter, giving way to more gnarled, less stately scrub and azalea. He wanted to get to the top of Grayson's Ridge and work his way downhill through Dengman Gap. He knew deer don't run downhill. It's too dangerous; their chests and necks and heads are more than half their weight. Their hooves are sharp and get driven deep into soft dirt; gravity wants to make their front legs buckle. They walk downhill. If he saw a deer, and the deer saw or smelled or heard him, and J.D. was above it, it would bound to the right or the left, its head and heart wide to his view, not a backside running away from him. J.D. thought about this as he walked up the steepening hill to the top of

Grayson's Ridge. At the crest on a butte looking three or four miles out over the Gap and down the Blue Ridge into North Carolina, he sat cross-legged and thought about animals only running uphill or sideways on a mountain and thought about the trees and how they get scrubbier, shorter, and more gnarled the higher up you go because there is less oxygen and the dirt is thinner and how many millions of acorns there were down below on the forest floor and how many more oak trees and fat squirrels there were going to be where the air and dirt were rich. He thought about the girl in the hardware store, her freckles and throbbing neck, and he watched her, quiet now, slowly, button by button, take off her shirt, and in between each thought, like a quick, hard yank on a chain, he thought about his mother and his father and what all might have happened. And why his mother wouldn't talk. Just drank and screamed and cried when she was alone. *What happened? Why won't anybody tell me? Is she the only one who knows? No, that can't be.*

The stillness in the air settled over him, around him like a blanket. One small plume of white smoke rose from a cabin chimney a few miles down the valley. The hills to the south were blue, and he knew it was the haze in the air that came from the trees, and it was that blue haze that hung about the hills and valleys that gave the mountains their name. Down the hill a ways in front of him, running crosswise, the grasses were beaten down in a narrow stip. A deer run. He watched a squirrel scamper up an oak, fidget about in the fresh acorns, and then scamper halfway down and stop stock sill, not blinking, not even a twitch of the nose as a hawk glided low over the edge of the scarp not far from the tree. J.D. thought he heard an almost infinitesimal breath from the feathered wings passing through warm air. In that instant, the squirrel was not a squirrel; it was a knot-lump, a brown carbuncle on tree bark.

The big bird canted slightly and swept off on a bow bend down the throat of the valley and off to another mountain ridge. The squirrel chattered and dashed for the ground.

The blue-brown valley was void of intrusion. All things there belonged there. J.D. tried to make his mind go placid, fearful that the ripples of his thoughts would disturb that perfect silence, but the more he tried to pull the peace into himself, the more his thoughts bumped about. The broad-winged hawk would surely not glide so smoothly through his disturbance. But no matter. There was nothing to be done with it. He had not come to hunt, to kill a deer in its own home and carve its guts out and then wonder what to do with the carcass. He had come to be alone with his thoughts in a place where no one knew where he was or who he was. He was in that place. His mother hurt, and that made him hurt. To try to think beyond that would do no good for anyone. He couldn't find a truth, not a single truth about it all. He couldn't find the eye of the needle. Most likely his father had left her with a hole in her soul, but he didn't know that either. Maybe he died with a hole in *his* soul. He wondered what would have happened if his mother had looked up from the floor of her bedroom and seen him standing there.

J.D. worried a rock loose from the ground, a potato sized rock, and juggled it back and forth from hand to hand as he thought about these things, and when he realized that someday he might understand as much as anybody about trees and ferns and forests, but probably would never understand people all that well, he threw the rock in a lobbing arc far down the hill into a patch of deep green-leaved rhododendron, and a screaming squealing fractured the still morning. Three or four or five big baby pigs ran helter-skelter from the bushes across the hillside slope, and a great sow boar lunged out of the low canopy, her head high, her massive mouth with razor-sharp tusks wide open, short legs pumping, thrusting her 500-pound body to the right, to the left, and then straight uphill as her pig eyes fixed on J.D. He jerked up, tripped backwards, jerked up, knelt down, and yanked and fought the gun strap cross-laced with the food bag strap, ripping his ear as he finally freed his rifle and slid his hand into the lever hoop, jamming it open to load the first shot into the magazine and spring back the hammer, the Winchester still pointed up into the Appalachian sky, and he knew he was too late. She was ten feet away and her mouth still wide open; she was lowering her head, lowering her tusks for the kill. As J.D. stumbled backwards, a great blast broke the air, and her boar head snapped to the side, driving her whole body, shoulder first, into the dirt two feet in front of him. The sow boar convulsed in a quarter-ton quiver, and blood pumped out of a hole in her head the size of a golf ball. Her legs gave a last jerk, her pig eyes went blank, and she died spewing brains and blood all over his feet.

J.D. jumped back, looking left where he was sure the shot came from, and he thought he caught a glimpse of something leaping from the scarp. He thought he caught a glimpse of a gingham shirt and a blonde braid as his heel caught a root and he fell flat backwards and the back of his head smacked hard on a rock.

As the horsemen come to the edge of the garden, they pull their black steeds up sharp where the flowers meet the dirt. They are muscular in sleeveless, leather jerkins with great, skillet-sized, brass peace symbols hanging from their necks. One has the head of a bear, one the head of a ram, and the lead horseman, whose mount rears up and blows hot feculent air through flapping, gaping nostrils, that one has the head of a boar.

He lowers his lance, the sharp spear just touching my mother's neck, and he grunts deep, growling, gasping grunts. My mother moves the point away with a gentle lift of the back of her hand, takes the single drop of dark red blood on her fingertip, and licks it off with a flick of her tongue. She is a naked child, and I am a baby on her back in a Guatemalan sack like a papoose. She stretches her arms out wide, draws a deep, deep breath, and blows pink air smelling like lavender into the horse's nose. They all, the men and their steeds, waft into nothingness, and she bends back to digging the black soil with her toes, letting seeds fall through her fingers into each divot. Junior Benoit has a white beard. He strokes it, standing at the edge of the garden, talking, but no words come. Only his mouth moves. Silent chatter. A vacuum. I can't hear anything. He is talking to me about my father. And then he says in a whisper so strong the flower petals, blinding bright red, shimmer and melt from the stem, dripping on the dirt like blood, "It isn't that you're not old enough to know this yet; it's that your mother isn't old enough to tell you. She's only six." And he walks away, wobbly-like.

J.D. felt a percussion throb in the back of his head. He was hot, very hot. He touched his chest with his fingers, and his skin was wet with sweat. He licked his lips. Dry as birch bark. He smelled meat cooking. He heard it sizzle. He moved his head, and something tugged around his ears. Something scratched on rough cloth. One eye eased open a slit. A bent man, an old man, hunkered over a wood stove. J.D. licked his lips again and swallowed.

"Where am I?"

"Well, shit a mile, little boy. I just knew the smell of fresh pig liver would bring you back from wherever you been. You're at the bottom of Dengman Gap, Galax, Virginia, in an old man's cabin. You got a hell of a bump on the back of your head, so you shouldn't be moving around quite yet. If you can sit up a little, I got fixed up some hot coffee and liver and eggs. You might be hungry by now."

"By now? What day is it? How'd I get here?"

"Let's see, little boy, I guess it's Thursday. I know it's the first day of October. I'm real sure on that. It's about midmorning, and yesterday early on I dragged you all the way from Grayson Ridge down through the Gap to my cabin, wrapped you up, got some opium down your throat, and put you to bed. Real opium, the good stuff. You were out cold for a while. Then you slept the sleep of the blessed." He was standing over a cook stove, fiddling with the food in a skillet. Spatula in one hand, fork in the other.

"Well, I thank you. That's a hell of a haul for an old man. What's your name?"

"My name? Old Man sounds good to me. Fits perfect. That'll do. And you, little boy, who are you?" The fresh liver fried, an egg cracked on the edge of the skillet, the egg fried.

"Little Boy sounds fine to me. We could just leave it at that."

The old man handed J.D. a glass of water and a tablespoon full of brown syrup. Then a cup of coffee. "That's a good idea. Why don't we just leave it at that. I'm Old Man, you're Little Boy. Leave it like that."

"Why did you have to haul me off the top of a mountain?"

"I was up there tending to my own business when I saw a wild she pig about to slice you to ribbons. I shot her dead just in time, but you tripped over backwards and broke your head open. I had to haul both of you down the mountain. That there on my skillet is part of the big beast. The rest of her parts and pieces are sitting in the shed in a crock full of salt brine. Want some food?"

J.D. folded the blankets down around his waist, sipped his coffee. *The old man must be at least eighty years old. Couldn't weigh more than 120 pounds, and he's bent and crooked.* He remembered the boar, remembered her lunging at him, and remembered the great blast from a gun. He sipped the coffee.

"I don't mean to be questioning the truthfulness of what you say, Old Man. Maybe you even saved my life, and here you are helping me out, but I can't really see you carrying me and a 500-pound pig down that mountain."

"Truth, Little Boy, is not like a lump of dirt that everyone sees the same way. It's a belief. Big lump to a flatlander, little lump to a mountain man. They're both right. Often, a pile of facts won't add up to the truth no matter how you arrange them. I didn't carry that boar down the mountain; gravity did. I just helped it along. So far as you go, I just tied you to the she boar and kicked you both downhill. Now listen close here. That's all there is to it. Nothing more." He turned face-on to J.D., pointing the spatula at him. "There is nothing more to it, son. Believe it, and it's true. Just like the Bible. Simple as that. Believe it, and—bingo!—by God it's true. Want some fresh cooked liver and eggs?"

"I have to call my mother."

The old man slid the skillet to a back burner, put his cooking utensils aside, wiped his hands on a checkered cloth, sat down in his rocking chair, slapped both knees, and began to laugh a loud, snorting chortle, shaking his head. "Don't that beat all! I suppose if I hit my head on a rock I'd have to call my mother right away too. Right away, that is, if she hadn't died a hundred years ago and if I had a telephone, which I don't. Now eat your breakfast, and we'll get to town bye and bye. *Have to call my mother now ... oh my goodness.*"

When J.D. awoke again, the sun had moved from the front windows to the back windows. It was a softer light, muted by the forest behind, a pale sun that had nearly spent itself for that day. There was a fresh glass of water and a small cup with brown fluid in it beside the bed. The old man was not there. It was unearthly quiet. He drank the fluid, drank the water, and put his feet on the braided rug beside the bed. He wobbled up.

There were scatter rugs in front of each chair and a large one in the kitchen corner. The cabin was one room; one big room with two windows in the front, two windows in the back, and one on each end wall. A sofa, chair, and a small, oval wood stove in one corner. He walked over to the stove. It was warm. Embossed on the cast iron front, it said Loth's Hickory—The W.J. Loth Stove Co.—Waynesboro, Va. Beside the stove was a bookcase. Paperbacks on the two top shelves, hard covers on the next two shelves, and tall books across the bottom. It stretched the entire length of the wall over and under the window. On either end, kerosene lamps hung from cast iron hooks. He walked slowly, holding his hand against the furniture. Past the front door was the kitchen. There was a small refrigerator with a chrome latch handle and chrome door hinges, a wooden counter, and soapstone sink with a pitcher pump. Under the pump spout was a bucket of cold water. J.D. splashed it onto his face and neck and dried with a towel hung through a wrought iron ring on the front of the counter. The dishes from his breakfast were washed and set in a wooden rack. Beside the sink was the cook stove, a six-plater with a hot water tank on the side. On the oven door, it said Glenwood-Model 207. He opened a simple board door beside the stove. Inside, wood was stacked chest high, arm's length deep. Off to one side was a board-walled shower stall with a slatted wood floor and a copper tank up above with a spigot on it. A pipe out of the back of the cook stove water tank went through the wall to a crank handle pump and up to the tank. Off the other side was a one-hole shitter with a swinging half-door. The cabin was neat. Not the neat of a tidy man, but the neat of a man who kept nothing he didn't want to put on his body, in his mouth, or in his mind. Spare and clean. J.D. ran his hand over the cabin walls. They were smooth, solid wood with a thin line of white chinking between each one. A log cabin built of chestnut logs. Chestnut beams, a foot square and thirty feet long. *Castenea dentata*. He could tell by the distinctive yellow sapwood at the edges of some of the beams. Those trees didn't exist anymore. In the early 1900s, they made up a quarter of all the trees in the Appalachian Mountains. They were all gone now. Gone to blight fifty years ago. He smelled them. They smelled of smoke and oil. *Chestnut*, he thought. *My God, these are huge timbers. They're worth a fortune as wood for furniture.* He opened the front door and peered out. The old man was sitting in the passenger side of his truck in the driveway, driver's side door opened.

"Time to get on over to town, get your truck, and call your mother." He chortled again and patted the driver's side of the seat.

"I don't need to call my mother because I need her," J.D. said, putting his hand gently on the back of his head. "I need to call her because she needs me. She might be worried I'm not home by now."

"No father, huh?"

"No. No. That's right, Old Man. I don't have a father. Now how's your truck going to get back here if I drive over? Can you drive back?"

"Not without ending up in a ditch." The old man jerked his thumb toward the flatbed. There was a tow bar on it.

Amanda Dixon hadn't even expected her son home yet. She

was thankful he called to tell her he might be a few more days. She was doing well and was quite happy. She didn't even ask him where he was. It must not have mattered to her. After he hung up, he began flicking his ear. Looking up the street and down the street, looking at Old Man sitting in the truck. He remembered he left his wallet in the hardware store, waved toward the old man in the truck, walked around the corner, stepped up on the porch, and said hello to Billy. Billy stared back blankly, eyes wide open, not a twitch. Like a photograph.

The girl was inside standing behind the counter adding up receipts. No, he hadn't left his wallet there. She shook her head, leaned over, and touched his shirt pocket. His wallet was in that pocket, but he was certain it hadn't been there yesterday. He had checked every pocket on his body. He never put his wallet in that pocket, and he never buttoned that pocket. J.D put his hands on the counter, leaning closer as she tapped his shirt. He looked again at her neck, so thin, and a simple silver cross hanging in the cleft between her collarbones. He pulled his eyes up and glanced around. One of the 10-gauge shotguns wasn't in the rack behind her.

"Where'd that big shotgun go?"

She looked back at the rack, moved some papers on the counter, licked her lips. "There was a bear ravaging the garbage out by the ball field. Mr. Harrelson went out and took care of it."

"Miss, did you help me out yesterday?"

"Sold you some shells and a permit. My name's Abby, by the way. Did you ever pull the trigger?"

"No," J.D. said. "I never did. That's all you did for me? That's it?"

"That's it, Mr. Dixon."

J.D., with Old Man riding shotgun, found his truck on the side of the road at the foot of the hill that led up to Grayson's

Ridge. He hooked up the tow bar, and they towed his Chevy all the way around the mountain, on to Cherokee Road, over the bridge, and back to the cabin.

There had been no time in his life where he sat and talked about all things he wanted to talk about. Maybe a little bit here and there but never any true words with a person who was not part of him, who hadn't seen any of the things he had seen, whose understandings of him were new, born out of just spoken words handed back and forth between each of them, having no root in anything already known except a trust that the gift of a word or a phrase was just that: a gift. Certainly no one had ever asked him how he felt about the fact that his father was dead (he said it didn't matter to him because he didn't know what it would have been like anyway, any more than he knew what it would be like having a brother or sister or two or three. Who knows?). Nor had he, nor would he ever have considered asking an old man why he lived alone and didn't have any pictures of any family or friends (he said he didn't have any family or friends, and it didn't matter to him either because, it sounds a strange thing, but he enjoyed being alone, not just being alone, but being left alone, like a cat curled up by a stove, but, by the way, he did have a friend, and he was sharing his company right now). Both voices were soft as air and seemed to waft from one to the other by the warm heat of the wood stove, like the birds on a thermal on Grayson's Ridge, unhurried, sure.

"A man on the moon."

"Pardon me? What was that you said?"

"I said there was a man on the moon, walking around just a couple of months ago."

"Aye-o aye-o, is that so? I didn't know you smacked your head so hard. I've heard that up in Roanoke there's a clinic that likes to talk to people like you about things like that."

"No, no, it's true. His name is Neil Armstrong. Walked around and put a flag up there too."

"My, my, you should tell that to the nice man in the white coat while you're lying on his sofa."

Every so often, when the stove needed a poke, J.D. would open the lid, rustle the fire about with the poker, add a stick, take the jug off the mantel, and they would take a sip just, as Old Man put it, just a sip to cut the phlegm.

"Did you say you were a forester?"

"Yes, I'm a forester, well not yet, but soon, soon I'll be a forester."

"You'll be a forester that knows what trees grow where and why. And people will listen to you when you talk about trees."

"Yes, Old Man, I hope they will."

"And what about your mother, Little Boy? What about her?"

"She's a geneticist. Studies genes and chemicals. I would prefer to wait until the words I choose to tell you about my mother are the right words. A week ago I would have thought I knew them, but today I'm not so sure." He took a swig from the jug.

"Next time," Old Man said. "Next time we can talk about her, and next time I'll tell you about my son. Shit a mile," he said, "you know what trees ought to be where, and your mother knows how people get like they are. That's perfect. Next time."

J.D. sat silent for a while, then asked about that girl, Abby, at the hardware store. "She's cute as a bug's ear. How long have you known her?"

The old man got up and crab-walked to the kitchen sink, splashed some water on his face, and crab-walked back. "I am pleased you met a pretty girl down here, but I don't know any girl at the hardware store named Abby. Don't know much of anybody over there."

It seemed as though the bird had tucked its wings and swung down fast off the warm wind, swung toward the ground to better see something that scurried about. It was past midnight.

4

Fighter Pilots

J.D. KEPT THE SPEEDOMETER AT EXACTLY SIXTY as he headed out of the high mountains toward his home in the northern hills and flatlands. He counted telephone poles, timing the count to see how many poles he passed in a minute and then figured out how far apart they were spaced. Two hundred and twenty feet. He wondered if he could figure out from that number how many telephone poles there were in the United States and how big a forest it would take to grow all those trees. He pulled off the road at one pole and looked at it carefully. Southern yellow pine. As he drove on, he began to calculate the number of miles of roads in the country, beginning with his own town, which he thought was a fairly normal, rural American town of about fifteen square miles with about forty miles of roads, and let's say the cities would have ten times that, and maybe 5 percent of the land in America, 3000 miles by 1500 miles, was taken up by cities of one sort or another, and he realized he was adding up trees to block out all his other thoughts. Everything: his mother, his father, the old man, Abby, the she-boar, the back of his head, his dream—everything had sprung wild, like birds out of a cage. J.D. tried to catch each one, one at a time, get it back in its cage.

He remembered when Uncle Danny, his father's younger

brother, had come to visit. It was over Christmas, and J.D., Jerry then, just five, was still in short pants. Gray, wool short pants with a thin, black belt and socks that came up to his knees. Jerry sat on the floor in front of his uncle and listened to stories about all the men who worked as US Marshals out in the hot, dry cactus land of west Texas. The hard men, brown and wrinkled from a sun that was a damn blast furnace in the sky every day, day after day, and they had to wear cowboy hats and tie rags around their necks to keep their head and skin from burning up. Had to drink five gallons of water a day to keep from drying up and blowing away across the desert like a big ball of tumbleweed. Tracking down one thief, one pervert, one murderer at a time. Just one at a time. Follow their tracks through the sand and the canyons and the scuffed-up arroyo beds and down into little, one-bar towns where they were always sitting at that one bar, half drunk or whole drunk, and you didn't even have to shoot 'em. Just show them your badge and ask the bartender for a napkin to wipe the puke-drool off their chin and take them away. Take them away for some judge to decide where to put their ass. Sometimes a gun would go off, and sometimes you'd get a little hurt, but not bad. He held out his left hand so Jerry could see it had only three fingers. The little finger was gone; nothing there but a stump. He let Jerry feel the stump and let him ask him if it hurt when it got shot off, and he said, "No, there wasn't any time for pain. If you jumped or blinked or cried out, like as not, you'd get shot through the heart. You might cry a little in the bar at night after you and your fellow marshals drank a few bottles of whiskey, but never there. Never with those guys. Too dangerous. Like my ear. That got chewed off by a half-Mex hired gun when I forgot to tell him who I was. Forgot to show him my badge. I just said, 'You'll have to come along with me now,' and he jumped up, threw his arms around me, and chewed my ear off. Couldn't cry about it there, but I sure did later." He pulled his long hair off to the side and let Jerry get up and touch the carbuncled flap that was all that was left. "Could have easily stuck me with his knife, so I suppose I'm a lucky guy. This is what it is, son," he said, leaning close to Jerry and putting his rough hand soft and gentle on his cheek. "Do the things you have to do, tall and straight. Don't cry, don't blink. There's plenty of time for all that when your work is done." He'd reach over and pat his mother's cheek and let his rough, three-fingered hand slide down her arm and give her hand a little squeeze.

His mother had a look about her that was different when Danny came and told his stories. She looked pinker than she usually did. She smiled the whole time. Pink and smiling, leaning forward, sitting out near the edge of her chair, pulling her skirt down over her knees. She'd do things like whistle a throaty, low whistle when he was done telling a story. It sounded like the cooing of the mourning doves that nested in the eaves of their carriage house. Jerry never heard her whistle when his father was talking. She always sat back in her chair with her legs crossed and just looked at him.

Little snippets of his dream came back to him as he drove. An opium dream. His mother a child in a garden, Junior talking in silent words, horsemen with animal heads. He remembered the colors in his dreams. Grass greens and reds, dripping blood reds, and Junior's white beard. His head hurt now that the brown syrup the old man had given him was wearing off and the miles were piling up behind him.

The last day his Uncle Danny was there that year, his father had taken him to the tennis courts at the university. He didn't want to go. He wanted to hear more stories, but his father said it was important for them to go and do something together. Just the two of them. It was the only time he could remember he had gone anywhere with his father without his mother being with them. There was no snow, but it was freezing cold. He had on winter boots, shorts, and a sweater. His father was dressed all in white clothes with a bright blue scarf tied around his neck. The very first ball his father hit to him went over his head, and he turned and ran after it, swinging his racquet with both hands, tripping on his boot laces, landing face first on the asphalt courts. He remembered crying but not letting go of his tennis racquet until his father knelt down, begging him to get up. He couldn't remember his father ever touching him.

He had to talk to Junior. Mr. Benoit was a chatterbox. Junior knew things that he needed to know. Old Man had figured out right away that he didn't have a father. How'd he know that? What does a boy who doesn't have a father do that makes everybody know that right away?

The old man knew other things too. There was a sense of fore-knowing in everything he said, as though each word was a footprint in a path he had walked many times. And there was no way that little old man hauled him and a giant dead pig down through two miles of forest. J.D. realized that the phone poles were getting closer together. They had more wires on them. He was coming up on a big city. Charlottesville.

Eight quarters and he got Mr. Benoit. "Junior's down to the garage yanking the motor out of his Mustang. Going to bore it and stroke it."

"Thanks, Mr. Benoit. Is he working tomorrow?"

"Tomorrow is Sunday. Nobody's supposed to work on Sunday." Mr. Benoit wanted to know how his mother was and how school was going and where he was and how life was treating him. J.D. answered each question with the politeness due an elder next-door neighbor, careful not to let any answer invite another question.

"You better believe it," Junior said to J.D. "I'd love to kick up some shit down in college town. Let's get us a hotel room to dump our stuff in and pound the streets all night long. I haven't been to the city in almost a year, and this country life is getting awful quiet for my tastes. Shit, J.D., the bars here close at midnight, and then the cops are driving the roads seeing who gets into what car. Having a good time is fucking dangerous around here." A compressor kicked on, and an air hammer battered away at some rusted bolt. A motorcycle engine screamed. J.D. envisioned Dickey, shirtless, revving up his Bultacco for another run up the face of the Bartlett Reservoir Dam. "And it's good to hear you talking as a friend, J.D. You know what I mean? I'll meet you at that Irish Pub near the fraternities at seven. How's that?"

J.D., leaning into the phone booth outside a gas station, pulled his jacket tighter around him as the wind picked up. He could see Junior in Dickey's garage, grease on his face and hands and arms, in a white T-shirt with the sleeves rolled up, big muscles, crew cut, square jaw, blue jeans, boots, smile big as a night sky. One afternoon when they were huddled together under a big pine by the shore of Long Pond, J.D. told him he thought about things all the time, trying to figure out how all the parts and pieces of life fit together. Junior said that life is easy to figure out. "It's like a barrel of pickles. Eat one and you know what it is. You don't have to eat the whole fucking barrel to see if you can find out more about what a pickle is. Like us," he said. "We're as different as you get, but we're still friends. Chewing on it longer won't get you knowing any better what it is. So stop worrying about it all the time. You'll be deaf, dumb, crippled, and blind before you ever get to the bowl of cherries. Half of the girls you could have fucked would've thought you're some kind of dickless egghead. So screw it; live now, think later."

"Yeah," J.D. said, "the Irish pub at seven sounds good to me. I'll be there."

They met at Hennessey's Pub, had a Guinness stout, then walked eight blocks to the underbelly of Charlottesville. There were a lot of places with cheap rooms. The Puritan Hotel, two blocks past the railroad tracks, was exactly what they hoped it would be. The sign outside said cheap, really cheap. Twelve bucks a night for a double. Getting in the front door meant shoving aside a passed-out drunk and stiff-arming a hungry whore in net stockings and a skirt no bigger than a sneeze. A ten-foot square lobby with busted linoleum floor tiles, one wooden chair in the corner, and a 400-pound Hawaiian, snoring, sound asleep behind a plywood counter. Junior leaned over the counter, stared at the fat man, looked at J.D. with an exaggerated gape to his mouth.

"Whoa!" he whispered. "Would you get a load of that motherfucker! Looks like one of Little Dickey's kinfolk."

Faster than a snake on a rat, he had Junior by the throat. Junior wriggled around and made squeaking noises. He stomped his foot. He slapped the counter. His eyes started to bug out. He kicked the counter. He clawed at the giant, hairless arm. The man's hand reached almost all the way around his neck. "You want a room?" he asked, looking at J.D.

"Yes, sir. A double if you have one."

"Twelve bucks." He let go of Junior.

The elevator around the corner was occupied by a young black man, shirtless with a floppy hat, sequined bell bottoms, and patent leather shoes. He was reading a comic book and didn't look up. The door was bent and off its track. They took the stairs, four flights up. J.D. got there first and put his stuff on the better of the two beds. Junior stared at his bed. There was a huge, salmon colored splotch in the middle of it. He put his finger on it. It was damp.

"Oh my fucking word," he said, rubbing his neck. "How did that possibly happen? I mean, Jesus, where did that come from?"

"Don't think about it, Junior," J.D. said, patting him on the back. "Sleep in your clothes."

"No, I mean, J.D., that just happened," he said, pointing at the splotch. "Whatever people were doing on this bed, they just did it! I think I'm going to barf." Junior went into the bathroom, saw a turd in the dry toilet bowl, puked all over the mirror, sink, and floor, walked out wiping his pale face and mouth with his shirt sleeve, picked up his bag, and went out the door. He motioned for J.D. to follow. Down the stairs past the kid still reading his comic and fast through the lobby, out the door. Junior turned back at the door. "Take your twelve bucks and shove it up your fat ass, Fat Man!" he bellowed and scooted down the street.

The Inferno Bar & Grill was two blocks down Prospect Street. Past a 24-hour check-cashing store, dead storefront, Liquor! Liquor! Liquor! neon flash. A cold rain that drove its way between the collar and the neck and drove the two boys close together, bumping shoulders as they walked past people driven into the shallow alcoves of the stores, huddled shirt to dripping shirt, trying to keep their feet up out of puddles, sharing a joint or a snort, sticking their hand out when the boys walked by. As they passed by the next storefront, some were laughing at a joke or absurdity, one laid on another, finding humor in a cold, wet, concrete world where the past, present, and future were unmercifully the same thing. Junior walked hunched with his hands jammed in his pockets. J.D. bumped him.

"How you feeling?"

"Like I just touched wet shmegma, somebody actually

crapped in a toilet with no water in it, and I barfed all over my boots. I need a beer or two or three right now. Right now."

J.D. held the door to the Inferno open for Junior, who walked in and lofted his voice over the din, over the backs of a dozen black drinkers hunched at the bar. "A couple of whiskeys and two cold Buds, barkeep." The bartender, white shirtsleeves rolled up, bald with a white apron wrapped around his girth, put his hands on the counter, staring at Junior. "What? What?"

"Okay, could we please, please have two shots of Jack Daniels and two Budweisers. *Please.*" They found their way to the only two open seats at the end of the counter in front of what had become the grill part of Bar & Grill: three large glass jars. One with beef jerky, one with hard boiled eggs, and the one right in front of Junior with gnarled, knurled, pinkish tubers floating in brackish fluid.

"Excuse me, sir, but what are those?"

"Pickled pig's feet," he said, putting down the two shots and two beers.

Junior closed his eyes. "I don't feel good again."

"Drink your beer," J.D. said. "You'll feel better."

"I don't feel so good. I'm going to vomit."

Ten minutes later, Junior was getting his third round. "You know, J.D.," he said, talking to his beer, "there's something about you that's like Steady Eddie. Test the water, test the water, slowly slide in, whereas me! Bang! Jump right in up to my neck. That's why I wanted to talk to you. Get some advice. I really need some good advice."

"You wanted to talk to me?"

"Yeah, that's why I said right off the bat when you called I said I'd meet you here. Shit, J.D., nothing could have been better than you calling when you did. I got to piss. Be right back."

The elevator kid with the floppy hat, now with a puffy-sleeved, wide-collared, white shirt open to the waist, came through the door, looked at J.D., and stood at the far end of the bar. J.D. asked the bartender if he knew a big Hawaiian guy who ran the Puritan Hotel. He shook his head and went back to pouring drinks. The man sitting next to J.D. leaned in close. "He's not Hawaiian; he's Tongan. Don't fuck with him. We all call him Mr. Mango. Mister being very important. Fuck with him, he will fuck you up."

J.D. took a pen from his pocket, a napkin from the bar, and wrote: *Dear Mr. Mango, We are very sorry for our behavior. We are from the country. Please accept our apologies. It won't happen again.* He folded a ten-dollar bill into the napkin, walked the length of the bar, stood beside the black kid, and gave it to him. The kid read it, put the ten spot in his pocket, the note on the counter, nodded to the bartender, and left. The bartender read the note, opened a Budweiser, and put it in front of J.D.'s seat.

"This is on Mr. Mango."

On the sidewalk in front of the white picket gate to Delta Zeta Sorority, Junior, watching girls spill out the front door onto the portico and lean their backs against the Doric columns, drinking beer, said to J.D., "Let's tell 'em we're from Harvard. That'll get their panties off."

A stout, square-headed guy came out and began joking it up with the girls. "Are you kidding, Junior? We tell them we're from Harvard, and that football player up there will stick our heads in a shitter. Let's tell them we're from Annapolis. That's better."

"Yeah, okay, J.D., you tell 'em. What the fuck's Annapolis?"

At the door they were met by a skinny, six-foot tall, sad faced, middle-aged woman with a long, droopy nose that seemed to have been leaking. "Do you have a chit?" she asked. They were both looking past her down a wide entry hall to a grand room festooned with balloons and dozens of pink and bouncy girls in mini-skirts and sleeveless blouses.

Junior elbowed J.D. "Oh, no, ma'am. I'm sorry. We don't have chits. We're from the Naval Academy in Annapolis. Fighter pilots. We only have two days' leave, so we just wanted to see, you know, talk to a few pretty girls before we have to get back in the cockpit. We're shipping out to Vietnam."

"Well," she said, "I'm the proctor here, and I can't let you in without chits. That's the rule." J.D. felt an arm slide around his waist and a breast push gently into the small of his back. The girl, blonde, was wearing an American flag blouse and a short orange and navy blue skirt with bright white stars.

"Miss Janowitz," she said like honey, "these boys here are fighter pilots. Fighter pilots, Miss Janowitz. They're going to risk their lives for our freedom. What kind of airplane y'all fly?" She looked up at J.D.

"F-4 Phantoms, ma'am."

"Miss Janowitz, they fly F-4 Phantoms for goodness sake. Don't we have a special little rule for special guests?" Her accent was peach-pickin' Georgia. The proctor looked disapprovingly at the cheerleader but stood aside. "Just this once, Shelly. Just this once."

J.D. put his arm around the Georgia girl and said, "Thank you. Who was that woman?"

"Oh, Miss Janowitz. She's actually really nice. She's a professor of forensic archeology in the medical school. A bone specialist. Human bones. You know, what kind of human, how old, how'd they die. That kind of stuff. I take one of her courses."

"You got that right, little missy," Junior was telling a petite girl with a button nose and thick, red lips, sitting next to him on the sofa. "We're supposed to wear helmets, but I always take mine off when I'm up around a mile in the air. Just feels better. More free. These little babies don't have steering wheels like a car. No sirree." Junior reached over and put his hand high up on her bare thigh. "No sirree. There's a big stick I got between my legs that I just push and pull gentle-like, and she goes up and up, and if I push it hard, she rolls over, and I jam that stick hard all the way, and man, oh man does that baby scream."

This was the second time he'd tried this story, but the first time he'd been standing up, and it was loud, and a black basketball player who looked a mile tall had leaned over and said in a voice that sounded like rocks running down a wooden chute, "Cut the shit, dick-weasel. That's my girl you're talking at." So he'd gone to sit on the sofa, and this time it took. This small thing started wriggling around, making little moaning noises, slowly took his hand off her thigh, stood up, and led him up to her dorm room.

It took three beers and a long time of tough talk about football and bullshit about fighter jets with five or six big guys until the peach-pickin' Miss America slid into the group in front of J.D., pushing her rump up tight against him and said, "That's enough of this boy-talk. This party's for us girls and, if y'all don't mind, I'd like to show our special guest around the premises." The premise consisted of a direct path to her room. She locked the door behind them. The walls were covered with posters of Mick Jagger and John Lennon and a hard-looking guy with long hair, a leather jacket, and an old guitar. J.D. turned to ask her who that was, but all her garments and undergarments were strewn on the floor, and she was kneeling naked on the bed, her eyes a little unfocused. She looked like Miss April, or May, or June—one of the pin-up girls on the calendar hanging in Lil' Dickie's garage. Slurring a bit, she said, "Okay, fighter-boy, fly me."

When Junior came downstairs, the little girl asked him if he was hungry and led him into the kitchen. A half a dozen girls were laughing and twittering and slicing up a pan full of brownies. A tall one, the one with the knife, looked at Junior and the little girl and said, "My, my, Susie, don't you look at bit flushed! Sounded like quite a religious experience up there. You want another? Maybe your friend here would like a brownie. They're dark and chewy with a pinch of a little something in them to make you happy and love God." She held a big one out on the knife.

"No, ma'am, thank you, but I'm not real hungry. I'll just take a half a one." He reached to the counter, picked up a square about half the size of a full brownie, put it in his mouth, chewed it, and began to swallow. All the girls went stone quiet, mouths open.

"Oh my sweet God!" shouted the tall one. "Oh my sweet Lord Jesus! He just ate a hundred dollars' worth of hashish! All our hashish! He ate the whole damn thing! That cocksucker ate our dope!"

Junior puckered up and chewed and chewed like a cow on its cud. "You girls got a little something I can wash this down with? A beer or something? Jesus but it seems stuck. Jesus," he squeaked, "having a little trouble here."

The tall one grabbed him by the neck and rammed her fingers down Junior's throat. Junior started flailing and pounding on the counter just like three hours earlier in Mr. Mango's place. The tall one pushed him away, slammed her hands down on the counter, screaming, "It's gone, this little prick ate it!"

"Jesus, somebody got a beer around this place," Junior squawked, and that's when all the commotion began. Junior, packing eight beers, three shots of whiskey, and two fat ounces of Lebanese Red Lion hashish, started getting the shit beat out of him by six half-naked sorority co-eds. Kitchen stools crashed, then living room lamps and tables. A general pandemonium ensued, and then the sirens came.

Junior groaned and put his fingertips to his cheek and nose. He rolled over on the concrete bed-shelf, swung his legs down, looking at J.D. and the bars of the cell. "Where are we? What happened to my face?"

"That would probably be a hundred-pound cheerleader. The lump on the back of your head," Junior touched his hand to the back of his head, "that there came from the cop you tried to push through the window of his own car. He didn't like that. His buddy didn't like me trying to help you out, either. We're in the drunk tank. Junior, you got to tell me, what did you do with that girl that made her think you owed her a hundred dollars? I mean, Jesus, Junior, a hundred dollars? Or was it two of them?"

"I don't remember."

"Junior, you got to remember something. Did you say you'd pay them? How many of them?"

"I don't remember."

"That thing about being fighter pilots, that sure worked," J.D. said.

"Oh yeah, I remember that part. That sure worked all right! Next time why don't you tell them we're fucking astronauts. Then they'd probably tie me down and chew my nuts off. Great idea."

He sat staring down at the back of his hands, fingers spread out fan-like, fingernails crusted up with the crud of a mechanic. "I look like a fucking grease monkey."

J.D. looked at his own hands. Clean and pink. "I look like a dickless egghead," he said. Their eyes met. It was quiet. They looked at each other.

"Okay, Junior, I have a question for you."

Junior looked back down at his hands and with one thumb tried to rub some grease out of the cuticles of the other hand.

"Junior, what do you know about my father?"

Junior rubbed more grease off his hand and then licked his fingers and rubbed them hard, nails down, on his Levis. "Why do you ask me shit like that? All I know is he was killed in a car accident. But you knew that. You told me that. So why are you asking me?"

"What else do you know? What did your dad tell you?"

"He didn't tell me anything. That's all I know. I don't feel good."

"He must have said some things to you. I know that your dad and his friends talk about it. I heard them laughing about it in your garage. He must have said something."

Junior looked back down at his hands. "God, I'm a fucking grease monkey. Probably always be a grease monkey. I feel like shit." He looked back up at J.D. "My dad tried to tell me something about how your father died, but I told him I didn't want to hear it. I didn't want to hear anything about it. You know why, J.D.? Because you and me are friends. Weird as it is, you're the best friend I have, and I don't want to know anything about you that you don't know. People can't be friends if one has secrets on the other. So I just walked away. Told him I didn't want to know anything. So I don't."

"Thanks," J.D. said. He picked up the roll of toilet paper and threw it across the cell, bouncing it off Junior's head. "Can you remember what it was you wanted to talk to me about? I mean, we're here, locked up, can't get out until somebody comes to get us. We can't even call anybody for another hour. We got nothing else to do. What did you want to talk about?"

"J.D., for the life of me I can't remember what it was that

was so god-awful important."

They talked about the she-boar, the old man, the girl, and the 10-gauge Westley Richards. Junior said that gun would drop a rhino dead in its tracks if you were dumb enough to get that close. "Ten-gauge ball packs a hell of a wallop, but it's so heavy it won't go very far. The kick on that shotgun would knock a grown man on his ass if he didn't know just what he was doing. Couldn't have been no old fart or some girl that pulled that trigger."

They sat in the concrete cell, each hunched over, elbows on their knees, looking at their hands, listening to the distant clanging of steel doors in the next cell block over, the muted commands of jailers, and the mumblings of prisoners being let out into the exercise yard. It came to Junior a half hour later while he was on the floor doing push-ups. "You remember Marie Cadieux?"

J.D. nodded. "Timmy's little sister. The little girl who played the violin? Yeah, I remember her. What about her?"

Junior rolled over on his back. "I knocked her up. She's pregnant. She missed her period last two months, and then she went and got tested. Christ, J.D. she's only sixteen." Junior went back to studying his hands.

"I have to call my mother," J.D. said.

"That's a good idea. She'll know what to do. Your mother's tough as steel. Don't get me wrong, I don't mean hard like a hammer head, I mean like spring steel. Bend and bend and bend to make everything as smooth as can be for other people. Bend but don't break. Never break. One of those people. Jesus, what the fuck was I thinking anyway? Fuckin' knocked up a baby."

"You're lucky, boy," the jailer said in a slow drawl, handing J.D. the telephone. "You're damned lucky. Chief could easy have charged the both of you with assault and battery on a police officer. You're lucky 'cause the chief was navy also. Naval police before he came here. If that schoolgirl hadn't called the station and told them you fly Phantoms, your ass would be sitting in State Pen for the next ten years. You got one call. Make it good." He left and closed the door.

"Hi, Mom, it's J.D. I'm really sorry about this. I'm really sorry, but me and Junior are in jail. It's a long story. I'm really sorry, but they won't let us out by ourselves. Somebody responsible has to sign for us and, ah, pay a fine. We wondered if maybe you could come get us."

"J.D., if I've told you this once, I told you a hundred times. Please listen to me. I don't want to ever say this again. Are you listening?"

He held the phone away from his head and squinted, his eyes closed. "Yes, Mom, I'm listening."

"It's *Junior and I*, not *me and Junior*. Of course I'll come get you. Which jail?"

That night at home, Amanda asked J.D. where he'd been and how it came to pass that he and Junior ended up in jail.

J.D. told her about the sorority party. Most of it. He skipped the part about Miss America. He told her about boar hunting and the old man in Dengman Gap. That there seemed to be a secret he couldn't crack. He skipped the part about the opium and his dreams.

"J.D., I thought you were on one of your three-day trips with your class. Weren't you? Why did you go down into Appalachia?"

J.D. got up and walked to the window, looking out into the dark woods. The night had become terribly dark, no moon or stars to give definition to any shape or any movement. And the darkness brought a quietness that made it dead dark. "No, the trip was cancelled. I just wanted to go someplace. Have an adventure. See something new. I ended up in the mountains. That's all." He was flicking his ear.

"J.D., is there something you're not telling me?"

"Yes, Mom, there is. I met a girl named Abby at a hardware store. She has copper skin and high cheekbones. Her eyes are like speckled purple plums, and she has long blonde hair. She's really sweet and really beautiful. She takes care of a boy who lives alone in the woods on sacred Indian ground. I might go back to see her."

"There's still something you're not telling me."

J.D flicked his ear a few times. "There are a lot of things people don't tell other people, even their mom. Sometimes there are probably things a mom doesn't even tell her son. Right?" He got up and walked to the foot of the stairs, looking back at his mother.

"Yes, Jeremiah, there are those things."

5

Songs

THE YARD, AS IT WAS CALLED, a quarter acre of fresh mowed, deep green Kentucky bluegrass in the center of a ring of five brick buildings, called houses, each with white columned porticos and balconies, gave the impression of Southern ease and grace. White wicker chairs were set about in groups of four around white wicker coffee tables. In the center of the Yard was a sculpture, a stone obelisk drenched in rivers of water running down all four sides to a circular bed of bricks surrounded by flowers. The waiters, as they were called, five of them, one from each house, wore creased and pressed white trousers with a black leather belt, sturdy black boots, and crisp, short-sleeved white shirts. They were all men in their mid-thirties. All well-built and neatly groomed, walking about with their hands behind their backs, occasionally serving someone a sweet iced tea in a plastic glass with a straw or replenishing a ceramic bowl of boiled peanuts.

Each house had a sign over the portico, under the ornate railing of the balcony. A wooden sign, with the name of the house written in black lettered script. They were named for Confederate generals from Virginia: Lee, Pickett, Jackson, Stuart, Hill. There were no doors leading out to the balconies, only windows covered by wrought iron bars bolted to the outside. Between the houses, the pie-shaped areas were closed off by similar ten-foot high wrought iron bars that curved both in and out at the top, also with no doors. It was not possible to intrude into this peaceful place.

Before the waiters could react quickly enough, a young man with curly dark hair, a straight thin nose, and fat lips, a young man everyone called Lord Poet, who sat talking with an old woman with a long, gray braid, smacked his narrow forehead onto the tabletop, jumped up, ran to the obelisk, careful not to step on a flower or a fern, pulled his shirt wide open, and bellowed. "Oh whooly, whooly wi' me, sir, you've woken me Bad Man! You've woken me second head! Today I have for all of you a poem from the great Maxwell Bodenheim. He wrote, to all of us, to all of us here he wrote," and Everett howled, "Like a vivid hyperbole / The sun plunged into April's freshness / And stuck its sparkling madness / Against the barnlike dejection / Of this dark red insane asylum / A softly clutching noise ..." By that point, his voice had taken on a trumpet-like tenor, and his arms and fingers were spread out wide, his head tipped back to the sky. One waiter got under his armpits, one got his legs, and they carried him flat out into Pickett House, his shirt torn asunder. He dribbled out two un-swallowed pills from under his tongue, down his cheek onto the grass.

No one seemed to notice much. They kept on rocking or mumbling or staring off at nothing. Through their Thorozine fog, the inmates at the Skinner Bluff Lunatic Asylum didn't care. Their entire universe was inside their head. Not much of it came out. Their eyes seemed muddled and opaque, their lips hung loose. They were an eclectic group: Negroid, Caucasian, Hispanic, and Asian. Everett Lord Poet did this almost every time they let him out into the Yard. The psychiatric attendants were never fast enough. Nor had any of them ever seen the little pills slip from his mouth to the ground. They were both, no matter fore or aft, always transfixed on the sheer strength of his body. He could hold it straight out like a board as he kept screaming out his insane quotations. It was, as Attendant Cobb always said, a thing of beauty. The attendants were not supposed to know anything about the inmates except their first names and medication programs, but they knew all about every one, and they loved to gossip among themselves and with their favorite inmates. With Everett's outbursts and soliloquies in the Yard and in the Pickett House sunroom, they all knew all too well what had happened to cause his mind to break.

The main floor of Pickett House, like all the other houses, had a wide corridor leading through to double doors at the rear entry. The doors were double locked. A nurses' station was set to the side by the locked doors. Across the hall were the bathing room, the therapy room, and a small sunroom with rocking chairs and a sofa. Behind the nurses' station were more iron bars in front of an apothecary. Once a week, Dr. Norfinger would come and write prescriptions for the inmates and affix his signature to the drug order for the house. From time to time, at the request of the duty nurse, he would see a patient to prescribe more or different medications or attend to the matters of their mind in the therapy room. The purpose of the lunatic asylum was to keep the inmates from the public eye, to keep them sedate and quiet, manageable and alive until such time as would be natural for them to pass on from this world unless there became a pressing need for space for more inmates, in which case some of them would pass on at an earlier age than otherwise would be natural. They would be cremated in the facility's crematorium and a small metal plaque with nothing but their first name placed flat on the ground in a corner of the field behind the complex. Kinfolk came to pick up the sealed tin box of ashes. If there were no kinfolk, there was no tin box. The ashes would be sent out with the day's garbage. There was nothing buried in the dirt in the field. Just metal plaques laid flat in the grass. There was nothing written, but ever since its founding in 1935, the owners had specified there would be no physical remains of anyone ever placed in or on any part of the facility. They hadn't wanted to tempt the possibility of spirits or specters or exhumations. To old Mr. P., the gardener who had placed the plaques in the field, about one a month for the last thirty years, no place on earth could have been emptier, more lonely, more haunted by nothingness.

The two attendants carried Everett into the main corridor. Nurse Pernie opened her log book of scheduled visitors to see if the woman who occasionally came to see Everett was scheduled for a visit any time soon. She wasn't. "Take him to bathing and then tomorrow morning, bring him to therapy," she said.

The bathing room had two tubs separated by a low, wide, rubber-topped table. There were sheets folded and stacked on a set of shelves. Everett didn't fight. He slowly undressed. They put on rubber gloves and dunked a king-sized sheet into each tub. The first tub filled with hot, hot water, just below scalding. The second with water so cold an occasional ice mush would puke out the faucet. They lowered him onto the table and wrapped him in the hot sheet, rolling him back and forth across the table. His skin turned bright pink as the sheet wrapped tight around him, and he grimaced, breathing out hard through tightened teeth, and then they whipped it off and rolled him in a freezing sheet as he gasped for air and his gonads shrunk back up into his body, and they whipped him out of that sheet and back into a scalding hot sheet and rolled him again and back into a freezing sheet and rolled him and rolled him. Ten times they did this until his brainwaves were as flat as the field out back and his central nervous system had given up transmitting any messages to his body. Attendant Cobb put Everett in a green johnnie coat, and they lifted him limp onto a gurney and wheeled him to the elevator and to his cot in the open third-floor bedroom, as it was called. Twenty beds for twenty men. Metal frame cots with thin, blue and white ticking mattresses, two sheets, a thick gray blanket and a thin gray pillow, and a foot locker for day clothes. A line of johnnie coats hung on a line of pegs like linen husks waiting to be filled each night by some skinny seed. It smelled like stink. Crazy stink of years of fouled breath, knotted hair, rotten feet, and urine. Crazy stink. Stark raving stink.

Dr. Norfinger stood by the open door of the therapy room when Everett was brought down in the morning. Norfinger was a hard man to look at. Short little legs, an enormous stomach that seemed to stretch all the way around his backside, causing his brown gabardine trousers to bunch up badly in the crotch both front and back, no neck, and a head small and pale, like a garbanzo bean. "Good morning, Everett. How are we today?" He reeked of rye whiskey, and his hands shook so badly he had trouble holding the door knob. Nurse Pernie had long been afraid that his herky-jerky hands and shot memory might just cook somebody, but so far, so good.

"Good morning, Dr. Norfinger," Everett mumbled, standing stiff in a white straight jacket, arms crossed in front, and two-foot-long cuffs tied tight behind. He was laid on his back on a wooden table and strapped down with black leather belts across the shoulders, waist, thighs, and shins. The attendant rubbed an oily gel on the temples of both sides of his head, and Dr. Norfinger placed two electrodes, held by a spring clamp, over his head. The doctor began to fill two hypodermic needles, one an anesthesia, one to dry up the saliva so he wouldn't choke on his own spit, but he shook so badly he couldn't get the needle in the vial. Everything rattled; the table, the jars, the glass tube needles. Attendant Cobb poked his head out the door and whistled softly for Nurse Pernie.

Strapped down, anesthetized, spit controlled and ready to go, Everett got 450 volts of juice at 1.2 amperes through his brain for five seconds. For a few weeks, he wouldn't remember anything at all that happened in the last month. He would be, day in and day out, reasonably content with the world, or what little he might recognize of it. In those times, the severed head of Professor Wentworth never came into his lap.

Two weeks later, Everett began to look forward to a visit in the Yard. He wanted to see Edith again. She was the old woman with the long, gray braid. Half-Apache she told him. She had a deep dent in her forehead, and her skin was scarred. Everett thought she was perfectly sane but had been put there because she had suffered a complete loss of memory and gone blind. Attendant Cobb had told Everett that she had suffered massive trauma from watching her children die in a fire and then being struck on the head by a falling beam. Two types of trauma minutes apart, and she had no idea who she was or where she came from and couldn't see a thing. She would sing about things that she could feel, like a breeze or the sweet iced tea. Everett knew trauma, and he knew that's why he was in the asylum. He told Edith he hadn't lost his memory, and for him, that was the problem. He had only lost his mind. He told her stories, and she would listen and pat his hand, and her lips would start to move, and she would pat his hand faster and then begin to sing a song about the story he had just told her. She always mentioned Kitty in every song she sang. Whoever or whatever it was, it seemed to be the only thing that had stayed with her. She didn't talk. She sang.

Visitors met inmates at the lunatic asylum in the front of the main administration building in a sunny, well-appointed room with floor-to-ceiling colonial era, Monticello type windows looking out over the bucolic fields beyond. There were books neatly arranged on bookshelves, upholstered chairs, pictures of Scottish hound-hunts on the walls, and two-way mirrors with attendants looking in. Inmates who were capable of meeting visitors—those sufficiently ambulatory, marginally lucid, and with no recent physical scars—were well prepped to meet visitors. They were scrubbed clean, combed, brushed, dressed up in normal clothes, given moderate doses of their medications, and escorted in as free and uncontrolled a manner as possible through the Yard, through the iron gate, and up the short brick walk to the administration building. Almost no one came to see anyone. Almost no one even knew that up on that vast bluff there were a hundred people dubiously certified as lunatics.

Everett loved these visits. They didn't come often, maybe once every four months or so, but he loved the feel of real, fresh, clean underpants with taut elastic bands and the loose swish of corduroys and a tucked-in cotton shirt with a button-down collar. And lace-up shoes. He loved the thorough brushing his teeth got and the mouthwash and the feel of the bristle-brush on his scalp as his shampooed hair was carefully parted. And he loved being partially cognizant with only a half load of medications.

"Good afternoon, Mrs. Wentworth. How are you?" he said as Amanda Dixon walked into the visitors' room. He stood and put out his hand.

She took his hand in both of hers and said, "I'm fine, thank you. And how are you, Everett? You look wonderful."

"I look wonderful because you are here. All the rest of the time I look like a mad dog."

"I'm sure, Everett, that can't be true. You are a handsome, fit young man."

"Mrs. Wentworth," he said, leaning toward her, his head a bit bobbly, "it's true."

He looked up to the mirrors and, knowing there were attendants watching them and microphones in the ceiling listening to them, he said, "But they're very nice to me here. They're very nice in the way they keep me from killing myself, you know, ripping my own head off if I could. They're very good about that. And some of them are quite smart. One of them even talks to me about my master's thesis on nuclear waste. I told you about that, didn't I? "

Amanda took his hands in hers and leaned toward him, her voice with an edge. "You are not responsible for my husband's death. He is. And he is responsible for whatever shame and misery and confusion you are suffering. Not you. Him."

Everett pulled back and began to mumble, his hands grasping, as though kneading a phantom ball in his lap, and his eyes closed, lips quivering. Amanda put her hand to his shoulder, knowing that she had tripped over the edge of his madness.

"How is your friend Edith? That's her name, isn't it? How is she? Have you seen her?"

He softened and sat up straighter, slowly came back from wherever he was. "Yes, she's fine. I see her in the Yard. That's where they let boys and girls, men and women, be together. In the Yard. We talk a lot if my mouth will work. You know, if I can put my lips together and pop them open to make a P sound. Or my tongue on my teeth to flick out a T sound. When I can do that, we can talk."

"Oh my goodness, Everett, I'm so sorry."

"No, no, Mrs. Wentworth, don't be sorry. Of all the people in the world, you are the one who should not be sorry. You are a good person. A really good person. Awhile ago, I told Edith about you. I told her about your son, J.D. That's his name, right?" Amanda nodded. "I told her about how he was a forestry student and had met an old man in Dengman Gap, down by North Carolina. Dengman Gap. Somehow that name stuck with me. Poetic, almost like James Dickey. And a pretty girl with eyes plum dark and little gold specks. That sounds more like art than poetry. And how you had said how happy you were for him to have found an old man at an Indian Reservation who could be like a grandfather to him. And there was a boy who lived alone in the woods on sacred ground, and he was also the old man's friend. The old man has some secret. That's what you said, isn't it?" Amanda nodded again. "When I said Dengman Gap, Edith sat right up like a bell had gone off. When I told her the rest, she scrunched her blind eyes closed, started tapping her foot, singing, *Dengman Gap, Dengman Gap, boy in woods, sacred ground, secret, secret, sacred ground.* Over and over. She began to sing it as a song. *I'm going to tell that to Kitty,* she sang. *Kitty will be pleased.* I don't know who Kitty is, and maybe she doesn't either, but the story of your son and the old man meant something to her. I think in whatever life she had before this place, she was a songwriter. I tell her stories, and she turns them into songs. Songs must be a memory of the heart, not a memory of the mind." Everett began rolling his head around in a circle, licking his dry lips, rubbing his thigh, and making small moaning noises. "Sometimes I think I'm the only one here who is truly crazy. Everybody else seems like they're just drug crazy. Like when the medications start to wear off, they start to seem normal. But I don't know what crazy is. I guess you're crazy if other people think you are. I would like to meet your son sometime. Talk about trees, maybe. Talk about something real. Anything real. Talk about something that isn't inside out."

Amanda had never heard him speak so much at one time.

She sat silent for a while, looking at him, then looking out the windows at the August sun in the sky above the open field, trying to sketch out a thought. She began to say that he meant a great deal to her when the door opened and the attendant said her half hour was up. "Dr. Dixon, it's time to go."

Everett jerked his head around. "You're a doctor? A head-shrinker?"

Amanda leaned over close and whispered, "I am not a doctor; I'm Mrs. Wentworth. People who work in these places get everything wrong. He doesn't even know what my name is."

Edith was the only inmate in the Skinner Bluff Lunatic Asylum who was completely blind and, even on the best of days, had no memory. The people who had witnessed her trauma were her husband's employers. Her husband was one of their most valued workers. To keep him on, to prevent any ugly legal recriminations, they had promised him a visit twice a year. The stipulations to the staff were simple. Keep her well. She will be picked up for a ride in the country twice a year on each equinox. She is to be heavily medicated on those two days. If any glimmer of her memory returns, even the tiniest shard, they are to be notified immediately.

On the morning of the autumnal equinox when the early fall day is the same length as the early fall night, a black Lincoln Continental with Texas plates pulled into the parking lot in front of the administration building. A tall man got out, ran his hand through his short, bristle hair, straightened the collar and sleeves of his black silk shirt, and walked briskly, straight-backed to the front door where he was met by a sparse woman in brown tweed with shiny, black hair pulled to a tight bun. She nodded, said something, and he came back a moment later and drove the car to a gate, a gate with sharp spikes on black iron rods bent both in and out at the top, a gate unlocked by an attendant. The passenger, also tall but with near shoulder-length, black hair, handed the attendant a five-dollar bill, and the car drove the service road inside a chain link fence along the backside of the five brick buildings and pulled into a parking spot behind last building: Lee House—Women's Ward—Medical Personnel Only. Two attendants wheeled a gurney out to the open rear door of the Lincoln and humped up Edith's flaccid body into the back seat, pushed her hanging dog-like tongue back in her mouth, wiped the spit from her chin, and closed the door. She slumped over sideways into a heap of big pillows as the car drove off.

6

Lupa and Bupa

THE OFFICE OF THE DEAN OF THE MEDICAL SCHOOL was spacious and airy with large corner windows. His desk was ornate and highly polished. It had two things on it: a telephone and a signed photograph of him shaking the hand of the legendary Gil Hodges, manager of the Washington Senators. In the photo, Dean Harris is wearing a knit vest, polka dot bow tie, and horn-rimmed glasses. He is beaming. Hodges appears to be scowling into his dugout, spitting out a seed. On an eighteenth-century, simple pine table, made with hand tools by a community of Shakers in Maine, was assembled a collection of anatomical sketches dating from 700 BC. On the wall behind the table hung two portraits in oil: on the left, Marie Curie, on the right, Albert Schweitzer, and in the center, in a gilded frame was a large reproduction of da Vinci's *Vitruvian Man*. Dean Harris thought that these three pieces pretty well summed up the kind of doctor he was. Rigorous in research, selfless in dedication, and precisely balanced. There was a knock at his door, and it opened. His secretary put her head around the corner.

"Dr. Harris, the men who requested the meeting are here. One is from International Chemical. One from the Justice Department, and I don't know who the third man is. He wouldn't say. He's wearing a uniform. I'm really sorry I don't know any more, but they wouldn't tell me. They just said it was urgent. And Maria Branoff from our legal office is here also. Is it okay to bring them in?"

"So, gentlemen, what is it you wish to discuss? My secretary was unable to provide me with an agenda or even something as simple as a topic so that I might be able to be sufficiently informed, you know, better prepared to help you." He was clearly irritated. "Mrs. Branoff, do you know what this is about?"

"No, sir. I'm sorry. I don't. The provost called and said I should be here."

"I apologize, Dr. Harris. I requested there be no notification. I think that the content of our discussion is best if it is just verbal among the five of us, nothing written. And totally confidential." The military man looked over at the other men. "You both agree, I presume?" They nodded. "I'm Colonel John Britt. I'm with the Army Biological Warfare Division."

"Fine," Dean Harris said and took his notepad and pencil off the conference table and tossed it onto a coffee table behind him. "What can I do for you? I assume you're not here to ask my permission to napalm children."

All three chuckled. "No, sir, we would not do that."

"What wouldn't you do? Ask my permission or napalm children? Now, gentlemen, why don't you just tell me what this is all about."

Colonel Britt took the lead. "This is Robert Hartford from International Chemical. The army has done a lot of work with his corporation over the last fifty years."

"Nice to meet you," Hartford said. He was tall with short hair and a military bearing.

"And this is Dan Logan from the Justice Department." The lawyer nodded to Dean Harris. The colonel continued. "The army is in the process of closing our biological laboratories. No new projects can be undertaken. We're here to ask for the assistance of your research people to conduct some independent studies of the effects of certain chemicals that were manufactured, under contract with the army, by International Chemical during World War I. They were never used on any populations. After the war, they were stored in secure, concrete underground bunkers on government land in Texas. However, there are now allegations that the Army *did* use these chemicals in at least one test site in New Mexico and that there have been detrimental effects on civilians living nearby. This is not true. There are no records to indicate that these chemicals were ever used in any way, but as Mr. Logan will explain, we need to know what the physiological effects, if any, might have been."

The lawyer had been told to give Dean Harris information that sounded as though it was highly confidential and the dean would feel important enough to be disposed toward agreeing to any request. Dan Logan put his elbows on the table, folded his hands, and spoke in measured, atonal statements. "A lawsuit has been filed in federal court by a very well organized environmental consortium on behalf of three families residing in a small town in rural New Mexico. The suit, naming as defendants both the Interior Department and the Department of the Army, alleges these chemicals have created birth defects in their children who live in or near this town. One thing is known for certain. These chemicals were never there or anywhere near there. Proving that, however, is quite problematic. And here I want to impress upon you the importance of the confidentiality of this conversation. Counselor, can we assume a privileged conversation here, attorney-client confidentiality?" Maria Branoff gave a short nod. He continued, "The chemicals in question were moved shortly after World War II to three different locations in the states of Oregon, Idaho, and Nevada. The difficulty here is that those site locations are shielded by statutes regarding national security and are known only to the military and International Chemical, which has a top secret clearance contract to monitor the sites. We would decline to provide that information to the court, even in sealed documents, leaving open the question of whether or not there is or was a site in New Mexico. We know as a matter of fact there isn't and never was. But we have no mechanism to prove it. There is a bunker nearby, but it was never used. It was built to store spent and excess plutonium from the Los Alamos Project, but the site, through a similar type lawsuit, was deemed to be the property of the Interior Department, and the trust documents in the original deed guaranteed public access to the land. Nothing was ever stored there, but these plaintiffs don't believe that. They allege material was stored there, subsequently moved, and the bunker sanitized. Not possible for us to prove otherwise."

Dean Harris had begun drumming his fingers on the table. "This is truly a problem of national security, isn't it?" They all nodded. "What can I do to help?"

"The only avenue available to us is to secure a dismissal from the court. The only way that can happen is to present evidence that the chemicals in question, singularly or somehow in combination, could not, under any circumstances, have produced the effects as alleged in their filing. Mind you, Doctor, these chemicals were produced in the early nineteen hundreds for agricultural use. No one has ever alleged any detrimental physiological effects. We don't dispute that the children of the plaintiffs have serious medical issues, but we need to prove that their conditions could not have been produced by exposure to these certain chemicals. That proof, that conclusive evidence, must come from the most respected research facility in the country. That is your facility, Dean

Harris. That is why we're here. To ask you to take on this project and assign it to a top scientist."

"Dean Harris," the man from International Chemical said, "there is a great deal of money available for this effort. Much, much more, many times more than would be necessary to conduct the research."

Amanda Dixon pulled her Buick into one of many empty spaces in front of a three-story brick building just across the North Anna River outside Charlottesville, Virginia. The sign beside the front door said in orange and navy blue: University of Virginia School of Medicine. Under that, in small, flat black letters, was written Biological Sciences Research Facility B. At the entry, she punched in a three-digit code and then, inside the vestibule, punched in a different code deactivating the alarm system on the second door. Raymond, the seven-to-three weekend security guard, was in his chair in an alcove, reading his fifth Louis L'Amour.

"Good morning, Dr. Dixon."

"Good morning, Raymond." It was Sunday, seven-thirty a.m. She worked Sunday, Monday, and Tuesday. She liked Sunday the best because there was no one else there. No one to chat it up with in the hall. Only a few lights were on. The linoleum on the corridor floor was shiny, bright from a night-time buffing. She used the stairs. On the second floor, halfway down the hall, she entered a four-digit code and went into her office and laboratory. The floors here had not been buffed. Janitors did not have the code for these doors and were permitted to enter only when the assigned occupant—faculty member, consultant, or visiting scientist—was present. Consequently, the rooms never received routine cleaning until they were vacant, awaiting a change of occupant. Immediate need of cleaning usually meant evacuation, lock-down, and specially trained people in white suits and gloves. Vans, which had no logos on the doors, would pull up quickly and quietly at the back entrance. No flashing lights. The regulations on spills or contaminations were rigid; anything other than water, coffee, or Coca-Cola, anything the scientist wouldn't willingly drink that found its way out of whatever container it was supposed to be in required instant notification. It wasn't that the university was so particularly scrupulous; it was the people who funded the research who were paranoid about it. From time to time, men in expensive suits would come by to talk about the progress of the experiments and the importance of security. They would meet with Amanda and the director of the program, Dr. Ken Norton, in a conference room on the first floor. They were always accompanied by a man in a cheap suit, not threadbare but the seat and thighs were shiny, and the jacket pockets bagged out. He was the only one who was ever introduced: Mr. Garfield, a minion from the Department of Agriculture. Amanda had no idea who the others were or what their interest was, nor did any of the other PhDs in her building. They were free to talk to each other, to swap stories and chat, but they were strictly prohibited from confiding the particulars of their research or collaborating with each other on their experiments. To maintain the aura of university-sponsored intellectual pursuit, they were allowed, even encouraged, to publish their findings in scientific journals. Alone and individually, each research project was normal for a medical or engineering school.

In a separate laboratory on the first floor, Dr. James Peters analyzed different chemical agents to determine the strongest and most effective available for the purpose of killing bacteria and fungi. His work did not concern itself with the well-being of people or foxes or salamanders. Just plants. The results of his research were, as was the case with all the scientists, delivered to Dr. Norton for him to decide which chemicals in which combinations would be given to Dr. Dixon for her part of the effort.

Amanda poked her head in the back room and said hello to her forty-eight white mice. She said hello to the grain group: first to Pod One, the wheat pod; then to Pod Two, the corn pod. Then she said hello to the tree group: first Pod Three, the fruit tree pod, and lastly the nut tree pod. Twelve mice in each pod. She had spent the last two months trying to determine the effect on the intelligence and motor ability of the mice offspring as it related to exposure to viral pathogens— chemicals used to control fungus in grains and different chemicals used to control bacteria in agricultural trees.

Phase One of the experiment was complete. It had involved increasing levels of exposure—air, skin, and bowels—to these chemicals. She knew this research had been done before, but she assumed the composition of the chemicals, both for grains and for trees, might have been altered to have better results, and someone needed to be reassured that they were still safe to use. Her conclusions were that the levels of concentration of the chemicals used in the routine process of farming had statistically insignificant effects on the baby's abilities to match their parent's abilities in navigating the maze. Amanda published her results in the *Journal of Agricultural Science*. She received fourteen responses: six from grateful farmers, three from "we already knew that" chemical companies, and five from environmental groups wanting to know who funded the research. She forwarded all responses to Dr. Norton.

Phase Two was much more complicated. For reasons she didn't clearly understand, the project description requested evaluation of the mental capacity of young mice whose parents had been exposed to incrementally elevated doses of both chemicals mixed in various combinations. "Why would a wheat farmer want to mix his anti-fungal product with an anti-bacterial chemical used by an apple farmer?" she asked Director Norton. He said he really didn't know for sure but he was led to believe that Big Agribusiness was looking for an effective bacterial and fungal treatment that could be used as a single product on vast farms, thousands of acres that grew multiple crops, without danger of creating genetic defects in the children of the farm workers.

"Nonsense," Amanda said. "That's really a stretch. Is that what those men told you?"

"No, they didn't. Not directly. I inferred it. I don't know who they are any more than you do. Why do you think that wouldn't be the case?"

"Because the big farmers have never cared one whit about the health of the workers. Why should they start now? Nobody is making them care. Most of those farm workers don't even speak English. If they cared, they would at least give them decent sanitation and teach their children to read. I think all they want is more crops so they can make more money, and I think they're in bed with the Agriculture Department. Aside from that, they irrigate the fields differently, they harvest the fields differently—why wouldn't they spray them differently?"

The idea of mixing the chemicals sounded harebrained to her. Dangerous. "There aren't many small farms left. You know, places where the farmer's own children work in the fields and play in the dirt. Where the farmer would actually care about what he puts in that ground and what it would be like twenty years from now when his son is the farmer."

"What are you worried about, Amanda? Earthworms too dumb to chew dirt?"

"Yes, something like that," she laughed, "but here's what I

don't understand: why isn't there some government agency whose only purpose is to make sure nothing bad happens to our soils, our water and air? Our earthworms. Somebody who can say no, or at least say, prove it and let everybody see the proof. Right now, it's just us and Big Business or whoever they are, and everything is secret."

She had been working on this experiment for almost three months. She had tested dozens and dozens of babies in the maze. There was no question that the parent mice became seriously debilitated by repeated exposure to most of the chemicals and even more so when the chemicals were used in combination. Cancers of all sorts—lung, brain, skin—developed quite rapidly with doses above a prudent level. Anti-fungals used for wheat and corn mixed with anti-bacterials used on fruit trees, mixed with common dilution agents such as sodium hypochlorite and ethanol, seemed to produce the most virulent and rapid growing tumors, but this propensity did not seem to be passed onto the offspring. Bryce Peters had told her that these chemicals had been around since the First World War. They were just stronger now with a wider spectrum of effect. She was closing in on a preliminary conclusion that indicated that the genetic transference resulted not in a diminished mental capacity to the offspring, but a significantly altered perceptive capacity. It was going to take more time to determine if these preliminary conclusions could be validated. She needed to re-test the control group to make sure her baselines were accurate. She needed to re-analyze the chromosomal characteristics of the test groups, but most of all, right now, she needed a cup of coffee.

"Hi, Loopy. Hey, Big Ears," she said to her two favorites as she went into the back room and filled her cup. "Hey, Lupa and Bupa, how you guys doing?" The two little baby mice stared at Amanda with identical blank expressions as she sat down and sipped her hot Columbian coffee.

She picked up the document Dean Harris had given her with the medical description of the disabilities of a few children in New Mexico. "Determine conclusively," he had said, "whether or not these chemicals could have caused these abnormalities."

She looked at Lupa and Bupa. Loss of motor control? No evidence of that. Significant retardation? "You know what, Lupa, Bupa, that isn't your problem, is it? You're not retarded. I don't think you're even slow. You two can figure out that maze as fast as all the other little guys. You just can't relate to anything: me, your parents, or any other mice." She reached in and touched their heads. They stared at her. "You two have a very strange disorder. Am I certain, like the dean wants me to be? No."

She remembered what Ken Norton had told her when she first started work there ten years ago. "Research findings that state a 100 percent certainty are almost invariably those that are later proven wrong."

7

Only Sixteen

J.D STOOD STARING UP AT THE SIGN OVER THE DOOR. *Lil'
Dickey's Garage: If it's broke, we fix it. If you're broke, we don't.*
It seemed mean-spirited, unfriendly. Dickey had painted it
himself when the garage first opened. Nor had he ever dared
ask Dickey why he called himself Lil' Dickey. It seemed so sure
to invite comments. And he wasn't little. He was normal
sized—normal height, even a little taller than normal, normal
weight, normal arms, legs, and head. Buzz cut and cigarettes
rolled up in his T-shirt sleeve. Normal.

The Lil' Dickey moniker had become clear last year when
J.D and Junior stopped by to borrow Dickey's timing light to
tune up Amanda's Buick. J.D. remembered it had been a very
hot Fourth of July. Dickey's whole family had gathered in the
parking lot of the garage for a holiday barbeque. There were
only ten of them: Dickey, his girlfriend, Marlene, his mother,
his father, his two brothers, their wives, and two teenaged
kids. Dickey had hauled a claw foot bathtub out from behind
his garage, filled it half up with ice and what looked to J.D. like
200 cans of beer. There was a grill fashioned out of the rusted
bed of a dead pickup truck and crisscrossed layers of hog fence
and angle iron. Thirty square feet of ribs, steaks, hot dogs,
hamburgers, and everybody there, everybody except Dickey
and his girlfriend, was gigantic. Mammoth. Dickey's mother

was using a Snoopy beach towel to wipe the sweat from her head, neck, and bosom, and it wasn't big enough to reach all the way around. The father was sitting on the hood of his Cadillac holding a beer in one hand and, with a sausage-like finger, stroking the head of a Chihuahua whose body was enveloped somewhere between his thighs and belly. The two teenagers were seeing who could lift the rear end of some customer's Ford Falcon the farthest off the ground. Dickey was the runt. That's why he painted himself on his sign as a smiling pip-squeak holding a screwdriver that was bigger than he was.

J.D. looked up at the sign again, wondering if he would ever dare paint a portrait of himself and hang it in a public place so the whole world could see what he thought of himself. No. That would not happen. It would probably be a picture of a guy with one ear the size of a baseball mitt. He picked up a piece of steel rod lying in the dirt and pushed the door open a few inches. Rommel the Doberman growled from inside the office. He poked his head in far enough to see if the dog was chained. It was. He walked in, dropped the rod on the concrete floor with a clang, and the dog sprang up snarling and barking. "Fuck you, dog," J.D. said. "Hey, Dickey, you here?"

"Fuck you too, Fixin' Dixon, you fuckin' pussy. How many times I got to tell you, the dog don't bite. Junior's out back under the Mustang." Dickey ran an automotive garage, but he was known throughout the whole area as a master welder and dynamite guy. He could blow anything up and weld anything back together.

"Hey, J.D.," Junior said when J.D. got around back, "you're right on schedule. Give me a hand here."

Junior had the hood off, radiator out, all the hoses, belts, wires, linkage, and carburetor parts cleared off, four chains bolted to the lifting brackets of the 289, engine mount bolts disassembled, and chain falls set up to a steel pipe tripod. He was underneath, flat on his back on a garage man's scooter, naked to the waist with grease smeared from his hair to his belt buckle. He told J.D. what he needed. "Pull the free end of the chain to put up-tension on the engine. Pump up the jack under the tranny just enough so it's supported by the jack, not the engine mounts. Get me a longer extension for this ¾ drive out of that box over there. When I loosen these bell housing bolts, put more tension on the chain falls, then grab the engine by the water pump pulley. Pull it forward as I loosen the bolts. Don't go up with it until all the bolts are free. Just get the gravity off it. Listen to me as I loosen these bolts. Grab it by the water pump pulley and jiggle it as I loosen them. Don't let the back end drop. Keep tension on the chain falls. I'm almost there. All bolts loosened, halfway out. Two out. Keep jiggling her. Six out. Got 'em all." He scooted out from under the car and got beside J.D. "Let's pull her free! Right to the cowling! Got it. The spline's free. Up on the chain fall! Jesus fuck-a wow man! We did it!"

They sat on the ground underneath a maple tree drinking cold beer. Nothing much moved. Late autumn and the leaves had mostly fallen from the tree, making a soft seat on the ground. Snow was a month away, but the high warm sun was a month gone by. It was a time between the seasons for the tree and for the sky and for the dirt and a time between the seasons for each of them. If they hadn't been next-door neighbors, they would never have known each other. They both knew that. If they hadn't hunted together, they wouldn't be sitting side by side under a tree waiting for the other to say something that would either make the sun hot or the snow fall. One or the other. The Mustang's engine hung by chains and pipes five feet in the air, yanked out of its car, waiting to get souped-up, bored, and stroked.

Dickey came around back with three cold beers. "Hey,

Dickey," Junior said, "you think *your* dad's a hippo, you oughta seen this motherfucker me and J.D. saw down in Charlottesville. He was a fuckin' Tongan. That's right, ain't it, J.D., a fuckin' Tongan. Made your pop look like a midget."

Little Dickey stopped, looked down at the two of them, and said, "Don't leave that engine up on the chain falls. I need them in the morning." He turned around and took all three beers back inside.

J.D. watched him walk away and thought, *The poor guy. He's really sensitive about it, and Junior's such an asshole.* He let some time go by in silence.

"My mom wants to talk to you, Junior. It's about Marie. She said she'd be willing to help you out, Junior. You need to go see her."

Junior stuffed his hand in his blue jean pocket, pulled out a piece of paper, and handed it to J.D. It was from the Selective Service System. It was a Pre-Induction Notice. *Report for a physical examination.* "On top of it all," Junior said, "I get this shit."

That night, J.D. sat on the bottom stair looking into his living room where Amanda and Junior sat across from each other, talking. It was late in the evening.

"She's pregnant. Do you know that for certain?"

"Yes, ma'am. The doctor said so."

"And why do you want to marry her, Junior?"

"Because she's a Catholic."

"You want to marry her because she is a Catholic?"

"Yes, ma'am."

"If she was a Baptist, would you still want to marry her?"

"No, ma'am, I wouldn't."

"Junior, do you love her?"

"I don't know that, ma'am. I haven't felt anything like

that."

"So you want to marry her because of her religion, not because of who she is. Is that right?"

"No, ma'am, that's not right. Who she is is a Catholic, just like everybody in her family, so I guess I want to marry her because of who she is."

"J.D., would you fix me a scotch and water? Junior, do want a beer or something?"

"Beer would be great, Mrs. Dixon. Thank you."

"And if she was, for instance, a Baptist, Junior, then what would you do?"

Junior lifted the beer bottle to his lips, drank nearly half of it, and put it down on the coffee table. Amanda picked it up, wiped the bottom, and put it on a coaster.

"If she was a Baptist, ma'am, I'd fix her up with an abortion and go to Vietnam."

Amanda rubbed the bridge of her nose with a finger, ran her hand across her forehead, pushing her hair off to the side behind her ear, and sipped her scotch. J.D. listened to the refrigerator kick on in the kitchen.

"So since Marie is a Catholic, she won't have an abortion?"

"I don't think I'd say *won't*, Mrs. Dixon. I'd say *can't*. They wouldn't let her."

"Junior, Marie is only sixteen. She's not old enough to be a mother. She's still a child."

"Well, ma'am, in some places she's old enough."

"Junior, you are not in 'some places.' You live in a perfectly normal town in the United States. Here, where you live and where she lives, she is not old enough to be a mother. Nor is it fair to cause her to lose the rest of her childhood. She's only in the tenth grade. My goodness, she doesn't even have an education yet. I understand she's learning to play the violin. If she were to have this child, she would never get an education.

She would never get a chance to become, who knows, maybe a concert violinist. She couldn't grow up and be the kind of person she chooses to be with the kind of future she chooses to have."

"Ma'am, she doesn't come from here. She wasn't even born here. She and Timmy and her mom and dad came up here when she was a baby. She comes from some little place called Fat Gap about two hundred miles south of here, way up in hillbilly country. J.D., it's near where you ran into that boar. Down there. I mean hillbillies, ma'am. That's where her people are. Cousins and uncles and aunts and grandparents. All of them. They speak English, but you wouldn't know it. Heard one of Timmy's cousins once. Didn't get a single thing he said. Lots of girls down there have babies when they're sixteen. That might even be old for most of them."

"What are you going to do for work?" J.D. asked.

"Her uncle owns a garage."

"Junior," Amanda said, "you have already thought this out, haven't you?"

"Yes, ma'am."

"Then why are you asking me for my advice?"

"Because you're a mother and you're the smartest person I know. If you understand me, then it's got to be okay."

"I'm not sure I do understand it all yet. What does your father think?"

"My father hates Catholics. Leastways from how he talks about them. Calls 'em mackerel snappers. I don't think he'd be all that thrilled with being a grandfather yet. He's only forty."

"So you haven't talked to him at all?"

"No, ma'am."

"Junior, is your name Elmer, like your father? Is that why you're called Junior?"

"Yes, ma'am, it is. Why?"

"I'm trying to help you. But I need to know you. I need to know who you are. I asked that question because you can't be Junior all your life. If you're going to be a father, I'd think you need to have your own name." She sat back and waited.

"I'm Elmer Benoit, Jr., Mrs. Dixon." He spun around to J.D. and, pointing at him, said, "If you ever call me Elmer, I'll beat the shit out of you! Excuse my French, Mrs. Dixon. Excuse my French. But, J.D., I'm serious."

"What do you think your mother would have thought about this?"

"I don't know. I didn't know her as a person. I only knew her as a mother. When I was old enough to know her as a person, well, you know, she couldn't talk anymore. So I don't know. But she had me when she was only eighteen, and I turned out all right. Well, kind of."

J.D. asked him if he could see his notice from the Selective Service. When Junior looked up at him, backwards over his shoulder, he knew that J.D. completely understood what had happened. He reached in his pocket and handed it to him. It was addressed to Mr. Elmer Benoit, Jr. Amanda watched her son read it, watched her son look at his friend, and went in the kitchen to fix herself another scotch.

"Junior, why don't you want to go into the army?" J.D. asked.

"How's that going to help anything? Doesn't seem like it would help anything. Still be the same situation. Marie with a baby and me gone off. Except I'd probably be like Eddie McKenna or my cousin Kenny. You remember them?"

"Yeah, I remember Eddie. I didn't know your cousin. You told me about him," J.D. said.

"Well, I'm just like them. Both of them. I know guns. I know how to hunt. I know machines. I'm tough. I'm really tough. You know that, J.D., and I'm the kind of guy that jumps in first and thinks later. I'm exactly the guy they would send into some rat-hole and get my fuckin' head blown off. Just like Eddie and just like Kenny. I'm exactly like them, and exactly the same thing would happen to me. And what the fuck for? What the fuck for?"

"You could tell them you'd do anything, just not go to Vietnam. Because of your cousin."

"J.D., you're shit stupid for a smart guy. You don't get to tell them anything. They tell you. 'Oh, excuse me, sir, I rather be in Vermont.' Well, you don't get to go to Vermont or anywhere else you think is nice. You get to be in a fuckin' jungle on the other side of the world with snakes and monkeys jerkin' off all over you and little people in pajamas with giant bazookas. That's where you get to be no matter what you want. They tell you. Not the other way around. You, J.D., you'd be an officer all dressed up in a uniform, telling people what swamp to crawl through. Not me. I'd be the guy doing it. I'd be the guy with the hand grenade and the M-16, in front of everybody else screaming shit like 'Die You Yellow Motherfucker!' running through the rice paddy. I'd be the guy coming home in a bag. Just like Eddie, just like Kenny. I know I would."

"So you knocked her up on purpose. I mean, you figured this out, then knocked her up, right?"

"J.D., I'll get what they call a 3A. Married with a baby. Then we can all come back up here, me and Marie and my kid, and shit, we can go boar hunting where you were in Virginia."

"So you knocked her up on purpose. Because she's Catholic and wouldn't have an abortion."

Amanda came back in, sat, crossed her legs, and leaned in toward Junior. The door to the kitchen had been open.

"I do understand, Junior," she said. "I have one piece of advice. You have made this child. Now go spend your life with one purpose and one purpose only and that is to be the best father and the best husband possible. Nothing else." She leaned forward, motioned to him to lean forward, kissed him on the forehead, and whispered, "Now go be a good husband, go be a good father. Nothing else matters."

After Junior had shaken Amanda's hand and given her the clumsy half-hug of a neighbor boy, he pointed at J.D. and said, "Don't ever call me Elmer. I'll knock your teeth out."

8

Blue Ridge Bar & Grill

THE FIRST POSTCARD FROM FAT GAP, postmarked out of Mount Airy, North Carolina, came two months later. It was a picture of a toothless old geezer with a floppy hat holding a jug with a skull and crossbones on it. The old geezer was cross-eyed. *Marie plays the fiddle all the time with her uncles and cousins. Tell your mom that's what she's learning how to do. She's really good. Got myself a coonskin hat last week. Got a lot of work. Nobody's truck runs worth a damn. Sure would be nice to go boar hunting ... Junior*

The second postcard came on the Ides of March. It was a cartoon drawing of a black bear playing an accordion. *Marie's uncle looks just like this guy. Marie and her clan are getting famous around here. They're playing in all the bars and restaurants. Everybody loves her. Her tummy is starting to bulge out. Shot a deer last week. I want to go boar hunting ... Junior*

The third postcard wasn't really a postcard. It was a photograph with stamps and writing on the back. It was a photograph of a huge bearded man with an accordion, an old, old woman with some instrument in her lap, and Marie Cadieux, very pregnant, angelic in overalls, playing the violin. It came in mid-May. *Didn't you say it was in Galax, Va. where the boar was? Marie's band Danseurs Lune (it means Moon Dancers) has been asked to play at a festival of fiddle music in Galax. Get a load of these guys. The baby should be here in two months so I'll go to watch the kid. We can go boar hunting ... Junior. P.S. I remember why those college girls beat me up. I ate their dope.*

J.D. sent a postcard back. It was a picture of a gigantic hog. It said: Deerfield Fair, 1965—Bad Boar Beanie—1,004 lbs. Biggest pig east of the Mississippi. *Dear Junior, I'm working at Bill Woodward's sawmill this summer humping logs. Time off not a problem. Great news about Marie. Give my love to her and your baby when it comes. I'll meet you in Galax at noon on Aug. 13 at the Blue Ridge Bar and Grill. We'll see if we can find Beanie up in the hills ... J.D.*

The juke box was playing Little Jimmie Dickens singing "Take an Old Cold Tater and Wait" for the third time in twenty minutes. It was Saturday, August 13, 1970. The bar was full, and it was noon. Everybody had at least one long neck Pabst Blue Ribbon in front of them. Most had a few, and some had shots of Jack Daniels set to the side. The bar was only ten feet wide; two feet for the back bar, two feet for the barmaid, two feet for the bar, two feet for the drinkers, and two feet behind to worm your way to an empty stool or elbowing and pushing and "Scuse me! Scuse me!" on down to the pisshole at the far back end. A handsome man, middle aged with thick silver hair, and an old man in bib overalls with a round, red face like a small pumpkin, one on each side of J.D., were arguing about whether Loretta Lynn was thirteen or fourteen when she had her first little baby and whether the lap joints of chestnut beam log cabins should be a dovetail cut, and the barmaid wearing tight blue jeans and a fringed leather jerkin was screaming at a bald toothpick of a man right behind the pumpkin faced man to stop using foul language in her bar or she was gonna call Sheriff Binkins to throw his wizened up, little sorry excuse for an ass out on the street. The etched glass mirror behind the bar spanned the whole thirty feet, and J.D. could see the faces of the men, quieting now, all quiet with just the last tail end of mumblings, all quiet and individual, singular, slack-lipped, looking into the mirror as Junior walked in wearing his coonskin hat, woodsman's boots, madras shorts, and a T-shirt with LBJ, droopy-eared and mushy-eyed with a bomb hanging out of his suit pants where his dick ought to be. "Hey, J.D.! We made it!" Junior squirmed his way past toothpick man and up to the counter between J.D. and the handsome man. "Hey, little missy, a cold beer for me and my friend," he said to the barmaid.

The first beer bottle off the bar was the rat faced man's. He lurched up, staggered a step, and swung his bottle in Junior's general direction, missing completely as the bar broke into cacophony and stools smashed into the wall in back of the drinkers and the barmaid screamed something about Sheriff Binkins, and then just as fast it went quiet. Strewn asunder but quiet. J.D. turned, looking at the door. The photo of Marie's uncle had not done the man justice. He was hairy all over and thick, and his nose and teeth stuck way out. He was big all right, bigger than any man at the bar, but it wasn't just his size that brought the bar down quiet. It was that he looked like a creature that had escaped from a zoo. He stood in the doorway, blocking all the light, and crossed his arms. He looked down the backs of the men, he looked in the mirror, down the whole length of the mirror at each face, then back up the bar to Junior. "Take that shameful shirt off. Now!" Junior took off his coonskin hat, laid it on the bar, took off his T-shirt and put it on the bar. He looked at his new uncle-in-law. The creature nodded, turned, and left the bar. No one said anything until toothpick man put a quarter in the juke box, pushed some buttons, and Buck Owens belted out, "Dang Me, They Ought to Take a Rope And Hang Me." It was still noon.

"Shit," Junior said, "I was hoping he wouldn't see my shirt when I got out of the back of his pickup. I knew he wouldn't like it."

The barmaid leaned on the bar in front of Junior, telling him, "Don't you call me Missy," and to get that disgusting hat and T-shirt off her bar, and, "Rules in this place are that you have to have a shirt on to be in here, so you better leave right now, come back when you're more presentable. There's a Dollar Store down the block. Now git!"

Out on the street, down the block around the corner by the hardware store, J.D. put his arm out, stopping Junior. There were two men in suits talking to Abby, and she was agitated, her face flushed, and pointing her finger at them. J.D. couldn't make out what she was saying. Junior asked, "Is that the girl you were telling me about?" and J.D. nodded. "Well then, J.D., go do something about it. They seem to be giving her a real hard time." He looked at Junior, and Junior elbowed him the ribs. "Go on! Do something!"

J.D. walked down the block, walked right in front of the two men, and with his back to them said, "Hi there, Abby. These folks bothering you?"

"Well, bless my soul. Jeremiah Dixon, you did come back to town, now didn't you. And yes, thank you for asking, they are bothering me. They want to borrow Billy for a little while. Of all the things. Borrow people? Have you ever heard of such a thing? How can you 'borrow' somebody? They say they're from some agency, but I got my doubts."

J.D. turned back to the men. One with short hair was trim and well over six feet tall. The other was just a few inches shorter, with long hair and very large hands. Both had the look of men who were used to coming out on top. "And just who are you?" the taller one asked.

"I'm the guy you're going to have to go through if you want to talk to this young lady."

"We're from the Bureau of Indian Affairs, as we told this young lady here. We have been advised that a young man she knows," he pointed to Billy's hay bale, "is living on Cherokee lands that are protected from trespass."

"You've been advised wrong." J.D. said and crossed his arms over his chest.

"We'll be back," the taller one said, "just to make sure." The two men turned and walked across the street to their car as Junior strolled away from the passenger side, whistling to himself. J.D. stood in the middle of the street, arms still folded across his chest, watching them drive away.

Junior said, "Fancy-ass brand-new Lincoln with Texas tags, QQQ–008. That's an odd one. There was one of those black doctor bags in the backseat."

J.D. turned to Abby. "I wonder how they know about Billy. And why the hell would government people drive a $20,000 car with no government plates and no government decal? From Texas? That doesn't make any sense."

Abby, her eyes fixed on Junior, shirtless in his boots, shorts, and coonskin hat, said, "Nobody will ever find Billy all the way out there any more than they'd find some particular squirrel, and don't swear, don't say *hell*, say *heck*, and who is that?" Junior took his hat off, swept it wide, long and under his waist, bowed low, and told her he was Mr. Junior Benoit, at her command, and she said, "If you are at my command, Mr. Benoit, then go get a shirt on. It's rude to be in public without a shirt on."

"Yes, ma'am," Junior said. He reached in his back pocket,

brought out two tickets, and handed them to J.D. "Eight o'clock. Center stage. See you there." He turned and walked off down the street.

Abby reached over and took the tickets out of J.D.'s hand. "Are you kidding me? Free tickets to Wade Ward? Kyle Creed? Bill Fletcher? Never heard of him. Vassar Clements? Oh my gosh! Marie Cadieux, never heard of her."

J.D. looked over her shoulder. "The guy who gave us those tickets, he's my best friend. His wife, Marie, plays fiddle. They're from Fat Gap, just over the state line in North Carolina. How about I pick you up at about seven-thirty?"

"How about," she said, turning around, her eyes looking up into his, her thin neck arched back, and two fingers touching his cheek, "you pick me up at six and take me out to dinner. How about that?" J.D. stared down at her freckles, her wide-lipped mouth, her speckled dark eyes. She took her braid from behind her neck and flicked it across his chin. She put both her hands in the back pockets of her blue jeans, stomped her boot in the dust, and stuck her jaw out. "Hey, how about that, Jeremiah Dixon? Some place nice."

J.D. went back to the Blue Ridge Bar & Grill, muscled his way past the drunks, up to the counter, and asked the barmaid, "If a guy was going to take a nice girl out to a nice dinner in this town, where would he take her?" There was only one place within an hour's drive. Bistano's Restaurant was ten miles out of town up on a ridge overlooking the whole of the Blue Ridge. He was in the front foyer of the restaurant a half hour after he left Abby, and he made a reservation. Six-thirty. The last table for two open on account of the music festival, but he got a table. He peered in the dining room. White linen tablecloths and candles. Men in suit jackets, women all dolled up. Wine bottles in silver buckets. He picked up a menu, looked at it, and then took his wallet out, counting his money. He reached in his pocket, pulled out a crumpled five-dollar bill, and put that in his wallet as well. *Close, very close. Need enough money for gas to get home. Need money for food for a couple of days. Need some money for bullets if me and Junior are going hunting. Maybe need five bucks for a present for Abby. Very close. Jesus, they want twelve bucks for a steak and potato. Wine is three a glass, but probably she doesn't drink. Beer's a buck. I'll go easy.*

J.D. drove his Chevy back to town, drove around the mountain and down to the bottom of Dengman Gap and up the long dirt drive over the plank bridge. He knocked on the narrow door of the old man's cabin. It was three in the afternoon.

"Well shit a mile in my hush puppies. Little Boy, what are you doing here?"

"Old Man, why do you have a pitchfork in your hand inside your house?"

"Saw that woodchuck. Come on in, Little Boy. Sit on down."

J.D. explained that he had a friend who got a girl pregnant and so his friend married her, and she, now his wife, was from Fat Gap, and she had become a famous fiddle player, and so he came down here to be with his friend when his wife got to play on the fiddler's stage in Galax with other famous musicians, and he ran into the cute girl named Abby who runs the hardware store and Laundromat in town. "You know her, right?" J.D. stopped and waited.

"You asked me that question last time you were sitting in that chair, and I told you then I didn't know her, and I'll tell you again, I don't know any girl named Abby who runs a hardware store. But if she's so fetchin', why are you sitting here talking to me instead of sidling up to her?" He poked J.D. in the knee with the handle end of the pitchfork.

"Because I need to clean up before I go and get her. It's a fancy restaurant. I need to shower, and I thought maybe I could do that here. I've been driving for a day and a half and sleeping in my clothes. I probably stink. Do you mind, Old Man, if I clean up here and maybe come back tonight and sleep on your sofa?"

"Well, Little Boy, I don't mind a bit if you clean up here. That's a good idea. And now that you mention it, you do stink. But, you know, I don't think planning on sleeping here tonight is a good idea. Matter of fact, it's a shit dumb idea. This girl's as pretty as a picture, and she wants to go out to dinner with you in a first-class place and then go stomp it up with ol' boys pickin' their claw hammers and this young girl screaming on her violin, and then you want to come back here and go to sleep? That's not a good plan. That's a dud. You got blankets and pillows in the back of your truck? It's a beautiful, warm night, the moon is full, and the hills and hollers are just waiting for young folks to nestle up into 'em. Go make 'em all happy. If you wake me up, knocking at my door in the middle of the night, I'm going to stick you with this pitchfork. Now g'won and get cleaned up. There's hot water in the cook stove tank."

J.D. stripped naked, went in the shower stall and turned the crank handle pump until the copper tank up above was full and opened the spigot. The floor was chestnut slats, and the walls were chestnut, and the water when it fell on him like a hot river made the whole room smell like fresh roasted chestnuts. He stood with his head tilted back, the water falling in his face until the last drop fell from the copper tank. When he came out, his clothes were gone. He'd left them in a pile outside the wood room door, and when he came out with a towel wrapped around his waist, nothing was there.

"Okay, Old Man, where'd you put my clothes?" J.D. walked into the big room, and there was a paper bag stuffed full of his clothes, and on the coffee table in front of the sofa was laid out a white shirt, black pants, a cowboy string tie with a silver cows-skull clasp, a black suit coat with gray satin lapels, socks, underpants, and his brown belt and boots all shined up. His wallet, keys, wristwatch, and knife were laid on top of the suit coat. There was a hundred-dollar bill on top of his wallet. The old man was sitting in his chair with the pitchfork still in his hand.

"My son was just your size. I've kept his clothes cleaned and pressed for all these years, knowing that someday they'd be handy for just this kind of night. It's on me. Now you g'won out of here and don't come back until tomorrow's sun is straight up in the sky."

"Yes, sir," J.D. said. In the front of his truck was a blanket folded up on the seat. It was a thick patchwork quilt.

J.D. parked his pickup across the street from the hardware store. It was six o'clock. The store was closed, and Billy wasn't there. He could hear Loretta Lynn belting out, "You Ain't Woman Enough to Take My Man" on the juke box from the bar around the corner and down the street. He sat in his suit on Billy's hay bale, stretched his legs out, crossed his feet in front of himself, stuck a piece of straw in his mouth, and admired his shined up boots.

Six-ten and no Abby. J.D. leaned over and pushed the buzzer on the wall. He pushed it again, and then he pushed it a third time. He put a new straw in his mouth, tightened up the clasp on his bolo tie, leaned back, crossed his boots again, and waited. He pushed the buzzer again. *Who is this girl? She's got more spark than a pinecone fire.*

9

Her Coif and Wimple

THE LITTLE GIRL'S MEMORY was like a few old, old photographs—black and white aged to sepia with curled corners. Even those bits of memory weren't any whole picture, just a little part of each picture, the rest having faded into nothingness. A little part, like a man's face that looks like a raccoon, all black across the middle where the eyes should be. Like a big white hand on a woman's neck. Like fingers with a big ring on a hand on the woman's neck and another slim and tanned hand gentle on her cheek, and in the corner of her crib a fire-breathing teddy bear. A teddy bear dragon. She doesn't know if those little snippets of memory are a bad man's hand on her mother's neck or if the tanned and gentle hand that slid fast off the cheek and was gone would be the hand of her father or what. And how does a teddy bear breathe fire? She only sees these parts of pictures just before she wakes up in the middle of the night sweating in twisted sheets, and it's then, just before her eyes open, the pictures flip in and out, and the sepia goes black, and she wakes up, and the first thing she always thinks is, *the neck with the hand on it must be my mother. Why else would I think it was? Why else would I think a tanned hand on a cheek was my father's hand if it wasn't? Why else?* And why is the same violin music playing very fast and very loud, every time, stuck in her head just after she wakes, so loud the inside of her head hurts. Abigail doesn't know. She has never met or seen anyone who said they were related to her in any way. She once asked a little girl who slept a few cots down who had a teddy bear if there were such things as teddy bear dragons that breathed fire, and the little girl had said, "No, you silly, the whole teddy bear would catch on fire, and then your cot would catch on fire, and then then the whole building would catch on fire, and everybody would die."

Abigail's cot was under a window that looked out over the front lawn and the parking lot. She would spend hours kneeling on her cot, watching people come and go from their visits with the mother superior. She would think about the teddy bear dragon and wonder if any of those people were coming to take her to a home of her own.

She sat side by side with Sister Valentine on a wide stone bench in a corner of the courtyard of the orphanage. It was like an English garden. There were rows of neatly trimmed hedges and beds of flowers. Bright, blooming flowers in tilled dark dirt and a few trees. An Anacacho orchid, a Texas redbud and a rough-leafed dogwood, each with tilled dark dirt in a perfect circle around the base. Every day, one of the sisters and Mr. Pops, the gardener, would come to the courtyard with four of five children from the orphanage to hoe and water, to trim, rake, and prune so that the courtyard was always kept and fecund. A refuge of beauty that smelled good and felt fresh. The children weren't allowed there except in the company of a sister so that the flowerbeds and hedges might not be strewn asunder by little feet playing tag, and branches or bones might not be broken by little daredevils climbing and swinging. It was a place for work and prayer, a place for solace and quiet conversation. There were two stone benches, one at either end of the yard, so that two sisters might have two conversations and their privacy not be compromised. Two stone benches, each just long enough for two people.

The sister had loosened her bandeau and wimple and pulled her coif back to free her ear and leaned her head in close so she could hear what Abigail was saying. Abigail whispered. Abigail always whispered. She never said anything out loud. "I would like to ask you a question, Sister."

"Please do, Abigail."

"Have I ever told you of the dreams I have?"

"Yes, I think you have, but I'm not sure I remember them all. Could you tell me them again?" The sister always said this because she had seen over the years that after the girl told of her dreams, she was peaceful, almost happy for a long time until it became necessary to tell the dreams again. In this courtyard. And always, always in the fall of the year and always when the moon that night was going to be full in the sky. She assumed that if the dreams held a germ of some truth, which, she thought, they might, then whatever happened most likely happened in the fall when the moon was full. But she didn't know any more or any better than Abigail knew. God knew, and when it was time for her to know, He would tell her.

Abigail whispered her dreams soft into Sister Valentine's ear, the hands and ring, the raccoon man, teddy dragon, and the loud, loud noise, and then she said, "I am eight years old now, and I want to go away and find out, and find out, I want to go, I think I need to go away and find out about me. Sister Paula told me this is not a convent. She said I can't live here all my life. She said, when I asked her if I could ever wear a habit and a coif, she said ..." Abigail leaned over in front of Sister Valentine, her angelic, little, high cheek-boned face all screwed up serious, and she said in a fake deep voice a shade stronger than a whisper, but still soft and low, a voice as loud as Sister Valentine had ever heard her use, "Sister Paula said, 'This is not a convent. It's an orphanage. Someday soon, sooner better than later, you are going to have to leave.' That's what she said. And then she said, 'Nobody wants you because nobody knows you and you won't talk. Nobody can hear you. You bother people that way. Speak up and you might find a home.' That's what she said. She said, 'You bother people. Speak up, child, and you might find a home.'"

One lonely blessed tear ran from the corner of Sister Valentine's eye, around her cheek bone, down past her bottom lip, bitten now by her teeth, and hung on the bottom of her chin until she wiped it off, tied her bandeau, her wimple, pulled her coif straight, put her arm around Abigail. "It's dinnertime now. Let's go back inside."

The orphanage was high up on the mesa in Ochiltree County in the Texas Panhandle, five miles from the Oklahoma border, not far from the Wolf River Canyon but very far from anything else. It was affiliated with the Sisters of Sacred Heart Convent in Lubbock, one hundred miles south and west. Affiliated or not, the director, Mother Francine, ran the orphanage exactly as she saw fit. She had been born in these parts seventy years ago to a slight, god-fearing white woman from Illinois who had been stolen from her missionary group, brutalized and impregnated by a Comanche brave, and left to die in the West Texas sagebrush. Mother Francine was weather-beaten, raw-boned, had taken her perpetual vows during the First World War, and suffered neither intrigue nor mischief among her sisters. Sometime after dinner, Mother Francine approached the corner in the hallway to the third wing, the wing where the young girls were housed, and she stopped, listening to a harsh, almost brutal interchange between two sisters regarding one of their children.

"You have no right to cause a young girl to fear …"

"You coddle that little half-breed child such that she will

never ..."

Mother Francine set her frock straight, pushing her hands from the bosom down to the hips, set her back straight, rounded the corner, and pointing upwards said, "Both of you, upstairs, in my room, right now." She turned or her heel and went back around the corner.

Her room was not her office. Her office had the usual accoutrements of an executive: desk, chairs, bookcases, pictures, and a side table with a water jug and glasses. Her room had nothing. Nothing, not even a window. It had nothing in it save a Navajo carpet that spanned from wall to wall. Mother Francine stood in the far corner, hands behind her frock, erect, regal, weather-beaten, black-eyed, and mad.

"Sister Paula, what breed of children would Jesus Christ our Lord prefer?"

"None, Mother Francine. The Good Lord loves all children the same."

"And, Sister Valentine, would our Lord prefer one child over another?"

"No, Mother Francine, the Good Lord loves all children the same."

"Then why is it you two, each of you, think that you know more about all children, or even one child, than our Lord Jesus Christ knows about them. Please tell me that." The sisters were silent. "Go now," Mother Francine said.

That was the way with Mother Francine. So tight, so taut, so clear that it was impossible for anyone, no matter how devout, no matter how disciplined, and usually no matter how connected or powerful, to break her simple grasp on the nature of the universe: love thy children and ye shall enter the kingdom of heaven. Nothing more. Because, as she saw it, children loved would love their children, and that was all the Hand of God needed to do to make this world a peaceful place.

Just touch one child born, one child pushed out of a bleeding womb onto the dirt floor of a mud hut and no person there to give the mother a splash of water on her lips before she died, before the men who heard the screams ran from their horses shouting, "Oh my good Lord, save the child!"

Mother Francine knew of Abigail's dreams, and she knew also that memories from infancy are the things that guide a child through the thicket of life to that place where they can spread their arms wide one day, look up into the benevolent smile of the Lord, and say, "This is who I am. I am yours." But you cannot give what you don't have. Little Abigail was eight now, very near of an age that adoption becomes impossible, and the poor girl had no idea who she was. She couldn't say, "This is who I am." She had nothing to give to the Lord. Mother Francine went into her office, picked up the telephone, and dialed a number.

"Yes, good evening, Father. This is Mother Francine. I'm sorry to bother you at this hour."

Whenever Mother Francine called, he began scratching himself, feeling as though ants were biting him. The longer the call went on, the more dire the condition became. Father Bruno was a vicar apostolic. The vast Texas Panhandle had never officially been designated a diocese so that in the College of Bishops he was a bit of a nobody.

"That is fine, Mother Superior. I'm happy to talk for a few minutes, but I do have a meeting very shortly. Oh, my goodness, look at the time. I'm almost late as it is. But never mind. How can I help you?"

"Father Bruno, we have a young child here who is eight years old and very shortly we will not be able to place her with a family. She is a beautiful young child but was physically scarred as an infant. She is not a good candidate for the convent. She has seen nothing of the world except the inside of this orphanage. The poor thing was left on our doorstep, burnt and wrapped in gauze in a plain brown box when she was probably less than two years old. We know nothing about her or where she came from. She doesn't speak except in the barest of whispers. She is blonde and fair-skinned, but her facial features are strikingly similar to those of an Indian. I would guess she is some part Indian, but we have no way of knowing."

"Yes, yes," Father Bruno said. "That's all very sad, but how can I help you?" This Mother was wholly in charge of where all her little people went, and he had never had anything to do with it, nor did he want to. And she was talking much more than she usually did.

"Father Bruno, there is a family that recently expressed to me a desire to adopt the girl."

"Wonderful!" he said.

"No, it's not wonderful, Your Reverence. The family is Cherokee from the Big Flats Reservation. It is a violation of Texas law to give a white child into adoption to an Indian family living on a reservation. For a child to be an Indian, it must be accepted into the Nation by the Tribal Council. She has not been, nor likely ever will be because no birth records exist. To do this, I will need your permission and your absolute guarantee that this will forever remain between you, me, and God. No one else." She paused. "Like the other secrets we have." She waited.

Father Bruno became confused. A secret shared between him and this woman? *It's illegal? What other secrets? What other secrets? Oh my, oh my, she knows about Brother Dominic. Oh my goodness.* He scratched his chest and neck. He cleared his voice once, twice, three times, checking his vocal chords. "Yes, yes, go ahead. You have my word. A secret. Yes, we'll keep it a secret. Can I go to my meeting now?"

"Yes, Father, thank you." And she hung up. *Poor Vicar Bruno*, she thought. *Poor man.*

Once a year, two men would come and ask to see the records of adoptions. It was also a matter of Texas law that these records were public information. Not the names of the children, not the families, nor any addresses or even states where they might live, but the numbers of adoptions, by age, were in the public domain. Mother Francine knew this, and so did the men who came. They made that clear to her on their first trip eight years ago. She could have made them request the information in written form through bureaucratic channels, but it seemed to her unnecessary and confrontational. They were the only people who ever came and asked for this information. Each year she would show them the numbers. They seemed particularly interested in Abigail's age group. Year by year, they followed that age group. Perhaps they were interested in Abigail. Mother Francine didn't know that for sure, but these men would never find out if she were sent out to the reservation. There would be no record of her adoption, and with children coming in and going out, the total number in the orphanage, month by month, was fluid. She was confident the men could not figure it out. Dealing with the sisters, particularly Paula and Valentine, was a bit more problematic. She needed to ponder this.

Within a month, young Abigail, at eight years old, went to live on the Big Flats Cherokee Reservation. The first week, her parents took her to see Chief John. He was brown and wrinkled with long white hair reaching down his back. He set the girl on his lap, pulled his hair back away from his ear, leaned close to her little mouth, and asked her to whisper her dreams into his old ears. She whispered her dreams just as she had whispered them to Sister Valentine. Then he asked her if she could whistle. "Yes," she told him. "Yes, I'm quite a good whistler."

"Whistle the music that is in your head."

First Abigail whistled a bit of "Ave Maria." "That's just to show you I can whistle." Then she whistled her song, a presto lullaby.

"Thank you," he said. "That was wonderful." And he whistled it back. "You are quite a whistler and quite a whisperer."

She said in her low voice, not loud, but a voice with a bit of timbre to it, "I don't need to whisper any more. I have a home."

She lived there, an only child known only as Abby, for nine years, huddled with the boys, fixing all manner of busted things because everything there in one way or another was busted, and flipping hubcaps like Frisbees and leaping over mangy, sleeping dogs, and when the little boy would yell, "Fetch this!" she would yell back, "Fetch it yourself, Little Billy Goat!" She and Billy Goat were inseparable. Every day, they played together. They went to school together. Abby taught Billy Goat how to read, almost. He wouldn't listen to the teacher, and whenever the teacher's words had even the slightest harshness to them, Billy would begin to cry. Abby would have to take him home because she knew that once Billy began to cry, it would be many hours before he was done with it unless she threw him hubcaps or challenged him to running races. When he was tired enough, she would sit with him at the kitchen table in her house and teach him that letters made sounds and, strung together, they made words, and those strung together made sentences. She would imitate a dog or grab a fork from the shelf or throw her shoe across the room, and Billy learned some of it. A little bit. Billy was not a bit slow. In most things, like numbers, he was sharp. With Abby's help, over a few years he got down the alphabet and all the sounds and a few words, but the letters always seemed backwards and disarranged. He just couldn't get from groups of letters to words on a printed page.

They came from the same orphanage. Abby hadn't known him there because he was three years younger, only five when she left, but when he was eight, Mother Francine came to the same conclusion about him that she had about Abby. No one was ever going to adopt a chronic bawler. She had called Father Bruno with the same results and called Chief John, and he was once again gracious about having a white child adopted into a family on the reservation. After two years with his new family, Billy stopped crying. He taught Abby how to whistle like a man. Like a cowboy calling for his horse. He called it the horse whistle. He pinched together his thumb and forefinger, pulled his lips over his teeth, pushed his tongue far back inside his mouth into a fat, wet curl, and blew out a tremendous shrieking whistle.

Abby lived there until her adoptive parents were both killed at noon on a Tuesday when a drunk from Dallas in a big red Cadillac ran into them head-on at ninety miles an hour on Highway 287, two miles south of Goodnight, Texas.

Abby sat alone in her family's *asi*, a small concrete block house with two rooms and most of a tin roof. It was neither stuccoed nor painted, and the steel windows the workers from the Bureau of Indian Affairs put in twenty years ago had rusted shut. She was waiting for the chief. He wanted to talk to her in her own house so that she had, as he put it, "belonging." When he came, he sat in a fold-out chair at the fold-out card table in the kitchen and told Abby he knew of the dreams she had when she came as a child to live here and hoped that she still had them. He hoped her dreams had not been caught and lost to the web but had slipped through the little hole in the middle of the dreamcatcher where good dreams know to go. "I know you must leave here to find a place for yourself in this world. To find that place, you must go back to the beginning. Listen for the music. The music you whistled to me when you were young. I have talked to a wise man in Tulsa who knows this music. I whistled it for him." The chief smiled. He whistled a bit. She smiled and nodded. They whistled together. "Where you find the music, you will find the raccoon, you will find the fire. Follow our trail of tears back to the place where they cried, where the mountains are tall and the trees are big and the air is blue like the sky and the water runs fast and clean. It is there you will find the music you hear in your dreams. It is there you will find the fire." He waved his arm toward the land where the sun rises. "Our people are buried in those mountains, and the wise man in Tulsa told me of the music there. It sounds like the music in your dreams. Go there." He put an envelope full of money and two bus tickets on the card table. He kissed her forehead and left.

Abby cried the rest of the day while she packed her things in a small leather suitcase with leather straps. She had her clothes, not many and not fancy, and she had one picture of her parents, Dallas and Wisika Hannah, and a bone handled knife with a deer-hide sheath and beaded tassels that Dallas had given her on her twelfth birthday. All packed and ready for the morning, she cried herself to sleep. She bit her knuckle and made squeaky little noises. At first light, she dressed, put on her silver bear necklace with the turquoise stones set around the center—her good-luck necklace—walked past the block house next to hers, whispered, "Goodbye, Little Billy Goat," then set off to Amarillo to catch the Greyhound running Interstate 40 a thousand miles east to Raleigh, North Carolina, then a second bus fifty miles north up into Appalachia. Up into Galax, Virginia.

10

Goin' to Git My Baby

WHEN ABIGAIL HANNAH CAME AROUND THE CORNER, J.D. thought he was seeing an apparition. An early evening mist had settled in, and the streetlight flicked on with an amber hue as she walked toward him. Her face glowed in the yellow light, and her mouth was in a straight, wide smile. Her hair was tied up on the top of her head with ribbons and beads. A necklace with a silver bear, green stones, and small brown and white feathers hung in the lacy V of a sleeveless, white satin dress. She wore leather sandals tied with rawhide high up her calves, and over her arm was a green, gold, and red fringed shawl. J.D. didn't move. He sat on the hay bale, transfixed. Mute.

She stood just off the porch step, straight-backed, her hands clasped together in front, and said, "You don't have to push the dang button forever. I'm not deaf." She waited through the silence, eyebrows up. "Jeremiah? Hello?"

He stood, stepped off the porch, and put his hand up, palm out, as if to say, "Stay," and then pointed to the ground as if to say, "Stay." He walked backwards across the road, still holding his palm out toward her, opened his truck door, took everything out of the front seat, and threw it in the back. With a chamois cloth, he wiped clean the entire cab. He shook his patchwork quilt and folded it, laid it out smooth across the back of the seat, smoothed it, smoothed it again, then walked back across the road, put his elbow out for the taking, which she took, and led her to the passenger side of the truck. He opened the door and, careful not to touch her, waited for her to slide in and comport herself, then closed the door.

The Chevy Apache had a 283 V-8 with dual exhaust. Two straight pipes and cherry bomb mufflers that Junior had modified to make her rumble. She did. She rumbled in a low, kind of earthy growl like a big cat. She rumbled up out of town into the hills and high up on a ridge and rumbled straight and smooth on a hard paved road along the ridge between tall oaks. Abby said, "Jeremiah?" He glanced over at her with his eyes wide and then rolled his window down and put his elbow out. When they pulled into Bistano's parking lot, J.D. shut off the engine and exhaled. She said, "Jeremiah Dixon, you talk just like a Cherokee. You don't say a dang word."

And he said, "There aren't any words in my language to say how beautiful you are."

She did drink. She let the waitress in her white waitress dress with a crisp, starched, white, frilly apron tied in the back with a great black bow tell her all about what wine would be best to drink with filet mignon. An Italian chianti. The waitress brought the bottle and a glass and poured just the tiniest bit into the glass and handed it to J.D., showing him the bottle. "I'm sorry," he said, "thank you, but I don't drink wine. I'm a beer guy," thinking how stingy they were with the beverages.

"Jeremiah, do you have enough money for this? I'm happy to just have a glass of wine and maybe share some small thing. This all might be a dumb idea, but I just wanted to feel special, but I'm sure fine with just a little special." He opened his wallet and showed her the crisp, new hundred-dollar bill. "Old Man," he said. "Old Man watching over us. It's a present from him."

"Us?"

"Yes, Abby, us."

"He sounds like Chief John."

"You mean, you don't know how smart he is, he just knows everything?"

"Yes. Just like that."

Abby ate and talked, ate and talked. All J.D. had asked was if she was born here. She said she didn't know where she was born, and she talked about Sister Valentine and Sister Paula and the courtyard. "Jeremiah, those two men who tried to take Billy, I've seen them before. I know I have. I can't remember where, and it was a long time ago, but I know I've seen them." She talked about Dallas and Wisika, fixing busted water heaters and doors and cars and the chief and the music. She told him that after she had been here a year and Mr. Harrelson had given her two jobs, Little Billy Goat had shown up one day and said that the chief had sent him to be her protector until she had a man of her own. "I think he thinks you might be that man." Every once in a while, she would dab her lips with the cloth napkin or reach over and dab J.D.'s lips with her cloth napkin. The waitress came to ask if she would like another glass of wine. She smiled at her with a brief nod of her head, pointed to J.D.'s beer mug, and talked about living on the edge of the reservation at the top of Grayson's Ridge looking down over Dengman Gap. And how Billy lived in town at first but then went to live alone far out in the woods on the sacred land, and he stopped talking, then stopped smiling, and then even stopped blinking. "He'll get better. He's like that. He gets better. And the crummy warshin' machines that are now truly starting to eat up nice people's clothing. I mean eat them up so shirts and dresses are nothing but rags when they come out. That is, if I can get them out at all without taking the whole dadburned machine apart."

"Did you shoot that boar?" he asked.

"What boar?"

The busboy came to clear the table. The waitress asked if they would like to see a desert menu. Abby said yes that would be nice. To J.D. she said that she had talked all the way through their delicious meal because she wanted to save the best for last, the dessert, and that was hearing him talk about his life. Her high cheekbones were flush with red wine. She ordered chocolate mousse. J.D. ordered another beer.

It surprised J.D. that when the check finally came, he was still talking, describing the bureau and the nightstand, the bedspread, the pictures on the walls, and the carpet on the floor of his mother's bedroom. The empty scotch bottle in the hallway. She had put her hand on his and squeezed. He didn't look up. He described her on her hands and knees, the size of her small fist. He took a deep breath, looking up at nothing, rubbed his face with his hand, and said, "The picture she was bashing wasn't a picture of my father. She doesn't have any of those. I can't even remember what he looked like. The picture she was bashing was a picture of Uncle Danny," and Abby squeezed his hand again, hard.

When he raised his eyes, she drew her finger across her lips. "Shhhhhhh."

On the way out, he offered Abby his elbow to make the way across the parking lot. She took his arm and put it up and over her shoulder, put her arm around his waist, and nestled her head against his neck. At the truck, Abby undid her beads and ribbons, ran her fingers through her hair, and pulled it back to a loose ponytail, leaving a shock of blonde hanging over one eye. "Jeremiah, do you have any rope?" J.D. fished a twelve-foot hank of rope from the bed of the truck and handed it to her. She put her shawl over her shoulders and wrapped the rope one time, two times, three times, four times, five times around her waist and tied it in a square knot, letting the short ends hang down loose on her hip. In a minute, she had gone from an elegant woman to a hillbilly girl. J.D. opened the door for her, and she slid more than halfway across the seat to a place that would be tight up against him.

The old wooden grandstands were in Felt's Park, just outside the downtown of Galax. The '58 Chevy rumbled along the ridge, down off the high ground and into the town. Abby nestled herself tighter and tighter into J.D. until he said, "Abby, you smell really good, but I can't steer."

In the parking lot, tailgates were down on the truck beds, doors wide open on the vans, and scores of musicians sat and leaned in small groups, fidgeting the thumb pegs on their fiddle, their banjo, their dulcimer. "Give me a G. Give me a G," and the man with the short, graying hair, wearing black trousers, cowboy boots, a crisp white short-sleeved shirt, and heavy, black horn-rimmed glasses would put his fingers to the neck of his beat-up Martin, look up at the Holy Father in the sky, and strum down one strum hard, and the others with their heads cocked to the side, ear down to the bridge, staring off at nothing, would fiddle with the peg, picking one open note, plink, plink, twist, plink, twist, plink, plink until all the notes on all the instruments were one harmonious union, and someone would say, "Well, by gum, I think we got it," and the fiddle player would go into a riff that hit fifty notes in ten seconds flat. The sheriff wandering by would say, "Lawd, Lawd, Jimmy Boy, you got any brakes on that thar thang?" and they'd all chuckle a little bit and say, "No sirree, Sheriff Binkins, our brakes done wore out long time ago," and then they'd bust into "Foggy Mountain Breakdown."

Abby and J.D. wandered around the parking lot, stopping here and there, listening until they bumped into Junior. They followed him through the gate where they gave the gate master their tickets, and the man whistled and pointed down at the front row. "My Gosh, Jeremiah," Abby said, "we're sitting right up there with all the special people." Junior still had on his coonskin cap and boots but was tucked in tight with blue jeans and a white T-shirt, sleeves rolled up. Abby sat between them.

"Ladies and gentlemen," the announcer boomed from the stage, "welcome to the final competitions for banjo and fiddle at this 43rd Annual Galax Fiddler's Convention. Over the last three days, you've all heard the finest Mountain Music in the world. Tonight you are treated to the best of the best. Three pickers, three bowmen just lightin' up a fire for y'all. The judges," he swung around, sweeping his arm toward the back of the stage, "are three of the finest in their own right. Let's hear it for Mr. Bob Whiddle, Mother Emeline Marsh, and Jerry 'Fast Fingers' Hurly. The contestants tonight, banjo first, are Kyle Creed, Bob Flescher, and Wade Ward. The fiddlers are Vassar Clements, Jimmy Coleman, and Marie Cadieux. She's the only lady on stage tonight, and what a lady she is. This is her first time with us, so give her a big hand when she comes on out. Each contestant can have up to seven back-up musicians, but each ensemble must have a fiddle and guitar and either a banjo or dulcimer. Two songs apiece, three minutes per song, more or less. Ladies and gentlemen, please welcome that magnificent neck-picker, Mr. Kyle Creed!"

After the claps and cheers and shouts, the music began. Kyle Creed had on a beat-up, narrow-brim cowboy hat and pens and pencils in his shirt pocket. The three of them, J.D., Junior, and Abby, sat still, unmoving, staring at fingers doing things that human fingers shouldn't be able to do. Still and unmoving through the banjos and the fiddles to the last when Marie Cadieux came on stage and Junior shot up like a rocket clapping and cheering until Abby noticed Marie patting the air with her hand as if to say, "Please, honey, sit on back down," and Abby, gently latching her fingers into his belt, pulled him back to his chair. She was a flower, a black-petaled flower of a thing. She pulled the microphone two feet down to her lips and said, "Thank you all, and I'd like to thank Mr. Grayson for introducing me as a lady, but as all you can see, I'm just a bit of a thing, not a lady yet, but someday I hope to be." There was laughter and applause. "But there is a lady here tonight on this stage with me. He was right about that. Would y'all please welcome out my great-grandmother, Granny Mae Cadieux, backing me up at ninety-two years young on the mountain dulcimer." Granny Mae wore a bonnet, and the house came down. Beside her stood her nephew, Uncle Albert, the bear, holding a bell-bottomed guitar that looked like a child's toy in his hands.

Marie began to play. J.D. thought the music sounded like a mountain stream running fast, clear water over rounded rocks. This mountain stream began in a gentle spring rain, clean and slow and easy, high on a ridge, then gathered and gathered to a rushing torrent down a steepening hillside gorge and cascaded with a thunderous roar into a still pond. She stood with her head bowed down, fiddle and bow held down by her sides, and the only sound was the strong, lingering bass note from Uncle Albert's big-bellied guitar. The audience was dead quiet until Vassar Clements, sitting off to the side, stood and began to clap. "The next song I'd like to play," she said after the noise died down, "is a tribute to your town. It's called 'Goin' to Git My Baby,' and it was written and played by Robert Jenkins who was born and died on the banks of your beautiful Chestnut Creek. I don't think there's any recording of it. My Granny Mae taught it to me."

She played up the neck and down the neck, hard on the bow and soft on the bow down to one long stroke of the final lullaby hum. Once again, she finished and bowed her head deep down low, and the grandstand was moonlight quiet. The only sound J.D. could hear was Abby's gasping sobs. She was squeezing his hand so hard he thought his knuckles would break, and she sobbed, "That's my song, that's my song. She found my song." And then the house came down again.

"That's my song." She was still crying. "I want her to play it to me more." When Marie, not even five feet tall, black curls bouncing, came on the stage to accept second prize, Vassar Clements reached his arm all the way around her, took her second prize out of her hands and, whispering something in her ear, gave her his. Everyone was on their feet, shouting and clapping. Except Abby. She was sitting, biting her knuckle, making squeaky little noises.

"That's my song," she whispered.

Junior met them in the parking lot and asked them to come down to Fat Gap in the morning and meet the baby. "Too late tonight and Granny Mae's got to get to bed." He nudged J.D. "Don't turn around," he said, "but those two guys with the black Lincoln from Texas who wanted to take the kid from Abby's store, they're at the other end of the parking lot talking to some hillbilly kid in an old Dodge Power Wagon with one of those piss-ant Yamaha dirt bikes in the back. I'm looking at them in the rearview mirror. You want to go have a word with 'em?"

"No, we'll do that later. Right now I just want to get Abby up to her house. See you tomorrow morning. Tell Marie she's fantastic. And, Junior, thanks for the tickets. Abby may be sobbing a little bit, but I think that means she loved it."

11

Down to the River to Pray

J.D. KNEW ONE THING FOR SURE. He did not understand people very well. It seemed that all the things of the world were simple and singular in their purpose. A pinecone fell, and a pine tree grew and stood in one place, straight and tall until it died and fell over and became the dirt the next pinecone would fall in. The animals slept, hunted, ate, slept, hunted, ate, fought, made babies, nursed their babies, slept, hunted, ate until they died and their bones became dirt. A perfect design. But people, he thought, people created worlds around themselves that were complicated, full of hurt, with things in them that made them fear and cry, things in them that were so unworldly that no one even knew what they were or where they came from. Things of the mind. No design at all.

He watched Abby kneeling down on the high mountain grass talking to Billy over the boundary wire. Wherever he lived out there, he could hear cars coming up to her shack or maybe he just knew when she was there. From the back in the moonlight, she looked like a gold-topped porcelain hourglass. She was telling him that she would be back in the morning. Everything was okay, just go on back out in the woods and go to sleep, and she'd be back when the sun came up. He reached over and touched her and then turned around and, like a deer, loped, bounded down the hill into the forest. Abby's house was a one-room log cabin with a tin roof. It was not more than twenty feet from the single strand of thick wire. The boundary of the reservation. There were hawk's feathers and branches hanging from the wire. A yellow sign, ten feet up on a tree, said: No Trespassing. Violators will be Prosecuted Pursuant to CFR 18 808 Sec 65.09. This property is Sacred Land owned by the Cherokee Nation.

Abby held the door open for J.D. He walked past a rusted sink on a stand with a mirror over it and a pitcher of water, soap, a toothbrush, and a hairbrush beside it. One room with a narrow bed, open shelves where her clothes were folded and stacked, a table with one chair. Kerosene lamps and a single gas ring on a wooden stand. Two small windows, one at either end.

"We can't stay here together," she said. "Billy wouldn't like it. He might do something odd."

"Are the other things he does *not* odd? Are they, ah, normal?"

"Perfectly," she said as she got back into the truck, slid across the seat and, once again, nestled tight against him.

They drove down the winding dirt road from the top of the peak. Halfway down the mountain, they passed by a truck pulled off in the woods. A 1952 Dodge Power Wagon with a motorcycle in the back. Abby said they were hunters most probably, but why would they be out past dark? J.D. didn't dare say a thing about the men and the boy in the parking lot. They drove on down to the paved road below. "Left," she said, and they drove over two hills and down into two valleys until they came to a river. "Right," she said, and J.D. followed the river on a narrow, rocky dirt path to a place where the sky opened up and the river turned and rushed down a ravine to a lake below. He parked at the base of a huge southern pine. The air was warm. An owl hooted. The bright moon made the lake look like quicksilver, as though it was thick and undulating. They sat snuggled as a soft breeze and the rumble of the falling water blew through the cab. A long time passed. The owl hooted and hooted, and another owl hooted and hooted back.

"Tell me why you cried when Marie played that song."

She leaned her face close to his ear and whispered her dream into his ear. He asked her if she knew who she was or where she came from, who her real parents were. He asked her how she knew the dream was real at all. A fisher cat, somewhere off in the deep woods, screamed its childlike scream. She slid to the other side of the seat. He rested his head on the steering wheel, looking over at her. He looked at her face, her neck, her breasts, her waist and hips and legs and back up, slowly back up to where the dress fell in a cleft between her thighs, and he breathed through his open mouth. He reached over and put his hand on her shoulder, letting it slide slowly down the smooth front of her dress. She moved his hand off, gave him the slightest shake of her head, and put her head back on the top of the seat, looking straight up, arms at her sides, breasts pushed out full, stretching the satin dress. She hummed one long, long low note like a part of a sweat lodge chant, then, in a jerk, turned her back to him and unzipped her white satin dress all the way down past the last smooth bend of her back, let her dress fall in her lap, reached behind, unclasped her bra and let it fall into her lap. She waited and then slowly turned to face him. All the skin from below her breasts to her waist was horribly disfigured, like a lava field solidified into ridges of dark, hard scars and raw-like soft spots and valleys. Red and pink and blue and almost quivering. All mottled except a hand's width of supple skin under the curve of her breasts where they rose from her ribs, as though the earth had heaved and grown after the lava flowed. As though she had become a woman inside a child's scars. Abby cocked her head ever so slightly to the side and looked at him with ancient eyes—round, black, unblinking. He bit his lip and ran his hand through his hair, and she shook her head again, pulled up and re-clasped her bra, turned her back to him, her smooth back with tiny, soft, white hairs in the deep rivulet by the base of her spine, and tapped the zipper on her dress. She arched her back straight while he struggled the zipper up, and then she put her two hands in her lap, legs together, staring out the wraparound front window of the old Chevy Apache truck, waiting, quiet, lady-like.

J.D. got out and went around the truck and opened her door. "Let's make a bed in the back and lie looking up at the stars and the moon." She nodded, and he unrolled a foam mattress, unrolled a sheet and fit it on it, took the quilt from the front seat and spread it out, smoothed it out and rolled his sleeping bag for a pillow. She climbed in the back, and he climbed in beside her. They lay on their backs and watched the clouds pass by the full moon, and when it was shadowed and darker, they could make out the Big Dipper in one side of the sky and Orion in the other. They nestled like spoons, listening to the wind and the creatures of the night. J.D. kept his loins away from her bottom, but she kept pushing it tight to him, and then she said that Little Billy Goat used to get a bulge in his pants, that's why she called him Billy Goat, and he'd tell her dirty stories until she threw rocks at him to make him go away, but one story he told was how she would always be a baby until a man was inside her.

"I don't want to be a child anymore, Jeremiah. Can you make me be a woman without touching my scars? Without lying on them? Without seeing my scars? Can you do that, Jeremiah?"

"Yes, Abby, I could surely do that, but your scars are a part of you. I don't think they're ugly at all. Everything that makes you so strong and beautiful is told right there. We all have scars. Lord knows, I have my own. I can make you a woman, Abby, but if I did, I would want to make you my woman, not just any woman." He kissed the nape of her neck, unzipped her dress, and gently pulled it off her shoulders. She rolled over, arched her back, unclasped her bra, and slid out of all her clothes.

J.D. undressed and knelt over her. He kissed her face, her neck, her breasts and nipples. He kissed her scars all the way down to the wetness between her legs, and then lying belly to belly, lips to lips, slowly slid inside her. He pushed up against a tightness and pulled back and then pushed soft again, and she said, "Harder, Jeremiah," and then the tightness gave, and she cried out, and he slid all the way deep inside with his arms wrapped tight around her, and she moaned that one low, long note, and the owls hooted back until the note cracked and the notes became higher and shorter, and it got darker as a cloud passed under the moon and then passed by, and the moonlight was bright and white, and they became gasps and gasps and gasps and the long shudder of a woman.

"There's blood on your quilt," she said at first light before the sun was up when the eastern sky was just a rosy smudge, as though a godly finger had rubbed a pastel hue along the horizon. "There's blood on your quilt. I've ruined it."

J.D. gave her a T-shirt, kissed her, and said, "This ought to cover you up enough. Let's wash off in the river. You haven't ruined anything. I'm going to leave it like that forever."

They went down to the river to bathe, her arm wrapped around his naked waist, thumb hooked in the elastic band of his boxer shorts, his hand on the hump of her bottom. She was singing softly.

As I went down in the river to pray/ Studying about that good ol' way/ And who shall wear the robe and crown? Good Lord, show me the way!

Up across the dirt path where the hill rose to a rocky promontory, the dirt bike was hidden behind a clump of small pines. The rider had been there all night, dozing on and off in his blanket, curled up on the bed of leaves and needles. The rush of the river had blocked out all sound, and the massive pine tree J.D. had parked beside blocked his view of the two in the bed of the truck. The rider, dressed in camouflage with a camouflage cap, was also awake at first light, and now, crouched beside the rock, one hand holding binoculars, the other rubbing his early morning stiffness, watched J.D. and Abby walk to the banks of the river. "My good Lord Jesus, wouldya jes look at the ass on that lil' thang." As J.D., in the river to his thighs, reached up the bank with both hands and fit them under her armpits, and she leaned forward to get lifted into the water, the T-shirt rode up her back to her waist, and the man by the rock promontory whispered, "I'mna pump that thang, I'mna stick it. I'mna gonna stick it big. I'm gonna pump that ass," and pulled his cock out of his army fatigues and stroked it. He watched them frolic and laugh and splash each other and kiss kneeling shoulder-high in the cold rushing water, and he watched them climb the bank back out of the river, and he focused the binoculars on the curve of her bottom as J.D. lifted her up into his arms, and he came all over the pine needles and oak leaves.

Five minutes later, the Chevy rumbled to life, backed up from behind the big pine to a clear spot, turned around, and nosed on down the dirt path. They were headed ten miles back to Abby's house to check on Billy and then down into North Carolina to Fat Gap to see Junior, Marie, and Granny Mae. To talk to Granny Mae. The roads were empty. It was early

Sunday morning, and those who were awake were putting out their flowered dresses and hats, their white shirts, shined shoes, and narrow black ties, getting ready to go listen to the preacher preach. The rider waited awhile, kicked some leaves over his spent semen, then fired up his bike and headed the other way, up over the hill and off through the woods to where he'd parked his truck, then into town to the Mountain View Motel.

Billy was not asleep in the woods. He was standing outside her shack, staring straight at the truck as it pulled in the drive, staring straight at Abby as she hurried out and over to him. He pulled up his shirt and held out his arms, and she knelt and looked him over, up and down. "They done it, Jeremiah," she said. "They done it. Those men have been here. Look at this." Jeremiah knelt down beside her and looked at Billy. He was cut and bleeding all over from his waist up and on his neck and face.

"Whatever it is they wanted, they tried to get it while we were down at the river. They chased him through the woods, but they couldn't catch him." She knelt beside him, put her arms around him pulling him close, tipped her head toward the ground, and mumbled, "Lot of blood passed out last night. Lot of blood. That must be where all the secrets are, Jeremiah, in the blood. Like Jesus. Blood of Christ." Her chin quivered, and he stroked her head.

"No. Abby," he said, "I don't think it's the blood of Jesus. I think it's the blood of you and yours."

She shot her head straight up and looked at J.D. Her eyes were full of tears, but her voice came solid. "Who's to know what all anybody wants. I sure don't. What did they want? What is so doggone important about Billy? I don't have the slightest idea about that. Let's take him with us on over to Fat Gap. He loves to ride in cars. Take us down to town, Jeremiah.

Take us to town and you can leave your truck there, and we'll all ride over in my car. Lot of blood" she said, "some taken, some given."

"Yes, Miss Abby." *Oh boy*, he thought, *oh boy, oh boy, Junior's going to love this guy.*

12

The Shorter the Better

FAT GAP, NORTH CAROLINA, WASN'T FAT, it was just wide, that's all. A long hollow between two tall peaks. The town was on two sides of one paved road: a Baptist church; Fat Gap Grocery with the post office inside; Uncle Albert's Texaco filling station with a round white sign with a big red fireman's helmet in the middle; Blue Seal Feeds and an abandoned factory with a dilapidated sign that said Jacob Bros. Rendering. A place that turned the fat of cows, pigs, sheep, an occasional bear, and who knows what else into lard and tallow. That's what they did. A rusted placard with an arrow pointing to the rear said Slaughterhouse.

J.D. pulled into the gas station, rolled the window down, and waited for the gas pump boy to come out. He was a scrawny, hatchet-faced boy of sixteen or so, wearing a grease-covered green shirt and grease-covered green cap, both with the fireman's hat on them, and a horrific case of acne.

"Do you know Junior Benoit?" J.D. asked.

"Shore do," the boy said.

"Do you know where he lives?" J.D. asked.

"Shore do," the boy said, then just stared at J.D.

"Well, would you mind telling me where that is?"

"Shore wouldn't. Wouldn't mind a bit," the boy said, smiling a huge toothy smile.

J.D waited. And waited. Finally, the boy, with a low voice, an eerily low voice for such a young face, said, "Har, har, har," poked J.D. in the shoulder, and said, "That's jes a lil' ol' trick I play on strangers who come around wantin' to know whereall some thang is at." He waited a while longer and then turned and walked back in the garage.

J.D. started to get out, mumbling, "That little shit."

Abby put her hand on his arm and said, "Don't say shit, say shoot," and pointed in the garage bay. Junior was sitting on a tailgate, grinning. Junior got in the truck, backed out, and drove off down the paved road.

J.D. followed. He patted Abby's leg as he drove off the paved road up a dirt track into the hills, spinning dirt, tailing Junior. "You're right, Abby, you're right. That kid's a little shoot-head with shoot for brains. He's also a fucking prick."

"Fudging prick," she said.

The road wound up and up a steep hillside through oak and beech and maple, all still green in the warm and wet summer, and over a bridge with high side rails and solid planking.

"Jeremiah, why is there always a bridge in front of everybody's house?"

"Because everybody needs a creek to get water, and everybody wants to be above the creek, not below it. Otherwise, you might drown. I think there's more to it, but I haven't figured it all out yet."

"Something I really love about you, Jeremiah, is that you say things in such a simple way that makes it easy to understand, but you never say you know the answer. I really love that."

The Cadieux house was nestled back in a pine wood. Front to the south, back to the north. It was a log cabin with a wraparound porch and a worn-out tin roof. Off to the side,

126

there were two hog pens: one for the boars, and one for the sows and piglets. All of them were grunting and squealing and rooting about in their hog troughs. One of the hogs, out around back where the others couldn't see, had his neck slit wide open, hung by hooks through his heels from a stout oak branch, a hog-hanging branch, over a dented copper bathtub full of bloody water. Uncle Albert was scraping the hair off the skin with a two-handled knife. Marie was standing on the porch holding up her trophy in one hand and her baby in the other. An old, ratty-eared bluetick coonhound, gray around the muzzle, sat in the dirt under a tree and howled as J.D. and Abby got out of the car. Howled an old howl, gave a weak woof, curled up, and went to sleep.

Junior peered through J.D.'s window into the backseat. Billy sat still, staring into Junior's eyes. Junior whispered into J.D.'s ear, "Who is that guy?"

J.D. whispered back, "Watch out, be very careful, he bites."

Junior opened the door and pulled J.D. out and off to the side. He pulled him close. "Somebody's gone off the deep end. This shit is creepy. He looks like a certified moron. Where the hell did he come from?"

"He's the kid those guys from Texas, the ones at the hardware store and in the parking lot, he's the one they wanted to take for a ride. Junior, they did it. Somebody snuck up to Abby's when we weren't there, found him out where he was in those woods, and chased him down. They didn't get him, but he's pretty well cut up and beat to shit from running so hard through the branches and the brambles. He's harmless, so don't give him a hard time and don't scare him anymore than he already has been. He may be a moron, but he's Abby's moron, and he's very nice. Just not smart like you. Or maybe he is. Maybe he just doesn't say anything, so you don't know one way or the other. Maybe he's way smarter than us. Maybe that's how you get when your brain's too huge. Who knows?"

When the girls—Grannie Mae, Marie, and Abby—were inside talking about babies, Junior, J.D., and Uncle Albert, taking a break from his pig skinning, sat on the porch with Billy. Marie had brought out iced tea for Billy and beer for the men. The old hound dog had curled up at Billy's feet, watching him sip his tea, and he watched the dog watch him. Uncle Albert, after hearing about grown men trying to borrow a young boy and then chasing him through the woods, thought it a good idea for Junior and J.D. to take the pickup and go find those men or leastwise whoever was driving the truck and set them straight about right and wrong up in these hills. "Find out what they were doing to Miss Abby's friend. A '52 Dodge Power Wagon? Sounds like Skinny Binkins' kid. Probably find him to the Roaring Gap Saloon couple of miles down the road towards Beullah. I'll tell the women you went off to do a piece of God's work. I'll send your girl on from here at sundown. Best if you're there before she gets home." He went to a shed by the pig sty and came back with a clear plastic tube. "Siphon hose. That ought to slow him down." Uncle Albert smiled his three-toothed grin.

The Power Wagon was at the saloon alongside ten or twelve pickups. A neon Pabst sign flicked on and off in the front window. J.D. stayed outside to siphon the gas from one truck to the other. The Binkins boy probably knew who J.D. was. Probably had seen him with Abby. But for sure he'd only seen Junior from the back across the parking lot or from the back in the stands at the music festival. Junior walked into the saloon with a twenty-dollar bill to give to the Binkins boy for a jug of shine, a small jug, not a big jug, just a small one so he could keep ten bucks as profit. "Get me to that shine and you get to keep half the money for your own self." As soon as the bar door closed behind Junior, J.D. stuffed the hose all the way down into the gas tank of the Power Wagon and began sucking. He sucked and sucked and flipped his thumb over the hose end to save the vacuum, then sucked and sucked again and spit gasoline from his mouth to the ground, flipped his thumb on the end, then sucked one more big suck and stuffed the hose into his own gas tank, spit gas onto the ground, and watched it flow, right as rain, through the clear tube from Binkins' truck to Uncle Albert's truck. Smooth and quiet. J.D. walked across the dirt lot to a side window of the bar, wiped the dirt from a corner of the window, and peered in. The place was rocking. Buck Owens droned hard and loud about pushing brooms for an eight by twelve four-bit room, and beery girls with misty eyes offered puckered lips over wet booth tables to unshaven men in cowboy hats, and Junior, shirtsleeves rolled all the way up, had a beer mug in one hand and the other arm around the shoulder of a lanky boy in camouflage clothes, a kid six feet tall who couldn't have weighed more than a hundred pounds. The twenty-dollar bill was on the table. J.D. went back to the truck, got his rifle out, jammed a round into the chamber, laid the gun on the front seat, checked the siphon hose to make sure it was dry, pulled it out, wiped the dribble off the end, and backed Uncle Albert's truck across the lot to the far side and shut off the engine. J.D. figured with the gas in the carburetor, hoses, and filters, they'd make it about a half-mile down the road.

Ten minutes later, Skinny Binkins' kid came out with Junior, fired up the Power Wagon, and headed north on the highway. J.D. followed back a ways. They made it almost a mile before they spluttered to a stop. He was cranking it over and over, trying to get it started again while J.D. crept low up to the driver's side door, crouched down, listening to Junior demand his twenty-dollar bill back. Junior had him by the collar when

J.D. stood up and, just like a year ago on Blue Top Mountain with the skinny girl, pointed the rifle straight up in the air, a foot from his head, and pulled the trigger. Skinny Binkins' boy jumped up hard. It might have been all the beer getting shaken around, fizzed up by his violent jerking, or maybe the tremendous blast of the gun busted the nerve wire between his mind and his distal sphincter, but, whichever, the boy sat slumped on the steering wheel, moaning, pissing out a gallon of steaming hot Pabst Blue Ribbon. He told them everything he knew, which wasn't much but enough to know that the two men from Texas were not nice people. And they were liars. They said they worked for the Department of Child Services, but even Skinny Binkins' boy was smart enough to know you can't do that in Virginia and come from Texas. He told them, "Even I'm smart enough to figure that. And government people don't go skulkin' around chasing boys in the woods and creepin' off in the night. I don't know who they are. They're gone now. They was at an inn in town, but they're gone now. Paid me fifty bucks to watch you and your pretty girl down at the river so I'd tell 'em if you were coming back."

J.D. leaned in the window, put his lips up to the boy's ear, and told him, low and slow, that if he ever said anything about what happened at the river to anybody, he would hunt him down like a dog in the night and cut his tongue right out of his mouth. "I couldn't see nothin'. Honest I couldn't. There was a big tree in the way."

They left Skinny Binkins' boy on the highway, out of gas, sitting in his piss-soaked pants, and drove back into Galax. Junior was chuckling. "How was she?" J.D. didn't answer.

Granny Mae sat in her rocker on the front porch with her dulcimer laid on the rail beside her. Her spit pail was five feet away in the corner of the porch. The tin bucket was half full of black goo, but the porch floor and corner post and railing were only slightly stained. She was a good shot. A careful, dead-eye spitter. She had been working on her spit for seventy years. A foil bag of Red Man tobacco, neatly folded tight across the top, lay on her lap. She slowly chewed her wad and spoke cleanly and slowly, not letting the juice garble her words. Abby sat at her feet, cross-legged, leaning back against the railing. She looked straight at Abby when she was talking, except when she turned her head the other way to spit. Just the two of them were on the porch. Her voice was like a stiff wind in the reeds—wispy but strong. Her words were so thick with mountain twang Abby could barely make out what she was saying. After a bit, Abby rested her head back, closed her eyes, and let the story be a mountain ballad.

"Child," she said to Abby, "you asked me to tell you who was Robert Jenkins who wrote that song we all played on that stage. And how did he die. I don't know all what it was, but I'll tell you what I know. In 1949, about twenty years ago, I was seventy-two then, my goodness, only twenty years back, seems like forever, that's what time feels like when you're happy to be alive, feels like forever. That was the year Robert died." *P-ding*, she spit, hitting the pail. "Anyway, back then the bridge going on up to his house, the bridge over Chestnut Creek, was a dangerous little thing. Two fat wood beams went from edge to edge, resting in deep pockets between huge, flat stones at both ends. I remember Albert getting down on his knees and peering down under that bridge just so he could tell me how bad it was made. The planks were laid across, but they weren't nailed so that when the creek rose up in a bad spring flood, the water would wash all the planks downstream but leave the big beams there. Beams were long and heavy, he said: men-folk could barely lift them, but the planking could be fished out from the pucker brush on the sides of the creek, carried on back, and put back in place. That's why Robert didn't nail 'em. So the whole bridge wouldn't wash away. I remember there was a tethering post in front of the bridge because no horse or mule would walk over it. They'd put one hoof onto the first plank and jump back with a jerk. It rattled something awful when anything passed on it, a truck or what have you. Most people were scared to drive over it. Most people parked in front of it, walked carefully, slowly down the center of it, and hopped off the last plank onto solid dirt on the other side. I know I did, and Albert, tough mountain man he is, why he'd walk just like a little ballerina." *P-ding*, she spit in the pail.

"We'd walk straight up, not looking back, as though everything was all right, then up the rest of the dirt drive to the front door of Robert's shack and rap that big ol' brass knocker he had nailed to front door. Robert would open the door, usually with a fiddle in his hand, and then he'd always bow deep like a gentleman, say, 'Come on in. Come on in, y'all.' We all had our own fiddles and dulcimers and violas or banjos or guitars, all of them slung over our shoulders on rope or cloth straps. 'Come on in!' he'd say, and 'Little Joe Bob'—that was Albert's boy before he died of the fever—'Joe Bob,' he'd say, 'would you g'won back down to the crick underneath that fine ol' bridge and fetch us out a little sompin' to sip on? Us folks likely to git a mite dry hammerin' on and hammerin' off. Grannie Mae, you got your holler bone slide with ya?' He always asked that, and I'd always say, 'Why yes, Robert, I do. It's rat har in my apron pocket.'

"That's how it was the last time I saw Robert. It was the Harvest Moon. Big, old, bright red round moon coming up in the sky in the fall of the year. I remember that clear. And we played music that night. Couple hours we played, and I think Jimmy Haskel was with us. Yes, yes he was, bless his soul. He passed a few years back. Jimmy played fiddle, just like Robert, and I had my dulcimer, and Albert, if I remember right, was playing on his guitar. My husband, Ernie, may God rest his soul, had his banjo. That's how it was. Robert wrote songs, new songs, beautiful songs that nobody'd never heard because he just wrote 'em and showed us how to play 'em. It was fresh and nice hearing new mountain music. It made me feel like the world would go on and on. Not just die out in some poor holler. One of the songs we loved the most was that song that made you cry, 'Goin' to Git My Baby.' You said you'd heard it before, but, child, I don't think you did. I don't think you could have. That song was never played outside the walls of Robert's house. Leastwise, not till I taught it to Marie a few months back. We did play it that night I do believe. I remember him saying, 'Well, Granny Mae, this is a lullaby, don't you think?' And I said, 'It sure sounds like something that'll make an old picker weep and put a baby to sleep.'" *P-ding*, she spit and just got the top rim, a little goo dripping down the side of the pail.

"That's how those evenings went at Robert Jenkins' house. He'd stoke up the fire in his wood stove and leave the front door of the house and a window or two open a crack so it was cozy and warm inside, and the evening breeze would blow through. There was something very clean and fresh about Robert. And something different too. He wasn't just some old somebody who played the fiddle and lived in a shack in in the woods. Lord knows there enough of us like that up in these hills. He was a thinker. Robert had a mind. He'd been to a university." *P-ding*, right in the bucket. "And he loved the Indians. Oh, how he loved the Indians. He used to joke that he was Robert 'One Foot' Jenkins. He'd lost most of his left foot at some army base to a dog when he was little. He said he'd jumped off a tin roof and landed in the guard dog kennel. One of the young guard dogs still loved to play with shoes. He was like that. Not one mean bone in his body and my, my, could he play that fiddle. Almost as good as Marie.

"That land there was his family's land, but they'd left it years ago when his papa became an army man. Then his papa died in the war, and his momma died a month later. Nobody'd lived there for twenty, thirty years when Robert came back and fixed the place up. Nobody really knew who he was or even that he was there. He kept to himself out there. Didn't venture out. He was a thinker, a book reader. He'd been to the university. He read books, and there was something about the Indian Burial Ground that he didn't like. Something about whatever all happened up there that he didn't like. He was fixin' to talk to people to get somebody to look into it all. He told us that that night we last saw him. Something about it up there he didn't like. I don't recall what it was.

"When we all were leaving, some other folks were coming in. I don't know who they were. Never seen them before. I remember him saying, 'Good evening, Doctor, please come in.' There was a man with wild white hair, a checkered jacket, like a professor, an Indian woman younger than he was who looked to be his wife by the way she held his arm, a younger man, and the younger man's woman carrying a little baby. A family they were for sure. We all nodded proper like to each other, and they went in, and we left to come on back to Fat Gap. I remember all that pretty sharp because that was the last time we saw him. That night or the next night or sometime there abouts, his house burned to the ground, and he was in it. Burned to death."

Granny Mae leaned way over toward the tin pail and spit the whole wad out to the bucket. *P-lunck.*

"Some days later, a deer hunter smelled all the smolder. The local policeman went out there, and then he talked to the newspaper for some reason that didn't make a bit of sense to me. Jimmy Haskell read it to me. That policeman said he figured whoever it was who lived all the way out there had fallen asleep, and a long, tin stove pipe, probably filled with creosote, had burned through, lighting the floor on fire, and he had died in the smoke and flames in his sleep. His body, he said, a burnt crisp, was in the basement rubble. No other bodies were found. He was alone, asleep, the policeman said. Stove pipe burned through. People shouldn't oughta have long stove pipes. The shorter the better. Keep 'em real clean.

"I remember clear as a bell Jimmy reading me that story because it didn't make no sense at all. I kept the clipping from the newspaper somewhere because it all was so sad and seemed so strange. Robert's stove pipe wasn't any longer than my foot. Jimmy Haskell told me Robert had that thing special welded up in town out of solid steel because he didn't trust the regular fittings we all buy at the feed store. That pipe didn't burn through. That's for sure. Policeman coulda seen that if he'd poked around a little bit. But he didn't. For some dang reason, he didn't. Didn't even bother. They just pulled Robert Jenkins' bones out and buried them up at the poor farm. That's what we heard. That's what people said they did, but who all knows what they did with that poor man's bones? They didn't even know who he was."

"Grannie Mae," Abby said as the old woman picked up her dulcimer and strummed a few notes, "Grannie Mae, how could I have heard that song?"

"Only one way, child. You woulda had to been at Robert's house."

Old Man was in the front yard leaning on a tree with a flashlight in one hand, shovel in the other, and a dead woodchuck at his feet. "Dadburned critter. Every time I plant a little something, he ate it. Two years I've had it out for him, and today I got him. Smacked him right on the head with my shovel before he could skittle away. Now he's got to get buried so he doesn't stink and the coyotes don't come. Then tell me about dinner with your girl." Old Man handed J.D. the shovel, patted him on the shoulder, and gimped off inside his cabin. J.D. watched the dull yellow glow of the gas lights flicker on.

Every once in a while, they passed the jug of Maker's Mark back and forth between them as J.D. described the tablecloths and fancy people and the wine Abby drank and how much it cost and, "Thank you for the hundred dollars. I'll get it back to you soon." How Marie, just a pipsqueak of a thing with bouncy black curls, a new baby, and a ninety-two-year-old great-grandmother took second prize, and Vassar Clements gave her his trophy. Skipping the part about the night in the back of the truck down at the river, he told as cleanly as he could the story of Billy and the men. The men and Skinny Binkins' kid. The parking lot, the chasing through the woods. When J.D. got to the recounting of what Abby had told him about Granny Mae and Robert Jenkins, the old man was no longer gently rocking in his chair. He was rigid on the front end of the seat, holding tight on the arms with his gnarled knuckled hands.

"Where was this bridge over the creek and this house that burnt down?" he asked.

"I don't know. She didn't say."

"Lot of drives go off the road over this creek. Could have been anywhere in a ten-mile stretch, I suppose."

"Yeah," J.D. said, "could have been. Old Man, I only have one question that I really need to know the answer to. I have to be at school on Monday morning, so I'm going to have to drive through the night, but I really need to know who shot that boar."

"Little Boy, do you promise to come back down on the first of October? That's less than three months away. Will you be here so we can talk more about this?"

"Yes, sir, I promise I will. Who shot the boar?"

"Might be that young fellow that lives in the woods. He might be deaf and dumb, but I don't think he's a moron. I think there's something else wrong with him that makes it so he can't communicate at all. Can't show emotion or talk or anything. I don't know what it is. I've never seen it or heard of it before. It's very odd. But I know he's not stupid. That's for certain. I would guess it was him." He got up, went to the sink, splashed water on his face, and went and lay down on his bed. J.D. smiled at him and tapped the old man's foot.

"Why did you lie to me about it?"

Old Man propped his head up on the pillow. "When I could still walk all the way up the hill, I used to go and just sit with him and watch the squirrels and deer. We would just sit, and he didn't mind that. I had this sense he knew everything that was happening around him. He had squirrel skins hanging from a pole, so he must have killed them, skinned them, and ate them. When I was there, he was always eating a bowl of some kind of mushed-up nuts. I'm thinking it must have been him. I heard a thumping outside, and by the time I got out there, nobody was there. Just you slumped against the cabin and the cut-up parts of an animal with a big boar head with a hole through it sitting in a tub beside the woodshed. I buried the head and put the meat in a crock of salt brine while you were sleeping."

"Why didn't you tell me?"

"That's sacred Indian land up there, Little Boy. Nobody's allowed to go there, let alone live there. Ever since he got out there, he's been helping me with work I do. That's how I know he's not a moron. I figured if you knew about him and you knew that I knew, it might get very bad. Now you've told me about your girl Abby who lives in that shack that used to be empty, those men from Texas and Robert Jenkins, and I think it might get very dangerous for all of us. That's why I got to think this through before I talk to you more. There's a story I want you, Little Boy, to know. Just you. You're like a grandson to me. You can make it come out all right, but I have to figure out all the ways it might end before I tell it to you. That's going to take a little while. Now go back to your schoolwork, and I'll see you October first." He rolled over.

"What kind of work do you do, Old Man?"

"Go back to school. Become a forester. I'm tired now."

J.D. put a blanket over him, blew out the lamps, and left.

13

A Momma's Boy

AMANDA DIXON CHOSE TO WALK A MILE from the public parking lot, across the entire campus of the university to the administration building of the School of Medicine. It was brisk but clear. She wore a black wool skirt, a tan blouse buttoned in at the collar, a scarlet jacket, and scarlet high heels. She wore no jewelry and didn't carry her purse. In the car, she had put on dark mascara and scarlet lipstick that matched her coat and shoes. Her hair was pulled back tight and pinned in a bun.

She gently pulled the walnut door closed behind her and gave it a final little tug. The latch clicked with the solid oiled click that comes with expensive hardware. Dean Harris didn't look up. He sat behind his desk, slowly turning pages of a document in a three-ring binder. He took a sip of coffee, turned back a few pages, knit his brow, flipped forward a few pages, and scowled. "Mrs. Dixon, have a seat," he said, pointing to a chair in front of his desk.

"I'm sorry, Dean Harris, it's Dr. Dixon. I'm not married. Amanda, if you prefer." She sat in a hard wooden chair in front of the desk. She pushed herself back in the chair but seemed to slide forward again. She pushed herself back again and slid forward again. She realized the front legs of the chair were shorter than the back legs so whoever sat there would continually be slightly sliding forward—nervous, uncomfortable, distracted. She got up and sat in a chair at the conference table. "Excuse me, Dean Harris, but there's something wrong with that chair in front of your desk. I hope you don't mind if I sit here."

"There's something wrong with your research, Mrs. Dixon," he said, closing the binder, looking down his nose over his reading glasses. "The people who fund this research expect a professional product. A complete product. Conclusive statements. Something that can withstand the rigors of peer review, the scrutiny of government, the withering analysis of corporate enterprise, and lastly, and don't ever forget, Mrs. Dixon, don't ever forget the smell test of a very skeptical public. This document would be eviscerated in the first inning."

Amanda glanced at the photo on his desk of him beaming up at a disinterested man in a baseball uniform. He was wearing the same bow tie that he was wearing in the photograph. Blue polka-dot.

"Dean Harris," she said, "Dr. Norton reviewed it and authorized me to finalize the findings for publication. He told me that the research, so far, was meticulous and the presentation solid. I only printed two copies of that document. One is filed in my office; the other was given to Dr. Norton. He still has it. They are titled, 'Preliminary Findings — For Internal Review Only — Do Not Copy.' I can't understand why you would come to exactly the opposite opinion reading only what looks to be a partial copy."

Ken Norton had told her that before he even got his copy, Harris had called and screamed about the "Preliminary Conclusions" chapter. That meant her office and documents were not secure. Someone had stolen her work. Someone had compromised the integrity of their program. Norton didn't know who, he didn't know why, but the dean was somehow involved. Her research seemed purely academic, innocuous, and yes, it was very well done. "Meticulous and solid," he said. "Did it state an absolute certainty? Thankfully, no." And then he told her that Dean Winthrop Harris had a stark weakness: he was afraid of strong women. Simple as that. He still lived with his mother. "Go after him," he had said. "Back him down and you'll find out what's going on. If he barks, don't just bark back. Bite. Remember, he can't fire you. You don't work for him. You have a contract with this research facility. He didn't sign your contract; I did."

Images of her dead husband came to her mind. A momma's boy. She saw his lower lip quiver when she demanded to know why her husband wouldn't touch her. She saw his back hunch and slump when she asked him where he went at night when he didn't come home. "You weren't in your office. I went there. The building was dark, and the doors locked. Where were you? Do you have a girlfriend? A professor's mistress?" He never answered with anything but a blubberish lie until he turned up dead in the morgue, and then she knew. She could have known much earlier, could have protected her son and herself if she had just batted him about a little bit, then slammed him with a clawed paw. He would have wept and told her all, and she would have moved away many years ago. She decided to stalk the dean, like a big cat in tall grass, to prowl about the edges until he smelled her scent and popped up scared.

"Dean Harris, could I ask how you came by a copy of a document stamped on every page, 'Do Not Copy'?"

"Mrs. Dixon, I am the dean of the School of Medicine. All that is done under the imprimatur of this institution is my business and my responsibility. The conclusions you have reached concerning the effects on human beings of a mixture of common chemicals is wholly inadequate. I quote from page

276: 'Second generation exposure resulted in 2 of 27 cases of identical male twins, neither able to interact with any other subjects. It cannot be stated conclusively that this condition is not a function of diminished mental capacity, but the statistical test results indicate it is likely some other disorder.' I underline the following statement. 'This condition has not been produced in any other clinical research known to this author.' That doesn't mean it doesn't exist, does it? I would like to see this change made to your report. 'No loss of motor control.' Fine. You established that. 'No loss of mental capacity.' Period. I know you can get there, Mrs. Dixon. That's what you are being paid for. To say things are either true or not true. Anything else, any other wavering is an egregious professional mistake. Am I clear?"

"Mice, Dean Harris, mice. The report says nothing about human beings. And you didn't answer my question. Who stole that document from my office?" She stood and waved her hand at the portraits on the wall: Curie, Schweitzer, and da Vinci's Perfect Man. "You seem to be a lover of truth, Dean Harris, so let's start here with the truth, right in your office." She walked to the portrait of Albert Schweitzer and peered into his eyes, then turned around and purred. "Who stole my work?"

"This conversation is over, Mrs. Dixon. Your contract will be terminated and a more professional replacement found. Good day." He stood behind his desk.

"Egregious is a good word, Dean Harris. It aptly describes you and your actions. Egregious professional misconduct and very likely criminal activity." She walked to his desk, leaned over at him, and growled, "You do know Dr. Marilyn Engleman, don't you? You know, the chair of the Standing Committee on Research Misconduct. You know Madam Hoffslinger, the University General Counsel? If I leave this office without the answers I deserve, those are the first two people I am going to see." She picked up the three-ring binder and slammed it on the edge of the desk. "Now, who stole my work, why do you have it, and why do you demand that it be so absolutely conclusive?"

Harris's eyes blinked shut, and his lower lip bulged out like a smacked child. He sat back down and inhaled a huge breath and blew it back out.

"The United States government removed that document from your office. They brought it to me. It has to do with the storage of various chemicals and potential lawsuits. The manufacturer of the chemicals funds your research. If your work is published as written, this school stands to lose a great amount of money and potentially suffer some very difficult, very bad publicity. I can't tell you more than that. Even that was told to me within the confines of attorney-client privilege. Please don't ask."

"Dean Harris, you can't terminate my contract; only Dr. Norton can, and he won't. You would have to fire him also, and then the truly frightening Madam Hoffslinger would be rifling through your drawers. This is what I'll do. I will re-run the last phase of the testing with a new set of second generation offspring. If the results come up the same, the report as written stands, no matter who likes it. If they are different, if they are statistically conclusive, the ambiguities will be removed. Deal?"

He kept blinking and licking. "Yes, that's fine as long as you never mention this to anyone."

"Unless I'm put under oath, Dean Harris, and only you can prevent that." She picked up the binder, tucked it under her arm, and left, clicking the latch firmly behind her.

J.D. was studying for his final exam. His course work was over. He was going to graduate a year early with a near perfect grade average. The last classes over the last three days had all been about tree blight. Fungi, bacteria, or bugs that attack trees and stunt them or cause them to die. The air-born, bird-born, bug-born blights that find a receptive host in trees of certain species with genetic characteristics that allow penetration of the leaf, skin, or bark. He was in his bed at home, pillows behind his back and head, textbooks and notebooks strewn across the patchwork quilt on his lap. He read a page, marked it with a bookmark, put it down, listened in his mind's memory to the professor's words, read his class notes, and made new notes on a clean sheet. Most of the material in the books and most of what the professor had said pertained to the Great Chestnut Blight of the early twentieth century. Four billion tall, broad, stout, beautiful trees gone to an invisible fungus brought over on a ship from Asia sometime around 1900. It was a fungus that clung to the feet and feathers and beaks of birds, that blew through the air and came in the rain, splashed up waist high, nestled into crevices in the bark, and grew around the vast girth of the tree into a sunken canker that choked off all life on its way from the roots to the branches. A few small trees survived in Pine Mountain State Park, in lands once owned by the Creek Nation. Occasionally, a sucker shoot springs from the still living root of a dead stump but never lives long enough to reproduce. The blight came to the forests in a thousand-mile swath along the Appalachian Trail from Maine through Georgia and within two generations wiped out the entire species. Four billion trees. The professor had said there was nothing more important for his students to do than make sure this kind of massive devastation doesn't ever happen again. *My God*, J.D. thought, *four billion trees*, and he closed his eyes, wondering how many trees there are and remembered the numbers that came to him as the telephone poles had whizzed by, and he pulled the quilt tight up to his chin and yawned and yawned again and felt soft and alone in his mind.

There was a garden, the rich dark dirt of the garden where it met the bright green grass, and he was a papoose again on his mother's back, and she was also a child. Junior, lying under a pile of naked girl bodies, just his head sticking out, stroking his white beard: "She's only six." His voice sounded gravelly, like car wheels turning in a driveway. Junior fought his arms free and clapped his hands once like a car door shutting, clapped again like a front door closing, and horses hooves, sharp on stones galloping off, sounded like the click of heels on a hardwood floor, and he smelled the lavender breath and woke up with a jerk.

Amanda was sitting on the edge of the bed looking at the patchwork quilt. "Where did you get it? It's beautiful."

"Mom, why do you look like Miss McManus? It's scary. You look really scary."

"Yes," she said, "I hope I do. I had to scare somebody today. Not you, J.D., not you, but someone. Someone important. And it worked. I scared him, and he gave me what I needed. Now where did you get this quilt? It's all hand sewn. Every one of these squares is hand sewn and crossed stitched together. Look at this," she said, holding a square up to J.D. "This is beautifully stitched. What kind of tree is it?"

J.D. looked at the square, looked at his open book, back to the square. "This quilt must be really old. All those trees died fifty years ago. That's a big chestnut tree."

"And what's this?" she asked, pulling another square up closer to her face. "It looks like a big, orange mushroom. And how did that blood get on it? It is blood, isn't it?"

"Oh that. The blood. I don't know. It was on it when the old man in Dengman Gap gave it to me." J.D. was intently staring at a square. "I don't get it," he said, pointing to a black 1958 Chevy Apache with a bright red stripe down the side. "How can that be? That's my truck."

"J.D., how do you know this is blood if it was on it when you got it? Did that man tell you it's blood? Maybe it's paint."

"Mom," he said, jabbing at the square, "that's my truck. How can that possibly be?"

14

Split-Finger Fastball

IT WAS THE DAY BEFORE THE AUTUMNAL EQUINOX. The sun had risen that morning at 7:10 and would set that night at 7:13. Tomorrow the sun and stars would share the day in exactly equal portions. Twelve hours for the sun, twelve hours for the stars. He had work to do to prepare for this changing of the seasons. He was punctual to the minute in preparation for the celestial shift. Tomorrow he would rise at precisely 7:11 in the morning (or at least when his wind-up clock dinged its alarm at 7:11 in the morning) and fire up the cook stove to make coffee and fry his eggs. At 7:11 in the evening, after having scrubbed his body from head to toe in a steaming hot shower, after having put all his clothes in a basket for the next day's washing, after having slipped into his flannel nightie, he would, tired or not, lean back in his chair with a pillow behind his head, whisper a shaman's prayer, and close his eyes. The equinox would pass in his sleep, and the next season, the next chunk of the year, the next chunk of his life would begin. His existence was measured in arcs of planetary orbit.

On this day, the day before the fall equinox—as on the day before the spring equinox—he was also busy with other things. Things that required a particular, ritualistic preparation. He had work to do to prepare for that precious time, that exact one hour that he got to see his wife. The old man pulled the trundle box out from under his bed. On his hands and knees, with a focus that transcended the stiffness of his bent back, the soreness of his knees and swollen knuckles, he moved a wooden hat box full of scraps of cloth and thread and pin cushions of needles off to one side. He fished out fresh sheets, a fresh pillowcase, and his fall blanket, a patchwork quilt he had sewn ten years ago. He put them all on a chair and stripped the bed of all its clothing. Stripped it clean down to the mattress ticking and beat the mattress with the handle of a broom. He didn't trip, stumble, or even shuffle. The old man's movements were crisp and economical, even graceful, like a crab on a rocky shore. *My God*, he thought, *I've done this more than forty times, and if I miss a step, if one corner of the sheet isn't tucked just as tight as all the others, if the dishes on the shelves aren't stacked in precise and determined order or the toilet paper roll in the one-hole shitter isn't new and full and set on its peg with the first sheaf hanging down the back side, not the front side, if any one of these or a hundred other conditions are not set to a perfect place, the next equinox will never come.* To the old man, God was in the balance, the order, the symmetry of all things in the universe, and if a man's spirit was out of balance with that symmetry, he would simply cease to be here. He would be sucked out of this circular, cyclical world and thrown down the rabbit hole into a parallel universe where everything was random, chaotic, linear. Where things traveled faster than the speed of light and all the creatures were strange and spoke gibberish.

The old man had devised this notion while sitting on a butte in the high New Mexico mesa watching the sun set, drinking a bottle of scotch and reciting parts and pieces of *Alice in Wonderland* with his best friend, Opie. They were both worried about two things: first, that their wives, Edith and Kitty, who were off on a fling in San Francisco, might never back come to them because they had upset the grace of living by never paying any attention to them as they labored day and night figuring out how to bust up a universal building block, and secondly, that God may not want them here anymore because they had busted up her building block and caused a cataclysmic chaos in her ordered universe. So they would have to go to a place where time went backwards or didn't move at all and nothing circled anything else, a place where there was no center to hold. And their wives would come back to this New Mexico place having fallen in love with other men— gallant, engaging, attentive, sensitive men—and they wouldn't be here to complain about it or maybe wonder at the beauty of it. They'd be off talking to the Mad Hatter and watching Humpty Dumpty go from a splattered mess on a stone sidewalk to a nice big egg on the top of a wall.

The old man sat on the mattress ticking and thought back through those years. Opie was dead now. He had been stuffed through the earthly rabbit hole by powerful people manically paranoid about Communism and had spent the last fifteen years of his life paying for it in an other-worldly purgatory for having, as the old man thought, shown the world what *energy equals mass times the speed of light squared* actually means to people in Hiroshima and angering those politicians. They had given him a Cassandra-like curse. He was the prophet. He knew what was going to happen because he had been to the other side of the mountain and seen it. But no one, not even his friends, would truly believe him or truly trust him. Ever. And his wife, his darling Kitty, would drink herself to death, and his daughter would hang herself in his own house. That is what Opie got for not tucking his sheets in tight enough.

The old man had refused to talk to the investigators, had refused to give up anything about his friend. He remembered looking at Opie passed out drunk on the mesa after the sun had set and the sky was turning from orange to purple and he was snoring with the empty bottle of scotch in the crook of his arm and a dead cigarette in his lips. He remembered thinking that it was better to get life without parole for being a good friend than getting twenty years for being a bad friend. So he didn't talk. Nor did Edith. Later on, by cruel happenstance, both of them got hammered into that parallel universe where caterpillars talked and everything was gibberish.

He stood up and beat the ticking again, with the handle of his broom, intoning with each stroke, *Blind mad men in a bomb-bunker room, Bomb-bunker kings with minds unstable, Added and subtracted from the Periodic Table. The Periodic Table, spun unstable, Landed in the belly of the Fat Boy tomb, Boomlay, Boomlay, Boomlay, Boom!* Making the bed was easier for him now. He didn't have to bend over; he was already bent. He smelled the fresh percale sheet, flopped it over the bed, and smoothed it out, making sure there were no wrinkles. He tucked in the first top corner, lapping one corner over another in a perfect forty-five, then tugging it tight across the top, lapped and tucked the second corner. He pulled the sheet to the bottom, grasping both sides in his hands and pulling until the sheet was taut and jammed it under, folding tight the hanging loose corners in a precise geometry. He patted it. Not a wrinkle, not a crease, and the sheet stood off the mattress by a half an inch everywhere, and the top sheet, loose on all sides, folded back the width of his hand-spread at the top, was smoothed to a similar perfection. "Perfect, perfect, perfect," he muttered. The patchwork quilt that he had spent an entire season sewing was designed in such a way that the squares aligned precisely with the edge of the mattress, and the border, a gray wool with satin edging, was eight inches wide on the sides and the foot. The top was all satin so it wouldn't scratch the neck and chin. Designed like this, it was easy to lay it on the sheet and have it hang over an exact amount all around the bed without fussing or repositioning. The squares on this quilt told no story. They didn't speak. They were blank squares of blue and green and yellow and black. It wouldn't do to have people think his fingers were talking about things he had agreed never to talk about. The pillowcase was an ivory colored Egyptian cotton Edith had bought in San Francisco's Chinatown when she was there with Kitty. The open ends were embroidered with fire-breathing dragons. By noon, the inside of the cabin was set in every way it ought to be set. The old man sat in his rocking chair and let his mind wind down. Bump, bump, bump, lump, lump, ripple, ripple, ripple until the waters were still, and he napped.

In the afternoon, after a sandwich of ham, lettuce, cheese, cucumber and a glass of milk, and after all of the detritus of eating had been cleaned, he paid the same attention to the outside of the cabin as he had to the inside. Every weed and spent flower was plucked, garden dirt turned and wetted, driveway raked. Before he went in, he hung a sign on the front door. A sign he hung there only on those days of equal length. It said Welcome and had a painting of a man dressed in ornate robes riding backwards on a donkey. It was the sign that had hung on the door of his office where he worked with Opie.

At 6:30, he finished his chicken noodle soup, rewashed and rearranged all of the dishes. After a hot shower, he put on his night shirt, took a book from his bookcase, and settled into his rocker, wrapped in a blanket. He would sleep there the whole night through. He opened the book and began to read. The book was titled *Symmetry Principles at High Energy*. Conference chairman: Dr. J. Robert Oppenheimer. He fell asleep in his chair with his book open to a chapter Old Man had written thirty years ago about the likely effects of splitting an atom in half: "Proton-Proton Scattering and the Charge

Independence of Nuclear Forces" by Dr. Karl R. Johnson.

The long-haired man stopped whistling and muttered, "Fucking bridge. This thing is dangerous. Somebody ought to nail this shit down." He was in the passenger seat of the Lincoln Continental. In the backseat, slumped into a pile of pillows, was a barely coherent Edith.

The driver said, "Vinny, shut up. This is a job we have to do because we fucked up twenty years ago. I don't like it any better than you do, but we made our bed; we have to lie in it."

"What's this we? I didn't do shit. It was you and that fucking monster, Ragnar. We don't have to do anything like this at any of the other sites. Only here."

The tall man said, "That's because we haven't fucked up anywhere else. This is a deal Colonel Britt made with our boss to make up for some vigilante bullshit. Now, like I said, get over it. You go through this song and dance every time we come here. Look at this," he said, checking his watch. "Noon, straight up. We're right on time."

Dr. Johnson was standing in the front yard leaning on his cane, his body bent over parallel with the center of the earth, smiling. The car parked. The two men got a folded up wheelchair from the trunk and humped Edith out of the backseat and into the chair.

"Dr. Johnson, why is the clown backwards on the donkey?"

"Hartford, I'm surprised you never asked me that question before. What makes you think it's the man who's backwards and not the donkey? Now please, may I go inside with my wife?" Hartford opened the front door and wheeled Edith inside. The old man followed, hobbling in a rapid shuffle, rapping his cane on the side of the cabin in an agitated manner when the wheel of the chair momentarily stuck on the threshold lip.

"Hey, hey, hey! Slow down there, you horny old toad," Vinny said, swinging his doctor's bag into the old man's bottom.

The old man waited until they were all inside and then, steadying himself with his elbow on the edge of the sink, making sure the taller man was out of the way, took his cane and slammed it into Vinny's knees, knocking him back to the door. "Get out of my house!" Vinny took a step toward him.

Hartford grabbed his thick arm and pointed the door. "Out." After the door shut, Hartford said, "I admire your spunk, Dr. Johnson. I know that may mean nothing to you, given where we all are, but I truly do. Here's your money." He handed him an envelope. The old man put the envelope in the kitchen drawer.

A few years after the war was over and the FBI had informed US Army General Leslie Groves, director of the Manhattan Project, that J. Robert Oppenheimer was a Communist sympathizer and quite possibly an agent of the Soviet government, and his wife, Kitty, was an actual member of the Communist Party, an agreement was reached with Dr. Johnson. Karl Johnson had spent two months leading up to the "agreement" being interrogated by the FBI. He had refused to give up one word about his friend or his friend's wife. Not one word. Not a thing for two months until one day, in a windowless room with bright lights, fold-out chairs, and a card table, they showed him a photograph that had been snapped of Oppenheimer and him sitting at an outdoor café in Boston with two men they said were British physicists known to be espionage agents of the Russians. Opie was drawing something on a paper placemat. They showed him a blow-up of the placemat. It was of a ball with little ridges in it shaped in a curving, mobius-like fashion. "Why," they demanded, "is Dr. Oppenheimer drawing them a picture of the detonating device used in the first atomic bomb?" He had stared at the photograph and looked back at the interrogators with a blank face. He remembered feeling a sense of both pity and fear. The sense you would get watching a rabid dog with red eyes, tongue hanging out, slobbering and wobbling toward you, stricken, oblivious to any reality. "Well, Doctor, Why?"

"Okay, you got me. I'll talk." Those were the first words to them in two months.

They both grabbed chairs, sat at the card table, and yanked out their notepads and pencils. One pushed the "go" button on a small tape recorder and snarled, "Give it to us."

"I don't think either of those men would like being called spies, though perhaps in a way they really were."

"That's for us to decide, not you. Keep talking," the bigger, older of the two snapped.

"Yes, yes, of course. What would I know about those things? We were in Boston to give lectures at MIT. We were drinking coffee at an outside table on Newbury Street. It was a beautiful day as I remember, warm and sunny, daffodils in bloom, when these two men walking by saw Opie. The came to our table and sat with us, apologizing for the intrusion, saying they recognized Dr. Oppenheimer from his picture on the cover of *TIME* magazine. They asked him if he could explain the physics of spin on a ball and how to throw one so it would drop straight down after fifty-two feet of travel at ninety miles an hour. You see, gentlemen, these two 'espionage agents' are actually Clemens Johann Driesewerd and, the one with the cleft palate, James Jacob Bagby, the two ace pitchers for the Boston Red Sox. What Opie is drawing is a baseball, which, to the uneducated, the paranoid eye, might look similar to the detonator used in Little Man. The curving ridges are thick thread stiches, not cordite explosives, and the lines you see are lift and thrust vectors, not wires. The equations are time/velocity calculations. Those two pitchers went on to the World Series using their newly devised weapon: the 'split-finger fastball,' or as Bagby called it, 'the third bomb.' Dr. Oppenheimer has had a huge effect on the course of human history. That morning was just one small example. Now, can I please go and will you please stop asking me inane and ignorant questions?"

The next day, a different sort of man came to see him: young, in his twenties, with an intelligent face that already had some laugh lines crinkling at the corners of his eyes. He wore the uniform of an army officer but only two bars on the shoulder. His name was Lieutenant John Britt. He said, "Those boys from Washington don't want to talk to you for a while, but watch out, now they really have it out for you. I heard the tape. It's hilarious. You made them look stupid."

"It wasn't hard. They were sure they were right. That's the surest way to be wrong."

"Doctor, how old are you?"

"What year is it now? 1948? Somewhere near seventy. Plus or minus. I don't know for sure. Everything washed away in a flood when I was very young. Including my mother and the Hall of Records."

"I'm sorry to hear that. What are you going to do now?" Britt asked.

"No idea, really. I'm too old to hire, and I don't have much money. My wife seems to have spent it all. Lecture, perhaps. I haven't thought about it."

"I have an offer for you. You would have your own house, a simple house, but in a very beautiful place. In the Blue Ridge Mountains. Your family could be there with you. All you would need to do for us is some work having to do with plutonium.

You would report back to me, by mail, once a week or so. That, and keep your work absolutely secret. Nobody is to know what you would be doing there. You would tell no one, ever. You, Doctor, are the perfect person for us. You're a physicist, you understand the isotope, you have top secret clearance, at least until the feds come back, and," he stood and put his hands behind his back, military-like, "you know what can happen to people who are entrusted with secrets and don't keep them. Work for us, Doctor, and they will leave you alone. If you don't, they will ruin you and your family. Are you interested in coming to some agreement about this?"

Dr. Karl Johnson nodded.

The old man moved his rocker in front of the wheelchair and laid his old hands on her knees. She slumped a bit forward. The squint of her eyes pulled the skin tight over her high cheekbones.

"Kitty?" she asked.

"No, Edith, this is Karl, your husband."

"No, no, not Kitty. The girl with blonde hair." The old man leaned his head close to her to hear her soft, song-like words. "The girl. She had eyes like plums with specks of gold."

The old man asked her if she remembered their granddaughter. "No," she said, "they told me about a blonde-haired girl."

"They?" he asked. "Who is they?"

"Kitty," she said.

The old man blinked back tears. Tears for all that had been theirs and now was lost forever. Edith was so far into another world she would never come back to him. Their son was dead. Their daughter-in-law, dear, dear Brigit, was dead, and their granddaughter, perhaps alive somewhere, didn't even know they existed. He laid his head on his wife's bosom and wept.

Hartford laid a hand on his shoulder. "Would you like me to take her back now, Dr. Johnson?"

"No, I'm all right. I just don't understand how God can be so cruel." He pushed himself from her lap and straightened a strand of her gray hair, pulling it gently from her face with a long, crooked finger, looping it behind her ear.

"How much time do I have?"

"Ten minutes," Hartford said. "About ten minutes."

Edith rolled her head back, her blind, brown eyes staring up at the wood ceiling, and began to sing in a voice as sweet and quick as a mountain warbler.

Dengman Gap, Dengman Gap
An ol' man lives in Dengman Gap.

He's got a friend they call J.D.
He knows all about the trees.
Another friend that can't be found
Lives alone in the Sacred Ground.

Sacred Ground, Sacred Ground,
That boy lives in Sacred Ground.

They got a secret big as the sky,
Might be the girl with the plum dark eyes.
Kitty knows, she won't say,
Don't know how it got that way.

Dengman Gap, Sacred Ground,
There are secrets all around.

Her head rocked forward, she closed her eyes and fell asleep with small, childlike snoring. The old man and the tall man stared at each other.

"Excuse me, Dr. Johnson, I need to ask Mr. Gravello to come inside." He opened the door and motioned him in. They stood huddled in the corner of the kitchen. The old man, watching his wife sleep and snore, wondered how that possibly could have happened. How did she know that? The men's voices came in and out. The old man knew that nothing good would come of this no matter how it had come to pass.

"That's right," Hartford was saying, "we don't have any choice. Somebody told her that. That means somebody else knows. Somebody at the asylum. Johnson has been coughing up classified information to who knows how many people. At least that kid in the woods and somebody else, probably more. Somehow it got out of here and up to her." He pointed at Edith. "Nobody is supposed to know even where she is, not even him. And she's not supposed to know where he is. This blows up, Vinny, and Colonel Britt is going to find out what we've done. Find out about Skinner Bluff. You know what? That's the end of International Chemical. Right then. Boom. Gone."

The old man lowered his head back into his wife's lap, looking away.

"Dr. Johnson, you'll have to come with us," Hartford said as Vinny approached him, preparing a hypodermic needle from the medical bag. The old man didn't move, didn't look as the needle slid in his vein and the plunger pushed the tranquilizer into his blood. He just nestled his head a bit deeper into his wife's tummy as he swirled around and around and down through the rabbit hole.

When the black Lincoln pulled into the parking lot in front of the administration building, the sparse woman in brown tweed came out to the car, leaned in the window, looked in the backseat, and said to the driver, "It's all set. Bring him to Pickett House first. Then drop her off."

"Yes, ma'am, will do. The old geezer thinks he's a nuclear physicist."

"Yes, I know," she said. "I talked to Mr. Huprin."

15

Dipshits Ride Donkeys

THE PLANKS RATTLED AS J.D. SPED UP OVER THE BRIDGE. His rifle rattled in the gun rack behind the seat. He gripped the steering wheel hard. Something wasn't right. Something was wrong. Up ahead, the cabin sat still, no smoke coming out of either stone chimney. It was too cold for no fire. Too far from summer for no smoke.

The '47 Ford flatbed was parked where the old man always parked it. The cabin door was padlocked from the outside, the curtains drawn. A sign hung on the door: Welcome, it said, with a painting of a prince on a donkey. That sign had never been there before. *What's that all about?* A car or truck had been there. There were tire tracks in the dirt that hadn't washed away in the light Indian summer rains. There were footprints, lots of them, and tread marks that looked like bicycles or a cart or maybe a wheelchair. Old Man got sick, and somebody took him away. J.D. sat on his haunches, stared at the tracks. He got his rifle from behind the seat, loaded it, and walked slowly around the cabin. He peered in through a slit between two curtains. Empty. Old Man's cane was looped over the back of his rocking chair. Where his friend had been, he wasn't anymore. Gone. J.D got in his truck and drove at a crawl, two miles an hour down the dirt road, blinking and flicking at his cauliflower ear. Old Man had said things might get dangerous. They might want to get Abby. That's what the old man was driving at.

The hay bale was on the porch, but Billy wasn't there. Harrelson's Hardware was closed. A sign on front door inside the screen said Closed Today—Very Sorry, but there wasn't any date. *Which day?* thought J.D. *Today or a week ago?* He walked around the corner to the EZ Clean Laundromat. It was opened, but a sign on the community bulletin board along with free kittens, odd jobs, and banjo lessons said No Attendant on Duty Today—Very Sorry. Do Not Use Washer #2 or #5. The lids to those machines taped shut with an X of black electrical tape. A large woman in flip-flops, lime green stretch tights, and a baggy sleeveless T-shirt was mating socks.

"Excuse me, ma'am, do you know if Abby, the attendant, was here yesterday?"

"What's it look like, Buster," she said in a nasty voice, pointing to a massive pile of clothes. "Look like I do that laundry every day?"

Look at things, for christsake, J.D. thought. *Don't ask dumb questions.*

Abby's car was in front of her shack. J.D. jumped out of his truck and hollered, "Abby! You here?" No answer. The door to her home was unlocked. It smelled fresh inside, citric fresh. There were candles set about on saucers, all the wax drippings cleaned off. Each candle had its own little tin snuffer on its saucer. Nothing was out of place. A paperback book, *East of Eden*, place-marked about halfway through, was on a bedside stand beside a kerosene lamp with her bone-handled knife. She hadn't left in a hurry. Nobody dragged her out. Nothing was ruffled.

J.D. pulled into the Texaco gas station and parked. There was no one in the service bay or the office. He went out back. The young kid was pumping diesel gas into a John Deere tractor. "Where's Junior?" J.D. asked. "And I didn't say, 'Do you know where Junior is?' I said, *where is he?*"

"I remember you. You didn't like my lil' ol' joke?"

"No. Now just tell me where Junior is. I'm not in the mood for any bullshit."

"It's his day off. Probably over in Beullah at the Roaring Gap Saloon or picklin' cucumbers up to his house." He stopped pumping gas. "Let's see," he said, holding out one hand palm up, looking at it, "Junior picklin' cukes or," he held out his other hand, looking at it, "Junior drinking beer? Saloon, fer sure."

"Thank you. That was much better. If you see him, tell him I went to Beullah looking for him."

The Pabst sign in the front window had lost its B. Pa st, Pa st, Pa st flicked on and off in the evening dusk. The Power Wagon, Skinny Binkins' boy's truck was parked next to Junior's. The parking lot was mostly empty. No music came from inside the bar. It was quiet. J.D. watched a doe at the edge of a clearing across the road nibble leaves from a sapling. Content. Ears and tail flickering. J.D. scuffed his boot in the dirt, and the deer was gone in a single bound. *That's odd*, he thought. *She didn't run at the sound of his truck or even the door slamming shut. She bolted at the scuff sound because she didn't know what it was. That's what I need to do if I'm going to find Abby and the old man. Stay relaxed, stay attentive, and know the difference between things that are usual and things that are not. Sounds or sights or words that don't fit in the place. And don't ask dumb questions.*

Junior was sitting alone at the bar, peeling a label off his beer, looking at the bottle as if he'd never seen one before. Two or three other guys were also at the bar, staring at their beer bottles, not talking.

"Jesus Christ!" Junior shouted when he saw J.D. "What are you doing here?"

"Oh nothing, just thought I'd drive a couple hundred miles to have a beer with my buddy. How's it going with you? How's the baby?"

"Baby's real good. Doesn't even cry at night anymore. Just kinda gurgles. Crawls around, too. Marie's great. Folks pay her a lot more money now to play that fiddle of hers. She shines up her trophy nearly every day. But what about you? How's school and really, J.D., what are you doing down here? Hey! Hey! Jimmy, you back there? My boy here's thirsty."

J.D. thanked Jimmy the bartender for his beer and looked over at Skinny Binkins' boy sitting in a booth in the far corner, staring out the window and pretending not to listen to them.

"Junior, let's go outside for a minute." Jimmy said not to worry, he'd put their beers in the ice bucket.

They sat on the tailgate of J.D.'s truck. "I'm down here, Junior, because I promised that old man who lives over in Dengman Gap, you know the one I told you about?" Junior nodded. "Well I promised him when I was here for the music festival that I come back down to see him on October first. He made me promise and said it was really important. There were things he needed to tell me. And he said it was dangerous." Junior tapped J.D.'s knife sheath, and J.D. opened it and gave him the knife. Junior began cleaning his fingernails. "The old man said it was dangerous because of something that had to do with those two guys in the big car from Texas. You remember them?"

"Yeah," Junior said, "those guys who wanted that moron. Creepy. That's why you wanted to sit out here. 'Cause of the Binkins kid."

"Right. Exactly. I told the old man about Abby and that kid—the moron, as you call him—and the old man said, I remember him saying this to me, 'It might get really dangerous for all of us.' Something like that. And now he's gone. The door to the cabin is padlocked shut, his cane is still there, and the place is empty."

"It's October second, not October first," Junior said.

"Yeah, I know. I'm a day late. Spun a bearing up on the parkway and had to fix it."

"It's not like you to be a day late, J.D. Bad shit happens when you don't do what you said. What do you want me to do?"

"Well, I can't find Abby. Her car's at her place, but she isn't there. Billy isn't either. The hardware store is closed, Laundromat says nobody on duty. I don't know where to look, so I think we ought to go to the old man's cabin and see what we can find out. I'd appreciate it, Junior, if you could get a hack saw or bolt cutters from your garage and meet me over there. Have a look around. I'd also like to tell that Binkins kid in there that we want to talk to him some more. I'll even pay a little something. I know he knows more than what he told us."

"I don't think you have to say you'll pay him anything. Just tell him you won't make him piss his pants again. I'll meet you over there. Finish my beer for me." Junior handed J.D.'s knife back to him, gave him a slap on the back, and got in his truck.

Junior was right. J.D. didn't have to pay him anything, and it was the kid who said, "Just don't make me piss myself again. That was bad to explain to my mom when she done the warshin'." He also told J.D. that those men were really scary. He'd heard them talking about how they might have to kill the retard and bury him out in the reservation so nobody'd find him. J.D. told the bartender the kid's beer was on him. He left the saloon and headed for Dengman Gap more worried than he had been when he got there. *Don't speed*, he told himself. *Relax. Be attentive. Watch and listen for things that aren't supposed to be there.*

Darkness was setting in. Junior had parked his truck thirty feet from the cabin, left it running with the headlights on. His rifle leaned against the door jamb. He was down on his haunches looking across the dirt when J.D. pulled up. J.D. parked beside him, set the brake, and left his truck running. He leaned his rifle against the other side of the door and hunkered down beside Junior. The lights of the trucks, skimming across the damp dirt, cast a clean shadow at the edge of any imprint. The tracks and prints stood out clearly.

"Let's look at these before we go up to the door and scuff 'em all up," Junior said. "Look at this." He was at the far side of the car tracks. He pointed to two footprints. "One, two. Going that way. See that. That's the driver getting out and, one, two. Going this way. That's the driver getting back in." He skipped and hopped over to the other side of the tire tracks. "One, two. One, two. Passenger side getting out and getting in. But lookee here. Look at these tracks. Definitely a wheelchair. Front tires skinnier and closer together than the rear ones." Junior scooted to about halfway to the cabin and squatted down again. He took a flashlight out of his back pocket and splayed it out across the dirt toward the cabin. "Look here," he said, pointing to sets of tracks, "wheelchair going in, loaded. Deep ruts. Wheelchair coming out, loaded. Wheelchair going back in, nobody in it. See, it barely makes a rut. Then here, wheelchair back out with somebody in it. Look at that. Clear as day. Two guys came in a car, not a truck. They wheeled somebody in, wheeled somebody out and went back in and got somebody else, and they put them both in the backseat. Backseat; it was a car."

Junior stood up, put his hands on his hips. "That's what it is, J.D., I'm sure of it. Am I fucking Daniel Fucking Boone or what? Jesus, I wish Dirk was here so I could teach him this shit."

"Your brother will be back," J.D. said. "You can teach him then." Dirk was deep in Vietnam, or Cambodia, or Laos. Deep in the war. "And yeah, Junior, you are Daniel Fucking Boone. I see it all. Let's go in."

Junior got a giant pair of bolt cutters from the back of his truck and shut off both trucks. Each arm of the cutter was three feet long. He had them spread out wide with the carbide beak open to the padlock when he stopped and peered at the sign on the door.

"What the fuck's up with this? That's a stupid sign." He snapped the lock.

It was dark inside. J.D. lit a match, found the gas lamps, and set a flame to them. The cabin was pristine, immaculate, and smelled of Murphy's soap.

"Boy," Junior said, "did he always keep this place so clean?"

"Well," J.D. said, going over to the shelf to fetch the jug, "he was always tidy but not like this." He pulled the cork and took a long swig.

"Are you shittin' me?" Junior yelped. "Is that what I think it is?"

"Maker's Mark." J.D. said, sitting down in the rocker. "The good shit."

Junior sat in the other chair. "Here's what I don't get. If you're so fucked up somebody has to take you out in a wheelchair, how'd your house get so clean? I mean, you said he lived alone. Sick people or dying people don't go crawling around cleaning up before they get hauled off, do they? And why'd they leave his cane here?" He handed the jug back. J.D. drank and wiped his mouth with his sleeve.

"Because they figured he wouldn't need it anymore?"

The two sat and talked, passing the jug back and forth,

just as J.D. and the old man had. Junior came to sense that his friend, while he surely loved his mother and maybe that girl Abby, really loved the old man. J.D. talked about the times they had been together, the things they had talked about, the mysteries that wrapped around the man, and from time to time he would choke up. He would get up, go to the sink, splash water on his face, dry it off, and come back and sit down. "That's what Old Man did when he didn't want to talk about something anymore. He'd do it just like that."

J.D. put his finger to his lips and jerked his thumb toward the door. "Shhhh. Something's out there," he mouthed.

"Oh, fuck," Junior whispered, "our guns are outside." He stood up slowly into a half-crouch. "You yank the door. I'll grab a gun." They crept over beside the door. "Ready?" J.D. nodded just as a knock came at the door. They both jumped back, stared at each other, frozen still. Another knock.

"Daniel Boone? Davy Crockett? You boys in there? This here is Annie Oakley." J.D. opened the door, and Abby stood there with an impish smile on her face, two blonde pig-tails hanging down, and a rifle in each hand. Billy stood behind her, at attention. She stepped in, handed both guns to Junior, threw her arms around J.D., nestled her face up into his neck, and kissed him. They murmured to each other. Junior turned away, put the rifles down, jammed his hands in his back pockets, and began whistling. Billy wouldn't come in. He stood with his hands at his sides, feet apart. Not budging.

Abby sat in J.D.'s lap. "How'd you know we were here? Why did you come here, Abby, if you didn't even know the old man or where he lived? I don't get it." J.D. took one last swig of the jug, put the cork back in, and handed it over to Junior.

"I don't know what's the matter with Billy, but about midday he walked into town and started tugging at me and pointing back up the mountain. So I drove up there, and he kind of tugged me out in the woods, down Dengman Gap to a big rock up beside this cabin. Must have taken an hour to get down here. I said okay, he wants me to know something, so we just sat there watching the deer and the squirrels and the birds until dusk came. I really wanted to get back home before it got dark in the woods, and then your trucks pulled in the drive, and we sat and watched you guys. Then we heard you talking inside, so we gave you some time to talk things over, just the two of you, and then I knocked at the door. Somehow, don't ask me how, but somehow Billy knew you were going to come to this cabin. It's a beautiful cabin," she said, looking around. "Beautiful."

J.D. said Billy had probably seen him there this morning and then maybe heard him when he went up the mountain looking for her.

"Abby, the old man knew Billy. I think he knew him really well. He told me he was definitely not a moron. That he was smart."

"Well," she said, "your old man got that right. 'Cause here we are, aren't we?"

"He also said he was probably the one who shot that boar that came at me and dragged it down the mountain. It's cut up and sitting in a salt brine crock out in the woodshed."

"I honestly don't know anything about that, Jeremiah. It doesn't sound right, but who knows what all happens in this world. Can't really be sure of anything. Who knows?"

"Don't ask me anything," Junior said. "The whole thing's too weird for me. I got to get home to my baby."

Abby went over and squatted down in front of him and put both her hands on his knees. "Thank you, Junior, for being such a good friend to Jeremiah. Would you give Marie a big hug for me and say hello to Grannie Mae? Tell them I'd love to see them soon."

Junior stopped at the door on his way out and peered again at the Welcome sign. "That's a stupid sign. Kings don't ride donkeys; they ride horses. Dipshits ride donkeys."

J.D. took some eggs and bacon and bread and butter out of the refrigerator and put them in a paper bag. He whittled a stick, carved a small notch in it, and after he closed the door behind them, he carved a small notch in the door, stuck the stick through the hasp hole, and aligned the two notches. He handed Abby the snapped pad lock and asked if her hardware store could find out what company made it and who sells them. He drove Abby home. Billy rode in the back of the pickup. When she got out, she told him he was going to have to sleep in his truck, down the road just a little bit so Billy wouldn't get nervous if he heard things in the night.

"How long before you think he'll get over it?"

"Hard telling," she said, "not knowing." She gave him a soft brushing kiss on the lips and mouthed, "I love you. Sleep well."

Sometime long into the night when it was black out and dead quiet, she crawled up over the tailgate and nestled tight up against him under the quilt.

"I want you again," she whispered.

Abby woke to the smell of bacon and eggs frying on a skillet over a fire between three rocks. J.D. had already made coffee, and he handed her a hot tin cup over the side of the pickup bed. She propped herself up, put a pillow behind her back, and sipped her coffee, watching him tend the fire. She pulled his quilt up over her knees.

"Jeremiah," she said, "I am so sorry I got blood on your beautiful quilt." She pulled it tight on her knee and rubbed the spot. She bent over and looked closer, then closer. "Jeremiah, would you please come here for just one second. Look," she said, pointing to the bloodstained square under the blood.

"Look real close. That's Billy."

"It sure is," J.D. said. "The old man must have made this thing himself. Look at this. That's my pickup, and look at this one, it's his cabin. I don't know what this ..."

"Jeremiah," Abby said, kissing his ear, "your bacon's burning. My goodness! Why are you cooking so much?"

He motioned his thumb toward the woods. Billy was sitting on a fallen log, fifty feet away, watching them.

"You know," J.D. said over his shoulder to Abby, "he might get used to us a whole lot quicker than you think."

After they ate, Abby scooted Billy away, and they spread out the quilt, looking at all the squares. There were 144 of them, each about six inches square. Diagonally, from corner to corner, they were blank black satin except for the very center one. It was bigger and set in the middle of the black X. It was a bird of some sort, like an eagle looking sideways. At each corner, also set in black satin, was something that looked like two bright, golden fiddlehead ferns with a cobalt blue ring where their stems crossed. The other squares didn't seem to have any pattern. Most were just pieces of cloth like a checked shirt or blue jeans or part of a worn-out dishrag. All around the outside were squares of an Indian teepee. Fourteen of the sixty teepee squares had the crossed fiddleheads in the middle of them. There was the one with blood on it that looked like Billy, shirtless, blue dots for eyes and wild red hair. One of J.D.'s pickup truck. Eight green ovals and four black circles each with an orange mushroom in the center. In front of each black circle was a tree. There were two squares of the fancy man riding backwards on a donkey, donkey facing donkey.

"Except for Billy and my pickup, I have no idea what any of this is or what it means," J.D. said, leaning his shoulder into Abby.

"It's a story," she said. "It's definitely a story, and these teepees all around the outside, it might be a story about Indians or maybe even this reservation. If you step back and look at it, it looks like your old man did not like that bird in the middle. It looks X'd out." She looked up. "Looks like it might rain. I'm going to town now before it starts. I really have to open up the stores." They walked back up the hill, holding hands, Abby still in her nightie.

"I'm going back over to the old man's place and poke around. Sometime today or tomorrow I have to head back up home to get ready to take my final exam," J.D. said, gliding his hand down the small of her back into the hollow of her waist and spreading his fingers out onto the curve of her bottom. She patted his hand off, and he and walked back down the road to his truck. He walked along the side of it, feeling the red stripe, muttering to himself.

The notches in the stick still lined up. No one had been there. J.D. looked at the footprints and tread marks in the drive. They had been much easier to see in the dark with the headlights played across them, but Junior was right: a car, two people, four trips with a wheelchair. J.D. ran his finger along the spines of the books in the bookcase. All the classics were on one shelf, alphabetically from Aeschylus to Zola. On the next shelf, half were recent Americans—Hemingway, Steinbeck, Faulkner, Fitzgerald—and the other half were religious books: the Bible, Koran, Torah, Bahagvad-Gita, *The Way of the Sufi*. He opened that one to a postcard. There was the man on the donkey. Underneath it said, "Nassredin, your donkey has been lost!" ... "It is a good thing I was not on my donkey or I would be lost too. From this day on I shall ride my donkey backwards. He will see where we are going. I will see where we came from. That way, we cannot get lost."

The third shelf had books with titles that made no sense

to J.D. He picked one out. It was called *P-Meson Articulation* by S.J. Stravitovich. Inside there were almost no words. Each page was filled with mathematical computations. Numbers and letters and symbols. J.D. recognized some of them from his calculus courses. He called them the hieroglyphics of physics. Another one, *In Search of a Unified Field Theory* had ten or twelve authors, all with foreign names, and whatever words were at the beginnings of each chapter were completely unintelligible to J.D. Every book on that shelf had the same stamp on the inside flap: Classified Document—Property of United States Government—Dept. of the Army—Los Alamos Nuclear Laboratory—Do Not Remove.

The old man was not just some old man. Somebody had been a nuclear scientist. There is no other way anyone could understand any of those books on the bottom shelf. Nor any other way they could have gotten them. Someone had been at Los Alamos. He remembered Old Man telling him about his son. That his son had died twenty years ago, murdered and buried it sounded like. He remembered how the old man's eyes had clouded up. How the pain of it was still with him. Maybe his son had been a scientist or a technician at Los Alamos or one of the other Manhattan Project plants. Super-secret. Had he known too much? Had he told people things he shouldn't have told them?

J.D. thumbed through every book, looking for a name. There were none. Anywhere a name might have been, the page had been cut or taken out. In the Bible, there was a drawing of the patchwork quilt at Deuteronomy; the passage at 27:15 was underlined: *Cursed be the man that maketh a graven and molten thing, the abomination of the Lord, the work of the hands of artificers, and shall be put in a secret place: and all the people shall answer, and say: Amen.* With it was a plot plan of the reservation showing the metes and bounds.

The property was roughly square, about two miles to a side. It had been prepared by the Survey Division of the Department of the Interior, dated June 12, 1919. He looked around the house, searching for a piece of paper, any paper—a receipt, a letter, a license or permit, a photo—anything that might have a name on it. There was nothing, not one scrap of anything that might say who the old man or his son might be. "Old Man," he had said, "that's a good name. Let's leave it at that." In a drawer in the kitchen, he found an envelope. In it were twenty new one-hundred-dollar bills. *Where does he get his money? Somebody must know him. Know he's here.* He went to the bookcase and put the envelope with the map in the Bible. J.D. found the trundle box under the bed. Sure enough, the old man had made the quilt. There was the cloth and the hat box with swatches and needles and thread. Abby was right; the quilt was saying something. It was a map of the sacred ground.

Out back, he walked through the woods to the place where the old man said his still had been before they burned it down. The foundation was there, barely visible under fallen leaves and needles that had rotted to soil, sprouting ferns and saplings, some of which had grown into trees reaching thirty or forty feet high. He could see some charred timbers from the burnt barn sticking through the undergrowth and bricks, probably from a chimney that hadn't fallen all the way in the hole. The sky had darkened quickly, and a bolt of lightning struck a tree up on the ridge illuminating, for one brief second, the entire forest in an eerie yellow flash. In that second, the whole of Dengman Gap looked primeval, undulating, and then a tremendous thunderclap broke directly over his head. He jumped and almost fell in the hole, and the forest was instantly awash in a hard rain. J.D. ran from the trees and back to the cabin.

Sitting in the old man's rocker, he rubbed his hands on the smooth cedar logs, looking at the cut pattern of the saw blade on the face of the wood. He got up and looked closely, running his finger up and down the kerf. The blade marks were vertical, not in an arc like a circular saw would have made. Vertical like a band saw would have made. He remembered Professor Dagget talking about saw mills and how, for more than a hundred years, first powered by water, then by steam, then diesel engines, the mills had cut logs using a circular saw. In the mid-forties, just after World War Two, the big vertical band saw mills were built in along the Pee Dee River in North and South Carolina. It was much more efficient because the bands could be ganged off one power shaft and cut a log into multiple boards in one pass. That mill was built somewhere in these mountains not more than twenty-five years ago. "This is not an old cabin," J.D. said out loud. "This is a new cabin. It has to be. If I can find out why the old man has to lie to me, I might find out what happened to him."

16

Hubie

J.D. REMEMBERED THE MAN WITH THE SILVER HAIR in the Blue Ridge Bar & Grill talking with his buddy about Loretta Lynn. He was also talking about chestnut beam log cabins. He needed to find the saw mill and make sure Professor Dagget was right. If he was, there was something wrong with Old Man's story about the moonshine still and Prohibition. If the professor was right, that cabin wasn't there then. It couldn't have been. The logs could not have been sawn that way.

Juke box and beer bottles. Laughter and back-slapping. Buddies clinking long necks, and everyone nestled up against each other, wriggling for room, talking about whatever that favorite thing was that they always wanted to talk about. Shouting above the music and whistling for the barmaid in her fringed leather jacket to set 'em up again. The only hole at the bar was where one of them left to worm his way back to the pisshole. If they were dumb enough to take their beer with them, their hole got filled, and they were left to elbow and shoulder their way back in beside some other friend or back shuffle into the men lined up against the wall. It didn't seem to matter who was next to whom; they all knew each other, they worked together, they lived near each other in the town in the hollows and the hills, they drank together, and they worshipped together every Sunday morning at the local

Baptist church. It was Saturday night, and they knew they'd see each other at nine o'clock in the morning, scrubbed and brushed and spit-shined, holding light on the elbow of their little missus as she gabbed her way down the aisle between the pews and took out the Good Book from the rack in front of her and laid it on her flowered lap, waiting for the preacher to make his way to the holy podium, waiting for the chorus to burst into hymn, shoulder to shoulder once again, waiting for a glimmer of God.

J.D. leaned between two heads and shouted out for a beer. He handed the barmaid fifty cents and asker her who the man with the silver hair was. "That there is the one and only, the truly special Appalachian gentleman, Mr. Willy Sherman, retired state police officer." She took his quarters, walked by Willy Sherman, and pointed back at J.D. The man nodded to her, and she brought J.D. a shot of whiskey. "It's on Willy," she said.

The man sitting next to Willy beckoned to J.D. He got up off his stool and shoveled his way through the throng, holding high a bottle of Carling Black Label, the only man in the bar to drink such a beer, special ordered for him. When J.D. sat down, Willy said, "That man there who just gave you his seat, that there is Bryce. These parts wouldn't be half what they are without him. What is it you need to talk about, young feller?"

"The first day I came in here, I heard you talking about log cabins made of chestnut. There's something I need to know about how the logs were sawed square for timber cabins. Is that the kind of thing you might know something about?"

"Well, young feller, it sure is. And I remember you. You were standing right between me and my buddy. When I was just a cub like you, I worked in two or three of the mills around here. That's how I got to know wood and machinery. That's how I got like this." He held up his left hand. It had only two and a half fingers. The pinky was gone at the nub and the ring finger gone from the knuckle. The chopped off ends were all bulbous and crusty. "Caught my shirt cuff. Ever since that day, whenever I work around machines, I roll up my sleeves. What is it you need to know?"

"I need to know if any of the mills around here are vertical band saw mills, and if they are, how long have they been doing it that way."

"I think there are two of them. Might be more that I never heard of, but I doubt it. I would've heard something, being in the business and all. One of 'em I've never seen. Started up north of Wytheville just a few years back. That's a small operation, man and his son with a two-band saw. The other is the big daddy of mills in these parts. It saws out probably five or six million feet a year. It's called Appalachian Mills, and it's over past Beuleah, about ten miles from here. I worked there every summer for seven or eight years. Good people."

"How can you tell if a log has been sawn on a band saw or if it was cut a long time ago with a two-man hand saw?"

Willy Sherman looked at J.D. long and hard. He breathed deep a couple of times and then, as if he had made up his mind to go one way or the other, said, "The kerfs, young feller, the kerfs." He took a carpenter's pencil out of his pocket and, on a napkin, drew vertical lines. "If'n they're wide apart like this and deep, that's an old hand saw—big teeth, wide set, long, slow strokes. If the kerfs are like this," he drew lines close together, "that's a band saw. Fast moving, narrow teeth. That's how you'd know."

"What I got then," J.D. said, "is beams cut on a band saw. If I wanted to talk to somebody who'd been at that big mill say, twenty years ago, who would I talk to?"

Willy Sherman signaled to the barmaid. "Jeannie, would mind gettin' me and this young feller here a shot of that good stuff your daddy keeps in the cupboard. Not that two-dollar stuff on the counter." He leaned on the bar and waved his finger around. "You see all these men here? They all go to church ever Sunday morning, and ever Sunday morning my wife tries to get me all gussied up and go down there with her, but I don't like going to church. I tried it once or twice, and I didn't like it at all. Don't suit me. So I get up early on church day and get out of the house before she wakes up. Take me a couple of six-packs and g'won up in the hills to where the old timers live. Listen to music and tell stories." He drained his shot and said, "Tomorrow's church day. If'n you want to go with me, you are certainly welcome to. I'd pick you up at seven in the morning. We could drive on down by Beuleah and go see Hubie Alley. He's run that mill since it first started. Me and him are kinfolk."

"I'd really appreciate it. That sounds perfect."

"Where do you live at?" Willy asked.

"I'm staying in a cabin over on Chestnut Creek just on the southeast corner of the Indian land. Cabin's about a quarter mile in over the bridge."

"I know where that drive is. My nephew told me. He delivers cordwood out on the road for a really old man that lives down in there."

"Yeah," J.D. said, "that's where I'm staying. The old man's a good friend of mine."

"He's a hermit, ain't he? I don't think anybody's ever even seen him."

At seven sharp, Willy picked J.D. up at the cabin. Just over the North Carolina line, Willy turned off on a dirt road that wound its way up a mountainside. He stopped at a plank bridge like the bridge to the old man's house. The creek under it was wide as a truck, and the water rushed down the mountain. Not a gurgle but a roar. "G'won out, young feller, and climb down the bank under the bridge. See what you find. If'n there's something tied to a rope, bring it on up." J.D. started carefully down the embankment, crab-like, and then grabbed a bridge beam, steadying himself. Hanging on a rope in a calm, bathtub-sized eddy built of a circle of rocks was a plastic jug with a cork in the top. J.D. untied it and scrambled back up the side of the creek. Willy took the jug and pointed to the top of the cork. There was a square and a circle in the square burned into the cork. "That there is what's called the maker's mark. It tells you who made this brew in such a way that only the people who live around here can know who the maker is. We know his mark. Don't have to say his name. This here's an old feller who lives a ten-minute walk that way along the creek." He pulled the cork out, took a swig, and handed it to J.D. It was hard and smooth, not ragged like J.D. thought it would be. "That jug hangs there for two purposes. One, so you can taste it to see if you want to buy some, and if you don't, just to say howdeedoo, welcome to the mountain. I think I'll get a little something for Bryce." Willy pulled the truck off the road, and J.D. re-tied the jug to the rope under the bridge, and the two of them set off on a path along the creek.

The mountain home was a log cabin with a wraparound porch. Two men sat out front, one with a guitar, one with a banjo, quietly strumming and picking. As Willy and J.D. came up close, one of the men nodded to them and kept on picking. They sat on the steps and listened to the music until the song was done. "Mr. Willy Sherman, how are you this fine morning? And who's your friend?"

"This here's a young feller I met in the Blue Ridge. He wanted to know about log sawing, so we're on our way down past Beuleah to see Hubie and stay out of the way of that preacher man. I thought we'd stop in here to say hello and he could see what a hand-sawn beam would look like. You did saw these all by your own self, didn't you?"

"I surely did, near on fifty years back when sawing a beam wasn't no harder than buttering a muffin. G'won and look about if you'd like to." He began picking a new tune, the guitar chords following the banjo. On the outside of the cabin, the logs were round, and J.D. could see the scallop marks where the bark had been shaved off. Inside, the logs were square, and kerf marks were wide and deep, just like Willy had said. Willy bought a jar from the man, and they set off back down the path along the creek bank.

"How do they learn all their songs if they don't have electricity to play records? Where do they hear them?" J.D. asked.

"Front porch to front porch, Sunday morning to Sunday morning all across this country. People stop by to visit each other and swap their songs. That feller playing the guitar, he's learning new licks. That's how."

The saw mill was gigantic. A pile of pine logs higher than a house stretched for hundreds of yards along the road, bookended by mountains of sawdust. There were dozens of drying sheds and milling sheds, forklifts and flatbed trucks, each with a sign on the door that said, Appalachian Mills— Beuleah, NC. The main mill building was the biggest building J.D. had ever seen. It was the size of a football field, open on both ends. It was all quiet, shut down, dead still, nobody there. "Big, ain't it? That's where I worked, over in that building running the V-match cutter."

J.D. got out and walked into the main mill. There were three sets of five gang bands. "Wow! Huge."

Judging by the outer appearance of his house and grounds, Hubie Alley was a rich man. The lawns, even in

November, were still a rich green and mowed in an even pattern and clipped right up to the base of each of the stately oaks that lined the paved drive up to his portico. The house looked like Monticello with Palladian windows and curved side walls. Two young black men were raking leaves. Mr. Alley was a round man in the finest tradition of portly, red-faced, white-haired Southern gentlemen. He was smoking a cigar, sitting in front of a fire in the library when J.D. and Willy were escorted in by a black maid in a white apron. "Willy, my boy, it's good to see you. How's my little girl?"

"Your niece if just fine, Hubie. She's paying a visit to the Lord right now, and that's why I'm out poking around the countryside. This young feller here has some questions about your saw mill, and I thought we'd come right over and let him ask them."

"Sit down, sit down. Would you like a cup of coffee or tea or maybe a glass of lemonade? LaToya, would you bring these gentlemen whatever libation they might choose?"

J.D. explained how he was a forestry student near ready to graduate and had come across an oddity. Something that didn't make any sense to him. "It's a cabin, sir," he said, "that's made out of one-foot thick chestnut tree beams. They don't have any nail holes or drill holes in them, so they don't look like they're re-used from some other place. They look fresh, but there haven't been any chestnut trees that size anywhere in this country for forty or fifty years. Maybe they're fifty years old, but here's the odd thing. They were milled out on a vertical band saw. Of that I'm sure."

"What's your name, young man?"

"My name? Jeremiah Dixon. People call me J.D."

"And where is this cabin?"

J.D. explained exactly where it was and about the old man who lived there and how he had gone missing three days ago.

He told Hubie Alley that he thought if he could figure out why the old man had said the cabin was there in the 1920s when it couldn't have been there that long ago, it might help him untangle the story, might help him find his friend.

"Come along, come along," Mr. Alley said. "I want to show you something." Willy said that he didn't think a whole damn tour of the place was so necessary; he just wanted to let this young feller know that there were a whole lot of chestnut logs that got sawed up into beams to make all kinds of buildings. Hubie paid no attention to him. He heaved himself up out of his deep leather chair and made his way down the hall and into a sunny arboretum. Orchids grew in black dirt. The wall below the glass was two feet high, and on top of it sat one-foot thick chestnut beams. The posts and rafters were all the same beams. "They look anything like this?"

"They look exactly like that."

He led them to the dining room. The table, curved in a gentle arc at both ends, was four feet wide and sixteen feet long. Set around it were twenty chairs, hand carved in the Queen Anne style, and a magnificent serving sideboard, all made of polished chestnut. J.D. ran his hand over the tabletop, bent down, and inspected the joinery of the chairs. "There are no screws in any of this. Everything is drilled and dowelled. This is worth a fortune." The table smelled of lemon Pledge and shone like a mirror.

"Let's all go back to the library and have a toast to a young man who truly understands fine wood and fine woodworking. I have a little story to tell you. LaToya, honey!" he shouted. "Forget the coffee."

They settled in to comfortable chairs set around the fireplace. He re-lit his cigar and poured them each a snifter of brandy. He swirled his around in the glass, sniffing it. "Old and sweet," he said, "just like that wood. Old and sweet." He told them a story.

"This saw mill opened in May of 1946. When the war was over, I was stationed at a new base in Germany. I was the procurement officer, and I had only two months to go before being discharged. I came across a factory there that had been set up by Hitler's men to mill wooden beams for train beds and caissons. They had run out of steel. Used it all for tanks and rail lines. Some brilliant German engineer had devised a saw mill system that could cut twice as much wood with half the energy as any normal saw mill. It was a multiple-ganged band saw with blades made of high-grade German steel. I made the arrangements to purchase this mill and have that saw shipped over here after I was discharged. That was the start of this business. About two months after the mill was up and running, a man came to me and asked if I would saw some beams for him. He said all I had to do was saw the logs. He would bring them here and take them away. I said most certainly, I charge five cents a board foot, and I could do it right away. The next day, a big green Mack truck showed up hauling a forty-foot flatbed loaded with four-foot diameter logs. The truck didn't have any signs or markings whatsoever, like a business or a man's name, but more than that, good golly Miss Molly, it didn't have any license plates or transport numbers or anything. He said he wanted twenty-five one-foot square beams thirty feet long and sixteen of them twenty feet long. I remember that because ... well, because, Willy, you remember, don't you? You were just out of the Army Corps of Engineers, concrete bridge construction, wasn't it? You'd hired on with the local police. You were here for some reason. Just come by to pay a social visit, I think, and you said what a good idea it was to saw all those logs up and get a good start on business. I remember that. I appreciate your help on that. I had no idea what kind of wood it was. Never seen it before, and by God's honest truth, I've never seen it since. I asked him what it was and where they came from, and he said, 'I have no idea what kind of wood it is, and where it came from is none of your business. Just saw the logs, and I'll pay you your money.' And, Willy, you said, 'These logs come from down in Georgia.' And then he said, 'This transaction is only between you and me. I'll pay you twice what you're asking if you promise to keep it that way.' 'Fine,' I said, and truthfully I haven't ever mentioned it to anybody. A load of reclaimed chestnut came in here one day and, bingo, then I knew what it was. Same grain, same pattern, same yellow sapwood at the edges, same everything. The issue has never come up until this day. Even the woodworkers who made that furniture never asked. They knew wood all right, but they didn't know trees. Not like Jeremiah here; he seems to know both, and by gum, seems to have a real stake in the answer. Anyway, that man had brought me twice as much wood as necessary to give him the beams he wanted, so I sawed what he needed, took his money, twice the usual, and kept the other half for myself. I didn't like that man."

Willy said, "I think that's why over all these years you've done so well, Hubie. You know the difference between telling the truth and not telling a lie. Most of us have a mite of trouble with that."

"No, Willy, nobody has a mite of trouble with that at all. They just pretend they do to make their own selves look more honorable. To me, it's sad that people think the truth is the same for everybody. Some folks like a good brandy, other folks can't tolerate it. What's the truth about that?"

"So you never knew just exactly where those logs came from," J.D. said.

"No, not exactly. Just somewhere down in Georgia, because that's what Willy said." He pointed his cigar toward J.D. "You seem like a strong and smart young man. Do you want a job? I have one for you if you want it."

"Thank you, Mr. Alley, but I think what I really want is to be a national park ranger."

"Done," Hubie Alley said. "That's an easy phone call. I need to call the good senator anyway. If I make the call for you, I'll expect you to get detailed out in these mountains. I might need a little help with logging contracts. Let me know when. I'm always here."

Driving back after the preacher was sure to be in regular clothes, Willy talked about his place, his Appalachia, these hills. and these people. How they didn't care much at all about whatever the rest of the world thought. They were, he said, all of a family. Almost everybody was somebody's brother or niece, and one thing that bound them all together was that life lived alone was hard, life lived with friends was easy. "People don't talk bad about each other out in these parts, and when the outside starts to come in, they circle up. Except," he said, "there are some people who live out in these hills who never mingle with anybody. Keep all to themselves. People don't even know who they are or just exactly where they live. Hard part about that is when something happens to them, nobody can help out. Nobody knows who they are or where they are. Lot of those folks out here. Not so much over in the flat lands; it's more civilized there. But out in these mountains, a lot of that."

He said he'd been out to that Chestnut Creek area at the bottom of the gap. He'd been patrolling the back roads looking for a young man from Roanoke who was wanted for rape, and someone said they'd seen him or someone who looked like him out on that stretch of road. He said he didn't know just where it was. "There are dozens of drives that go off that road, over the creek and up into the hills. I drove up one of them, and you know what was out there? There was a negro man living out there. Now you'd think somebody would've known about that. Very few of those kind of folks live out here, but nobody had ever said anything about it. Nobody knew he lived way out there. All alone. Dangerous out there all alone in Dengman Gap. Anyway, young feller, watch your own self out here."

17

The Booby-Trapped Chair

AMANDA DIXON WAS AT THE MEDICAL FACILITY sitting in Ken Norton's office discussing with him what to do about her findings. She had finished the studies, including the additional research she had agreed to do for Dean Harris. A copy of the conclusions to her work, six pages typewritten, lay on Dr. Norton's desk. The original was in her lap. Since she had the encounter with Dean Harris, she had brought every piece of paper home with her every day after work. She left nothing in the file cabinet or anywhere in the office.

"If it was the government," she was saying, "that was interested in this, then it must be that they had used the chemicals for something and were worried about political fallout if people had developed diseases or genetic mutations from exposure. They were surely using Agent Orange in Indochina, but that was different. That was a defoliant that acted immediately." The chemicals she had been working with were used to kill bacteria and fungi over a long term and were certainly never intended to be used together. They were for totally different purposes. That's why, she said, she didn't understand why they had wanted her to do this research in the first place.

Ken Norton didn't know either. He thought the conclusions would be solid enough for Dean Harris and shouldn't present any significant problems. But since he couldn't figure why anybody would want to know this, and particularly why they needed to know it absolutely, he didn't know how Dean Harris might react. It seemed to him it was like spending tens of thousands of dollars to find out what the effect would be of mixing weed killer with rat poison. Who would do that?

"What time is your meeting?"

"Well, if you say my work meets your professional standards, I'll have these conclusions delivered this morning. He wants to see me at three this afternoon."

"Amanda, do you mind if I go with you? I don't want it to seem like you need your boss there, but I'm really interested in seeing firsthand what his reaction is. I might ask some questions to see if I can figure out who's funding some of our research here."

"I would be pleased if you came with me. Ken, I've known people like him all too well, and if he said something I took offence at, I might just stick him through the throat with a hat pin. I find the man odious, and I don't think I'm done running over him."

"I'll plan on being there, Amanda. If for nothing else, just to watch the show, but I suggest you show a bit of restraint. He is the dean after all."

The dean's secretary let them both into his office as soon as they arrived. He was, as he had been before when she came to see him, behind his desk flipping through the pages of her report. Flipping forward, flipping back, making marks. He didn't stand up when they came in.

"Have a seat," he said. "Dr. Norton, good of you to come. Mrs. Dixon, good to see you again."

She leaned on the front of his desk. "I have told you three

times, my name is not Mrs. Dixon. Nor is it Miss Dixon. I am not married. I have been married, and it wasn't to a Mr. Dixon. The only name I have for your use is Dr. Dixon. Are we clear?" She saw the same eye blinking and fat lip-pucker she had seen before, and she knew she still had him. "Dr. Norton," she said, "I suggest we sit at the conference table. The chair in front of this desk is booby-trapped." Ken Norton visibly winced at her complete absence of professional etiquette.

"Thank you, Dean Harris. It's nice to see you again as well." He sat down and kicked Amanda under the table. She smiled her most coquettish smile.

"Well, well, well," the dean said, sitting down, "we certainly have some interesting findings from your research. I am very pleased with the new results."

"Why, Dean Harris, would you be pleased or not pleased by a scientific fact? That seems contrary to the whole notion of science. What is, is. What is not, is not."

"*Dr.* Dixon," he said, "I do not want to engage in a nasty fight with you. Perhaps 'pleased with the new results' was the wrong way to put it. I am pleased that additional tests were done, at my request, and the results have corrected what could have been seen as a lack of professional rigor."

Amanda closed her eyes and said a private little prayer in her mind. *Dear God, please don't let me murder this sanctimonious sack of dog shit.* "Yes, Dean Harris, I am happy to have been given the opportunity to tighten up the findings."

"Ken," Dean Harris asked, "have you reviewed the research and the report?"

"I have. Dr. Dixon has done exactly what she was asked to do and done it with a high degree of professionalism. The work meets all standards of excellence set by the facility for this type of research. I can't understand, however, why anyone would want to know any of this. That has me mystified. Do you have any idea?"

"I don't ask funders why they're asking for the research. That they want it and are willing to pay for it is enough for me to approve the work."

"What if," Amanda interjected, "they wanted to know so they could wipe out a whole race of people? Wouldn't you want to know that before taking their money?"

Ken Norton kicked her under the table again, and this time Dean Harris saw it. "Okay, you two, let's be straight up about this. As I told you, Dr. Dixon, it was the government that, somehow, I don't know how, got into your office and took your original conclusions. I told them that I believed that to be a serious breach of both our security and our agreement. Do you know what they said? They said, 'Oh so sorry. We're in a bit of a rush here.' That's it. They are the United States Army. They don't tell people why they want to know anything, and even if I were to ask they would say, 'Oh, so sorry.' End of conversation. If the army wants to wipe out a whole race of people, that's an issue to bring up with the president, not me. Now, for my edification, could we review, in brief, exactly what these findings are?"

Amanda stared at him. The army? He hadn't said that before. She knew he was lying.

"Dr. Dixon?" Norton said.

"Yes, yes, of course. I'll keep this brief. Is five minutes okay?"

Twenty minutes later, she wrapped up. "There is no evidence of loss of motor control. The anomalous physiological condition created by ingesting a mixture of anti-fungal agents intended for use on wheat and corn and anti-bacterial agents intended for use on trees appears to be temporary. It appears to persist during the time the mixture is ingested. Not exactly, it may linger in diminishing effect for some time afterwards, but after two weeks of a regular diet, the effects I identified—near total lack of ability to communicate or respond to other mice—seemed to dissipate, and the test subjects eventually returned to a statistically normal state. Their cognitive capacities, their statistical intelligence, did not ever seem to have been compromised; just their social, interactive, and communication skills were seriously diminished. I don't know the chemistry of it. Bryce Peters has studied that. He told me that when these agents are mixed, they produce a distinct chemical not found alone in either of the two. I don't know what it is, you would have to ask him, but to me, it's almost as though the mice were administered a psychiatric drug. However, none of the effects alleged to have occurred in the children in New Mexico were found to be present in any mice subjects when administered the chemicals as described in the medical report."

"Thank you both," Dean Harris said. "I'll forward these findings after I get a final copy." On their way out the door, he said, "Oh, by the way, Dr. Dixon," pointing to the chair in front of his desk, "my mother gave me that chair."

"What a sweet mother you must have," Amanda said, pulling the door shut with crisp tug.

Dean Harris dialed up International Chemical before the two were in the elevator.

Amanda shut her car door harder than it needed to be shut. She didn't like the feeling of being used and lied to, but more than that, she was angry with herself for having responded like a mean-spirited, petulant teenager. Over the last six years, she had worked hard at leaving behind all of the vitriol that had filled the fractures in her soul. After William died and it became suddenly clear why he never would even kiss her, not even on the day they were married, and why he consummated their union with young boys in ten-dollar motels, she had been like a cracked jug. Nothing stayed inside of her. It all oozed out like some toxic juice. People, friends and relatives, had come to see her at first to offer their condolences. They didn't know anything about who her husband was or what he had done to others in the innocence of their youth. They didn't know how he died. They just came and brought cookies and casseroles and sipped tea with long faces steeped in sympathy until they saw and smelled the noxious seepage and stopped coming by. It had driven her son, a shy and reclusive child anyway, into the attic. She had worked hard to glue up the fissures, to make herself whole again, with compassion—to be an adult. And now this. Ken Norton had suggested she take some time off. The next research project wasn't quite in the pipeline yet, he had said, and it might be a good time to take a vacation. He hadn't come out of that meeting with jovial guffaws and back-slapping about how she had really gotten to the dean and what a heinous liar he was. Oh, no. He had come out of that meeting concerned about her. He had seen the cracks, smelled the vitriol. Amanda was angry with herself and scared. She didn't want to break open again, particularly over someone as unimportant as Dean Harris.

The first step was to stop thinking about herself and do something nice for someone else. She put her pocketbook on the kitchen counter and poured herself a glass of scotch and added some ice cubes. She sat on a barstool at the island counter, going through a list of people she could do a favor for. Elmer Benoit? No. He would want to put his hands on her. Miss McCloud at the library? Poor woman. She lived alone, and nobody liked her. She always snapped at people, especially the children, and her girdle and stockings made a horrible rasping noise when she walked, and now she had brain cancer. No. She wouldn't see it as kindness; she'd see it as something else.

Lord knows what. Old Gerald Lovejoy who just lost his wife. *That's it. I'll bake him a casserole. Oh dear God, bring it to him and sip tea and tell him how sorry I am. I can't do it.* J.D. came in through the back door, whistling.

"I finished my exams, and I'm pretty sure I aced them. I'm a college graduate," he said, puffing out his chest.

"J.D.," Amanda said, pouring her scotch down the sink drain, "how would you like it if I took you out to a fancy dinner. Just us, to celebrate." He leaned against the refrigerator, stroking his chin. "I'm sorry," she said, "you're probably going out with your classmates."

"No, Mom, I'm not. I'm the only one who took the exam. It's September; everybody else takes it in May. I finished school eight months early, remember? And I'd be happy to go out to dinner. How fancy?"

"Suit jacket, no tie," she said.

The waiter poured her wine, twisting the bottle as he finished with an affected flourish, and brought J.D. his beer in a tall glass. He didn't like beer in a glass, he liked it in a bottle, but that's the way it was in these places. "Tell me about your girl down south. What's she like?" J.D. talked on and on about Abby and then about the old man and how worried he was because he had gone missing. That there might be something dangerous about it or some mystery to it that he couldn't figure out. There were wheelchair tracks, but he didn't have a telephone and nobody ever went there. And he told her about Junior and Marie, how she had won the trophy at the fiddler's convention and how Junior was always there for him. A really good friend. Amanda realized that her son had grown up while she wasn't looking. *He's going to move away, and I'll be all alone in that big old house. There I go again*, she thought, *feeling sorry for myself instead of happy for someone else.* She had been fidgeting with her napkin since they sat down.

"Mom," J.D. said, "something's bothering you. What is it? Is it your work?"

"Yes," she said quickly, wanting to avoid talking about those dark things that still lingered inside her. Her son did not need to know about that. Not yet, anyway. While they were finishing their dinner, Amanda told him about the experiments she'd done with the mice and what a foolish waste of money it was. She began to talk about Dean Harris, what an awful man he was, when J.D. interrupted. He wanted her to go back to the mice, to describe them. When she finished, J.D. asked her if she would like to come down to Galax and meet Abby. Then he told her about Billy. She made him go over it twice, and then said she would meet him there tomorrow at three in the afternoon.

"There's a motel in town," he said. "I forget the name, but it's right on main drag. I'll try and set up a room."

18

Bear Traps

J.D. RESERVED A ROOM FOR AMANDA at the InnTowne Motel. It was mid-fall, and the tourist season in the Blue Ridge was over. After the fiddlers' convention ended in August, many of the visitors hung around the town and camped out in the mountains in Virginia and North Carolina, playing music with the old timers and their children who lived in the gaps and hollers and up in the hills. They bought and sold instruments and swapped tunes, keeping the tradition of mountain music alive, infusing into the legacy new riffs and lyrics from the songs of the folk singers from the cities. Dozens of people from Maine and New York, Georgia and Alabama, and even a family of six from California found their way to Fat Gap looking for Marie Cadieux, just to meet her in person and maybe pick a tune or two with her on the front porch. Uncle Albert didn't like it. He was busy raising hogs and picking corn. Granny Mae would only come out to the porch to play if there were children there. She'd sit them in a circle at her feet and sing them simple ballads. Marie loved it and made Junior stop that awful kid at the gas station from playing his dumb jokes on everyone. She made him hack out a clearing by the creek just before the bridge and build a fire pit and keep it stocked with dry split wood. Junior would show them where it was and collect five bucks a night per tent. "Don't leave peanut butter outside," he'd say. "Lots of bears in these woods. Smell it a mile away." October brought cold air, and their tents had come down and their motel rooms vacated. J.D. booked his mother a room for three days.

He checked on the cabin. He sat in the rocking chair and forced himself to hear the old man's words, forced himself to see him scuttle about. It was too easy for it all to become memory, like a rainbow after dusk. He knew that Old Man was somewhere, and he knew he would find him. It took being watchful and attentive. To see how pieces fit or didn't fit. Something would surely be out of place somewhere. As much for himself as for the old man, he needed to get him back in his cabin. His cabin was nothing without him. It was empty as an old wooden box. When he realized he was biting his lip and flicking his ear, he knew how much he missed him. He pushed himself up out of the rocker, closed up the cabin, and fired up the '47 flatbed. He made four trips in and out, bringing the cordwood from the roadside and stacking it in the woodshed. He brought the gas cylinders in and swapped them for the near empty ones. J.D. drove to the Food Mart in Mt. Airy and told them he was the old man's friend. He talked to the stock boy who delivered the food to the end of the dirt drive each week and asked him if he'd seen anything different or odd. No, the kid had said, last week the old guy just didn't drive out to get his groceries. First time ever he could remember that happening. J.D. told him the old man went away for a while and not to bring food again until he called him. He bought a bottle of Maker's Mark and drove back north.

Amanda and J.D. walked from the motel down the main street. It was a small town but a town that anyone could live in or live near without having to go anywhere else. Men in bib overalls sat on benches on the sidewalk talking things over. There were very few cars, mostly old pickup trucks. The movie theater was the big attraction. *Gone with the Wind* had been playing since June, but the marquee promised *Dr. Zhivago* "Coming Soon." On Main Street, there were three music shops: one that sold instruments like banjos and fiddles, one where an old man with a very long, gray beard made instruments with hand tools in the shop, and one store that sold records and posters. J.D. tugged his mother in the door and pointed to a poster on the wall. It was of Marie and Grannie Mae and Albert ripping it up on stage at the Felt Field grandstands. Beside the poster was a newspaper article from the Carroll County Gazette: "Youngest and Oldest Take Second Place."

"That's Junior's wife right there playing the fiddle," J.D. said.

"Oh my gosh." Amanda bent close to the poster. "She's precious!"

"And that," J.D. said, "is her great-grandmother who's ninety-two and still playing the dulcimer."

"J.D.," Amanda said, "does Junior have one of these?"

"Oh yeah, he sure does, a couple of them. There's even one pinned up in their outhouse. Junior told me that Marie shines up her trophy almost every day, and someday she's going to be the most famous fiddle player alive." Amanda pushed a wisp of hair back behind her ear.

"It's so nice to be wrong sometimes. It washes things clean." She bought herself a poster and a photocopy of the newspaper article, all rolled up together.

They stopped in the Koffee Klatch to get iced tea to go. It smelled like bread and pies. J.D. ordered, and the girl asked him if he wanted his regular or unsweetened. "Regular," he said. "And how about your girl? What does she want?" J.D. turned to his mother. She smiled and batted her eyes. She looked about twenty-five, and he was nearly a foot taller than her and hadn't shaved that morning. He turned back and said, "My girl wants it sweet."

They walked down the street, and Amanda said hello to anyone they passed. Most of the men tipped their hats, some said, "How y'all do?" They walked to the window of the EZ Clean Laundromat. About midway down the line of dryers was the bottom half of a girl, blue jeans and boots sticking straight out into the aisle, the other half from the waist up was completely inside the machine. The center agitating spindle was lying in a pile of wet clothes on the floor. J.D. opened the door and followed his mother in. The girl was yelling, "This dadburned piece'a shoot! I've 'bout had it with this crud! Fudge it all!" And there was a banging like a wrench being smacked about in a tin barrel. Amanda pulled J.D.'s arm toward the door, but he walked up to the girl and patted her on the bottom. Good solid pats. The wrench banged, and her head banged on the lip of the machine hole as she heaved herself out, her hair all wild and askew, and the green-gold flakes in her eyes on fire. She came out holding the wrench as if it were a cudgel, stood in front of J.D., blinked a few times, dropped the wrench on the floor, threw her arms around him, and began to cry. Between her sobs, she waved her hand at the woman standing there staring at them and choked out, "G'won now, please. Come back in a while." Amanda left the Laundromat and sat on a bench on the sidewalk out front, smiling to herself and looking around.

"Abby," J.D. said, untwining her from around his neck, "does this place have a bathroom?"

She backed up, kicked the pile of clothes on the floor. "No it don't; you go right ahead and pee in that machine, see if I care."

"Abby, can you clean yourself up just a little bit? That's my mother you just scooted out of here." He pointed to the bench out front. "My mother ... that's her."

"Jeremiah Dixon, how could you—"

He held up his hand. "It's okay. Do you have a small bucket just to put some water in to wash up with? Your face is all covered with spindle grease."

She nodded, nodded, nodded. "Right," she said, "small bucket, towel, mother. Yes. Over here, mother, bucket, get the bucket, Oh my gosh!" and she disappeared into a back room.

J.D. hopped outside and said to Amanda, "Do you have brush and a small mirror?" Without looking up, she fished them out of her pocketbook and handed them up to him.

"She's beautiful, J.D.," she whispered.

Amanda knelt down in front of Billy on the front porch of the hardware store. She asked him questions about what it was like where he lived and was he happy and what kind of food did he eat. He stared at her, unblinking, without expression. She knelt there looking into his face. He didn't seem to mind. Every once in a while, she would tap her fingers on the porch boards to see if he looked down. Or stand up to see if he looked up. He didn't.

Abby poked J.D.'s arm and pointed to the inside of the store. She closed the screen door quietly behind herself, put her hands on her hips, and breathed deeply, blowing out hard at J.D. Then she said, "I want to have a mother like that. Jeremiah, I really want to have a mother just like that."

"Abby, we'll talk about it."

The Blue Ridge Bar & Grill on Main Street was packed with local boys. J.D. and Junior had bellied up to the only open space at the far end of the bar by the pisshole. The barmaid brought them each a Pabst and told Junior it was nice to see he'd bought himself a decent shirt and left that flea-bitten rat-hat at home. He said, "Yes, ma'am," and that he surely did appreciate her straightening him out of that score.

"I'm growing up, J.D.," he said. "It's scary. The little missus has me washing dishes and changing diapers. Hardly get a chance to shit-kick anymore. Uncle Albert still thinks I'm a pissant from up north, so I just steer clear of him. But I got my 3A card from the government, and I got a good wife and baby, so I don't really give a shit what he thinks. That's what I mean. A year ago, anybody, I don't give a fuck how big they were, anybody talked to me the way he does, and I'da laid 'em out with a two by four. Now, I just let it go and stay out of his hog pen. That's what I mean; I'm growing up. Take that barmaid. See how nice and polite I was."

"I think I like you better the other way," J.D. said. "I've done enough growing up for both of us. Sometimes it feels like I never was a kid. Just went from being a mouse in the attic to a man. That's the reality. One day my mom says, 'Here's a gun. Go hunting with Junior Benoit, shoot things, and grow up.' So I did, just like that. Bang! Shot things. Not a kid anymore. Talking about reality, my mom came down today. She wanted to meet Abby. Meeting up with Abby in the Laundromat was a bit of a shit show, but they're fast friends now. She's up at Abby's seeing where they all live, talking girl talk." J.D. didn't mention the mice. He didn't want to get Junior started on Billy.

"Your mom's here? That must mean you and Abby's getting kind of serious. Is that it?"

"No, Junior, that's not it. She just wants to see what I've been doing down here and what the people are like. She really wants to meet Marie and see your baby. She bought a copy of your poster today. I told her about the old man going missing, and she thought since she's a medical research person, she might be able to help. How, I don't know. She didn't say. Aside from that, I think she gets lonely up north all by herself."

"Well I'll tell you this about your mom, J.D. If anybody asked me who is the smartest person I know, I'd say your mom. And if anybody asked me who's the most grown-up person I know, I'd say your mom. It's almost like she doesn't have anything wrong with her."

"Yeah," J.D. said, "it's almost like that. Almost."

Junior asked the barmaid, "Would it be possible for you to please bring us a couple more beers? We'd sure appreciate it." She brought them, and Junior said, "Thank you very much, ma'am."

And she said, "Cut the bullshit, buckaroo." Junior smiled and winked at her.

"If your mom's here, maybe you and her and Abby can come over for supper. We got corn and squash and hog ribs coming out our ears. Maybe your mom could tell Uncle Albert, all nice and polite like, to go fuck himself."

"My mom doesn't tell people that. Well, actually I'm not so sure of that. She doesn't tell people to fuck themselves when I'm around, but in her business, maybe she does. I'm thinking she's a pretty tough duck. Shit, Junior, things are happening fast. Maybe we should've spent more time being kids, doing things like banging those sorority girls. That was fun."

"Fun?" Junior said. "Fun? You call it fun getting the shit beat out of you by a pack of half-naked girls?"

"No, I didn't mean that part; I meant the part before that happened."

"Oh, yeah, I remember her. Little bit of a thing, but, man, was she ever a screamer. I'm surprised they didn't call the cops while I was porking her. It was like being in one of them Pentecostal churches with her screaming, Oh God! Oh God! Jesus, I almost went deaf."

"Well, who knows," J.D. said, "maybe we'll go out and have some more fun sometime. Hopefully this growing up thing takes longer than we think. Could be it just feels like we're all grown up, but we really aren't."

"Could be," Junior said, "could be. Sure hope so."

Skinny Binkins' boy came in the bar and squeezed and bumped his way behind the barstools and in and out of the men in the three-foot aisle. One of the men slapped him on the back of the head and said, "Hey, Binkins, how's the sheriff?" Binkins had his eyes on J.D. and Junior and kept weaving his way until he scrunched in beside them. J.D. waved to the barmaid and pointed at Binkins. She brought him a beer, and J.D. paid.

"You the sheriff's kid?"

Binkins nodded. "But," he said, "that don't mean jack shit. I don't never see him. Those men are back in town. They found me and paid me another fifty bucks to watch the road where that girl lives. They didn't say nothin' about what all they was doin', but I know there's something mighty bad smellin' about those two. This time they got guns. I seen 'em in the backseat of their car. I mean they paid me the fifty bucks, so I gotta do it, but like I said, you all's local, so that why I'm telling you."

"Binkins, sounds to me like you're playing both sides of the fence here. Is that it?"

"Man's gotta eat," Binkins said.

"When are they coming?" J.D. asked.

"Tomorrow morning, crack of dawn. Seven o'clock. I'm supposed to go up there and tell her Mr. Harrelson wants to see her right away, and he don't want no moron coming with her. It's about business, and the moron's been hurting business. People don't feel good about him just sittin' on the porch staring at 'em, and so they ain't comin' to the store. He wants to see her all by himself, right now. That's what I'm supposed to tell her."

"Binkins, thank you. We'll make it right for you. Don't

worry about that. What time do you think they'll be going up there?"

"'Bout seven-thirty. They said they'll be lookin' for her car coming into town, then head up right away. I'm supposed to park in the woods down to the bottom of the hill, and anybody comes wantin' to g'won up, block 'em and pertend my truck done died. That's all what my job is."

"Binkins, we don't want anything to happen to our people. They're not hurting anybody." J.D. signaled the barmaid for three more beers. The three stood sipping their beers, elbows on the counter, not saying anything, thinking their own thoughts. Binkins tipped his beer all the way back and drained it. He pushed himself upright, getting ready to go.

J.D. said, "I do have one more question before I forget it. Is getting chased around by government people normal around here? I mean, does this happen to a lot of people?"

Binkins looked at J.D. with a serious look, peeled the label off his beer bottle, rolled it around into a ball, dropped it in an ashtray. "Nope, I'd have to say it's not normal."

It was fresh and clear early in the morning when J.D. and Junior parked their trucks at the old man's cabin. J.D. checked the notches on the hasp peg. They were just as he'd left them. "Did you get the traps from Albert?" Junior reached in the back of his truck and pulled out two gigantic steel traps, each with five feet of chain and a steel ring carabineer on the end.

"Bear traps," he said. "These little babies ought to slow them motherfuckers down." He took a stick as thick as his arm from the truck and laid it down. He pried one trap open, open, open until a little cog clicked on the edge of a flat disc the size of a saucer.

"Yikes," he said, stepping back, "ain't that thing ugly looking." Pointed teeth sprung open in a circle like a serving platter. He took the stick and, holding it a foot above the plate, dropped it. Bang! The steel jaws snapped shut on the stick, its teeth digging deep into the wood.

"Oh my God," J.D. said, "that fucker's dangerous." Junior set the second trap and dropped the stick. Bang! It snapped shut.

"Here's what we got to do." J.D. knelt down and drew with his knife blade. "I've done a lot of thinking about this. We both go halfway up the hill. You set a marker on the fence and go into the res, straight in, ninety degrees to the fence. You go in five hundred paces, about a quarter mile, get out of sight, and wait. I go all the way up and wait for the car. After those guys start down the hill, out of sound and sight, I take Abby's shovel and bury these babies beside the Lincoln." He drew the car in the dirt. "One here, just where you have to step to get in the driver's side door. The other I put here." He drew a circle in back of the car, centered on the trunk. "I bury them both, cover them up with leaves that are spread all over the driveway anyway, and latch both rings to the drive shaft. Driver guy gets snapped. Other guy either runs around back to see what happened or runs to the trunk to get a tire iron to pry the fucker open and—Bang!—got 'em both. I can probably set and bury and cover these things in about five minutes. The two guys will be going down through the woods real slow, spreading out and being careful. I'm going to set these and then take off down the hill outside the res, fast but quiet. When I get to your marker, I'll turn in five hundred paces, and we should hook up. Then, Junior, my man, we herd them up through the funnel, just like a couple of bucks. At the top, it won't be Dirk; it'll be these two bad boys." Junior pulled a red bandana out of his back pocket, and J.D. nodded. "Our whistle to each other will be a Phoebe whistle, okay?"

They took their rifles, slung them across their backs, each

with a bear trap slung over a shoulder, and started climbing up the hill up through Dengman Gap. They had decided not to tell Abby what was going on. She might decide to get Billy out of the woods, and the Binkins' kid would see them both driving out, and the men would never come.

If J.D. and Junior were going to find out what these men were doing and why they wanted Billy so bad, they were going to have to catch them and scare it out of them. They didn't look like the types that scared easy, but way out in these woods with your leg half chewed off and clamped in a bear trap, who knows? Even the toughest guys might blink. That's all they needed.

The oak and pine sapling growth was thick. They stayed away from the reservation boundary wire, but both of them kept peering into those lands, and both of them had the same feeling of strangeness about the place. They could see a few mounds, round on the top and round on the ends, about the size of a railroad car, far off through the woods, none near the boundary. There were some huge trees out in the forest, but J.D., from that distance, couldn't make out what kind of trees they were. Every once in a while, Junior would stop, look at J.D., wiggle his fingers by his face, and mouth the words, "Weird, creepy," and by natural impulse, they would go on veering away from the sacred forest. A doe with two fawns, nibbling on young leaves, watched them make their way up the hill until some exact moment that her mind said bolt, and she and her fawns bounded, leaping with their legs straight out in front of them and straight out behind, with awesome grace and speed, under the wire and into the burial grounds. *That's why it's a wire, not a fence*, J.D. thought. *So the animals can come and go.*

Halfway up the hill, Junior took his bandana off his neck and tied it to the fence wire. He handed off the other trap to

J.D., and they both said "Good luck" to each other at the same time. Junior headed off at a right angle to the wire, into the sacred ground, crouching low, zigzagging around trees, counting his paces. J.D., doing his best to keep the claws from banging on the chains, walked fast, off and up the hill toward Abby's shack.

As J.D. neared the ridge, he heard the rumble of the Dodge Power Wagon coming up the other side of the hill. He checked his watch. Seven o'clock. Binkins was right on time. He moved quietly now, hunkered in a half-crouch so he wouldn't alert Abby, close enough so he could see her shack, but far enough away so he couldn't be seen. He pulled off the bear traps and gently put them down in the leaves, unstrapped his rifle, and lay down on his belly behind a large, sloping granite boulder. Skinny Binkins' boy parked and went to Abby's door and knocked. She opened the door still in her nightie, with a cup of coffee in her hand. He wasn't close enough to hear what Skinny said to her, but he heard loud and clear what she said to him. "What do you mean Mr. Harrelson has a problem with Billy? Why does he have a problem now and not a year ago? And I got a problem with his stupid warshin' machines. When did he tell you this?" Binkins backed away toward his truck, shrugging his shoulders and waving his arms, palms up. He got in his truck, backed it around, and sped down the hill.

Poor girl, J.D. thought. Abby came out dressed. She went to the wire and put her forefinger and thumb in her mouth, spreading her lips wide, breathing one deep breath, tilted her head back to the sky, and shrieked out her horse whistle. She waited and did it again. A few minutes later, Billy came running up the hillside, nimble and fast. She gave him a quick hug and waved her arm out toward the forest, pointing down the hill to where he had come from. Billy stood while she drove off and then turned and bounded back through the trees. J.D.

waited, quiet, flat down on the backside of the rock, wondering how he had gotten to a place in his life where he was going to purposefully cause someone horrible pain. If he was lucky. *That's what it is*, he thought. *Abby and the old man. That's why I have to do this. For them.*

The black Lincoln eased up the drive and turned around, facing down the hill. It was quiet, rolling over the fall leaves still damp with morning dew. The men wore camouflage, and each had a holstered pistol riding on their hip. The long-haired man had a pair of handcuffs on his belt. They closed the car doors carefully. A firm push and click. At the wire, they whispered to each other, the tall man pointing to the right and to the left. They checked their watches and ducked under, spreading apart, moving very slowly and quietly, half crouched.

J.D. waited until they were well out of sight, slung his rifle over his back, and dashed to fetch a shovel that leaned against Abby's shack. He spread the leaves away from beside the driver's door and behind the trunk and dug two shallow holes. He got the traps and set each one into the hole, crawled underneath the car and snapped the fat rings onto the drive shaft, knelt by the first trap, and pried the circular teeth apart until the cog clicked on the trip plate. He set the second and then spread the leaves over each trap and chain, returned the shovel, and sprinted off, out and around the far edge of the reservation, moving as fast as he could without making noise, darting from big tree to big tree almost a mile down the hill along the wire to the red bandana. He knew he was much further down than the men. They would be moving carefully and slowly. J.D. turned straight in and, keeping low, began to count his paces.

The sun streamed through holes in the forest canopy, bright with moist air, making narrow shafts of light like beams through the branches to the soft, leafy floor. It was too early for dry air, too early for the snap and crack of twigs. His movement made only a rustling noise. The squirrels and birds had begun their morning chatter. Three hundred paces in, J.D. came upon a burial mound, taller than him and long as a house, tubular, round across the top and sloping round about the ends with trees and bushes growing on it. He moved slowly sideways and across the front, not wanting to touch it, seeing invisible spirits in the light beams, hearing silent incantations in the dull rustle, the hair on his neck and arms bristling. Sacred ground. Some other world. He quickened his pace, scooting ape-like until he came upon the trunk of a massive tree, four feet in diameter, with a huge, majestic, curving crown. He rubbed his hands on the bark, mumbling to himself. He backed up, looking to the leaves. He picked up a nut from the forest floor. *How can this be? I must be wrong. This is a chestnut tree. It's supposed to be dead.* He was standing there straight up staring into the leaves when he heard the Phoebe whistle.

"What the fuck are you doing?" Junior whispered hard. "There are guys with guns out here, and you're standing around staring at the trees. Jesus, J.D., focus!"

"It's a chestnut tree. They're all dead. That's a huge, healthy chestnut tree."

"Oh, yeah? Wow! Guess they're not all dead, Mr. Tree Expert. Did you get the traps set?"

"Yes, set and latched onto the drive shaft." They fanned out a little. "They should be coming this way. And yeah, they have pistols. One of them has handcuffs on him, so they are definitely going to try to take Billy out of here. Where is he?"

Junior pointed off down to the bottom of the Gap. "I saw him running, and I whistled to him and shooed him off down to the old guy's cabin. He seemed like he understood, but who knows if there's anything upstairs in that head. But he took off like a deer. Did you see the grave mound?"

"Really spooky. Why do you think these guys want Billy out of here? What's their problem?" J.D. asked.

"Don't know. Only way to find out is to ask them, nice and polite, while their foot's locked in those steel jaws. Let's spread out and move uphill, side to side. When we see one of them, I think we got to shoot, not to kill but maybe hit a rock or a tree next to them. They won't know how many of us there are out here, so if they're smart, they'll turn back and get the hell out of here. Make sure no one in front of you can see you. Don't be standing out there staring up at the trees like some stoned hippie. This is serious shit, J.D. If I see one, I'm shooting. You shoot too, just up in that general direction. Then they won't be able to figure it out. How many rounds do you have?"

J.D. checked his cartridge belt. "Twenty."

"Me too," said Junior. "That should do it. Let's stay about a hundred yards apart, and for chrissake, don't shoot sideways. I'll be over there. Let's go."

As the sun rose higher in the sky, the light shafts disappeared when the moisture burnt from the air, and the woods became speckled with light and shadow. A soft breeze blew, and the whole hill seemed to shimmer. The leaves and sticks were beginning to dry. They moved back and forth across the hill, staying low, going from rock to tree to clump of rhododendron. J.D. saw a shadow cross a light spot and moments later, cross another. He scrunched forward behind a mossy rock, unslung his rifle, pointed it in the direction of the shadow, and waited. It was a man. The long-haired one. Fifty yards uphill. J.D. aimed at a thicket of bushes just off to the left and pulled the trigger. The man jumped and hit the ground. J.D. jammed the lever down and fired again. Junior's gun fired, once, twice, three times. The bush thicket came alive with squealing as the man was clawing up the hill on hands and knees, crashing through thickets, and J.D. saw the boar come right at the long-haired man, blood on her shoulder, head down, tusks out level, and gore him in the side. The boar thrashed her head about, backed up, and gored him again, and the man screamed, shrieked and screamed.

J.D. hunkered down, and Junior came up beside him. The taller man was sprinting across the slope—light, dark, light, dark—as he ran through the shadows and the sunlight, his pistol drawn, firing at the boar, missing, and the boar charged off away around the base of another burial mound and down into the bowels of Dengman Gap. Little boars scrambled behind, squealing, one scrambling on three legs, and then the woods became quiet again with only the moaning of the gored man and the grunting of his buddy hauling him up the hill. Another scream came from up on the ridge. A high-pitched scream and a rhythmic pounding. J.D. and Junior ran to the edge of the reservation, under the wire, and up the hill toward Abby's shack.

Skinny Binkins' boy had stopped screaming and pounding on the car when they got there. He was lying on the ground, whimpering. J.D. and Junior pried the jaws loose. The cuts were deep. J.D. snapped the other trap with the shovel, crawled underneath, and freed the rings from the drive shaft.

"We need to get this kid to a doctor. His shin bone's broke."

Junior said, "You get Binkins down the hill to his truck. I'm not going through all this without finding out who these shitheads are. G'won. I'll be all right. Lookee there, the doctor's bag's in the backseat." The door was locked. With his rifle butt, he smashed the glass and took the bag out. He fished around and found a vial of pills that said, *Take two every four hours for pain.* He gave a handful to Binkins. "I'll meet you back at our trucks in a couple of hours." J.D. put Binkins' arm around his shoulder, told him to stop his fucking bellyaching, and they hobbled down the drive. Junior took the traps, stashed them in Abby's shack, and waited.

The long-haired man did not look good. Blood was running out of his thigh and hip, and his face was the color of cement. The tall man hauling him was breathing hard and grunting. It had taken him a long time to get up the hill. He saw the broken window, reached through it, opened the door, and began to stuff the wounded man into the backseat. Junior walked up behind him, put the rifle barrel in his back, and said, "Do not turn around. This is a 30-30 in your spine. Turn around, and I pull the trigger. Now reach in that guy's back pocket and get out his wallet. Throw it over your shoulder." The wallet landed in the leaves. "Now, Mr. Man, reach in your own back pocket and chuck your own wallet on the ground. G'won, do it!" He did. Junior said, "I'm picking these up. Do not turn around or reach for your gun. You do and you're a dead man."

The man said, "You're going to get a fast trip up to Skinner Bluff."

Junior picked up both wallets, grabbed the black medical bag, and sprinted into the woods.

All the contents of the medical bag were laid out on the kitchen table at Marie's house. Scalpels, sutures, gauze, tape, needles, syringes, iodine, a roll of duct tape, the vial of Demerol that Skinny Binkins' boy got some of, two vials of liquid medicines—one marked Thorozine, one marked Vitrastenol—and a pair of handcuffs. Amanda poked them around with a plastic spoon.

"These medicines, J.D., are only administered at psychiatric hospitals. There's something sinister here.

Something's very wrong. I need to know more about, what's his name? Billy. I need to know what Billy eats." Billy was sitting out on the front porch, the old bluetick coonhound curled up at his feet. Abby said she thought he ate nuts and berries, and sometimes she gives him some vegetables. She sat cross-legged on the bed staring at the driver's license photos. Marie was reading them to her. "Robert John Hartford, Florida driver's license. Robert Hartford, Director, Environmental Security, International Chemical Corporation. Robert Hartford, Senior Case Manager, State of Texas, Child Welfare Protection Agency. That one has a gold seal and the name of the governor on it. Robert J. Hartford, Investigator, Bureau of Indian Affairs. Five crisp new one-hundred-dollar bills and some small bills. My gosh, the guy's got three jobs. He works for some chemical company, the federal government, and the governor of Texas. How's that happen? This other guy who got attacked by the hog is Vincent R. Gravello. Oklahoma driver's license. Another one with the governor's name on it. Dr. Vincent Gravello, MD. Consulting Physician, Child Welfare Protective Agency. And here we go again. Dr. V. Gravello, Staff Physician, International Chemical Corporation. Vincent Gravello, Investigator, Bureau of Indian Affairs. Same problem. Three jobs—two government, one private. How can that be? Look at what this one says, Mrs. Dixon. 'Vincent Gravello is a Licensed Pharmacist in the State of Texas. License #12867 Expiration Date 04/09/64.' Whoever he is, he's not a doctor; he's a guy who sells pills, and this thing ran out five years ago. Who are these guys? Why are they trying to steal Billy right out of an Indian Reservation? I mean, gosh, with handcuffs and guns. Do government people do that? Do they drive big fancy cars and wear camouflage clothes and hunt people down? That doesn't sound right at all."

Uncle Albert said, "That ain't right. That ain't who they are."

Abby said, "Remember, Jeremiah, I said there was something familiar about these guys. That I thought I had seen them before. I have. I remember now. I was little, in the orphanage. I would kneel on my cot and watch for people who would come to the front door. I wanted somebody to come for me. I remember seeing these two, maybe more than once, come to the orphanage. That's where I saw them. This guy, he had more hair then, but the other guy looked just like this. That was, gosh, fifteen years ago, but I'm pretty sure of it. These are the same guys."

Amanda sat next to Abby on the bed. "You told me yesterday you didn't know who brought you to the orphanage, but you had burn scars when you got there. Is that right?"

"Yes, Mrs. Dixon, that's right. I don't know anything about how I got there or why I was there. I only know that I was only one or two years old because that's what Sister Valentine told me. She said God gave me to her all wrapped up in bandages and baby clothes."

"What was the name of the orphanage?"

Abby furrowed her brow. "This may seem funny, but I don't know. Nobody ever told me that, and my parents on the reservation never said."

"Junior." Amanda touched his arm. "What did you say the man said when he gave you the wallets?"

He said, "You're going to get a fast trip up to Skinner Bluff." Amanda asked Marie if they had a phone.

"No, ma'am, we surely don't."

"Junior, could you drive me down to the garage? I need to make a phone call. There's a phone there, right?"

"Yes, ma'am, there is."

"Operator, Could you please get me information for Houston, Texas. I need the number for the United States Marshals

Service." The operator connected her right away.

Ten minutes later, Uncle Danny had agreed to do some poking around in Texas. He thought he'd look into that corporation, see if he could track down the orphanage, find out what he could about Skinner Bluff, then get on a flight out to Virginia. He figured he couldn't be there for three or four days.

"Have to wrap up a case here, and then I'll take some vacation time. It's good it's Indian land. Marshals have jurisdiction there. Tell J.D. to get his girl out of there and someplace safe, and, Amanda, it'll be really good to see you. I miss you."

19

Colonel Britt

"GENTLEMEN, IF WHAT YOU HAVE JUST TOLD ME is even partly true, I have to take you both off this site in Virginia. I've talked to Jack Huprin, the CEO of International Chemical, your boss, and he has agreed that the circumstances you have created are intolerable for both his company and the United States government. It is appalling to me that two young boys and a deranged kid are close to derailing our national security. Is it true, don't answer that, I know it's true, that you got gored by a boar, your wallets and medical bag taken, and then you drove to the county sheriff's house, not his office but his own home, and, Bob, you honked your horn in his driveway and asked him to take Vinny to the hospital? I can't believe it. We, all of us, are not supposed to do shit like that. I am a colonel in the United States Army. Do you know what that means? Do you two have any idea what that means? It means that one, maybe even two generals are growling at me all the time. But now, they're not growling. Oh no, they are barking in my face. Because of you. Because you're under contract with the Department of Defense, and you have caused the potential for a serious breach of highly classified information. I don't want either of you ever to go back to that site. If Huprin wants you to keep monitoring the other thirteen sites around this country that I, not you, have responsibility for, then so be it. I can't change that without terminating International Chemical's contract. I can't do that without Congress getting into it. Nobody wants that. I don't know what Huprin will do with you, but you're done in Virginia. Is that clear?"

Colonel Britt got up from his desk, poured himself another cup of coffee, his fifth in two hours, and looked out the window over the grounds surrounding the Pentagon in Arlington, Virginia. It was peaceful out there. Green, mowed lawns and trees with circles of black mulch around them. The parking lot had shade trees every twenty feet so the cars wouldn't get hot in the summer sun.

Dan Logan from the Justice Department sat quietly. Hartford and Gravello were in front of him across the table. Britt talked with his back to them. "Do you remember the first night we met? Do you remember looking at that carnage out in those woods? I should have known then that you two were cowboys. But I was young, just a lieutenant, and the army had a contract with your company. Since World War I, the army has had a contract with your company, and General Groves said, 'Go with it.' So I did. I should have known. My God, I should have known. But the general said, 'Go with it. Our national security is more important. Get the local sheriff to help us out.' He turned back, opened the drawer to his desk, took out a bottle of scotch, and poured some in his coffee. "God, I should have known better. We were supposed to have been a team, you and me. Now all across this country, fourteen places where Americans live and work and raise families, I have the possibility of this shit to deal with. And that little girl you put in the orphanage eighteen years ago, you don't have a clue where she is, do you? You don't know, and you don't even know how to find out. Goodbye, gentlemen." Gravello limped toward the door, leaning on his cane. Hartford nudged past him.

After the door shut, Attorney Logan, leaning his elbows on the conference table, clicking a ballpoint pen, said, "Colonel, this is really bad. The situation is this: the National Environmental Coalition has prevailed in their preliminary motion to subpoena certain employees of International Chemical. But they've done something really smart. Since there's no federal agency overseeing the various environmental laws passed by Congress, only the individual states, they filed against the Department of Defence in federal court under the property provisions of the Fifth Amendment. Now it can't be remanded back to a single state. It gives them national scope. Do you understand?"

Britt nodded.

"The judge is a Kennedy appointee who clerked for Earl Warren and then taught law at Harvard. Not good for us. And they've hired Russell McNary, a really smart, seasoned civil rights lawyer. It was very smart on their part to file the suit in New Mexico and not Washington, DC. Two reasons; the chances of getting this judge were fairly good, and any appeal will be heard in the Ninth Circuit. The Ninth Circuit, Colonel, does not like the army. Those two geniuses who just left your office are going to get subpoenas for depositions within the week. You won't because you have immunity, but they will and probably Huprin as well. Here's the nut of it. They don't know what's where. That goes for both International Chemical and the Environmental Coalition. As far as McNary knows, they're only talking about kids on reservation land in New Mexico, and they don't have any proof of anything. But, Colonel, they depose these Hartford and Gravello guys, and those bullets are going to find some mark. I know you know this, but I'm going to refresh your memory. After the First World War, Americans by and large came to think that chemical warfare was something heinous that the Germans did, not us, and Congress got on board and tried to defund and disband the Biological Warfare Division and the entire Chemical Corps. In the rush to disposal, so we could keep these weapons but keep them out of the public eye, the only records they kept were what was shipped out, not where it was going. Now watch this. I'm Russell McNary, you're Hartford. Your shirt is soaking wet. You've already sweated about ten pounds of really foul sweat, and your face is the color of a nice ripe tomato." Logan got up and stood over Britt with his arms out wide and screamed out in an incredulous voice, "Are you telling this jury that hideous chemicals that cause, as experts have said in sworn testimony, that cause human mutations, cancers, and death are buried somewhere in our country? And you don't know where you buried them? Are they under our school playgrounds, in our National Parks, or at the bottom of our rivers and lakes? Where? Mr. Hartford, what are they and where are they?" He paused. "Now, Colonel, we, you and I, know that all there is at the Virginia site is uranium and plutonium. That's correct, isn't it?"

Britt poured himself another cup of coffee. His hands were beginning to shake. "Yes."

"Colonel, I got your memorandum about Dr. Johnson and your decision to have Huprin's people 'relocate' him. By the way, where do they relocate people to?"

"I don't know. I didn't want to know, so I never asked."

"Right now that's very good for everybody. What struck me as odd is the trigger for that decision. Here it is." Logan pulled a piece of paper from his briefcase and laid it out on the table. "You said that Dr. Johnson's wife somehow knew of a person named J.D., and this J.D. person, whose name by the way is Jeremiah Dixon, knew what Dr. Johnson was doing in Dengman Gap and that he was protecting this other child who has some kind of serious disorder. Security had been breached, you said. I can understand that. He's been monitoring potential leakage, right?" Britt nodded. "And there hasn't been any, right?"

Britt nodded. "That's right."

"Here's the odd thing. You also sent me a copy of a research paper that was done by a University of Virginia scientist, at your request, concerning the chemicals in question out in New Mexico. Am I still right?" Britt nodded again. "That paper concluded that there was a possibility that the chemicals, the very ones that were likely stored together, could produce an extreme psychiatric disorder which, incidentally, is the very same condition that this kid that Hartford and Gravello were hunting down seems to have. She, the research scientist up in Charlottesville, wouldn't know any of that of course. She wouldn't even know the kid existed. But if that kid has this disorder and it's caused by these chemicals, if for some strange reason, International Chemical stashed chemicals with the plutonium without telling you, or stashed plutonium where there already were chemicals, this is no longer a civil case about stored chemicals. It is a criminal case, everything Attorney McNary needs to bring down the entire army program and you with it. No immunity in a criminal case. But she wouldn't know about that kid, Colonel, would she? Would she? Of course not, how could she? But, Colonel, look at this." He took the report from his briefcase.

"The author of that report is Dr. Amanda Dixon. She's the mother of this Jeremiah Dixon. Somebody hasn't connected the dots. Isn't that right, Colonel?" He went back to clicking his pen over and over again. It sounded like a big clock ticking.

"What do I do?" Britt asked.

"Rule number one. Never ask your attorney what to do. Suggest something, and I'll give you whatever legal advice I can."

"Councilor, what's our best position here?"

"Well, if McNary doesn't know anything about Virginia, he might not ask Hartford questions that would bring that up. From a legal standpoint, we have to keep this a civil case. The only hope we have of prevailing is getting a dismissal out in New Mexico. National security, no hard evidence, all circumstantial. That kind of thing. At this point, we don't want to know anything about what International Chemical might or might not have done. But the only way we can be sure this stays a civil case with a chance of dismissal is if the woman, her son, and that disabled kid don't exist. At all. Never did. How to get that done, Colonel, is a military decision. I really can't give you any advice on that." Dan Logan closed his briefcase, shook Britt's hand, and left the Colonel standing, looking out over the perfectly manicured lawns, wondering what names those two were going to take after they got their subpoenas, if they ever did get served. He punched the intercom for his secretary. "Get Hartford and Gravello back in here."

"Vinny, how long is your leg going to take to heal?"

"It's not as bad as it looks. I should be okay in a few days."

"Good. As soon as you can walk, the two of you get back down there. Find Dr. Amanda Dixon, find her son Jeremiah Dixon, and find that demented kid. Make them gone. Nobody dead but all of them gone forever. And this time, take Ragnar with you."

20

Speak up, Child

AMANDA BEGGED HER SON not to go back on the reservation land. J.D. was adamant. "There's a chestnut tree, a huge chestnut tree out there. Those aren't supposed to be alive anywhere in this country. Professor Dagget told me, and the text books said, there's not one living specimen of this tree bigger than a sapling that has ever been found except in one park in Georgia, and those are puny. I have to go back and see if there are more. I have to know so I can tell Professor Dagget about it. I'll take Billy with me, if he'll go. I'll be fine. There's a boundary map of the land in the old man's cabin. That should help. We'll be fine. Those men are gone, and I can guarantee you they won't be coming back in any hurry."

Abby said she was going too. So did Junior, but Uncle Albert said if Junior didn't get some work done down at his garage, he was goin' to fire his ass. Marie said, "Junior Benoit, you had better be earning some money to feed your baby. Lord knows, it isn't right for me to have to earn our keep by playing my fiddle."

Grannie Mae smiled at J.D. "It's good for young folks to find out the truths. To know what God's world is made of."

Amanda took Abby aside. She put her hands on her shoulders and said, "Abby, you cannot stay in your house until we all know what those men were doing out there with their guns trying to kidnap or kill Billy. It's too dangerous. Can you stay here with Marie?"

"No," Abby said, "I don't want to be in their way here. They got a little baby, and I got Billy. Maybe I can stay with Jeremiah in the cabin. Oh goodness, Mrs. Dixon, I didn't mean for you to think—"

Amanda interrupted, "That's a very good idea, Abby. You'll be safe there."

The old man's bed was too narrow for two people. It was so perfectly made that neither of them wanted to rumple it. Billy wouldn't come in, but they weren't sure where he was going to sleep, out in the woods or just outside by a window. J.D. spread blankets and sheets and quilts on the floor, and they cuddled up tight. When the night was black and moonless and the cabin dark, J.D. pressed himself against her. She whispered, "Shhhhh," and kissed his lips. She softly rubbed his chest, his belly, and took him in her long fingers and stroked him.

At first light, J.D. lit the gas ring and boiled water. He sliced ham and cheese and cucumbers and set a plate outside the door with a mug of coffee. He dressed and waited for Abby to wake. He checked outside the door, and the plate and cup were empty.

J.D. hadn't noticed the boundary wire before. It wasn't more than a dozen yards into the woods off the side of the cabin. He found the corner of the reservation. They spread the quilt out on a rock. Kneeling shoulder to shoulder, they sketched out a path on the survey map up through the forest to a place near her shack, over across the top of the ridge and back down to the bottom. J.D. pointed to where he thought he'd seen the chestnut tree. It was very close to where a tree square was on the quilt. About a mile up and a half mile in.

"What are these?" Abby asked, tapping the square with

the black circle and the orange mushroom. There were four of them.

"No idea. Let's go find out." He had his rifle, his knife, and a tape measure from Old Man's tool box. All the way up the first pass, they saw nothing. No big trees, no mounds. Just a ten-point buck standing watch on a hillock. Tall, square, magnificent.

When they got to Abby's shack, they went in. Abby looked at the bear traps, shaking her head. "You guys," she mumbled, "are brutal." J.D. took the bear traps and put them behind the outhouse. Abby came out with a cloth bag of food over her shoulder, high leather boots laced up over her blue jeans, a bandana on her head, and her bone-handled knife on her belt. "Better," she said. "Let's go find Billy and your trees."

He pointed off to the south and west. "About a quarter mile that way."

The chestnut tree was bigger than he had thought. It was not more than twenty feet from a burial mound. "We're not supposed to be here, Jeremiah. People are buried here, and their spirits live in this ground, in these trees, in the air. They're here watching us."

"I don't believe in spirits," J.D. said, measuring the circumference of the tree at his shoulder height. He wrote down 198" on the boundary map at the mark he had made for this location. "This is virgin growth, Abby. This tree is at least five hundred years old. They're fairly fast growers like the larch and beech, but to get this big takes a long, long time, and for some reason the blight didn't come here. Why? Why did it skip this place?"

The chestnuts that had begun to fall from the tree in the cool autumn nights were the size of plums, green, spiny, and some split open, ripened from the dampness of the ground. Abby said, "The blight skipped this place because it didn't want to mess with the spirits, that's why."

"I have to do this, Abby. You know that, don't you? We'll be okay as long as we stick together."

The first mound, shown as a green oval on the quilt, was identical in size and shape to the one he had seen by the tree. J.D. had it figured out—exactly how to go from one point to another by taking rough measurements from the quilt and following the sun in the sky. Every once in a while, they would see Billy standing immobile in the woods and watch him dart off. He would always be near a mound when they came upon it. He knew where they all were. He knew what they were looking for. "He'll show us where he lives pretty soon," Abby said. "I know he will." Through the canopy, they caught glimpses of hawks gliding on the rising air, down through the gap. They stopped and watched a black and white woodpecker with a bright red crown rapping on a dead tree. It was as long as J.D.'s forearm. "Pileated woodpecker," he said. "Big bird."

By midday, they had found all eight green oval mounds, and J.D. had marked the locations on the survey map. Throughout the forest, there were stumps of trees that had died decades ago, with small shoots growing out of the roots but no more full-grown chestnut trees. They decided to find the three other black circles. They were near the bottom of the hill, and the three circles were all above them. They began the climb and found the first mound on a flat plateau. It was shaped just like all the others; same size, same curves. There were two massive chestnut trees and three smaller ones. The bark was furrowed, winding up around the trunk in a spiral fashion, the ground again littered with spiny nuts. J.D. measured all of them, writing down the circumference on the map. The largest was over two hundred inches around, five and a half feet in diameter. The next mound was similar. Two big trees, four small ones. Near the top of the ridge, about a half mile down and in from Abby's shack, they found the last mound. There were three huge chestnuts and four smaller ones. Underneath the canopy, below the massive crowns, shielded from the sun and rain, was Billy's lean-to.

J.D. said, "If that boar hadn't attacked that guy yesterday, they would have found this place. They probably wouldn't have found Billy, but they would have known where he lived. Then they could come and get him anytime. Thank God for she-boars."

"You're so right about that, Jeremiah. Thank God for she-boars."

The lean-to was a crude stick roof and two walls. Billy sat inside, cross-legged, watching them both with a blank expression. There was a fire pit made of stones, a bed of leaves and moss with two thick blankets covered by a tarp. A bow, hand whittled, strung with bailing twine, hung on one wall. Four arrows—straight, skinned sticks with blue jay feathers and points sharpened and burnt hard—leaned against the wall. Most of them had blood on them. Squirrel skins were stretched tight and pinned to the wood. A cast iron pot with a stick spoon in it sat on two short iron bars above the fire pit. Outside the shed there was a large pile of green, empty, hollowed out chestnut shells and rodent bones. Abby stirred the pot around and scooped out a spoonful. "He eats squirrels and chestnuts," she said. "Your mom wanted to know that. Except for what I bring him sometimes, like some vegetables, it seems to be nothing but squirrels and chestnuts. That's all." She sat beside Billy, rumpled his hair, and wrapped her arm around him, hugging.

J.D. walked around under the big trees, occasionally stopping to pick up a nut, examine it, and drop it back down, muttering to himself. He pulled out the map and looked at the notations and location of the chestnut trees. "That's odd," he mumbled. "Something's funny about this." He watched a squirrel rummaging around in the leaves, scritching, scratching about with its forepaws, gathering nuts. "That's strange. Why is that? Abby," he said, "I need to go back to the mound we were at before. It's not too far. Let's stick together. Come with me. There's something I need to check out." She nodded, got up, patted Billy on the head, and went off down the hill with J.D.

At the other mound, it was the same. J.D. checked the nuts on the ground. All of them. All around. He began muttering again, walking off to an oak tree and picking up acorns, kicking shells about with his foot. Abby stood next to him and whispered something, pointing up at the mound.

He brushed past her and said, "Don't bother me. I'm thinking. Anyway, I can't hear you when you whisper. If you want me to hear you, speak up."

Abby turned and stared at him as he walked away. Then she ran toward his back and launched herself into him, knocking him down face first in the leaves. She straddled his back and pinned his arms down with her knees and leaned over by his ear. "Don't ever tell me not to whisper. Don't ever tell me that I'm bothering you because I whisper. Don't ever tell me to speak up." She began to sob, and J.D. stopped moving. "Sister Paula told me no one wanted me because I bothered them with my whispering. That's why no one wanted me. I'm out here in this sacred Indian land where nobody ought to be because I want to be with you. I want to help you and be with you. I have nothing in this world but you. Nobody but you and Billy. I don't have a mother like you do or a father or a brother or even a friend except Billy, and there's something really wrong with him. Billy, my only friend, and there's something really, really wrong with him. I don't have anything except you, and I thought you wanted me. I thought I was wanted." She was lying flat down on him now, her face resting on his head. "I thought you wanted me, and then you say, 'Don't whisper, you're bothering me.' Just like Sister Paula. Just like Sister Paula. 'Find a voice,' she said, 'find a voice, and somebody might want you.' Well I found a voice, and now nobody wants me anyway." She got to her knees and struggled up. "And, Jeremiah," she said, standing over him, "what I did for you last night in the dark? I'm not doing that anymore. Go do it yourself!" She walked slowly, shoulders slumped, up the hill.

J.D. rolled over and watched her walking away. He ran after her and put his arms around her, turning her to him, brushing the hair out of her face, and he kissed her and tipped her head back. "I will never say you bother me. Never again. And you can whisper all you want. I'll lean in and listen. I do want you, Abby. I really do. More than that ... I love you." He kissed her forehead, the tears on her cheeks, her eyes.

She put her arms around him, nestled her head into his chest, and said, "Nobody has ever said that to me. In my whole life, nobody ever said that. Do you mean it?"

"Yes, I mean it." They stood, arms wrapped around each other, listening to their breathing, listening to the blood pump in their veins.

"Tell me what you were whispering. I want to hear it. I'll listen."

She waited and waited and then said, "If you tell me you love me one more time, I'll tell you what I said. Just once more."

"Abby," he said, "I love you."

"Okay." Then she whispered, "Cherokees don't put rocks in their burial mounds."

She led him by the hand back to the mound and pointed. "Look, look at that tree root sticking up on top of the mound.

That root has grown out and over something like a big rock. That's not right."

J.D. hesitated and then said, "I have to do this," and climbed up on the mound. He dug around with his fingers. Abby broke a branch from a limb on the ground, sharpened the end with her knife, and tossed it up to him. J.D. dug the dirt away until a corner under the root was showing. It was not a rock. It was concrete under dirt. He dug out a little way straight down the face and brushed the dirt clean. Behind the tapered ends of the mound was a steel plate.

"Jeremiah, you don't need to worry about any spirits up there; this is not a Cherokee burial mound."

J.D. jumped down. "Where's Billy?" he asked. Abby pointed. Billy was standing fifty feet away, watching. "You stay here with Billy. I'm going to run up to your house and get a shovel. And, Abby, look at the chestnuts on the ground. None of them have been eaten by squirrels or pigs or anything. There are no empty shells. The squirrels rummage around and collect the acorns from the oaks. Nothing eats these nuts. Only Billy. And one other thing, these chestnut trees only grow at the mounds that are the black circles with the orange mushrooms on the old man's quilt. Like this one. They don't grow anywhere else out here. They don't grow at the other mounds."

When he got back with the shovel, Abby was standing by the mound with Billy. Billy had a pen and small notebook in his hand. Abby pointed down at the ground. There was a round brass and chrome dial the size of a donut. The dial had markings from 0 to 100. The needle stood at 2. Abby handed J.D. the notebook. On each page, there were four numbers, most were 0, some were 1, a few were 2 or 3.

"That's what Billy is doing with the old man," J.D. said. "He's out in these woods every day writing down the readings on these dials. There are only four each day. Four mounds. The four black circles on the quilt. Abby, you're right. They're not burial mounds. There's something else in them. Something the old man monitors. For someone. Something he wanted me to find by finding the trees."

An hour later, J.D. had shoveled some the dirt from the front of the mound. It was two thick steel doors, hinged at the edges, welded shut in the middle. They went back to all four mounds where the chestnut trees grew and found, at each one, a brass and chrome dial on the side, covered by leaves. J.D. took the sharpened stick and shovel and poked and dug enough to know they all had steel doors. "Let's get out of here," Abby said. "Now we know why the men were here. They know about these, and they don't want us to find out. They were going to take Billy away forever, or kill him."

"Abigail," Amanda said, "you must get Billy out of there. Far enough away so he won't be eating chestnuts. There must be something about them that's causing his disorder, just like my mice, Lupa and Bupa. The same disorder. My guess is that there are chemicals inside those vaults that are leaking into the roots of the chestnut trees. That's why the squirrels won't eat them."

"Mom," J.D. asked, "what kind of chemicals were you working with?"

"Anti-fungal and anti-bacterial developed for agricultural use on grains and trees," she said.

"If that's true and those chemicals are in there, then that's why the trees didn't die in the blight. Their roots are sucking up anti-fungal chemicals. They only grow at those four mounds, nowhere else. How are we going to find out what's in there?"

Amanda raised both hands up. "You're not going to find out. It's too dangerous out there. You're not going back."

Uncle Albert paced back and forth on his porch in front of the others. "If'n those men didn't even want your Billy kid out there, they don't want nobody knowing what's behind them steel doors. Nobody. There ain't nobody going to open them doors. Why would they? That there is supposed to be sacred ground to the Indians. Can you all imagine just what a hullaballoo it would be if'n somebody put chemicals out there without telling the Indians. Without telling nobody. Good God Almighty, there would be one hell of a rumpus. They ain't gonna open those doors all on their own selves. Never gonna happen. But listen up here. Those fellers find out that J.D. here dug it out and knows what all's in there, they'll come to get him. They'll come to get him unless," he held his think finger up, "unless the doors are opened. Then they wouldn't dare do nothin' 'cause they wouldn't have no way of knowin' how many people knew. Problem is, ain't nobody within a hunderd miles would even think about goin' out there, let alone cuttin' open steel doors with God knows what inside. My Jesus, it might just blow up. Explode." He waved his bare, hairy arms around. "Boom!" he shouted. Grannie Mae jumped in her rocker, and a bit of tobacco juice squirted down her chin.

J.D. and Junior looked at each other and said the same thing at the same time. "Little Dickey."

"Excuse us, Uncle Albert and Billy. Excuse us, ladies, but we got some work to do." They got in Junior's truck and drove to the phone in Albert's garage.

"How we going to pay him?" Junior asked. "He's going to want some money. Lose two days of work and all, he's going to want some money."

"I know where there's a lot of money," J.D. said. "I can borrow some. Let's offer him twice what he normally makes. Let's offer him twenty bucks an hour, including driving time. He'll do it."

21

Lil' Dickey's Rig

LITTLE DICKEY'S RIG was a red, dual wheeled one-ton '64 ford with boxes on both sides of the bed. Between the boxes were tall, steel tanks of oxygen and acetylene, each canister chained upright in a rubber-wheeled dolly. There were hoses, an arc welder, metal saw horses, bar clamps, C-clamps, pry bars, a big anvil, a little anvil, and a giant vise bolted to the bumper. In the boxes were gauges, welding heads, cutting heads, tips, sockets, ratchets, grinders, hack saws, ten different kinds of hammers, pliers, screwdrivers, and a collection of old *Playboys*. On the roof was a flashing yellow light, and on the front bumper was black and white sign that said *Lil' Dickey*.

Dickey eased into Uncle Albert's Garage, pulled up to the Texaco pump, and said to the boy, "Fill 'er up. Put her on Junior's tab. Where is he?" He had an unlit Camel cigarette hanging out of the side of his mouth, the pack rolled up in the sleeve of his T-shirt, and a three-day growth of beard. The boy stood there scratching at a pimple. "I said where is he?" The boy pointed into the lift bay and jumped to the gas cap.

"Hey, Junior, what the fuck's going on down here?" Dickey said, slapping the fender of the car Junior was working on. "Must be pretty near knock-off time. It's Friday night for chrissake. Anywhere we can get a beer around here so you can tell me what the fuck I'm supposed to be doing? Let's go, come on, it's Friday night." He slapped the fender again.

The Roaring Gap Saloon was packed. Skinny Binkins' boy was there hobbling around on crutches, a cast on his leg, blathering about how he stepped in a bear trap. Junior bought him a beer, put him on a stool, took his crutches, spun the stool, spun it again, and grabbed him on the chin when he came around. "Now you just shut your mouth, okay?"

"My daddy's on to you two. Your dickhead friend left me at the hospital to get this here cast put on and took my truck away. My daddy come in with those two men, one of 'em stuck rat in the leg by a pig. I had to ride home with 'em, and my daddy, the miserable fuckin' prick, my daddy beat me half to death with a stick. Cocksucker. I hate that man."

Dickey, Junior, and J.D. found a booth in the corner. Jimmy the bartender brought them each a Pabst, and Junior told him to keep them coming until closing time. "Got a lot to talk about, Jimmy. Lot of catchin' up to do," he said.

"So let me get this straight," Dickey said, draining his fourth beer, "you two jerk-offs want me to go out in the forest where it's against the law to go and there are Indian bones all buried out there, and even the Indians won't go there 'cause the place is spooked. And you want me to drag hundred-pound tanks and hoses two miles down a hill, just stopping along the way to cut open inch-thick steel doors that just might have dynamite or poisonous gas and shit behind them, and then, if my ass hasn't already been blown to Kingdom Come, then, quick like a bunny, I'm spossed to hop on out of there before two evil motherfuckers or the sheriff catches me. That about sum it up?"

"Jesus, Dickey, I always known you was a fuckin' genius. Smart too. You nailed that right on the head. Hey, Jimmy!" Junior yelled. "Gettin' a little dry over here!" Binkins hobbled over on his way out and put a mason jar of moonshine on their table. J.D. gave him a ten.

All three had ridden up the hill in the front seat of Dickey's rig. The other two trucks were down below at the old man's cabin. All three had massive hangovers: dry-mouth, the shakes, tunnel vision, four cups of coffee, and the runs. J.D. stuffed a roll of toilet paper from Abby's outhouse in his Guatemalan food bag, considered getting food from her shack, but the thought of it made some hot bile creep up his throat. After they humped the tanks on their dollies out of the bed of the truck and coiled the hoses, J.D. shuffled off a few feet, knelt down, and barfed all over the driveway. He wiped his mouth with a wad of toilet paper, and Dickey grabbed the roll from him and waddled off into the bushes. Junior took a can of Budweiser from the truck, cracked it open, drained it in gulps, crushed the can, threw it in the woods, and yelled, "Come on, you pussies, let's do this thing."

They roped a gallon jug of water and two shovels onto one canister, another gallon jug and a four-foot-long pry bar onto the other, and Dickey, wearing his leather apron, gloves stuck in his back pocket, looped the hoses over his shoulder, carrying the cutter head, gauges, and mask. Junior took the oxygen tank, J.D. the acetylene. Getting under the wire was a problem. They had to lower the tanks flat on the ground and, on their hands and knees, push them forward. They were heavy. Each one, with the dolly, shovels or pry bar and chains, weighed as much as they did. The wheels were made for asphalt, not rocks, leaves, and sticks. The first vault was a quarter mile away. It took all their strength to keep the tanks from rolling away downhill or pitching over sideways at lumps in the ground. Here and there were swales where they had to get in front of the tank and pull it up a hill, pulling against gravity with their heels dug in. "If that acetylene gets away and crashes into a rock and blows, our little honeys will be out here a month searching for all our body parts," Dickey said. He hung way back so he could smoke.

Halfway there, Junior dropped his tank, fell to the ground, and started wriggling around on the ground like a split-open snake, screaming, "Cramp, cramp, my leg, I got a cramp in my leg! Ow! Ow! Fuckin' Charlie horse! Oh my fuckin' word my leg, I'm dyin' out here, I need water. Christ, I can't breathe!"

J.D., slowly, dully, untied a jug of water they had brought to put out fire from the torches. Junior drank and drank and poured some over his head, stretched his leg and pounded his thigh, got up and danced in place, a boxer's dance, jabbing at the air. "All right, I'm good, let's go."

The first mound they came to was where Billy had his camp. Billy wasn't there. He was with Abby and Amanda down in Fat Gap. The old hound dog had taken such a liking to him, always lying at his feet with his jowls on the porch boards, old eyes looking up at Billy, that they decided Billy should stay there until all this "rumpus," as Uncle Albert called it, blew over. Everything was how J.D. and Abby had left it two days ago. Dickey took his leather apron off and sat on the stump by Billy's fire pit and watched J.D. and Junior shovel the dirt away from the front of the mound. They were stripped to the waist and drenched in sweat. When they got halfway down, Dickey said, "Hold it, boys. You said the top was concrete, right? I think I want to cut the top half of the door free while all this dirt is still on the bottom half. That way, if she's going to blow, she'll blow the top off instead of blowing the doors right back at us. I got a better chance of not getting killed. Level out that dirt so I got a flat place to stand and cut me a notch off to the side to set the tanks on. The hoses will reach ten feet. Cut it right here." He pointed to a spot on the slope. "Cut it square and level. Then take one of your shirts and wipe the center of the door down clean so I can see the joint." He began to unchain the tanks from the dollies and fit the hoses to the cylinders. When J.D. and Junior were done, he took off his shirt. "Whenever I ride my Bultacco up the face of a dam, I do it bare-chested. I don't know why, but that's how I've always done it. Die with your boots on and your shirt off, I guess. I'm going to do this one just like that." He cinched his belt a notch tighter on his blue jeans and put the apron back on. He put on his welder mask, flipped up so he could see, put the strike-starter in his back pocket, and climbed up the face of the dirt. Standing on the level spot, the top of the steel doors about chest high, he said, "Okay, wiggle both those valves a little this way and that to make sure they aren't stuck. Both of them. Then tell what the gauges say."

Junior fiddled with the valves and said, "Fifty-two on the oxygen, five on the acetylene."

"Close down the oxygen till it's forty, open up the acetylene to eight."

Junior turned the valves a little bit, a little bit, a little bit and said, "Got it, forty and eight."

Dickey put on the gloves, flipped down the mask, turned open the brass knurled knobs on the cutting head, and said, "Tell Marlene I love her." He struck the strike-starter right at the end of the cutting tip, and a yellow-blue flame shot out, a foot long. He turned one knob down until the gas was bluish and eight inches. He pulled the cutting head lever, and the flame honed shorter, brighter—6,000 degrees of bright blue heat hissing like an angry cat.

As the flame moved slowly up and down the first few inches of the door joint, the steel turned orange and then red, morphing from a solid to a liquid, flowing like lava, and Dickey shouted "We're going in!" and squeezed the oxygen blast lever, and the flame blew the molten steel into the vault. He shut off the torch, flicked his mask up, and stood waiting. He put his ear near the hole, then his nose. "Stinks in there, but nothin' popped. Nothin's burning. I think we're all right." He re-lit the flame and started heating and cutting the doors apart, all the way down to the dirt. He heated the hinges on the sides to free the post from the sleeve. They moved the tanks, and J.D. and Junior shoveled, casting the dirt out and back in a semi-circle. They reset the tanks, wiped down the doors, and Dickey, starting again chest-high, heated and blew, heated and blew the steel all the way down to the bottom. It was a clean cut, straight and pencil wide. A stench wafted out, pungent, acrid, chloric.

They shoveled all the dirt away as far as the door was wide, and J.D. fit the tang end of the pry bar into the gap, set his feet into scuffed-out divots in the ground, breathed deep, and pushed on the bar with everything he had. The hinge pins squealed as the door moved. Junior grabbed the edge and pulled, and J.D. set his body on the other door and pushed until it was wide open. All three pulled the other door open and stood staring at a sinister mass of boxes and barrels, the floor dripping with yellow-green ooze. In front were dozens of tall, narrow, square red boxes. In black letters on each box was painted: ! DANGER ! — Radioactive Materials – Do Not Move — ! DANGER !

Roots of the chestnut trees had busted through the concrete floor slab and humped up into the goo on the floor of the vault. "Shhhhh. Shut up, listen," Dickey said. "Listen ... you hear that? What's that clicking noise?"

"That clicking is coming from back there," Junior said, leaning forward, head cocked with his hand to his ear. "Back over there," he said, pointing to the side of the vault, midway back.

J.D. started shoveling dirt on the floor, covering up the

ooze. "I'm going in around the side."

"You're fucking nuts," Dickey said. "You touch that stuff, and you'll turn into a giant mutant. Like a four-hundred-pound beetle or something."

J.D. shoveled in a dirt path all the way around the red boxes. He threw the shovel back out and stood immobile. The barrels, rusted and leaking, had painted labels, one entirely readable. "Holy shit, these barrels say: ! DANGER ! – Biochemical Hazard – Do Not Move — ! DANGER !

"There's a little box down here that's making that ticking sound. It's attached to the back of one of the red boxes. One of the boxes marked Radioactive." He slowly backed up, backed away, staying on the dirt, careful not to touch anything, then turned and sprinted twenty feet to a rock and sat down. "I think I'm beginning to understand what's going on here. We have to open the other three doors. We have to do it today, now." He pulled out his map and pointed through the trees. "That way," he said.

They re-chained the tanks and shovels to the dollies and set off at a quicker pace this time. Careful but purposeful. They found the second mound and began the process exactly as before. Shirts off, sweat, level platform, notch for tanks, and doors wiped clean. Junior rechecked the pressure, made a minor adjustment, and said, "Eight and forty. Ready." The torch began to melt the steel. The oxygen blast blew it in. Same stench, same clean line. Same heat to the hinges to free them up. They shoveled out the rest of the dirt, graded it clean, and cut to the bottom. The doors swung open, and the contents were identical. J.D. shoveled in dirt to a path and checked the red boxes. Exactly like the first mound. Same ticking.

After the third vault was open, Dickey was done. It was late afternoon, and they hadn't had any food all day. The water jugs were empty. Each one of them had puked at least once, but their bowels had firmed up. They still had a little bit of toilet paper left. The third vault was the same as the other two, and he was sure the fourth one would be the same. J.D. asked Dickey how much money they had promised to pay him, and Dickey said, including the drive back home, if they left now, they'd be into it 440 bucks at twenty bucks an hour. J.D. said if he opened the forth vault, he'd pay him six hundred; if he didn't, he wouldn't pay him a cent.

"You're a prick, Dixon. You know that? A first-class prick." J.D. flicked his ear and blinked at him. They chained everything up and made their way down to the last vault. The going was easier because the tanks were getting emptier, lighter. When they began to shovel, the sun had passed beyond the forest canopy and only filtered through the tree trunks in soft, thin rays. "This door has been cut open before and then welded back shut," Dickey said. "There are two joints." By the time the cut to the bottom of the doors had been made, it was dusk and getting hard to see. A moon had risen, and the forest was bathed in a gray iridescence. They pried the doors open. Junior jumped back, falling down, screaming, "Jesus Christ!" J.D. backed away, making grunting noises.

Dickey stood there agape, arms hanging at his sides, then grabbed a dolly and threw a tank onto it. "Just like I said, I'm going to hop like a fucking bunny right the fuck out of this place. Right now!" Leaning up against the front of the red, radioactive boxes, stained green from the ooze, were three skeletons sitting in a row, their empty eye holes staring at the boys. Each skeleton had a hole the size of a bullet in the center of the forehead.

They scrambled. J.D. kicked a shin bone with a foot attached to it out into the leaves and then pushed both doors shut and shoveled some dirt in front of them. Chains, tanks, hoses, they grabbed them all, and J.D. checked the whole area to make sure they hadn't left a single thing that might identify who they were, wrapped the bone in his shirt, grabbed his dolly, and ran, bouncing and lurching after Junior and Dickey who were at nearly a full-bore run out of the woods. "That way!" he screamed. "More to your left! Go left!"

At the cabin, they heaved the equipment and the wrapped leg bone into the back of J.D.'s truck. J.D. dashed inside and grabbed the envelope full of money out of the Bible. Dickey got into Junior's truck, and Junior said, "Dickey, I'm really sorry, but when I get to the end of this driveway, I'm turning right and driving out of this state into North Carolina, and I'm not coming back. You'll have to ride with Dixon. He's got your money. Sorry, man, I got to go. This is bad shit. Bomb stuff. Dead people. Bad shit." Dickey got out, and Junior spun dirt, squealed over the bridge, down the driveway, onto the Cherokee Road and off to Fat Gap.

Dickey got in J.D.'s truck and started pounding on the door panel through the open window.

"Dixon, for chrissake, let's go!" J.D. stuck the stick back in the hasp, aligned the notches, and sprinted to his truck.

At Abby's, they backed the trucks up, tailgate to tailgate, and slid the tanks and equipment into the red Ford. Dickey slammed his tailgate shut and stuck out his palm. J.D. gave him six crisp, new, one-hundred-dollar bills. Dickey said, "Dixon, don't you ever forget this. This is real important. I was never here. Never seen this place." He stuffed the bills in his shirt pocket, gave J.D. a soft punch on the shoulder, and drove off, leaving J.D. staring down into the sacred ground, wondering how this all possibly could have happened.

22

Chewed Off By a Murderer

THE OFFICES OF THE UNITED STATES MARSHALS SERVICE were located on the top floor of a brand-new, glass and steel federal courthouse in downtown Houston, Texas. Deputy Marshal Daniel Wentworth was third in charge of a twenty-man force. The US Marshal for the Southern District of Texas was John Wilson, a thirty-five-year veteran who wouldn't retire. He wasn't seventy yet, so he didn't have to, but more than that, he had nothing to do to if he did. No wife, no kids, didn't play golf, and didn't want to do anything except catch bad guys. He had been on the force at the tail end of the FBI's assault on bank robbers in the thirties, and almost all of the robbers were fugitives from justice in one way or another. That gave Wilson jurisdiction in their apprehension. He never stood in the way of Hoover's guys making the arrest, but he was always there to take custody of the reprobate when the newspapers took their pictures and wrote their stories. He still wore a loaded gun on his belt, every day, all day while he sat at his desk in his office reading newspapers. Dan Wentworth's immediate superior, the chief deputy marshal, was Jane Hightower, the highest ranking woman in the service. President Kennedy had appointed her the day before he died in Dallas. She had been with the Texas Rangers in charge of the detail guarding the governor's wife and children. She didn't wear a gun. She didn't need to. Her father, a Louisiana politician, had raised her on bourbon and alligator meat.

"Chief," Dan Wentworth said, "I need to take a few vacation days. I have a friend in Virginia that's in some trouble and needs a little help. I wrapped up the Magbie and Hughes abduction case and have some time coming. I'll spend the next day or two here, on my own time, Chief, doing some research and then head east for a week or so. That okay with you?"

"Sure," she said. "Sounds fine."

Jane Hightower knew that Dan Wentworth, at least according to her best friend in the Dallas FBI office, spent his off-time camping, fishing, hunting, and having a twenty-year love affair with his brother's wife. "She's pretty," he had said, moving his hands in an hourglass shape. "Redhead. Smart, too. PhD."

"Have a good time, and, Dan, don't do anything I wouldn't do."

"Chief, I truly hope to do a few things I know you wouldn't do."

Wentworth confirmed that the office central fax machine, a fifty-pound beast in the center of the secretarial pool, was available to receive documents. He checked his notes from the conversation with Amanda and then called the headquarters of the FBI in Washington and asked if they could please send him any information on Robert John Hartford or Vincent R. Gravello. An hour later, documents came through. Bingo. There was an outstanding arrest warrant from ten years ago for a Robert J. Hartford issued by the federal district court in Fargo for failure to appear on charges of aiding and abetting in an assault on a tribal police officer and criminal trespass on Sioux Indian Lands in North Dakota. He had been identified by a second tribal police officer a mile away who had taken down the license plate number of the speeding car with two occupants as it left the reservation. A police sketch accompanied the warrant with a visual description of Hartford given by an employee of Western Rental Car. The employee hadn't seen the second man. Hartford had used an Ohio driver's license to rent the car. No such number had been issued by the State of Ohio, and the trail went dead. Gravello was wanted on six outstanding state warrants, all in California. Five pertained to illegal distribution of controlled substances, and one was for fraudulent representation in the procurement of a license to practice as a pharmacist. He called the California Registration Board and yes, they did have a photo of Mr. Gravello as part of his original application, and they would fax it right away.

Wentworth called the Bureau of Indian Affairs. No person by either name had ever worked for the agency. The same was true for Texas Child Welfare Protection Agency. He called International Chemical and was transferred to the office of Mr. Fred Britton, Director of Personnel. He said he was a college buddy of Bob Hartford and was trying to track him and his friend down for a college reunion back east in southern Virginia. He heard they were working there. It took the secretary two minutes to tell him neither of those people worked in any capacity for International Chemical. The corporation did not have any records showing contracts for work in anywhere in Virginia.

The Child Welfare Protection Agency did have a list of all orphanages in the state. There were six, three operated by the Catholic Church. After checking with their main office in Austin, he was given the name and number of a Father Bruno, Vicar Apostolic of the Texas Panhandle.

"I do not intercede in the operations of those facilities. You will have to ask the Mothers Superior themselves. Thank you and God bless you." When reminded that he was speaking with a federal marshal, the Vicar went silent. Then in a tremulous, shaky voice, he said, "That would be the Wolf River Orphanage run by Sister Francine. I do remember something about two children being given into adoption to that reservation you mentioned. And please, Officer Wentworth, could you please keep this conversation private. That information is, how should I say, it's, it's a secret." The man sounded downright terrified of this Mother Francine.

It was a twelve-hour drive from Houston to the orphanage near Wolf River Canyon in Ochiltree County. Wentworth decided to make it two days or he would arrive in the middle of nowhere in the middle of the night with no motels within fifty miles. International Chemical was located in downtown Dallas just off Highway 45. The answer he had been given about Hartford and Gravello had been quick and perfunctory. Not enough time to even check any files. He would have a look around and see if he could shake anything out.

The building was a three-story concrete structure with dozens of small windows, like gun ports. A high chain link fence ran around the entire property, and the entrance was gated with a guard post. Wentworth did not want his arrival announced. He clipped his "Star in a Circle" pin on his shirt pocket, took his .38 revolver from the glove compartment, and slid it in his holster. He pulled up and immediately got out of his car and met the uniformed, armed guard face on at the gate. "Do you have an appointment?" the guard asked.

Wentworth pulled his badge out, lifted it up face high, a foot in front of the man, and said, "United States Marshal's Service. We do not make appointments. Open the gate and do not announce my presence. That just might constitute obstruction of justice. Am I clear?"

The guard looked at his cowboy boots, blue jeans, and denim work shirt, then his wallet badge, his shirt badge, and his gun. "Affirmative, sir. Covert. I understand." Wentworth asked if there was another security station inside the front entry.

"Yes, sir," the guard said.

"Call them and tell them to let me through when I get there. Same drill—just let me through. No questions, no calls."

The guard gave a short snap of a salute. "Ten-four, will do, sir." He slid the gate open.

The two internal security guards also saluted as he came through the front doors. They were both in their late twenties, and, like the guard at the gate, had the young, the eager, the scrubbed, and clipped looked of army privates. "Where is Mr. Fred Britton's office?" Wentworth asked.

They directed him to the elevator, third floor, left at the end of the corridor. "But I'm sorry, sir, he left about an hour ago, and his secretary's out sick. Don't know if anybody's up there."

"Good," said Wentworth.

The girl sitting at Mr. Britton's secretary's desk was a young, plump, coiffed girl in her twenties. She wore glasses with rhinestones set in the upper pointed corners and had a chatty sense of humor, even when being confronted by a federal marshal. "I don't know much," she said. "I'm just sitting in for Brenda. She's sick today. I usually work in the car pool office. You know, signing cars in and out and setting up rentals." She touched the badge Wentworth was still holding out, running her finger over it. "Wow," she said, "you're those guys who ride horses and never say anything."

Wentworth figured that was a great image and he'd stick with it. He laid the drawing of Hartford and the photo of Gravello on her desk and tapped his finger on them, saying nothing. "Sure," she said, "that's Bob McCoy and Vinny Stoner. Lousy drawing of Bob, no offense of course, but it makes him look like a porcupine." She giggled.

Dan Wentworth decided to keep it going this way. She looked up at him, and he raised his eyebrows and pointed his finger right and left. "Oh, no, they wouldn't be here now; they only show up here every couple of months." She smiled at Vinny's photo. "Good looking, isn't he? He always brings me a gift and takes me out." Wentworth raised his eyebrows again. "Don't get me wrong; he's not married. Me either. He's just really nice. Likes to have a good time."

"Known him a long time?"

"Oh yes. When I was a little girl, I used to watch him at church on Sundays. He was one of the altar boys at Saint Paul's. He always looked so tall and handsome in his white robe."

"What work do they do here?"

Some alarm bell finally went off inside her. She pushed the pictures back to him across the desk top and said, "I really shouldn't be talking to you. I'm just a fill-in, and Mr. Britton's not here. I don't know anything anyway, so, I don't mean to be rude, but could you please go now? Maybe you could come back when Mr. Britton's here. What did you say your name was?" She picked up a pencil and pulled a notepad to her.

"I didn't."

Wentworth placed a collect call to Washington from a pay phone on the street and asked for any information the FBI had on McCoy and Stoner. "Call back in three or four hours," they said. He knew that distances in Texas were not measured in time but by how many cans of beer it takes to get from one place to another. He didn't drink when he drove, but he figured it had to be at least a six-pack, probably two, from Dallas to the northern edge of Ochiltree County. He arrived at the orphanage in the afternoon. The buildings and gardens, the trees rising up out of the enclosed center courtyard, were like an oasis in a desolate land. A fertile touch of brightness in a place owned by the scorpions, rattlesnakes, buzzards, and sagebrush. Mother Francine answered the door when he rang the bell. He showed his identification, and she let him in. "You look more like a roughneck than a policeman," she said, touching his elbow and leading him into a sitting room off the entry.

"Same thing, Sister, same breed."

When he showed her the drawing and photograph, she said, "Yes, those two men used to come here twice a year to check on the numbers of children who had come in, remained in, or had been placed out. They were from the Child Welfare Protection Agency."

"Did they ever show you their identification?"

"Yes, the first few times they showed me their cards and driver's licenses. I wouldn't have talked to them at all if they hadn't. Why do you ask?"

"What, Sister, do you mean, 'wouldn't have talked to them at all.'"

"Well, Marshal Wentworth, not just anybody can drop in and ask for that information. But they were from that agency, and all they would ask me for were the numbers of children coming and going, as I said. They never asked me the names or anything about specific children. I always gave them the numbers because that information is reachable in the public domain with any formal request. I'm not permitted to withhold it. It always struck me as odd that they drove all the way here to ask me those questions instead of simply sending a request from the agency."

"If you had received a request from the agency, would you have forwarded any and all information requested?"

"No, only the numbers. Any request that involves a child's name, or where they might have been placed by adoption, requires an official letter on the agency's letterhead bearing the director's signature on the agency's raised seal stamp. Also odd to me was that if they were interested in a specific child, why didn't they bring me a sealed letter with that request?"

"I am going to try to ask these questions in such a way as not to compromise your legal obligations, but at some point that may get tough."

"Marshal, I am not afraid of tough. Look around at where we live and what we do. None of my sisters are afraid of tough. If I can answer the question, I will; if not, I won't. Please, go on."

"Do you think they were actually interested in a certain child?"

"I always had the feeling they were because they seemed most interested in a certain age."

"If you felt that it was a certain age, how old might that child be now? Can you say?"

"Surely. I would guess the child to be somewhere around twenty or twenty-two years old."

"Okay, Sister, I'm going to cut to the chase here. I believe those men were not associated in any way with Child Welfare Protection Services, and I believe that they were not the people they said they were. Their names were not Hartford and Gravello. And I believe they may have been looking after, if you will, or better said, following, a particular child. I don't have any idea why or what their interest was, but a possible connection has come up. They couldn't ask you directly because, without the official letter, you wouldn't tell them, and if they had given you a letter, real or fraudulent, you would have called the agency headquarters to verify it. And you would not have asked Father Bruno to do that, would you?"

"Oh dear," said Mother Francine, "you certainly have me pegged, don't you? I think I'll get myself a glass of lemonade. Would you like one?"

"You don't happen to have a beer, do you?"

"You're a very funny man, Marshal."

"Thank you," he said. "Do you have a phone I could use?" She pointed across the room. While she was out, he called his contact at the FBI. In three minutes, he had the information he needed on McCoy and Stoner. Both wanted, both unmarried. She returned from the kitchen with a glass of lemonade and a cold Lone Star beer.

"Good old Mr. Pops, our gardener, still puts in a full day of work, but he drinks a bit. I'm sure he won't mind."

Dan Wentworth cracked open his beer, took a long swig, and smiled at Mother Francine. He could feel an intense strength in her and not a strength born solely from her devotion to her Lord. She has seen the hard side of life, he thought: the dirt, the stench, the rawhide. And she has chosen to take care of children out in a dangerous and forsaken place with no men around, except, he took another swig, good old Mr. Pops.

"The connection between these two men and your orphanage centers around two children, both of whom, it seems, we're not certain, but it seems were here during the time those men made their visits. You, or possibly one of your sisters, are the only ones who could make a possible association between the children and those men. I am here to ask you to travel east with me to Virginia to see these children and hopefully see these men and verify the connection. We can't tie it together without a statement from someone who knows what all four persons look like. Someone who can recognize and identify all of them. Will you do it?"

"It is absolutely impossible for me to leave here for any

length of time."

"Four days?" he asked.

"Not possible."

"Sister, your children may be in grave danger. I can't help them without you helping me."

"Who, Marshal Wentworth, are these children?"

"One is a young boy, probably seventeen or so. He's called Billy, and he has some kind of psychiatric disorder. That's all I know about him except that two men, and likely these two men, are trying to either kidnap or kill him. The other is a girl about twenty or twenty-two. She doesn't know how old she is. She was apparently found on your doorstep in a box, burned and wrapped up. Her name is Abigail." Sister Francine pushed herself back in her chair and didn't say a word.

"Sister, I don't expect you to say anything. I would prefer it if you didn't. This is not an official federal investigation. Yet. It may become one. But until then, you shouldn't tell me anything that violates your legal obligation of confidentiality. I am aware that both of these children were adopted into families on the Big Flats Cherokee Reservation. I am also aware that that is likely a violation of state law. I am a federal officer, and I don't care about state law. To me, I would guess you did that to protect these children from becoming wards of the state, kicked around from foster home to foster home. I truly respect that. But right now, a young man I am very fond of seems to have fallen in love with Abigail, and Abigail has been nurturing and protecting this Billy fellow for three years. All three of those young people are directly in harm's way, and they don't know it. Both of the men spent six years in Folsom Prison for attempted murder. One is currently wanted for assault on a police officer, the other for drug violations. Will you help me?"

Mother Francine said, "Father Bruno has irritated me."

She left the room. She came back with another nun. "Yes, Marshal, Sister Valentine will travel east with you. She knows those men, and she knows the children. God bless you and please protect them from harm." She put her hand on his shoulder and asked, "What happened to your ear?"

"It got chewed off by a drunken murderer in a bar outside El Paso."

"That's what I thought," she said. "You can sleep in Mr. Pops' room. He's off in Lubbock." Her robes swirled in a queenly fashion as she swept out the door and down the hall.

Wentworth turned to Sister Valentine. "Is your Mother Superior always funny like that?"

The sister had a little knit to her brow. Her eyes took in his boots, empty gun holster, pin badge, long wavy hair, all six feet three inches of him, and settled on the little flap of an ear lobe, mouthing the words, "Chewed off by a murderer."

"Yes, Sister, it was a perfectly good ear, but he chewed it off while he was hugging me. I don't know for sure, but maybe he was drunk and hungry."

She squinted and scrunched up her nose. "I am not sure I believe you. Did the Mother say your first name was Marshal?"

"If she did, she was wrong. My name is Dan. I am, however, a federal marshal, hence, Marshal Wentworth."

"Oh my goodness," Sister Valentine said. "Now I understand. Yesterday I was in the office, and a phone call came for a man named Marshal Wentworth. I told the woman nobody with that name was here or had been here. She left a message. I am so sorry I didn't tell Mother Francine. It didn't seem important. I didn't realize it was for a policeman. Shall I get it for you?" She clasped her hands in front of her robe, bit her lower lip, and blinked her blue eyes.

"Yes, Sister, I would appreciate that."

She scooted out of the room, giving him a wide berth, her

head tipped down, mumbling to herself, "Murderer chewed his ear off."

The message said, *Call Jane Hightower immediately. Very important.* It listed her home phone number. "Excuse me, Sister Valentine, but I need to make a confidential call on this phone."

"Dan," his boss said, "you didn't tell me or anybody else where you were going, so I really couldn't find you. But the day you left, I got a somewhat frantic call from Amanda Dixon. She said it was very dangerous there in a place called ... hang on, let me find it ... in a place called Dengman Gap, near Galax, Virginia. The boys, she said, I don't know which boys, she didn't say, but 'the boys' found vaults of biochemical and nuclear waste stored on an Indian burial ground, and there were skeletons of people with what looked like bullet holes in their heads in one of the vaults. Dan, what is going on here?"

"Chief, I didn't know any of that. I only knew there were people trying to kidnap or kill a young disabled boy who is a friend of my nephew. That's all I knew. I have found out since the men are both ex-cons and both federal fugitives. This sounds really bad. Amanda doesn't exaggerate."

"Your nephew, Dan? She said to tell you to please get there as soon as possible and that you won't be able to reach her because she and Jeremiah Dixon will be up at the Skinner Bluff Lunatic Asylum, back in two days. Dan, what is this about?"

"I don't know any more than you do. She said I won't be able to reach her?"

"That's what she said. And she said it purposefully. She sounds very nice, very smart, and very scared. When are you going to get there?"

"Tomorrow at two I fly into Roanoke with a nun from this

orphanage. She knows the kids, and she knows the men who are trying to harm them. She can ID all of them. I should be in Galax by six."

"Okay, Dan, here's what it is. Mrs. Dixon and her son, Jeremiah, will be back in town by then. You get there and find out if any of this is true. By 0800 the next morning, you call me. If it is true, I'm calling in the chief marshal in Washington. They take over. You get off the case. Too close, way too close. Oh, she also gave me some advice."

"Shit. Okay, what advice did my sister-in-law give you?"

Jane Hightower laughed. "She advised me not to call the Bureau of Indian Affairs. She assumes they're in with whatever is happening. She sounds really nice, and the FBI says she's a real pretty redhead. Take care of yourself. There will be a car for you at the airport. Get the keys from airport security. Call tomorrow, 0800."

"Chief, is there any agency in charge of who puts chemicals where?"

"Not that I've ever heard of, but, Deputy, I am not concerned with that. What I am concerned with is skeletons with bullet holes in their heads. Tomorrow morning, 0800." The line went dead.

At eight in the morning, Uncle Danny, Deputy US Federal Marshal, and Valentine O'Shea, Sister of the Order of Sacred Hearts, boarded a plane in Amarillo bound for Roanoke, Virginia.

23

At the Nut House

DOWN AT THE CAMPING AREA Junior had cleared for transient fiddlers, Amanda and J.D. sat on a log at the edge of the creek, shoeless with their pants rolled up and their feet in the cool water. It was still, and a warm thick mist hung in the air, mixed with the oak and beech smoke from Granny Mae's cook stove. The creek gurgled around rocks and by the rough edges at the banks. Amanda was telling her son, slowly, her words raw and burnt, that William Wentworth III was not his father. That he had married Amanda when she was twenty-two for the sole purpose of diverting attention away from his perversities so that suspicions wouldn't arise that might jeopardize his tenure at the university. They slept in separate bedrooms, and he never touched her, even on their wedding night, except for a fleeting pat here or there when they had company or were out in public. She had no more tears for herself; those dried up years ago. She only had tears for her son and tears for Everett, a young graduate student whose mind and life had been ruined by Professor Wentworth. She couldn't bring herself to tell J.D. the specific details of the horrific accident, just that it happened at a motel frequented by people having sex for money or favors. Favors, she said, that's what he traded. A master's degree where the poor boy would have gotten one anyway. He was a brilliant student of geology, almost finished with his thesis on the disposal of nuclear waste.

The creek bubbled, and the mist thinned from the rising sun. J.D. began whittling a stick, waiting for his mother to go on. She had told him only half a story, but she seemed content to sit in silence and watch the water and the trees, to smell the air. He could hear Abby and Marie laughing on the porch. Somewhere far out in the gap, Sunday morning church bells rang. "Mom?" he whispered. She pulled her feet up out of the water and leaned back on outstretched arms. She described the lunatic asylum and what Everett looked like and how deep his psychosis was. That it wasn't likely he would ever recover enough to lead an independent life. She had called the asylum the day she got here and made an appointment to see Everett. She went to see him every few months because ... because ... because, she really didn't know why well enough to put it into words, but it was something she had to do. The appointment was for today, this afternoon, and she wished that J.D. would go with her to see him. She had told Everett all about him and Abby and Billy. "The poor lad had said he would love to meet you and—how did he put it?—talk about trees or something real, not all inside out." Amanda told J.D. where Everett was and that the name, Skinner Bluff, was the same name the man had said when he threatened Junior. She thought there was some connection between that place and this place, and maybe J.D. could figure it out if he went with her. She talked about Billy and, if her research had any validity to it, he might start to become normal again in some weeks or months. The roots of the chestnut trees, drinking up insecticides, making them impervious to blight, might have caused the nuts to have the same combination of chemicals that she was experimenting with. Might, she said. She didn't know, and she began to ramble on about what a delightful girl Abby was, how she and

Marie were becoming fast friends.

"Mom?"

She waited, looking up at the clearing sky, and told him they must be back here tonight so they could see Uncle Danny, who was flying here maybe tomorrow morning to help figure out what has happened in the burial ground. "Uncle Danny," she told her son, "is my true love. He is not your uncle, he is your father." J.D. threw the stick he was whittling into the creek and watched it wiggle and skip its way down through the little rapids. She put her arm around his shoulder and squeezed. "I hope when this sinks in, you're happy about it. Dan Wentworth is a strong and wonderful man."

"Uncle Danny? My father? Does he know?"

"No, he doesn't. If he did, he wouldn't live in Texas. I'm sorry it took so long for me to tell you, but in all these years, it has never seemed to be the right time. Once you really grew up and started being your own person and spending lots of your time outdoors, you seemed at peace with yourself and the world. It seemed like you didn't need to know. That it would just confuse things. But now you're going to need him. You're going to need his strength, and I can't be with both of you without you knowing and without him knowing. I wouldn't be able to look at you two together at the same time." J.D. smelled bacon cooking at the house and heard the piglets' frenzied squeal when Uncle Albert dumped their slop in the trough.

"No, J.D., he doesn't know, but yesterday when I talked to his boss, a woman named Jane Hightower, I got a strong feeling that she knew. I'm sure of it. She asked how you were holding up, and I said you seemed to be doing well, and she said, 'Well he certainly comes from strong stock, doesn't he?' Those people, policemen, make it their business to know everything about everybody except themselves." She stood up and ruffled his hair. "He's a wonderful man, your father is.

We'll see him tomorrow if all goes well."

"So it's true about my ear? That's where I got it, right?"

"Yes, that's where you got it. From your father."

"From Uncle Danny. I think I'll always call him Uncle Danny. Anything else would be strange, like Dad, or Daddy, or Father, or Dan, or who knows what? My God, Mom, what do I do now?"

"Nothing. It'll all be fine. Let's go meet Everett so that part of our life is behind us."

"Or in front of us, Mom. You said he studied disposal of nuclear waste. Maybe he knows something that could help us figure this all out."

When they passed by Charlottesville, J.D. pulled off the highway and down a few streets to the sorority house where Junior ate the hashish. "Wait here in the car," he said to his mother. "I'll be back in a minute." She watched him walk the path, holding something wrapped in a shirt. The door opened, and a bright blonde co-ed flung her arms around him. He struggled free and pointed back at Amanda. She disappeared inside and returned a few moments later with a skinny middle-aged woman. They talked and talked, and then the woman took the shirt from J.D. and wrote something on a piece of paper. The co-ed kissed him, and he jogged back to the car.

"Bones," he said to Amanda. "That's a bone I grabbed from the vault, and that woman there is one of the country's leading experts on bone forensics. She teaches that here. And guess what? She's running tests tomorrow on a whole batch of bones, and she's going to do mine with them. Call her in two days. Hot dog! Might find something out."

"Like what?" Amanda asked.

"Like how long has the person been dead," he said.

Everett was escorted into the visitors' room, scrubbed, clean, and coherent. Amanda gave him a hug and introduced J.D. They shook hands. Everett wouldn't let go.

"What's your favorite tree?" he asked.

J.D. said, "If you let go of my hand, I'll tell you. It's an easy question." Everett sat down and crossed his legs. "Up until yesterday, I had three favorites. In order: red oak because the furniture that comes from it is so beautiful, sugar maple because the sap is so sweet, and ash because it is so strong and supple."

"I only met you two minutes ago, so this may be somewhat presumptuous of me, but I think you just described your mother."

J.D. laughed. "Yep, I sure did, didn't I? Funny about that. What is your mother like?"

Everett sucked in his breath with a gasping, squeaking noise and pounded his fist once on his thigh as though he was trying to start his motor. "I don't know who my mother was. I grew up in my father's house with his girlfriend. Her name was Geisel, and she spoke with a very thick French accent. She was a horrible person. I think she was addicted to some kind of drugs because most of the time she would sit for hours in a chair with a stupid grin on her face, and then later she would turn into a monster throwing things at me and screaming terrible things. Truly despicable things."

"I am so, so sorry, Everett. I didn't know that," Amanda said.

"Oh don't feel sorry for me. I turned out fine. I'm fine … just fine."

The three were silent. Everett flicked lint from his lint-less trousers.

"Let's talk about Edith," Amanda said. "She's Everett's

friend here, and they see each other in the courtyard every once in a while. How is Edith?"

"I haven't seen her since the day she sang me that lovely song about Dengman Gap and all the secrets. For some reason, they don't let her out anymore." He turned to J.D. "Does your girl really have plum dark eyes?"

"Yes she does. With gold speckles."

"She sounds beautiful. Someday ... someday ... maybe someday ..." He went back to flicking lint.

"Everett, do you know anything about nuclear waste stored in Dengman Gap on Cherokee land? That's what you were doing your thesis on, isn't it?"

"No, no, I don't know anything about that." He straightened and spoke in flat tones, as if reciting. "I was researching naturally occurring uranium lignite deposits near Billings and Bowman, North Dakota, and heard about the possibility that spent uranium was stored in above-ground structures on Sioux Indian lands. Above ground, not in natural deep-ground stone apertures that would be reasonably safe for centuries. Nobody wanted to give me any hard information about it. I couldn't wrap up either part. But I don't want to talk about it. It's gone from me."

Everett was rocking back and forth, hands clasped in his lap, looking at J.D. "You want to know why I did those things with your father. Whether I did those things with men all the time. I didn't. Just with your father. He promised he would have my thesis finished and I would get a degree. And then the police found me sitting with his severed head in my lap."

"He wasn't my father, Everett. He wasn't anybody's father."

"Everett," Amanda said. "Just because I was married to him does not mean he was my husband. He wasn't that either. Husbands are called husbands because they care for their wives. He was an evil, self-centered man who didn't care what happened to people as long as he got what he wanted. He wasn't evil because he slept with men. Sometimes there's nothing wrong with that. What *was* wrong is that he lied to his wife and cheated on her and let the world believe he was the father of a beautiful son. He wasn't, and he knew it."

"No more, Mrs. Wentworth, no more of that. I can't ..." He turned to J.D. "You said up until yesterday you had three favorite tress; now you only have one. Why is that?"

"Yesterday I found some trees that don't exist, or at least everyone believes they don't exist. They are huge, thick, and tall with a canopy as big as your courtyard down there. They have spine-covered nut pods and a curving spiraled bark. They are now my favorite tree because I know about them and no one else does. And they're beautiful."

"Chestnut trees?" Everett asked.

"How ... did ... you ... know ... that?"

"There's a new patient here in my house, Pickett House. He's quite elderly. He sits in the sunroom and mumbles about those trees all the time. He's quite nice but very old. He says he's a nuclear physicist, but he won't talk about any of it, just the trees." He looked around the room and up at the ceiling. "Mrs. Wentworth, they must be busy. They can't be listening to me talk or they would have come to get me. We're not allowed to talk like this."

Just then an attendant came in the room and took Everett by the arm. "Time's up, folks. Everett, let's go."

J.D. got up. "Excuse me, sir, but I would appreciate just a few more minutes with Everett. Just a few more minutes. Would that be okay?"

"No," Attendant Cobb said, "that would not be okay. Come on, Everett, back to your house." He yanked Everett's arm. J.D. stood in the doorway, blocking his path. Amanda had left the room. Agitated voices were coming from across the hall in the director's office. He heard Amanda demanding that Everett be released to her custody, right now! Everett was behind the attendant, pointing at J.D., then at himself, at J.D., at himself, and then at the front door that led out to the parking lot. He made a fist and pointed at Cobb.

Amanda came storming across the hall. "I don't know what's the matter with these people. They are rude and mean. J.D., please, let's leave now. Everett, thank you."

J.D. took one step forward, and the attendant gave him a hard shove back, and Amanda moved between them. "Let go of Everett's arm, young man. He will go peacefully. If you touch my son again, I will call the police." As they passed by the director's office, Amanda opened the door and said, "You should be ashamed of yourself."

Grannie Mae's was the one place that no one would know about. Not the people from Skinner Bluff, not the men in the Lincoln Continental. It was night black and moonless when the headlights from Amanda's Buick found the front porch of the house in the woods. The lights were on. Uncle Albert stood on the front steps with a flashlight and a shotgun pointed at the windshield. "Who are ya?" he bellowed. J.D. shut the car off, got out, and put his hands up. Albert played the light on his face, uncocked and lowered the gun. "Come on in."

In the kitchen, sitting at the table, both in their nighties with playing cards strewn out in front of them, were Abby and Marie. Abby held the baby, his head nestled over her shoulder, patting his back. "Jeremiah Dixon, I want one of these little things. I want me a baby just like this little baby. He is so cute," she said, kissing his neck and making cooing sounds.

Billy sat on the floor in the corner with the old dog curled up at his feet. The hound dog arched his eyebrows up, blinked his rheumy eyes, gave his tail one wag, and went to sleep. J.D. said, "I'm sleeping out in my truck. All of you can figure everything else out." Amanda winked at Abby, and Abby winked back, smiling. Amanda jabbed J.D. in the ribs with her finger. "Oh, right," he said. He gave Abby a kiss on the forehead.

Marie pointed to her cheek, and he gave her a kiss, and she said, "Jeremiah, would you be a real sweet pea and take that little baby off your honey's shoulder and lay him down nice and gentle in his crib over there. Pull that blue blanket up around his chin and give him a little goodnight kiss. That would sure be sweet of you. Abigail, I'm so sorry, honey, but with all these visitors, we might come up a bed shy," she said, pushing the cards across the table. "It's your deal."

24

Bone Density

UNCLE DANNY RECOGNIZED THE BLACK CHEVY PICKUP with the red stripe along the side. He pulled the US Marshal Service car into the parking spot beside it in front of the InnTowne Motel. He and Sister Valentine walked up the outside wooden stairs and along the second-floor balcony to room 218. For an hour, J.D. had been practicing in front of the mirror, going over and over every possible thing he might or might not say when Uncle Danny got there from the airport. With his hand held out, going up and down simulating a handshake, he said, "Hi, Dan." "Hello, Dad." "Hi, Uncle Danny, guess what? You're my Pop." Then he got to a place where he thought it best to let his mother tell Uncle Danny however and whenever she wanted to. He would just say, "Uncle Danny, it's really good to see you." Ultimately, that seemed cowardly so, in front of the mirror, he squared up, stuck his hand out, and settled on, "Hello, Father." When the knock came, J.D. opened the door and didn't say a word. He just stood there staring at his father with a badge, a gun, half an ear, standing beside an angelic nun in full nun garb. "Hello, Father" didn't fit at all. It was instantly wrong. He didn't say anything. Uncle Danny didn't say anything either. It was as though all of the strange circumstances wrapped into one certain point in time sucked them both into dumbness. The marshal stood with his thumbs hooked in his holster belt until the sister poked him. "Well, I guess we might have a little catching up do. Is your mother here?"

"No, sir, she isn't. She's over in Fat Gap." J.D. turned to the nun and held out his hand.

"Hi, I'm Jeremiah."

"Jeremiah, it's very nice to meet you. I'm Sister Valentine." She shook his hand, unable to keep the smile and the twinkle off her face. She was looking at his cauliflowered ear and then back at the marshal's ear. "Perhaps I could go get us all some coffee. I'll be back in a little bit." She turned and walked behind the marshal, a foot shorter than him, patting his back as she passed by.

"That's Sister Valentine from the orphanage?" J.D. said slowly, drawing out each word, staring after her. "Where did you find her? Why did she come here? Abby is going to go nuts!"

"I found her at the Catholic orphanage. That's where they live. She came here because I asked her to." He walked past J.D. into the motel room, sat on the bed, and asked, "How are you holding up? I hear you've seen some pretty ugly things."

"Yes, sir, I have, but I'm doing fine. I'm not alone. Mom's here, and I have some good friends who've been in all this with me."

"How about we don't do the 'sir' thing. It makes me feel old. You're a grown man now. If just plain 'Uncle Danny' is good with you, it's good with me. What about you? J.D. or Jeremiah or Jerry?"

"Uncle Danny. I'm good with that. For me, J.D., that's what Mom usually calls me. The old man called me Little Boy. He never asked me what my name was; he didn't seem to even want to know. I kind of liked hearing it that way. He never told me his name either. There was something, I don't know, something special about not having names."

"You really like that old man, don't you?"

"Yes, I do. I remember him saying to me after I said I had to call my mother, 'So you don't have a father, do you, Little Boy?' He knows things and not just things about all this weird stuff with chemical vaults and dead people. He knows things about the universe. I want to find him. Get him back to his cabin."

"We will. We'll do that," Danny said.

By the time Sister Valentine had returned from the Koffee Klatch with two coffees, an iced tea, and three jelly donuts, J.D. had told Danny the whole sequence of events. He had started his story with the afternoon he had come home from school and found his mother alone, drunk, and nearly hysterical. "I just left," he said, "and that's how I ended up here." He then talked about every event, methodically, right up through seeing Everett at the nut house.

"J.D., let me get this straight. You actually set bear traps for these men to step in? That's brilliant; I wish I'd thought of that. Could have used it a dozen times. Bury some of them in a circle in the soft desert sand and put a whiskey bottle right in the middle. Would have saved a whole lot of aggravation."

"You two are talking about causing people to step into bear traps and suffer incredible pain, all alone in the desert. What would the poor people do? Just lie out there and die?"

"Nope, Sister, they'd drink the bottle of whiskey and never know there was anything wrong with their leg. I'd come by in the morning and round them up. But I have to know why you bought jelly donuts. That doesn't seem like something a nun would do at four o'clock in the afternoon. Or any other time for that matter."

"All the time we were on that airplane, I could only think of two things: one, how wonderful it was going to be to see little Abigail, and two, eating a jelly donut. I haven't had one of these for twenty years." She bit into it. The bluish-red filling squirted out and splotched on the front of her bright white habit, "Oh dear! Oh my goodness!" she said. "That must be why Mother Francine won't let us have jelly donuts."

The weight of knowing that this man had come to help him and to help Abby and Billy, and that he had brought Abby's most special person with him and that this man was his father, all of that was beginning to envelop him. He was transfixed by his father's clumsy roughness and strength and by the giddy innocence and honesty of Sister Valentine.

"You know when I was telling you about how I first met the old man, how I had left home because Mom was drunk and smashing a picture on the floor and I had to get out? Well, it wasn't until I was having that fancy dinner with Abby and telling her about it that I realized that Mom didn't have any pictures of William Wentworth. It was a picture of you she was smashing."

"Alcohol can sure have a nasty effect on people from time to time. I have no idea why she would be smashing my picture." The faucet in the bathroom sink dripped a steady drip. The under-the-counter refrigerator hummed. A car horn barked on Main Street.

Sister Valentine said, "Eat your donuts; they are very tasty. Jeremiah, did you know that Marshal Wentworth's ear got chewed off by a murderer?"

"I've heard that." He flicked his own ear and took a bite of his donut. "I can see how easy it would be for that to happen when your ear is sticking out there like this fat jelly donut. I'm going to make a call from the office to the bone lady and see if she knows anything yet."

Out in Fat Gap, Amanda paced on the front porch. She had wanted to go into town to meet Danny when he came in from

Texas, but Uncle Albert had said, "Nope. Bad idea. Who knows what all those men might have got figured out. J.D., you g'won over and bring your rifle." J.D. had loaded five rounds into the magazine of his 30-30, slung it over his shoulder, kissed all the women, including Grannie Mae on the top of her bonnet, and had driven off into town.

Amanda, alone on the porch, pacing, leaned over the railing and beckoned to Uncle Albert out in his hog pen. When he came over, she whispered, "Albert, do you have a little something to calm me down? I don't know what's got into me, but I'm getting very nervous." He reached up and patted her hand and walked off around the house. He came back with a ceramic jug with a cork in the top, uncorked it, took a swig, and handed it to her. She looked at the jug and said, "I've never done this kind of thing before."

Albert said, "You never been here before."

She tipped it back and swilled a shot. "Thank you. That's better."

Two cars rattled over the bridge and up the drive. J.D.'s truck was first, followed by the Marshal Service car Wentworth had picked up at the airport. They pulled up side by side in front of the porch, and Amanda ran down the steps and into the arms of Danny. J.D. scooted around his truck and opened the door for Sister Valentine. She stood and adjusted her wimple and coif, smoothed the front of her habit, avoiding the donut stain. A scream came from inside the cabin. The screen door burst open, and Abby came running down the stairs. She stopped short of Sister Valentine, and they took each other's hands. Abby began to sob, bowed her head, and whispered, "Sister Valentine, I didn't think I would ever see you again."

The sister kissed her forehead and said to Danny, "This is my Abigail." They walked arm in arm up onto the porch, and they knelt together in front of Billy. He stared at them blankly. The sister reached up gently and pushed his sleeve up over his elbow. In the crook of his arm was a birthmark shaped like a dog. "This is Wilbur."

Uncle Albert stood in the doorway and watched all the conversations going on at the same time: Amanda, Abby, and Marie and Sister Valentine; Junior and J.D. Grannie Mae was in her rocker between Billy and the baby's crib. Danny moving from group to group, from person to person, asking questions.

Uncle Albert boomed out, "Do I got this right? Six months ago, it was nice and peaceful around here, and now my house is full of what all? Cops and babies and nuns and lady scientists and … and deadbeats and morons and, my God Almighty, it's like I got a damn circus goin' on in here. I'm goin' to my hog pen." He walked out, slamming the screen door. Everyone hushed.

Grannie Mae said, "Don't pay him no never mind, he likes to sleep with his hogs."

Uncle Danny leaned on the kitchen counter and said, "I need to ask a few more questions here. For those of you who've been too polite to ask, I'm J.D.'s uncle." Amanda shot a glance at J.D. He shrugged and gave his head a single shake. She looked up at the ceiling and exhaled. "I'm a federal marshal, and I'm out here to see if what I've been told is happening out here is true and to see if an investigation by federal authorities is warranted. I need to call my office at eight tomorrow morning to give a report on the situation and let them decide what's going to happen. Before dark, I need to go with J.D. to the Indian land and verify what they've told me about the vaults. But I need to get clear on some things first. Sister Valentine, you can verify that these two," he pointed to Abby and Billy, "are children from your orphanage and they were both given to adoption on the Big Flats Reservation."

"Yes, Marshal, that's true."

"Amanda, you said the chemicals you were doing experiments with produced in mice a condition similar to what you witness in Billy. Who was that research done for?"

"I don't know. I only know that when I had finished the preliminary findings, they were purloined from my office by the US Army. I was told that by the dean of the school."

"Junior, you mentioned that you thought the local sheriff was somehow involved with these men who seem to be trying to hide the existence of these vaults. Why do you think that?"

"Because Sheriff Binkins' boy told us he was beaten by his daddy for letting us know that they were coming to the vaults to find Billy and that it was the sheriff who drove the guys to the hospital after one got gored by a boar. So we figure they're in it together."

"J.D., you said you took a bone from one of the skeletons in the vault. Just to point out, if this does get to be a federal investigation, someone might have a problem with you taking away part of the evidence. Did anyone, Junior or this Dickey fellow, see you take the bone?"

"No, sir. No one saw me, but the bone lady said the person died somewhere around twenty years ago, and she said it only had half a foot and the person was probably a negro. Something about bone density."

"A negro? That's odd. All right. Do you have the medical bag and wallets and identification you got from them? Are they here?"

Junior brought them out of a back room. The marshal spread the contents out on the counter, separated out the identification documents, and asked Sister Valentine to look at them. "Are these the same men who came to the orphanage to get information on adoptions?"

She looked at the photos. "Yes, that's them. They were

younger then, but these are definitely those two men."

"If these men reside in Texas, are employed in Texas, are wanted or have conspired to commit federal crimes in Texas, my office in Houston has the authority to hunt them down wherever they are and bring them to justice. Amanda, do you know anything more than you have told me about Skinner Bluff Insane Asylum?"

"Only that they seem to give Everett a lot of drugs, and the woman who runs the place is very nasty. I don't like her one little bit, and I don't trust her."

"Funny thing about that place is that I couldn't get any information about it. Either there are no records, local, state, or federal, or they're all blocked somehow. No local or state tax records, so it must be federal property, but the FBI couldn't find anything. Zero. J.D., could you get that quilt you said was some kind of map? Let's take a look at it."

J.D. fetched it from his truck and spread it out on the kitchen table. The marshal stood back staring at it. He rubbed his fingertips on some of the squares and then tapped the center one, the one that looked like an eagle. "That's the insignia of a full bird colonel in the US Army. That old man must be saying that whatever this operation is, it's being run by an army colonel. This here," he said, tapping the symbol of the crossed fists, "is the insignia for the military's Biological Warfare Division. Look at this. There are four of these inside the border. How many vaults did you find?"

"Four," Junior said. "We found four, and this is really spooky."

"There are, let's see, fourteen of those at the tepees with that symbol around the edge. Anybody want to guess what that old man is saying?"

"Oh my God," Amanda whispered. "There are fourteen of these sites at Indian Reservations around the country. Why wouldn't anyone know about these or have raised a stink about it? How can nobody know?"

"Bingo," Dan said, "exactly. There are fourteen of them. This is not the only one, and there *are* people who know about it. The problem is they're all at that lunatic asylum."

"J.D., didn't Everett say something about nuclear waste on a reservation in North Dakota?" Amanda asked.

"Yes, yes he did. He said he heard about it, and nobody would talk about it. He said it was Sioux land."

"I'm going to have to talk to this Everett fellow. You told me he said something to lead you to believe the old man might be there too. That right?"

"Yes, sir, oh, sorry, yes, Uncle Danny, that's right."

Amanda looked at her son and his father and rubbed her eyes and the bridge of her nose, blowing out air in little puffs.

"All right," Dan said to everyone, "I'm going to go with J.D. up to the top of the ridge where Abigail's house is and then work our way down to the cabin where the old man lived, stopping at each of the vaults. I hear that's a lot better than walking uphill. Junior, could you stay awake until we get back and make sure Albert's got his rifle in that hog pen. Don't let anybody near here. Is there anything anybody here knows that they haven't said that we need to know before tomorrow morning?"

Abby said, "I forgot to tell J.D., but he asked me to find out from Mr. Harrelson where the padlock that was on the cabin came from. He said you can't buy those. It was made by a company called Brighton. They only make hardware for the military."

"That," Danny said, "is not a good thing."

Amanda tugged at his arm as he moved to the door. "I need to talk to you about something, Dan. It's important."

She took his three-fingered hand and led him to a back

bedroom and closed the door. She looked at him about to speak. He put his arms around her and kissed her neck. "My God, is it good to see you. I've missed you," he said. "You smell good, you are good. And strong. Amanda, I love you very much."

She felt his breath on her neck and closed her eyes, realizing that was all she wanted to hear. *He's going off to something very dangerous with J.D. He doesn't need to get distracted. Not now.*

"That's all I wanted, Dan. Just to feel you. Be safe. I love you too."

He ran his hands through her hair and kissed her on her lips, her nose, her forehead. "I'll be fine, and I'll take good care of J.D. for you."

"For us, Dan, for us."

They took both the truck and the marshal's car, left the truck at the end of the old man's dirt drive, and took the car around the mountain and up the hill. Abby's shack was just as she had left it. Nothing seemed out of place. Dan had J.D. show him where the car had been and where the traps had been set.

"Brilliant," Dan said.

"Didn't work, though," J.D. said.

"Oh it would have, given the chance." Dan stood at the wire reading the sign. "That doesn't make any sense." He read it out loud. "No Trespassing. Violators will be Prosecuted Pursuant to CFR 18 808 Sec 65.09. This property is Sacred Land owned by the Cherokee Nation.

"Trespass on Indian lands is a tribal law offence, not a federal offence. It's prosecuted by the tribal police." He took out a notebook and wrote down the Code of Federal Regulations number. They had about two hours before dark set into the hills. J.D. recognized certain rock outcroppings, swales, and small stream crossings. He saw the crown of the chestnut trees blocking the bright of the sky from hundreds of yards away. The trek from the shack to the first vault was easy. The doors were open, just as they had left them. Dan inspected everything, making notes. He drew a picture of the dial outside the vault and got down on his hands and knees and looked at the name printed in the center of the black and white disc: Brighton. He picked a nut from the forest floor, rubbed its spines off, and tossed it to J.D. "Give that to your mother. She might be able to tie it to something."

The second and third vaults were the same as they had been left. An hour had passed before they got to the place where the boar had charged Vinny Gravello. Dan wanted to see if anything had fallen out of their pockets or off their belts. The blood was still there but nothing else. They could see twigs and branches snapped in a path up the hill where Hartford had dragged his bleeding buddy, and they followed the path up for a short way and then turned back to get to the last vault before dark set in.

The doors were shut, but the dirt J.D. had shoveled in front of them had been moved. The skeletons were gone. "They were right there," J.D. said, pointing at the red containers. "Honest, Uncle Danny, they were sitting right there staring out with bullet holes in their heads. Look at all the footprints in the goo. They took them."

Dan looked at the tracks and scrapes in the dirt in front of the vault and unsnapped the cover strap on his pistol. "They're here or just left. Come on, J.D., which way out of here?"

The notches didn't line up. Danny motioned J.D. back against the wall, leveled his gun chest high, and eased the door open. It was empty. But they had been there. All of the books were gone. The shelves were bare, not even an atlas or a Faulkner or a Bible. The bed that had been made so taut and perfect was rent asunder, and the mattress ticking and the pillows and seat cushions were all slit open end to end and side to side. The trundle box below the bed had nothing in it. The rest of the cabin seemed untouched. The refrigerator was cold, and all the food was there. The one-hole shitter was immaculate, undisturbed from the old man's efforts to make his world so perfect. In the drawer where the envelope of money had been was another envelope. J.D. picked it up and told Dan it had not been there before. That's where the money had been, and he had taken that out. He still had it in his back pocket. "This envelope was just put here." Dan took a knife from the silverware drawer and the cloth from the ring in front of the sink. Holding the envelope by the corner with the cloth, he flicked open the unglued flap. With the other corner of the cloth, he pulled out a note. Written in pencil in block letters, it said: *Whoever is reading this note, make your peace with the world.*

"Sounds an awful lot like threatening a federal officer, don't you think?"

Dan went out first—quietly, carefully, his pistol leading the way down the dirt road to J.D.'s truck. They talked quietly as they walked over the bridge and down the drive. He needed a telephone, he said. He needed it tonight. He told him to go to his car, then go back to where his mother was. He said he was staying in the motel tonight so he could look around the town. He wanted J.D. and Junior and Albert to sleep shifts. "Keep your rifles loaded. Don't let anybody near the place. That old man is the only one who knows why all this is happening. He might have told someone. Who, other than you, knows him? Anybody?"

J.D. told him about Willy Sherman. "He's a retired state trooper. His son just joined the force. He seems a really good person. He didn't say he'd ever seen the old man, but he did talk about hermits who lived somewhere out here. He might know more than he said. Sometimes you can find him at the Blue Ridge Bar & Grill. Tall guy, very handsome, with wavy silver hair. Fourth stool in from the door."

"Chief, I'm sorry to call you at home, but here's what I know." He started from the beginning, detailing everything he knew in a chronological order, piecing it all together from what he had been told and what he had seen. He ended with the cabin ripped apart, the old man gone, and the note. "These people intend to kill to keep us from knowing about what's in those vaults and others on reservations around the country. And, Chief, don't forget, skeletons of murdered people. I need back-up here, Chief. We need some marshals down here right away. People's lives are in immediate danger."

"Dan, you don't need back-up. I told you, remember? You're off this case if it's going to be a case at all. Remember? And, Dan, how do you know that there were bones there at all? You didn't see them."

"The leg bone my nephew brought to the forensic expert will have the same chemicals on it that are leaking all over the floor of that vault. That's how. It's a goddamned good thing he took it when he did."

"Call me back in an hour. Collect."

Willy Sherman was sitting on the fourth stool in from the door. It was early yet, and some of the barstools were empty. Dan sat next to him. "Marshal, how are you doing? What brings you here?" Sherman asked, looking at his shirt badge and scarred leather-skin face.

"I'm looking for a man named Mr. Willy Sherman. Retired Virginia State police officer."

"You found him."

Marshal Wentworth leaned his elbows on the counter and began to talk in low tones, just above the noise of shoveled ice, the pop of beer bottle caps, and the murmur of early evening, sober conversations. Jeannie the barmaid kept trying to get the marshal's attention, but he didn't respond. He was telling a tale very carefully and slowly, making sure that Sherman knew enough to be helpful and not enough to become a problem.

Willy interrupted him. "I think Jeannie here either really wants to meet a bona fide US federal marshal or she thinks you shouldn't be taking up a stool without buying a beer."

Dan looked up and said, "Pleased to meet you. Bourbon, two ice cubes," and went back to his story. Their voices rose incrementally as the bar filled up and the folks had dispensed with their "Shore good to see ya's" and moved their chatter into second gear. Every once in a while, Willy would nod and add a piece of information or an anecdote.

When it came time for the marshal to leave and make his phone call, both men stood and shook hands. "You can count me in, Marshal. I'll be there. I've been waiting a long time for something like this," Willy said.

Jeannie leaned on the bar, extending her hand out, and said just as sweetly as she could how truly honored she was to make the acquaintance of an honest-to-God US federal marshal. Dan Wentworth, shaking her hand, said, "Thank you, ma'am." He winked and left, looking for a phone booth.

"Get off the case? Just drop it and walk away? That's insane. People's lives are in danger here, and somebody put toxic chemicals and nuclear waste on Indian land, and you're telling me that jerk-off in Washington ordered me to go home and pretend nothing happened? Did you tell him what I told you?"

"Dan, stop screaming. That jerk-off is everybody's boss.

Now you're not really supposed to know this, but he got a call from a general. A general, Dan. There aren't a lot of those guys around, and they talk to people like the president, so if you're smart, you'll gather up that little nun of yours and get your ass back here."

"Chief, help me out. This is my family. My only family." He waited, listening to her breathe.

"Okay. Okay, Dan, I'm way out on this one, but I do know that the only return flight from Roanoke to Amarillo is on Sunday. I'm entering in my log, sending confirmation to Washington, and noting for the file that I immediately ordered you to take the next available return flight to wherever you left the Marshal Service car and to report to work on Monday morning. If you're not here, Dan, you're fired. Period. Watch yourself; I don't want you to get killed or sent up to an army brig. Of those two, killed is best for me."

"You're a sweetheart, Chief. One more question. Do we still have legal authority to deputize citizens? I have one .38 caliber pistol. If I got these guys right, they're both federal fugitives, both wanted for Class One felonies, and probably are murderers. There are a few guys out here who know these woods and can shoot the eye out of a squirrel at a hundred yards. What do you think?"

"No family, no women, no lunatics. Don't call me sweetheart. Take care, see you Monday morning 0800."

It was eight o'clock at night when Dan left for Skinner Bluff. He had driven to each motel within ten miles of Galax, asking the office clerks if anyone named Hartford or Gravello, McCoy or Stoner had checked into any rooms, and he had cruised the parking lots and all the streets downtown looking for a black Lincoln Continental. Nothing. It would be ten at night when he got to the lunatic asylum, long after lights out and long after the nasty woman in charge had locked up the office. That didn't matter. She lived somewhere, and he would find where that somewhere was and ask her a few questions.

The bone. He remembered the bone when he saw the exit sign for Charlottesville. He found Delta Zeta sorority house on the campus of the University of Virginia where J.D. had described it. He rang the front door buzzer. It was quarter past eleven on a Thursday night, and the lights that were on were all on the second floor in the rooms of the girls studying for tomorrow's classes. He rang again and again, and then Miss Janowitz, in a brown bathrobe and pink slippers, opened the door. He showed her his badge, and she brought him in to the front sitting room. Miss Janowitz told him there was a high probability the bone was Negroid; it was more dense than either Caucasian or Oriental. The extent of decay of the marrow cavity indicated approximately twenty years from death to the present, but the chemicals might have had an effect that skewed that determination. If they did, she told him, it would have been a longer time span, not shorter. The only certain chemical that could be isolated was Phenomizol, probably resulting from a combination of anti-fungal and anti-bacterial agents. That was all she knew. She wasn't a chemist. The bone was in the laboratory three miles from there and, if he would give her a few minutes to get dressed, yes, she would call building security and arrange for the lab to be opened so he could pick it up. She got in the front seat of the marshal's car. On the way back to the sorority house, Dan handed her a pad of paper and a pencil and asked her to write down everything she had told him and sign it. Sign it Dr. Janowitz.

There were six or eight cars in the parking lot of the Skinner Bluff Lunatic Asylum. The administration building was locked. Only outside security lights were on, and the other buildings had a dim yellow glow coming from the middle of each first floor. It was silent there, the gates all locked and no one outside. He decided to stand at the gate to the courtyard and shine his flashlight back and forth across the front doors of the buildings until someone got curious enough to come out to see what was going on. No one came out, but the courtyard exploded in a flash of light as bright as an operating room. Still no one came out into the courtyard. He stood drenched in white light, seeing nothing, until a voice from behind him said, "Do not turn around. Put your arms on the fence and spread eagle. Now!"

He could feel the cold round steel of a gun barrel pressed into the flesh behind his ear. A pair of hands unsnapped his holster strap, lifted out his pistol, and took his wallet and badge from his back pockets and then patted his legs up to his waist, around his stomach over his back and chest, across his shoulders and down each arm. There were two of them. "I am a federal police officer," he said. They said nothing. Handcuffs snapped closed on each wrist and then snapped closed on the metal bars of the gate. He was locked in crucifix. The gun barrel pulled away from his neck, and a walkie-talkie growled static. "Miss Harbone, do you copy?" "Copy." "Courtyard gate, federal cop." "Name?" "Deputy Marshal Daniel Wentworth." "Hold him there." "10-4."

"Mr. Wentworth," her voice was bitter and sharp, "you are the brother-in-law of Mrs. Amanda Dixon Wentworth. Is that true?" Dan leaned his head against the bars. "Well, it doesn't matter if you're going to talk or not. We know that to be true. For all this time, we thought having Mrs. Wentworth come and visit Everett was a good idea because her dead husband's brother was a big-time federal marshal and that would give us an added layer of support should we ever need it. But no, oh no, that isn't what happened. You aided and abetted an attempt to abduct a certified mental patient from a certified institution, and you just committed criminal trespass on private property without a warrant. Now do you want to say anything?"

Dan's shoulders were beginning to ache. He shrugged them up and down and rolled his head to the other side, hoping to catch a glimpse of her or one of the men. He could only see part of one black leather shoe. "Mr. Wentworth, the authorities having jurisdiction over this institution are going to want to talk to you. You'll have to stay with us until they can get here."

"Who are they?"

"You will get to know them in the morning. It's a long drive from Washington." She said to the two men, "Get Nurse Griswell up here to give him something to calm him down. Take him to Stuart and lock him in holding." Her heels clicked on the brick as she walked away.

It was in the voice. The insanity in it. He'd heard those voices before from inside cells, in courtrooms, on witness stands. Voices of women being tried for hideous crimes. He remembered Amanda saying she thought they had their own crematorium here. He knew he was never going to wake up in the morning. His car would be in parts and pieces in a back alley chop-shop, and they would be all over the Gap hunting down Amanda and the rest of them, and he would be ashes before the sun rose. It was far better to go out with a bang than in a puff of smoke. He needed to stall. He twisted his wrist and looked at his watch. Four minutes before ten. *Hopefully I can live for four or five minutes. They can't just shoot me here; somebody would wake up, there would be blood all over. They've been told to get the needle in me. Got to stop that. Five minutes. That's got to be enough.* He flexed his shoulders, arms, fingers, stretched out each leg, and arched his back until the spine knuckles cracked then relaxed, breathing deeply. He did it all again. He had to make sure both feet didn't come off the ground at the same time or it would pull his arms right out of their sockets and snap his sternum clean in two.

The walkie-talkie hailed Nurse Griswell. She copied, and the voice told her to come to the administration building and then to the courtyard gate and bring her bag. "Strong stuff. Got a big guy here. On the double."

Dan kept stretching and flexing and breathing deep. He saw her when she passed out of the courtyard glare walking hurriedly, almost jogging along the back service road. She was carrying a small black satchel. She looked short and thick. *Good*, he thought. *Wider, lower target.* He heard the plimp, plimp of her nurse's shoes on the brick walk as she came up behind him. He heard the click of the strap lock on the satchel and the rattle of vial against vial in the bag. "I'm going to go in the neck," she said. "It's quicker." Dan waited until he felt her elbow brush his back. He leaned into the bars, lifted his knee up waist high and like a horse to a dog drove it straight back as hard as he could. It must have caught her in the pelvic bone. It felt hard, and she screamed, and then there was the thud of her head hitting the bricks.

"Holy shit!" one of the men shouted, and Dan lifted his other leg and shot it back, his boot just barely catching something, and headlights burst on them, and a flashing blue light spun around the courtyard. A shotgun blast broke the night.

"I'm going to count to three, mister, and you're gonna drop that gun or I'll blow your guts all over this place. One, two," and the gun dropped on the bricks. "Very good. Now I'm counting to three again, and you're gonna unlock those cuffs. One, two," and one of the men grabbed Dan's wrist and stuffed a key in the handcuff lock. Miss Harbone came running down the path as the second handcuff was opened up. Dan turned and watched her run right up to the barrel of the shotgun, screaming obscenities into the face of a fully uniformed Virginia State police officer. He gave her one push with the barrel, and she fell over backwards on the grass. "You listen to me, little missy, my name is Garth Sherman. That's my father," he said, jerking his head toward Willy. "This is federal property. I don't have any jurisdiction here, but that man does. Marshal, what do you want to do?"

"I want to leave this place for others to deal with later. And believe me, they will. But first I need to know something." He crouched down beside Miss Harbone. Her face, naturally skinny and sharp, was screwed up tight. Her eyes were narrowed, and her upper lip was pulled up over her teeth. She looked just like those women in the jail cells. He took the collar of her blouse and wrapped it tight in his fist, pulling her shoulders up off the ground, and put his own face an inch away from hers. "Where is the old man who was brought here last week? And where is Everett?" She squeaked, and her face became red. Dan loosened his grip, realizing he had shut off her air. "Where are they? I'm taking them with me."

"You can't take them with you. The old man is with his wife, Edith. They both passed away. They were old, very old. Their ashes are in the graveyard, not far from Everett's ashes. Everett had an accident in the therapy room, poor boy."

Dan slammed her head down and let go. "You will meet your maker, and he will judge you. Let's get out of here. Give me my wallet and badge." He holstered his gun, looking down at Nurse Griswell. She looked a little cross-eyed, and there was a small pool of blood behind her head, but she was breathing. "Get her a nurse. She doesn't look good." He started to walk away, back to his car.

Willy Sherman said, "Marshal, I truly don't mean to tell

you what to do, but this situation is not right. It doesn't fit with anything I know. There are four men standing on their feet and two women, busted up, lying on the ground. That ain't good no matter who they are. It ain't right."

Dan turned. "You're right; this is unseemly. Would you help Miss Harbone up?" He knelt down beside the nurse. Her hypodermic needle was in the grass. He picked it up, held it vertical, and pushed the plunger until a drop of clear fluid tricked out the hole in the top. "I'll give you a little shot of this sedative, and you should feel better. It'll ease the pain."

She jerked and screamed, "No! No!"

"That's right, isn't it, little girl. This isn't a sedative; it's a death sentence." He put the needle in her medical bag, snapped the bag shut, and said, "We'll take this with us." He lifted the girl in his arms and handed her to the bigger of the two guards. "Take care of her," he said, "and I have a piece of advice for all of you. Go to your locker, change your clothes, get in your cars, and leave here and never come back. That includes you, Miss Harbone. If one more poor soul dies here after we walk up that path and drive out of here, you're not only going to be looking at premeditated murder, you're going to be looking at me. And you don't want any part of that. You're all," he said, sweeping his arm around, "guilty of attempted murder of a federal officer. The only way you don't do life without parole is to take one step toward doing the right thing now. Tell those people down there to protect and care for those patients and walk on out of here. We'll find you later." He picked up the medical bag and walked up the path.

25

A Truly Ugly Man

DAN DROVE BACK WITH WILLY SHERMAN and the black bag. They now had two black satchels, two wallets, a bone, the bone doctor's statement, and the block-letter note. Dan dropped Willy off at his home in town. Before he got out, Dan said, "By the power vested in me by the United States Congress, I hereby appoint you deputy marshal of the US Marshal's Service. You are obligated to uphold the Constitution, all the rules and regulations pertaining to this Service, protect the health, safety, and well-being of the American people, and to defend this country against all enemies, foreign and domestic." Willy asked what he was supposed to do if there was a conflict in all of that. Dan, somber as a deacon, said, "Should any conflict arise among those obligations, you are hereby ordered to use your common sense. Goodnight."

The midnight-shift office clerk, rousted out of a sound snore, said no one had come into the motel looking for him, and he hadn't seen any black Lincoln come into the parking lot. He was a truly ugly man, Dan thought, huge and ugly. No wonder he had to work there in the middle of the night. Nobody would want to have him as part of their team out in the light of day. The man kept rapping a big finger ring on the countertop. It was two in the morning when Dan locked the door, set the security chain in place, turned the light out, and put his head on the pillow. It smelled clean, almost medicinal, like a swimming pool or a doctor's office. He drifted off into a sound, sound sleep. The wake-up call was to come at six. He was to meet up with Willy at six-thirty, everyone else in Fat Gap at seven.

Willy Sherman pulled into the parking space in front of the InnTowne Motel office at ten minutes of seven. Dan's cruiser wasn't there. He asked the woman at the desk if she had seen Marshal Wentworth that morning. No, she hadn't. His car wasn't there when she opened the office at 5:30. She spoke in a thick Eastern accent. Willy asked if the night-time attendant was still there, and if not, could she please get that person on the phone. No night-time attendant, she told him. "See sign: Office Closed 1:00 a.m. — 6:00 a.m." After Willy brought out his expired state police identification, she unlocked room #218 and let him in. None of Dan's things were in the room. The blankets were on the floor. There was a chlorine smell. He sniffed the bed and pillow. She sniffed and said, "Smell bad. Not my pillow." The security chain was cut in half.

Sister Valentine asked everyone to please bow their heads for a moment of prayer. "And yes, that includes you, Uncle Albert, and also you, Mr. Sherman." She had read something in Willy's eyes that told her he had not yet brought the Lord into his heart, and she knew that now, at this time, with all that he had just said, that didn't matter. The Lord would find his own way in. She just needed to clear the path. To let him know he was not alone.

"*Neither shall the wicked dwell near thee: nor shall the unjust abide before thy eyes.*

"*Thou hatest all the workers of iniquity: thou wilt destroy all that speak a lie. The bloody and the deceitful man the Lord will abhor.*

"But as for me in the multitude of thy mercy, I will come into thy house: I will worship towards thy holy temple, in thy fear.

"Conduct me, O Lord, in thy justice: because of my enemies, direct my way in thy sight.

"For there is no truth in their mouth: their heart is vain.

"Their throat is an open sepulcher: they dealt deceitfully with their tongues: judge them, O God. Let them fall from their devices: according to the multitude of their wickednesses cast them out: for they have provoked thee, O Lord. Amen."

"Sister, do you know that entire book by heart? I mean, do you remember every word in the whole thing? That's a long book."

"Mr. Sherman, I picked that passage, part of Psalm 5, just for you. I thought it might help for you to know you are not alone. And no, I don't know every passage of Holy Scripture. I memorized that psalm twenty minutes ago from Grannie Mae's Bible, the Douay Version of the Old Testament. Marie helped me. I needed to find something that would help you know that ..."

She turned to Marie, extending her arm out from her gown, palm up, and Marie said, "The Lord has your back."

"Sister, I'm sticking with you. Or more like, you're sticking with me. Here's what I want to do. We're in this thing alone, well, according to the good sister, not quite alone, but Marshal Wentworth made two things clear. One, there are people here who want all of us gone, and two, they have very powerful connections and we're getting no help from anyone. That includes the Virginia State Police. They will not authorize my son to take any direct action to assist us in any way. We could all get the hell out of Dodge and hope it all goes away, but it won't. They will hunt us all down and either kill us or put us all in the lunatic asylum. Dan appointed me a deputy marshal, so I'm required to uphold the Constitution and protect the American people against enemies here and abroad, foreign and domestic. That means … that means … Sister, what does that mean?"

"Conduct me, O Lord, in thy justice: because of my enemies, direct my way in thy sight."

"Right, that's what it means." He looked tired and worried. He ran his hands through his hair and rubbed the back of his neck. "Here's what we're goin' to do. Search everywhere. Every nook and cranny within ten miles of here to find Marshal Wentworth and these guys, to trap them, to corner them, to cause them to come to justice. I'm very sure they're still here because all of you are still here. They won't go back to that asylum. Not after yesterday. They have to assume the state police are still around." Willy Sherman was very tired. He hadn't much sleep, and he had to pee, but Albert had been in the bathroom for ten minutes. "I'm going outside to relieve myself," he said. "Are there any rules about that?"

"Twenty steps," Marie said.

Amanda was sitting at the table with her arm around her son. Both their faces wore the shadows of sadness. Abby leaned across J.D.'s back, her head nestled into the crook of his neck. He was whispering to her. She stood up and looked across the room at Grannie Mae.

"Grannie Mae," she said, "do you recall the story you told me about the fiddler, Robert Jenkins, whose house burned down, and you all played that song, 'Goin' to Git My Baby?'"

"Why, yes I do, Abigail. I do remember telling you that story."

"Grannie Mae, is there anything important that you left out of that story? Anything at all?"

292

"Nothin' important that I can think of. What is it bothering you, child?"

"Grannie Mae," Abigail scrunched down beside her, "was Robert Jenkins a negro man?"

"Why, yes, yes he was, but that's not important. Color of a man's skin shouldn't make no never mind about who they are."

J.D. poured himself a cup of coffee and spoke to his mother. "The old man's cabin isn't old. It was built some twenty years ago with chestnut logs that came from the sacred ground. Chestnut trees that didn't die because they were sucking up insecticides. And that burned-down moonshine still behind the cabin? That wasn't a still. That was Robert Jenkins' house. These men needed him gone for two reasons. One, because Robert Jenkins knew something about what they were doing, and two, so the old man could live there right at the edge of the reservation so he could monitor possible leakage from the nuclear waste. Something went wrong, and the house burned down. Robert Jenkins didn't die in that fire. Grannie Mae, just like you told Abby, that house didn't catch on fire from a burned-through stove pipe. They burned it down because they had to have a story about what happened to Robert Jenkins. He couldn't just disappear. Somebody might get curious. They shot Robert Jenkins and two other people, set the house on fire, and put the bodies in that vault. They knew where the bones were. They put them there."

"Grannie Mae, do you remember the name of the policeman who talked to the newspapers about that fire? The one who said you shouldn't ought to have long stovepipes?" Abby asked.

"I shore don't, honey. It's in that article. I got it stowed away somewhere in one of my trunks."

J.D. sat down beside both of them. "If I said a name, might that jog your memory?"

"Might. Might not. I'm awful old now. Can't remember like I used to."

"Sheriff Binkins."

Uncle Albert, buckling his belt, slammed his palm down on the kitchen counter. "That dadburned weasel. He was sheriff then, and he's still the sheriff. Can't seem to get rid of the rodent."

"No," Grannie Mae said, "that name doesn't ring a bell, but I'll go right now and find that old newspaper clipping. I'm sure it's in that old trunk at the end of my bed."

Willy Sherman back came in from outside. He took a map of the county from his back pocket. "Sister, like I said, I'm sticking with you. We're going to take Grannie Mae, Billy here, and the baby to my house. My wife is there, and my son took a few days' vacation. He's there. The rest of you, I want you all to split up so they won't recognize any couples. Little edge. Not a big edge but a little. J.D., you take Marie in your truck, Junior, you, and Abigail. Albert, you take Amanda." He spread the map out on the table and drew four wide circles for each of the four groups. "Here's what we're lookin' for. That black Lincoln first and foremost and Marshal Wentworth's cruiser. Very likely they're both still around here. Might be at a motel, might be at a campground, might be anywhere. The county dump. J.D., that's in your circle. Look for a bag of bones or a bag of stuff from the cabin. Junior, most of the motels are in your circle. Check the parking lots, ask the office clerks, check their dumpsters. Albert, you're down here where all the campgrounds are. Go through them all, check everything. Me and the sister are goin' to pay Sheriff Binkins a visit. We all meet back at Albert's garage at noon. Don't nobody come back here or go to the old man's cabin. That comes later." He wrote down his home phone number on three scraps of paper and handed them out. "G'won now, get the things you need, and fire up your trucks. Sister, get your crucifix. We're going to need it."

"With all due respect, Mr. Sherman," J.D. said, "I'm not letting Abby or my mother out of my sight until we're all safe again."

Junior said, "Same goes for me and my bride. Sticking together."

Albert said, "I'm goin' alone. Don't want no company."

J.D. had a pocket full of cash. He stopped at the gas station and had the boy fill the tank. He re-wrote the phone number down and handed it to him, telling him if a black Lincoln or a federal car came in there or passed by there, call that number right away.

The county dump was like every other county dump. Weird people lived there, and it stunk. Bad stink. A young boy, ten or so, with a face as flat as the moon, sat on top of a rusted tractor, shooting rats with a .22 rifle. The rats, big and gray like skinny cats, scurried from pile to pile. Abby and Amanda rolled the windows up and sat in the truck. "How did we ever get here?" Amanda waved her arm at the putrid piles of garbage.

Abby pulled her shirt up a little bit and pointed to her pustulent scars. "I think it's all my fault. I think I was in that house that burned down, and they took me away. And then I came back because Chief John said to, and Billy followed me and went out in those woods to live. That's how it all started, and now look at us. They want to kill everybody, and we're sitting in a rotten, stinking dump, looking for bones of dead people," she cried, biting her knuckle, "bones who are probably my mother and father!" She put her head in her hands and wailed, "I'm so scared."

J.D. came back from the last far pile of garbage and looked in the window. Abby was lying across the seat, her head in

Amanda's lap, sobbing. Amanda, stroking her hair with one hand, waved to J.D. with the other: *Go away.* J.D. went back to the first heap that was mostly a small mountain of household garbage and used baby diapers. He kept looking back over his shoulder at the truck until he came across a plastic bag that was wiggling around. He peered closer. There was a dead dog sticking out the end with a rat chewing on its neck. He threw up all over it, and the rat kept on gnawing. He ran back to the truck, took his shirt off, wiped his mouth, threw the shirt in the back, jumped in, and fired it up. "Fuck this!"

Abby, still sobbing, looked at him, bit her lip, and said, "Yeah, Jeremiah, that's right. Fuck this!"

Junior came out of the second motel office, shaking his head. "It's like who stays in these rat holes is some kind of national secret. They won't tell me nothin'. I can't remember the name of the place that Skinny Binkins' kid told us they stay at, but, like as not, that's where they'd be at. I don't think it was either of those. Those places probably got fleas."

"Well then why don't we go on down to that saloon where you like to go and see if he's there and ask him." Marie patted his knee.

Skinny Binkins' boy was at the saloon. When they walked in, one of the men gave a little whistle when he saw Marie. Not a rude whistle, just a short, little, one-note, "Boy is she pretty" kind of whistle. Binkins did not want to talk. "My daddy gonna beat me to death, he finds me talkin' to you all."

Marie nudged Junior aside and stood close to Skinny's boy. "You don't have to tell us a thing," she said, handing Jimmy the bartender a piece of paper and a pencil from her purse. "Tell him."

They stepped down to the end of the bar, and Jimmy brought them the paper. *Mountain View*, it said. Junior gave

Jimmy a five-dollar bill and pointed at the kid.

Marie went into the office of the Mountain View Inn. The clerk was a middle-aged stout man with very thick horn-rimmed glasses. She went to the end of the counter where it was low so you could fill out the forms. Marie, bouncy, bright, cute as a button, smiling as though nothing in the world was wrong, asked the man if two men driving a Lincoln had checked in recently.

He said, "Sorry, but we don't give out that information to the public. People deserve their privacy. Marie licked her plump lips and smiled at him, leaning over the counter far enough so her loose blouse fell a bit open in the front. She looked up at him with her eyes wide, and he was staring down at her new-mother breasts. "Can't you just take a peek down at your log and see if a little something pops out? I won't ever tell a soul." She wiggled her shoulders and giggled. "Just between you and me." He grabbed the file box from the shelf and tried to flip through the registration cards, but he couldn't take his eyes off her long enough to read them. "Here," she said, sweet like honey, "I'll do that for you." Marie began flipping slowly through the cards. The man tried to say something to her, but he couldn't bring himself to do it. He just stared and blinked. "Why, I guess they just aren't here. Those rascals must be at some other establishment." Standing up straight and tucking her blouse in tight, she thanked him, blew him a kiss, and walked out.

"They aren't here," she told Junior. "They aren't at any of these motels. It's quarter past eleven. I want to stop at Mr. Sherman's house to quick feed the baby before we go on over to Albert's garage. I'm getting real heavy with milk."

Junior was talking with Garth about the difficulties of law enforcement at the state level when Grannie Mae motioned him over to her. She took a very old newspaper clipping and put it in his pocket. "Please make sure you give that to Jeremiah when you see him at the garage." She patted his cheek. "You're a plum lucky man. You have a beautiful baby and a beautiful wife."

"Yes, ma'am, I'm sure all men would agree on that."

Sister Valentine was there, Dan had told Willy Sherman, for the sole purpose of making a positive identification of Abigail and Billy, and McCoy and Stoner to tie them to federal crimes in the state of Texas. "If that happens," he had said, "my boss will have no option. She will be required by law to open an official investigation no matter what the big-wigs in Washington want." If she didn't, and things blew up, Congressmen would drum her out of the service. "We need," he had said, "to get the nun close enough to these guys to see them. Nobody argues with a nun. They're not like other people; they don't lie or make shit up. Nothing but the truth, so help them God. We got three days. That's it."

Sheriff Binkins was at the county courthouse in Wytheville. Willy and he had known each other for years. They didn't really like each other, but they were cordial. The sheriff attended Baptist church every Sunday and professed to be a god-fearing man. Willy's wife told him that in a vain effort to make Willy feel small about running out of town every church day morning.

"Skinny, how are ya?" Willy said when they found him in the corridor outside a courtroom, talking with the public defender. "Can I have a small moment of your time?" They went around the corner by a drinking fountain. "Skinny, this here's Sister Valentine. She's from Texas, but she's here to help out on an issue about them two men who keep goin' on that Indian burial ground. We wanted to ask you if you've seen them around in the last day or two."

"Nope," Skinny said. "Can't say as I have."

"Sheriff, does that mean you haven't seen these two men recently?" Sister Valentine asked.

"Yes, ma'am, that's what it means."

"Well, all righty then," Willy said, slapping him on the back, "that's all we wanted know. And Skinny, tell that defender out there he ought to stop goin' to the mat for deadbeats he knows are guilty as sin. Ain't that right, Sister? Let the Good Lord judge 'em. C'mon now, I'll take you back to my house. You'll like my wife. You two oughta have all kinds of things to talk about."

Sister Valentine looked at him quizzically, wondering why they drove all the way to Wytheville just to have Sheriff Binkins say, nope, he hadn't seen them. What did Mr. Sherman think the sheriff was going to say?

They all met at Albert's garage at noon: Willy Sherman, J.D., Abby, Amanda, Junior, and Marie. Albert never made it. The last to leave the house, he ran out of gas in the driveway. He decided to hitchhike to the garage. He got picked up by a small delivery truck with a box on the back. Albert lumbered up to the driver and shouted, "Only goin' to the Texaco." The driver pointed to his ear, so Albert said softer, "Texaco." The man smiled, nodded, and jerked his thumb toward the back box, and Albert climbed in and closed the door. Twenty minutes later, Albert began pounding and kicking on the inside of the box and bellowing, "Hey, you, stop this dang thing!" The truck didn't stop. Albert opened a box of pamphlets: *Appalachian School for the Deaf*, Chattanooga, Tennessee. Two hours later, the truck stopped. The driver opened the door, grinned, and pointed to a squat, white building that had a sign above the door: United States Post Office, Tellico, Tennessee.

"J.D., you did check Abigail's house at the top of the hill, didn't you?"

"Yes, sir, we did. They haven't been there."

"That means the likely place for them to be," Willy said to the group, "is that old man's cabin. Can't call the police because we aren't sure about it. Not really sure about it at all. If the police went out there and they weren't there, they probably wouldn't come the next time we called them. If they are there, they'd be long gone out in the woods what with all the lights and sirens. Everything might come unglued. We got to know for sure. And we can't just drive in there or they'd pick us off like ducks in a pond. We need to go on foot, through the woods, but I think only me and J.D. and Junior. You girls need to stay here." He went on describing how they were going to park the cars out on the paved road and circle around.

Junior handed J.D. the newspaper clipping from the *Carroll County Gazette*. He read down through it. It was just like Grannie Mae had said. It ended with the quote from the policeman. "'People shouldn't have long stove pipes. The shorter the better. Keep them real clean,' said Officer William Sherman." J.D. stared at Willy. Officer William Sherman.

The voice of Hubie Alley came into his head. *Willy, you remember, don't you? You were just out of the Army Corps of Engineers. Concrete bridge construction, wasn't it? You'd hired on with the local police.*

26

The Rickshaw

THEY HAD GAGGED DAN WITH A PAIR OF SOCKS. He was slumped, his chin on his chest, but he had come to enough to hear the murmur of their voices. Enough to cock one eye open. He stayed slumped and made gurgling snoring sounds. There were three of them outside the cabin door. The door was open, the window curtains drawn. There were three different voices. He only recognized one. The voice of the ugly man at the motel. "Hartford, you and me should have shot that old man when we shot the kids. None of this would have happened. Ain't that true?"

"Yeah, it probably is true. Britt still doesn't know about the chemicals. That's why this whole thing went south. The old geezer figured it out, and that kid turned into a moron from being near that shit. Britt's a soft son-of-a-bitch. Give the old man a decent break, he said, and we end up having to bring that baby girl all the way to Texas and hauling that blind lady down here twice a year. Soft. He can't bring himself to hurt the old guy. Just like what he told us yesterday, 'Don't kill anybody, just move them away until we can get this place cleaned up.' He still thinks that old black fiddler died in the fire. Now we got the bones, they'll never know."

A third man spoke. "Britt doesn't know the vaults had always been here, that Sherman just made them bigger for the nuclear stuff?"

"No," the second man said, "but I got to tell you, Sherman is doing a hell of a job making them think he's their best buddy, their goddamn savior. Setting it up chummy with that Dixon kid, taking him out to the saw mill and everything and just waiting for the marshal here to come to him. Brilliant. Now let's go wake up our cop. Sherman should be here in about ten minutes. Within an hour, we should have all six. Vinny, get a bucket of water. That ought to do it. Then you two go out to where you're supposed to be. And, Vinny, stop that damn whistling. You're bugging me."

"It's that song they played at the festival, that same song the black man was playing on the fiddle the night we first came out here. Haven't been able to get it out my head for twenty years. Every time I come to this cabin, it seems like that's all I can hear."

"Get the bucket of water and keep quiet."

Dan braced himself, sucking air in through the socks, and then pinched his lips tight shut. One of them threw a whole bucket on him and then took the gag off. It was Hartford. "Hey now, Mr. Marshal, how you doing?" Dan tried working at the handcuffs that held him locked in the old man's rocker. They were too tight. One ankle was chained to the bed frame. It was a clever set-up. He couldn't push the chair over to try to wiggle free. His head was still full of cotton from the chloroform, but it was clear they didn't want him dead. That would have been easy. Hartford sat in the other chair, watching him. The other two had gone outside, one under the bridge, the other inside the burned out house foundation. Each of them had a twenty-five round semi-automatic machine gun with a pistol grip. It was one o'clock. They were waiting for Sherman to bring them the two boys through the woods and then go back to fetch the three girls. They would have them all.

"Mr. Hartford, or McCoy, whichever." He spoke slowly, slurring. "What do you intend to do with six people? You can't possibly think that you can kill all of us and get away with it. That's insane."

"Mr. Wentworth, I have never killed anyone, and I have no intention of doing that now. We aren't even going to harm a hair on anybody's head. You're all just going to disappear. Poof! Here one minute, gone the next."

"Like the old man who lived here. Poof! Gone up to your own private insane asylum and then into your own private crematorium. Like that?" His lips were numb.

"No, not like that. Aside from that, Harbone lies. Dr. Johnson's not dead. Now shut up."

Junior hugged Marie, telling her not to worry, he was going to be fine. "I'm the toughest guy you know, aren't I, sweetheart? We got these guys once; we'll get 'em again, this time for good. Tell little Dirk I love him, to be strong. And, honey, I love you an awful lot."

J.D. hugged Abby. He whispered in her ear, "Don't look up, don't look around, don't flinch, don't say anything. Sherman is one of them. He's bad. I'm going with him because if he thinks I know, they'll kill us all. We won't have a chance. I'll somehow tell Junior, but I want you and Marie and my mom to figure out some way to get a big diversion up there at the cabin. They're there, and Sherman knows it, and we're walking into a trap. Think about getting something to happen that might throw them all off, maybe give me and Junior a second to do something. One hour, be there in an hour. And, Abby, I meant what I said out there in the woods. I love you. I meant it then, I mean it now, and I'll mean it tomorrow. Don't cry, don't blink, don't do anything, just figure something out. You can do it. Those people killed your parents. I'm sure of that."

He kissed her on the lips, and she closed her eyes so she wouldn't blink. J.D. gave his mother a hug and a kiss on the cheek. "Let's go," he said to Junior and Willy. "Let's do this thing."

They parked Willy's car and J.D.'s truck out on the Cherokee Road a ways beyond the drive to the cabin. Willy holstered a .38 pistol, and Junior and J.D. slung their hunting rifles over their backs, and they climbed down an embankment and up into the woods near the reservation boundary. They'd have to cross the creek, but it was still safer than going in on the drive. It was the shortest path to the old man's cabin. They spread out and crouched down, moving quietly and quickly. J.D. let Willy move ahead so he could whisper to Junior, but he couldn't get close enough. He considered just putting a bullet in the guy's back, but he figured that it wouldn't help in the long run, and he'd probably go to hell for it. *Play it out. See what we get.* Fifty feet from the cabin, they got a hail of machine gun fire. J.D. spun around and fell, grabbing hold of his leg. Willy Sherman stared at Ragnar and his gun poking out of the foundation hole. He slowly turned and pointed his pistol at Junior's face. "Drop the rifle, boy." J.D. was bleeding badly from his thigh. They cuffed Junior to the bed frame and put a tourniquet on J.D.'s leg and then tied him to the back of the chair his father was in, manacled and gagged.

"I'm scared of big people," Junior said to no one.

Abby said to Marie and Amanda, "We don't have much time. Jeremiah told me that Mr. Sherman is one of them. He's working with those people who have Uncle Danny, and Jeremiah knows they're walking into a trap. He wants us to somehow get out there and make some ruckus so him and Junior have a chance to do something. Give me some ideas. He said to be there in an hour. What do we do? Get the police? Make a bomb? How do we get their attention off our men long enough for Junior and Jeremiah to do something?"

They put their arms on each other's shoulders, heads touching, huddled, and they mumbled together. Marie was talking. Amanda stood straight up.

"I am absolutely not doing that!"

"Me either," Abby said.

Marie said, "Let's talk that part over with Grannie Mae. She might know something else. But all the rest of it, are we good on it?"

"I don't like it, but I can't think of anything better. I'll do it," Amanda said.

"Me too," said Abby. "It just might do the trick." She broke out of their huddle and said to Albert's gas station boy, "What's your name?"

He said, "Pete."

"Fine," Abby said. "Pete, you see that chair over in the corner of the office? Get it and put two long bars along the side of it and make us a rickshaw. You ever heard of one of those? Over in China they carry the queen around in one of those. Me and Marie, we're going up to Albert's house to get some things. Mrs. Dixon is your boss. Do what she says. Right now. Make the chair. Don't be looking at me stupid-like. Get to work."

Abby and Marie ran out to Junior's truck, jumped in, and screamed up the road to Marie's house. "We need my fiddle, Grannie Mae's dulcimer, and that bone she puts on her finger. We need that thing. And two long coats, like trench coats. We got those. Albert's got a couple of them." Marie and Abby ran into the house and grabbed the things. Five minutes later, they were on the road to town. Marie was driving the curves at sixty miles an hour. Abby's knuckle was bleeding from all the biting on it. When they turned off Main Street, Abby fished in her pocket and got out the keys to the hardware store. It had been shut and closed for two days. A *So Sorry* sign hung on the door. She dashed in and came out with a rolled up saddle blanket. They wheeled around the corner, down two blocks to a quiet street lined with simple houses and small, simple lawns. "That one," Abby said. "There's Billy out front."

"Grannie Mae, we got trouble. Big trouble. We need you to come with us. And Sister Valentine, you too. Where's Albert?"

"Hold on just a minute here," Garth Sherman said, looking at Marie and Abby. "I'm sorry, girls, my dad said these folks were to stay here until he got back."

Grannie Mae walked up to him and said into his chest, "Young man, I am ninety-two years old, and I decide what I'm goin' to do, and this here nun is a Sister of the Order of Sacred Hearts, and I can pretty much guarantee you she don't take her orders from mortals like you. Now you be a good boy and get out of our way. Mrs. Sherman, thank you for your hospitality. Could you please look after that baby just for a short little while? Thank you." She hobbled past the state trooper and out the front door, followed by Sister Valentine, Abigail, and Marie. Abby whistled to Billy and pointed to the back of the truck, and he and Abby hopped in. They all headed off back to the garage to pick up Amanda and the rickshaw.

"No Albert. Wonder what happened to him," Abby said to herself. "We'll have to take that Pete kid even though he don't seem to have the brains of a toad."

Pete's rickshaw was a thing of beauty. He'd taken a hack saw and cut two steel pipes off the lumber rack of a dead pickup and, under Amanda's exacting tutelage, lashed them to the sides of the chair with stout rope. She had made him put one end on the tailgate of the truck, sat in the seat, and told him to pick up the other end. She had jumped and wriggled around and pronounced it sturdy and safe enough to carry the old woman. She said, "Pete, take off your belt and put it with this rickshaw. We'll have to strap her in." They had just finished when Junior's truck screeched to a stop a foot from the gas pump. Sister Valentine was clutching her crucifix and mumbling prayers. Grannie Mae had pulled her bonnet down over her eyes.

Billy and Pete got the rickshaw into the back of the truck, and then Pete stood off to the side laughing his eerie laugh, and Abby said, "Stop your dang laughing. Shut the pumps off, lock the doors, and get in. Fast. Move." Pete scrambled into the open bay, pulled the door down, shut the breakers off, and dove in the back with Billy, Amanda, and Abby.

Marie parked in front of the bridge, and as quietly as they could, they unloaded the rickshaw, put Grannie Mae in it, strapped the belt on, and put the violin and her dulcimer in her lap. "Now, Grannie Mae," Marie said, "I need to ask you a good hard question." She glanced at Pete and Billy and leaned down and whispered the plan in her ear. Grannie Mae grunted and signaled Amanda and Abby over, beckoning them down toward her mouth. She whispered to them, and they both shook their heads. Then she said, loud and firm, "Do you love your man? If'n you do, you must do everything it takes to keep them from gettin' killed. Now you two girls just g'won and do it!"

Abby closed her eyes and blew her breath out. "Okay, Grannie Mae. Okay."

Amanda and Abby put on Albert's trench coats. Abby unrolled the saddle blanket and took out both Westley Richards 10-gauge shotguns and a fistful of shells. Ten-gauge slugs. Big and heavy. She opened the breech on her gun and slid in a shell. She handed a shell to Amanda. Billy reached over and took the gun, took the shell, loaded it, and handed it to Amanda. He put the rest of the shells in his pocket. Abby said, "Billy, you and Pete stand behind me and Mrs. Dixon. Right tight behind us so we won't fall over and so they can't see you. All they'll see is girls." She and Amanda slid the guns inside their trench coats. In a silent, somber procession, they crossed the bridge with Billy and Pete carrying Grannie Mae like the Queen of Sheba.

Grannie Mae said, "I always told Robert to fix this dang thing. It's not a good bridge."

"Shhhhhh," Marie whispered in her ear. Grannie Mae nodded, patted Marie's cheek, and spit a bit of juice over the side of the bridge.

Abby was in front. They were still out of sight of the cabin when she heard the door slam. She held out her arms, and everyone stopped, holding their breath. She caught a glimpse of someone running off the other direction through the woods. She thought she saw Willy Sherman's silver hair. She motioned them on. When the front of the cabin came in view, they all stopped. They could hear talking and banging noises coming from inside. Abby turned around and said in the quietest of voices, "Sister Valentine, would you whisper us a prayer? When you say, Amen, we go. Fast. Marie and Grannie Mae, play your hearts out."

"*O Lord, we commit ourselves to your bosom. Forgive us our sins. Amen.*"

They ran as best they could with their loaded shotguns, their long and jostling rickshaw, their instruments. The boys set Grannie Mae down, Marie handed her the dulcimer and bone and then spread her own legs wide, tucking the violin into her quivering chin, and said, "And a one and a two," and she pulled the bow hard across the stings as Grannie Mae hammered down on the mountain dulcimer to the tune of "Goin' to Git My Baby." Sister Valentine stood between them holding her crucifix straight out in front. Amanda and Abby stood on either side. Billy leaned into Abby's back, bracing her, reached down, cocked the hammer back, and slid his finger over hers on the trigger. Pete, watching him, did the same with Amanda.

The cabin door shot open, and two men came out, each with an evil-looking weapon in their hand, and each with a stunned and muddled look, their eyes locked on the five women, trying to comprehend. Ragnar's eyes squinted, he gave a single shake to his head, and his gun lifted up from his side. Pete leaned harder into Amanda and said soft behind her ear, "Shoot, lady, shoot!" In that instant, as if a part of the music, as if a part of the play, two long shiny barrels of the shotguns swept up and out of the fold of the trench coats, level to their waists, and the orphan and the widow pulled their triggers. The leaves and the grasses all up the hillside quivered in the mighty blast. Ragnar's gun spit bullets in the dirt and up the side of the sister's holy habit as his lower leg flew back into the cabin, separated from his body just below the kneecap. Hartford's pelvis was plastered on to the door jamb. They both collapsed, screaming.

Vinny Stoner stared at the blonde girl, up to her face, and he knew those big, round, plum dark eyes, and then into the face of the sister from the orphanage, into her crucifix, and he knew the sister. He knew the song, and he knew who they were. He saw Ragnar's gun creep out from under his body, and Vinny, the altar boy at St. Paul's, fired one round straight into the back of the one-legged Bulgarian and then dropped his gun, kicked the bloody half-leg off his boot, and began picking pieces of bone and flesh off his shirt, his neck, his pants, mumbling Hail Marys.

The garage was locked; no one there. Willy Sherman picked up a piece of pipe left over from Pete's rickshaw and bashed the glass in the office door window, reached through, unlocked it, went in, and picked up the telephone. "Garth, call your boys out. Get the captain to send three squad cars, fast. If they're not nearby, get a park ranger. These guys are armed and very dangerous. You know where this cabin is? Good. It's not on Indian land. Fast." He slowed down, waited. "Listen, son, I got to say this to you right now so you understand why I'm doing what I'm doing. When you were just a baby, they made me help them violate that sacred ground. They made me do it, and then they made me lie about it. I've been waitin' years to get back at them for what they did. I think it's all set up now. Bring out the boys. I'll meet you there."

Ten minutes later, two Virginia State police cars and a park ranger truck barreled down the dirt road and over the old bridge, blue lights flashing. They called in for three ambulances, for Hartford, J.D., and Sister Valentine. For Ragnar, they called Dr. Heath, the county coroner. He had died of a single .25 caliber bullet wound from Vinny's gun that entered from the back, three centimeters below the scapula, passed through the heart, and exited between the fifth and sixth rib of the thoracic cage.

Willy Sherman leaned against his car, talking to Dan Wentworth. Dan motioned over one of the state troopers and asked if he would please call in and have a couple of officers go up to Skinner Bluff Insane Asylum and pick up an old man and drive him down here to his cabin. "He's old, he's bent over," he told the trooper, "walks with a cane. His name is Dr. Johnson. See if his wife is there. Her name's Edith. She's blind. And look for a young feller named Everett. Bring 'em all down here if they're alive. Better bring a couple of cars. Might need a shotgun or two."

27

Tribal Ceremonies

THE FLIGHT FROM AMARILLO TO WASHINGTON touched down on the Dulles International runway at two in the afternoon on a cold, gray day a week before Thanksgiving. Chief John had never flown on an airplane before, and for the entire flight, he had been certain his body and spirit were going to be dashed into dust in some remote place, some place his people had never even been to, never even heard of. When the agent from the Bureau of Indian Affairs met him at the gate, the deep copper hue of his face had turned a light brown mud color. He was wearing his finest hat: a white, tall-crowned fur blend Stetson with a silver-studded rawhide band and tassel. His snakeskin boots were shined, and his wife's favorite Mexican serape hung loosely over his old shoulders. He was being taken to a government room somewhere to talk to people about how, as the white man had said, "to appease the angry spirits and allow them to return to peace."

Chief John wasn't sure the spirits were angry at all, but if the white men wanted him to tell them that a good water and wastewater system, a recreational facility, a new elementary school, and guaranteed education at a public university for all children on the Big Flats Reservation would do the trick, he was happy to tell them that.

Chief John had talked this over on the telephone with four

other chiefs: Iroquois, Blackfoot, Sioux, and Delaware. These were some of the tribes that owned lands on which these terrible poisons had been stored. They were the chiefs who had been selected by the Council of Nations to speak on behalf of all tribes whose lands had been violated. They had all agreed that this was what they needed to tell the men sitting on the podium in the great domed building in the Capitol. They decided also to tell the Great White Men that if the spirits were not appeased in this way, then when they died, their bodies would simply disappear, and no one would ever remember that they had ever lived. Don't say it as a threat, they decided; just say it as a sad fact. One of the sad facts among many sad facts that they, as "Medicine Men," were burdened with.

Chief John was on his way to meet with the other chiefs to hone their thoughts. In three days, he would be driven in a very big car to the place where the Trail of Tears began, where they cried, where they followed Chief Going Snake, where the mountains are tall and the trees are big and the air is blue and the water runs fast and clean. Where his people were buried. There he would see Wilbur and Abigail. She had found her song there. He wanted to hear her whistle it again.

Vinny Stoner was also in Washington. He was sitting at a long, narrow table in a windowless room in the second-level basement of the Justice Department. Beside him, on his right, was a robust Irishman, Jake Hennessey, the sole proprietor and only attorney ever to work for the law firm of Hennessey, Hennessey, Brandies & Black. International Chemical had withdrawn any legal support for Vinny when he turned state's evidence. In the middle of the table was a camera on a tripod. Across the table sat six Justice Department attorneys all dressed in similar black, charcoal, or gray suits and all with narrow black ties. Vinny was in the fifth day of deposition. "Mr. Stoner, how many of these sites are there?"

"In the United States, fourteen that we were in charge of. There might be more. I don't know, but I don't think so. I heard there were twenty-one in other countries."

"Mr. Stoner, you heard that from whom?"

"It was in a meeting in Dallas where Mr. Huprin, the big boss, told us that."

"Mr. Stoner, did International Chemical own and operate Skinner Bluff Lunatic Asylum?"

"Yes."

"Who were the inmates?"

"Anybody and everybody from around the world who might spill the beans on all these secret sites."

"So these people in that asylum weren't insane; they just knew too much. Is that right?"

"Well, maybe they weren't insane when they got there, but they sure were after a month or so."

"Mr. Stoner, did Colonel Britt know that there were toxic chemicals stored at these sites, in particular, the site in Virginia?"

"No, sir, he didn't. He only knew about the uranium and plutonium. At least as far as I know, he didn't know that those vaults had been built in the 1920s to stash away the insecticides. He didn't know that Willy Sherman just made them bigger to fit in the nuclear stuff. I know that because Mr. Huprin made us swear we would never tell him that."

"Mr. Stoner, why did International Chemical put all of these deadly chemicals on Indian land?"

"Well, that's easy. Because nobody who amounts to anything is ever allowed to go there. It's like the perfect hiding place. No white people ever see anything, and nobody believes the Indians when they complain about anything. It's perfect."

"Why did it all come apart in Galax, Virginia?"

"Because that old man who Britt hired to live there was

smart enough to figure it all out. At the other sites, the guys who monitored them were just kind of average people. They had security clearances and all like that, but they weren't geniuses. This old guy was smart enough to figure out that nobody would believe him, they'd think he was just a crazy old goat, but they sure would believe a smart young kid and the smart kid's scientist mother. The guy was a nuclear physicist. He wasn't any dummy."

"Who shot Mr. Jenkins, Dr. Johnson's son, and his wife?"

"I need a cup of coffee. Can somebody get me a cup of coffee or something?"

"No. Who shot them?"

On the deposition tape, Vinny's face is not visible. His head is down on his chest. Only the top of his head shows. His attorney is telling him to look up into the camera and just tell them what happened. "It's the only way, Vinny," Hennessey's voice says. "It's the only way you're going to stay out of prison for life."

"Nobody meant to kill anybody. We were told just to get the black guy out of there and get him up to Skinner Bluff. He knew way too much. He was playing his fiddle really loud. We didn't know Dr. Johnson was there. When we saw the car by the bridge, we figured we had to go in anyway and just grab the black guy and get everybody else out of there. We put on masks like Zorro masks and walked in. Jenkins picked up a fireplace poker and slammed it into Ragnar's neck. Ragnar shot him, and he fell into the stove. It was a tall stove, and the whole thing fell over, and the fire came out and lit the rugs on fire. There was a baby in a crib, and the fire jumped into the crib, and everybody was screaming, and Hartford started shooting. I don't know who shot who. Nobody was supposed to get killed, but then all of a sudden I'm grabbing the baby and she has her teddy bear in her arms and it's like the thing is made of plastic or something and they're both on fire and I run out with the kid. The whole place is on fire, and Hartford and Ragnar come out dragging the old man and his wife, and then Ragnar runs back into the fire and drags out three bodies. All dead."

"Who, Mr. Stoner, put them into the vault?"

"I don't know any of that. What vault?"

"Who shot the three people: Mr. Jenkins, Dr. Johnson's son, and his wife? Who shot them in the forehead and sealed them into the vault? Who?"

"I don't know anything about that. I was just hugging the baby to put her fire out and drove out of there to call Colonel Britt. That's all I know."

"What do you know about Willy Sherman?"

"All I know is this: I thought he was working with us. I never met any double agent before. That is one smart-ass hillbilly. That's all I know. Here's the thing of it. There were too many smart people barking up our tree at the same time. When that happens, all the money in the world can't hide a lie. That's how the world works, that's how God made it."

"Thank you, Mr. Stoner, you can go now. We'll see you here tomorrow morning at eight."

He had agreed to do this in exchange for ten years, out after six, but after eight long ten-hour days of staring into the camera and drinking a dozen cups of coffee before noon, eating only pizza, being locked in a cheap motel room every day after testimony, his mind was shot. All six lawyers had taken turns asking him questions. A lot of times, the same question was asked a different way by a different lawyer. Over and over again. After eight days, he couldn't remember anything. *Colonel who?*

But they had what they needed. They had everything the chairman of the Armed Services Committee wanted to once and for all shut down the Army's Biological Warfare Division, but to have the rest of the army come out looking okay. They had everything the attorney general wanted to force International Chemical to do nothing but sell fertilizer to farmers. The world's largest chemical company might be able to turn a profit in Africa, Indonesia, or South America, but not here. Jack Huprin had bankrolled George Wallace's campaign, and President Nixon wanted his nuts in a vice.

Hubie Alley made good on his promise. After an hour on the phone with Senator Rudolf Jessup, after Hubie had explained all the goings on down in the Blue Ridge and the heinous invasion of the sacred ground of the Cherokee Nation, extoled the virtues of one Jeremiah Dixon, and talked about the difficulties of securing decent logging contracts that would, in his words, "make these precious forests more healthy for many generations," the senator had agreed to convene public hearings on both matters and to have a chat with the superintendent of the Nation Park Service.

"And, Rudy, can't you get some folks up there in Washington to put together some agency or department or something that's in charge of keeping our land and forests clean so we all can stay healthy and make a decent living? I mean, Rudy, what the army and that chemical company did out there in Dengman Gap is just a plain and simple violation of God's will. It's despicable. Somebody needs to be in charge of them. Teddy Roosevelt would do it."

Twenty minutes later, Hubie's phone rang, and the superintendent of the Park Service told him that there just so happened to be a temporary, one-year position available for an Assistant Deputy Director of Forest Management for the Shenandoah, Blue Ridge, and Great Smokey Mountain federal lands. If Hubie were to give a personal recommendation, his young friend could certainly be appointed right away and be in a good position to receive a full-time civil service appointment a year down the road.

Senator Jessup had a letter drafted to the president, urging him to move quickly on legislation to establish a new agency charged with the protection of the American environment. All of it: land, air, water, and creatures. An agency with authority over all private and public entities, including the military. He got eleven of his colleagues to sign on. He called the governor and convinced him to have his national guardsmen stand sentry around the perimeter of the sacred ground until the mess could be cleaned up. Jessup also coordinated hearings for three separate Senate Committees: Public Works, Indian Affairs, and Armed Services. The star witnesses for each, Jeremiah Dixon, five chiefs of the Indian Nations, and (Retired) Colonel John Britt, were all lined up to testify. The Justice Department was pursuing three trials—one civil, two criminal. The civil trial, a suit against International Chemical, would likely take years and might have a settlement of hundreds of millions of dollars. The federal criminal trial pertained to Skinner Bluff and involved charges of kidnapping and attempted murder of federal officers. That trial might take many months. Jack Huprin, Edna Harbone, and Robert McCoy were being tried in state court on seventeen different charges including first-degree murder. The jury in that trial would likely have rendered its verdict before the vernal equinox.

Chief John arrived in a big, black limousine. Old Man met him at the door, and the two exchanged a long, still, and silent greeting. Then they shook hands.

"Thank you," said Chief John.

"No, thank you," said Old Man.

The chief looked at the Welcome sign on the door and

said, "Where you're going doesn't mean anything unless you see where you've come from."

"You are very right about that, Chief. Doesn't mean a damn thing."

Card tables and boards on saw horses had been cobbled together and covered with Grannie Mae's tablecloths. It all fit in the cabin, but just barely. There was enough room, with all the other furniture moved out of the way, to walk around the ends and sides. Sister Valentine said a Thanksgiving grace while they all—Old Man, Grannie Mae, J.D., Abby, Junior, Marie, Albert, Amanda, Dan, Billy, and Chief John—held hands. Beside the old man was a small stool with Edith's favorite scarf draped over it. On the scarf was a plain metal plaque that said "Edith." Nothing else. On a stool beside Amanda was a similar plaque that said, "Everett." Nothing else. Old Mr. P. had made one last trip to that place on earth that could not have been emptier, more lonely, more haunted by nothingness.

Abby leaned close to Old Man and took his gnarled knuckles in her hand and said, "Guess what, Grandpa?"

"What is it, Little Girl?"

"Pretty soon you're going to be a great-grandpa."

After the table was cleared and the leftover food wrapped and divvied up, they all made their way to the near corner of the sacred ground. Junior and Billy carried Grannie Mae in her rickshaw, the old man shuffling along beside it. J.D. and Sister Valentine hobbled on their crutches. Abby had on her silver and turquois bear necklace, and her bone-handle knife in its tasseled sheath hung on the rope wrapped around her satin dress. Jeremiah's National Park Service officer's uniform was pressed and spangled with shoulder patches and a big bright badge. Chief John performed a tribal marriage ceremony, joining together Abigail and Jeremiah, which is all the spirits had ever really wanted anyway.

ACKNOWLEDGEMENTS

MOSES DURGIN was an old, old man who lived on a farm in New Hampshire. He was unworldly wise. When I was young he told me things that only Medicine Men know. He treated me as a friend, with respect, until one day that changed a bit. I told him that a man had flown up to the moon, got out and walked on it. He became openly suspicious of my mental health.

CHARLIE HARMON always called me 'Little Boy' whether I was working for him on his construction crew or on the phone each Christmas for years afterwards. He was a truly fine Appalachian gentleman who gave me the inspiration to write about the strong and independent people of the Blue Ridge Mountains. To the folks of the Blue Ridge Bar and Grill, I hope my recollections have done you justice. It was and still is today, a really special place.

MARY IRONS is, statistically speaking; I mean if you do the logic on it, the finest first grade teacher in the United States. She is also a top drawer First Reader and a good enough friend to speak her mind. That's a good friend.

ELIZABETH DAY of Blue Root Editing has done a fantastic job of proofreading this book as well as a re-published (8/2013) version of Hoover's Children. I really should have paid more attention in grammar school when Mrs. Winslow was going on and on about syntax and semi-colons. Thanks, Elizabeth.

TOM HOLBROOK, my publisher, has done all the hard work of taking these hundred thousand words and giving them form, context, and clarity; giving them physical being, as he did for my first book, 'Hoover's Children'. I am indebted to Tom and to the folks who work with him at RiverRun Bookstore. Thank you all.

About the Author

Tony Irons was born at a Manhattan Project reservation in Richland, WA where plutonium was enriched for use in the H-Bomb. When he was ten, his father died. His mother, a poet, moved the family of seven children east to Exeter, NH. During the heart of the Vietnam War, he served three years as a Conscientious Objector working with soldiers addicted to heroin. He dropped out of college after nine months and became a carpenter, a contractor and taught himself architecture. He became one of the last self-taught architects in the country, becoming licensed in California in 1994. Mayor Willie Brown appointed him City Architect of San Francisco. In 2000, Tony was awarded a Loeb Fellowship in the Graduate School of Design at Harvard University.

At Harvard, Tony studied creative writing with Anne Bernays through the Neiman Foundation. He and his wife Lee lived in a small apartment just off Harvard Square. It was there that Tony wrote many of his short stories about his experiences in Mississippi and Alabama during the Civil Rights Movement. He and Lee live in NH.

CPSIA information can be obtained
at www.ICGtesting.com
Printed in the USA
LVHW030459161221
706294LV00002B/203

9 781939 739018